YOU
WILL
REMEMBER
ME

Also by Hannah Mary McKinnon

Sister Dear
Her Secret Son
The Neighbors

HANNAH MARY McKINNON

YOU WILL REMEMBER ME

mira

mira™

Recycling programs
for this product may
not exist in your area.

ISBN-13: 978-0-7783-3181-0

You Will Remember Me

Copyright © 2021 by Hannah McKinnon

This edition published by arrangement with Harlequin Books S.A.

For questions and comments about the quality of this book, please contact us at
CustomerService@Harlequin.com.

Mira
22 Adelaide St. West, 40th Floor
Toronto, Ontario M5H 4E3, Canada
BookClubbish.com

Printed in U.S.A.

To Mum—
who always said being stubborn, ahem, *persistent*, would pay off

To Carolyn & Emily—who turn dreams into reality

YOU
WILL
REMEMBER
ME

Know thyself? If I knew myself I'd run away.

—Johann Wolfgang von Goethe

1

THE MAN FROM THE BEACH

Cold. Cold was the first word that came to mind. The first thing I noticed when I woke up. Not a slight, uncomfortable chill to give me the shivers, but a cramp-inducing, iced-to-the-bone kind of frozen. I lay flat on my stomach, my left ear and cheek pressed into the rough, grainy wet ground beneath me, my entire body shaking. As my thoughts attempted to assemble themselves into some form of understandable order, a wave of icy water nipped at my bare toes and ankles, my instincts pulling my feet out of reach.

I had a sudden urge to get up, a primal need to take in my surroundings and assess the danger—was I in danger?—but the throbbing pain deep in my head made the slightest effort to shift anything seem impossible. Lifting a finger would be too much effort, and I acquiesced, allowing myself to lie still for another few freezing seconds as the frigid water crept over the balls of my feet again. When I blinked my eyes open, I was met by a thick, fuzzy darkness enveloping me like a cloak. Where the hell was I? And wherever it was, what was I doing here?

When I lifted my head a fraction of an inch, I could barely make out anything in front of me. There was hardly a noise, either, nothing but a gentle, steady rumble in the background, and the cry of a bird somewhere in the distance. I made my brain work its way backward—bird, rumble, sand, water—and the quartet formed the vaguely cohesive image of a beach.

Searching for confirmation, I inhaled the salty, humid air deep into my lungs as another slosh of water took aim at my calves. This time the discomfort was enough to push me to my feet, and I wrapped my arms around my naked torso, my sopping board shorts clinging to my goose-bump-covered thighs. An explosion of pain in my head threatened to send me back to my knees, and I swayed gently, wishing I had something to steady myself with, willing my body to stay upright. As I pressed a hand to the side of my skull, I let out a quiet yelp, and felt along a two-inch gash in my scalp. My eyes had adjusted somewhat to the lack of light, and my fingertips were covered in something dark that smelled of rust. Blood. How had I...?

Another low rumble made me turn around, shuffling slowly in a semicircle. The behemoth effort was rewarded by the sight of a thousand glistening waves dancing under the moonlight like diamonds, the water stretching out and disappearing into the darkness beyond. As my ears tuned in to the rhythmic *whoosh* of the waves, my mind worked hard to process each scrap of information it took in.

I'm definitely on a beach. It's nighttime. I'm alone. What am I doing here?

Before I could answer the single question, a thousand others crowded my brain, an incessant string of chatter I couldn't stop or get away from.

Where is everyone? Never mind them, where am I? Have I been here long? How did I get here? Where was I before? Where are my clothes? What day is it?

My legs buckled. Not because of the unfamiliar surroundings, the cold burrowing its way deeper into my core, or the pain in my head, which had increased tenfold. No. My knees hit the sand with a dull crunch when I realized I couldn't answer any of the questions because I couldn't recall anything. *Nothing.* Not the tiniest of details.

Including my name.

2

LILY

A frown settled over my face as I put my phone on the table, pushed the bowl of unfinished berry oatmeal away and stretched out my legs. It was Saturday morning, and I'd been up for ages, too eager—too hopeful—to spend a day at the beach with Jack, but those plans had been a literal wash-out. The start to the summer felt capricious, with this second storm in the last week of June poised to be much worse than the first. I'd convinced myself the weatherwoman had exaggerated or got her forecast completely wrong, but clouds had rolled in overnight anyway. As a result, I'd been unceremoniously woken up at two thirty by a trio of bright lightning, deafening thunderclaps and heavy raindrops pelting against my bedroom window.

At first, I'd pulled my pillow over my head to deafen the noise, and when that didn't work, I rolled over and stretched out an arm. The spot next to me was empty and cold, and I groaned.

Jack hadn't come over to my place as I'd hoped he would, slipping into bed and pressing his naked body against mine. I'd buried my face back into my pillow and tried to ignore the tinge of disappointment. We hadn't seen much of each other this past week, both of us too busy with our jobs to spend more than a night together, and I missed him. Jack had called the day before to tell me he'd be working late, finishing the stain on the cabinets he'd labored on for weeks before his boss had to let him go. Apparently expensive custom kitchens weren't in as high demand in Brookmount, Maryland, as originally thought.

"But you got laid off," I'd said. "It's your last day. Why do you care?"

"Because I made a commitment. Besides, it'll help when I need a reference."

Typical Jack, always keeping his word. He'd bought a lottery ticket once, and the clerk had jokingly asked if he'd give him half of any winnings. Jack had laughed and shaken the man's hand, and when he won ten bucks on the ticket, had promptly returned to the store, and paid over the share as promised. His loyalty was one of the many things I loved about Jack, although part of me wished he weren't quite as dedicated to his soon-to-be ex-boss.

"You could come over to my place when you're done," I said, smiling slowly. "I'll leave the key under the umbrella stand. I don't mind you waking me up gently in the middle of the night...or not so gently."

Jack laughed softly. The sound was something I'd fallen in love with eighteen months ago after our eyes had met across a crowded bar, the mother of all uninspired first-encounter clichés, except in this case I'd been forced to admit clichés weren't always a bad thing.

"It'll be really late, Lily," he said, his voice deep. His English accent was something of a rarity in our small coastal town, and still capable of making my legs wobble in anticipation of his next words. "I'll go for a quick swim now, then finish up work. How about I come over in the morning? Around nine? I'll bring you breakfast in bed."

"Blueberry pancakes from Patti's? With extra maple syrup?"

"This time I'll order three stacks to make sure I get some."

"Pancakes or sex?" I said, before telling him how much I loved him, and whispering exactly how I'd thank him for waking me with sweet weekend treats. I'd hoped it might change his mind and he'd come over earlier, except it was ten now, and he still hadn't shown. It was odd. Jack detested being late as much as he loved being early. He often joked they set Greenwich Mean Time by his father's old watch, which Jack had worn since his dad passed a little over a decade before we'd met, when Jack was only twenty.

I checked my phone again. Jack hadn't answered either of my calls, another anomaly, but I tried to talk myself into believing he'd worked late into the night to make the final good impression he wanted, and overslept. Maybe there was a line at Patti's—the restaurant was slammed every weekend—and perhaps his phone was set to silent.

I picked up my bowl and wandered to the kitchen. My place was the smallest of six apartments, a tiny but well-maintained one-bedroom in a building a few miles from the beach, farther than I'd planned, but the closest I could afford. I'd lived there for almost five years, had furnished it with an eclectic assortment of third-hand furniture, my favorite piece a royal blue microfiber sofa I'd bought for fifty bucks, and which Jack swore was the most comfortable thing he'd ever sat on. Whenever he sank down into it and pulled me on top of him with a contented sigh, I'd tease him about what made him happier: the squishy, well-worn cushions, or me.

The image made my frown deepen. Where was he?

Peering out of the kitchen window, I stood on my tiptoes, craning my neck to get a clear view of the spot on the corner where Jack always parked the ancient, faded silver F-150 he'd persuaded Sam, his landlord, to let him use. Apparently Sam hadn't argued, saying as long as Jack stayed in the apartment and made rent on time, paid for the vehicle's upkeep and rock-bottom insurance premiums, he could use it until he'd saved enough cash to buy himself a different truck. Sam's generosity had surprised me until I'd met him and I'd realized the gesture was the epitome of his personality.

I pushed myself up onto the counter, toes no longer touching the linoleum floor as my eyes swept the area outside again. No matter how hard I stared, the parking space remained empty, save for a lake-sized puddle from the incessant rain. An uncomfortable sensation sneaked its way down into my belly, refusing to be quietened by my silent words of reassurance Jack was running late, and there was nothing to worry about.

Over an hour later the rain hadn't let up. Neither had the feelings about something being wrong. If anything, they'd both increased in intensity, churning my breakfast so I could feel it in the back of my throat. I called Patti's Pancakes.

"Haven't seen him all morning, darlin'," Patti said after I explained I was looking for Jack, and I imagined her wide brown eyes, her giant silver hoop earrings swinging left to right as she shook her head.

"Are you sure?" I asked, already knowing there was no way Patti would have missed him. We were regulars, and she always made time for a chat, never failing to comment on Jack's "ridiculously gorgeous" accent that reminded her of her long-deceased grandfather, another real gentleman, and one she remembered fondly. There was no doubt if Jack had been at the restaurant this morning, she'd know.

After I hung up, I phoned the place where he worked. No answer. My brow furrowed again as I tried Jack's cell once more, listening to the standard factory voice-mail message he'd never bothered to personalize. We weren't the kind of couple to live in each other's pockets. Both of us gave one another, and ourselves, enough space to breathe while enjoying every moment we spent together, but I knew Jack. Something was wrong.

I couldn't hang around in my apartment any longer. At the risk of him making fun of my paranoia, I grabbed my jacket, keys and bag, and dashed outside. With a cough and splutter, the on-the-verge-of-death engine of my old Chevrolet gained a little more self-confidence when I backed out of the driveway and headed toward the center of town.

The most direct route to Jack's place took me past Patti's, and I stopped the car outside regardless, craning my neck. All the tables were taken, and while the line of weather-braving, hungry brunchers huddled under the ruby awning was only two rows deep, there was no sign of Jack, or the truck, anywhere.

I set off again, turned left on Marina Road to his apartment. Fat raindrops splattered against my windshield, making me go slower despite my impulses ordering me to put my foot down. Judging by the empty streets, most of the town's few thousand souls had decided to wait out the storm in the comfort of their homes. That was Brookmount—sensible and quiet. Even at the height of summer, most tourists wouldn't venture down this way, preferring the fun-filled attractions Ocean City had to offer. The mentality suited Jack and me fine. We'd found our separate ways here because we'd needed a change and had tacitly agreed not to push each other for too many details. In my experience, people always had a couple of ghosts in their past, skeletons in closets best nailed shut.

I focused on the road, slowed down some more when I passed what had now officially become Jack's prior workplace. Maybe he hadn't been able to finish the job last night after all, and had returned this morning, but my theory didn't add up. First, he'd have called me, or picked up their phone. Second, his truck wasn't parked in the front or at the back. Third, all the lights were off, and—although I didn't need a fourth—the red-and-white *Open* sign had been turned to *Closed*.

The fearful, panicking voice in my head, the one I'd attempted yet failed to silence, whispered he'd gone to the beach last night. For a *swim*. I pushed the thought away, trying to shut it up, but it ignored my efforts, bounding around my mind like a bunny on speed. "He's *fine*," I said out loud, startling myself. The words did nothing to placate my trembling fingers, or stop the hairs on the back of my neck from standing sentry and sending freezing shivers down my spine.

A few minutes later I arrived at Jack's place, the last house on Bay Court, where he rented the apartment above a double garage. Sam owned the house on the other side of the large driveway and was a veteran pharmaceuticals sales rep, often gone weeks at a time. The testament to his successful career—a bright yellow Porsche—was the only vehicle parked outside. I got out of my pathetic excuse for a car, held my jacket over my head in a pointless attempt to avoid the steady downpour and sprinted up the wooden steps to Jack's front door, where I rattled the handle. Locked. I banged on the glass.

"Jack? Are you home?"

I knocked another few times, waited awhile for a reply in case he was in the shower. I so desperately wanted to hear him in the hallway, imagined him with sopping wet hair, a towel wrapped around his trim waist, and muttering something like, "All right, all right, mate, keep your hair on." He'd open the door and I'd fling my arms around him, then take a step back, put my hands on my hips and ask if he had *any idea* how worried I'd been. The imminent feeling of relief made me hold my breath, but when there was still no answer, I had to let it go.

Forced to concede Jack being in his apartment when the truck wasn't there made no sense, I nonetheless invented stories. Maybe Sam had borrowed it. Unlikely, considering Jack had both sets of keys. Perhaps the Ford had broken down and Jack had got a ride home, or he'd parked the truck down the street for some reason, and I'd missed it when I'd driven by. Whatever the case, in all these scenarios Jack was inside either taking a shower, or fast asleep. I knocked again, cupping my hands against the frosted glass, peering inside and calling out Jack's name, but the place remained dark and silent.

I thundered down the stairs and ran to Sam's oversize front door, where I pressed my finger on the buzzer. I didn't let go until Sam stood in front of me dressed in red-and-blue-striped pajamas, his thick white hair sticking up like fuzzy antlers above his temples.

"Hey, Lily," he said as he rubbed his eyes, his yawn turning into a smile. Sam was always happy to see me. He'd once told me I reminded him of his daughter who'd moved to Los Angeles a few years ago. When I'd mentioned my parents lived there now, too, he'd declared it a sign and given me a bear hug. His fatherly affection was welcome, and more than I'd received from my mom and dad in years, ever since they'd banished me out of their lives and onto their pretentious look-at-our-perfect-family-just-don't-ask-about-Lily Christmas card list.

Sam ushered me inside. I wasn't sure how he did it, but although his house was large enough to fit an entire family, complete with kids, pets and a few sets of football gear, it was always cozy and inviting. Somehow the air smelled of freshly baked muffins despite Sam's self-described inability to boil an egg. He grabbed a towel from the powder room and draped it over my shoulders, making me notice for the first time how cold and shaky I felt.

"Did I wake you?" I said, my teeth clattering an indecipherable symphony as I clutched the towel, bringing it closer to my chin.

Sam waved a hand and grunted. "Freaking storm kept me up half the night, so I slept in. I had no idea how late it was and..." He looked at me, rubbed the stubble on his fleshy cheeks with an equally meaty hand, as a puzzled expression crossed his face. "What's going on?"

"Have you seen Jack?"

"I assumed he was at your place."

"No, and he's not answering his phone."

The look on Sam's face changed from half-asleep to fully alert in a split second. "That's not like him. That's not like him at all."

His confirmation made the panic billow and mushroom inside me. Fear traveled up my throat, thick as molasses, threatening to suffocate me in the hallway, turning my next words into a strained whisper. "I can't get ahold of him. We haven't spoken since last night when—"

"I'm sure he's fine—"

"He went swimming, Sam. At the beach."

"We'll take my car."

I didn't argue, didn't think I'd be able to get my hands and legs to cooperate well enough to drive. Sam grabbed his sneakers, threw on a jacket, and we were on our way to Gondola Point, the secluded beach where Jack preferred to swim any day the weather would allow. It was a ten-minute drive. Sam made it in seven.

"There!" I yelled as we turned the last corner, pointing to the truck at the far end, but the relief was swiftly replaced by more rising anxiety when we got closer and I saw the vehicle was empty. Before Sam came to a full stop, I jumped out, ran over and tried the handle, but the truck was locked. Undeterred, I searched underneath the front bumper, found the set of keys that Jack often hid there, something I made fun of him for because it was the most obvious place a thief would look. Except now I didn't think it was funny. It wasn't funny at all. I unlocked the truck, reached under the driver's seat and, when my fingers closed over Jack's wallet and phone, let out a whimper. Sam stood next to me now, and when I turned around and he saw me clasping Jack's things, the fear I knew he'd worked hard to hide was splashed all across his face.

"Where's Jack?" I shouted, my voice carried away by the wind. "Where is he?"

Sam put his hands on my shoulders. One look and I knew what he was going to say. I wanted to press both of my hands over his mouth, forcing his words to stay inside. Once he said them, they'd be out there. They'd make this nightmare real.

"No," I said, trying to back away so I wouldn't hear, but Sam held firm.

"Lily, honey," he said, his voice gentle. "We have to call the cops."

3

THE MAN FROM THE BEACH

I woke up with a start, needed a moment to figure out where I was before allowing myself to sink back onto the mattress, my mind retracing the events that had led me here. After I'd staggered away from the beach, I'd come across a dusty, four-foot-wide track. Trying yet continually failing to regain focus, I attempted to force my brain to decide which direction to take. I stood by the side of the path forever, my mind spinning. Unanswered questions piled on top of each other, layer after stifling layer of uncertainty. When I couldn't bear it any longer, and for no discernible reason other than gut instinct, I turned right.

As I'd limped along, forcing one foot in front of the other, the sky had clouded over, taking away most of the moonlight and visibility, making everything around me more ominous. I picked up the pace, ignoring the pain in my temple, which ordered me to slow down, to *sit* down, and kept walking. About a quarter of a mile later, a fat water droplet bounced off the top of my skull. A flash of lightning followed, and not long after I heard the sound of rolling thunder in the not-too-far-away distance. Shivering, I upped my speed some more, hoping to find refuge before the heavens opened and dumped the brunt of the approaching storm on top of my aching head.

The track had been deserted. Not a single pedestrian, cyclist or anyone in a car I could ask for help. As I walked, my feet thudding in a steady rhythm on the path, I'd asked myself the same question over and over, saying it out loud, as if making a demand would suddenly provide the answer. "What's my name? What's my name? What. Is. My. *Name?*"

Fear came and went like waves on the beach. One minute my mind screamed at me to find shelter and get warm, but the next, the question returned, running through my head at a maniacal speed. *What's my name? What's my name? What's my name? What's my name?*

I'm not sure how long I walked. An hour? More? Bombarded by the frigid rain, barefoot and wearing nothing but shorts, my head still pounding and no recollection of…*anything*, I needed to find help. I ordered myself to keep going. *Keep going.* Those two words became my new mantra, the only way to drown out the voice in my head bellowing this was all wrong, I was in trouble. Serious trouble.

When the track veered to the left and I'd seen a flickering light in the distance, I'd wanted to run to it. My legs refused. They were at least twice as heavy since I'd started out, making me walk more slowly as I tried to ignore the sharp pebbles and stones digging into the soles of my feet. Getting closer to the light, I could make out the faint shape of a single-story home and I let out an exhausted grunt. Almost there, I told myself. Hobbling up the long driveway, I staggered in the direction of the front door, but when a flash of lightning illuminated the skies and the car parked outside, my feet stopped dead. I squinted at the large blue-and-white letters on the side of the vehicle. The word *POLICE*.

I scrambled, toes and heels searching for traction, as if they, not my brain, sensed danger. It didn't make sense. An officer might be able to help me, except I knew—I *knew*—I couldn't knock on that door. Couldn't ask whoever was inside for assistance. I had to get out of there, and so I turned and ran this time, disregarding the stinging in my feet and the searing in my lungs as a primeval fear deep within me took over, urging me to put as much distance between me and the house and police cruiser as fast as I could. I kept going for longer than I thought possible, didn't slow down until the track widened some more and changed into smooth asphalt. That was when, doubled over from the effort, I finally caught my breath for long enough to steady the pounding of my heart.

I still had no idea what was going on, what had happened to me or why I was so afraid. I racked my brains, but no answers came, and it was still pitch-black when I'd made it to the outskirts of a town. I couldn't bring myself to knock on anyone's door. I didn't recognize any of the landmarks, street signs or houses, had no clue who lived in the latter, but understood they'd call the cops if they were woken up by a half-naked man who couldn't tell them who he was. Although I knew little else, I was certain I couldn't take that risk.

When I saw a set of headlights coming my way in the distance, I'd crouched behind some leafy bushes to stay out of sight. I rubbed my face with my hands, noticing the watch on my left wrist for the first time. It looked older, had a plain white face with black roman numerals, and the glass cover and silver metal band were scratched and worn. The time said five fifteen, and as the first rays of sunlight crept their way across the skies above the clouds, I decided it had to be morning. I examined the watch, willing myself to recognize it and remember where it had come from, but only found a blank static space in my mind where the knowledge should have been. Heading underneath the nearest streetlamp, I released the clasp, took off the watch and examined it from every angle, ran a finger over the engraving on the back.

To Brad
All my love,
Rosalie x

"My name's Brad?" Hearing my voice was like listening to a stranger. "My name's Brad." I made it a statement this time, trying to convince myself with certainty. Now I had my name, I hoped other things would fall into place. I stood there with my arms bent, palms facing the sky, as if expecting a miracle. Nothing. Everything remained as strange as it had been since I'd woken up. My name sounded unfamiliar on my tongue and as for Rosalie, I had no idea who she was, or if I loved her back. Was she out there searching for me? Why couldn't I remember someone who was obviously an important person in my life? My pulse accelerated again as I tried to process yet more questions I didn't have the answers to. They frustrated me so much I slipped the watch back on my wrist and kept going, repeating *my name is Brad*, in the hope it would have the desired effect if I said it enough.

A little farther down the road I'd reached a single-pump service station with a store that had a bright, wooden *Jim's General & Deli* sign on the door. Perched above it on the front of the roof was a giant, weathered plastic sculpture of a fish my brain somehow identified as a sturgeon. Another sign near the door caught my eye, some company proclaiming they offered the best fishing charters in Maryland. *Maryland.* Instinct combined with logic told me that's where I was, although I didn't know how I felt so certain, or why I somehow also knew this wasn't where I belonged. I looked around. Two cars were parked out front, one with a teardrop trailer attached to the back. Great. I knew the species of a plastic fish and what kind of trailer this was but couldn't remember my own name or what I was doing in Maryland. There had to be some comedic value in that—too bad I couldn't find it. I shook my head, immediately regretting the gesture because of the sharp stabbing pain it caused in the side of my skull.

Staying low, I crept to the vehicles. My immediate and not particularly brilliant plan was to find water, clothes and shoes before retreating someplace else, getting warm and figuring out what to do next, but as I got closer to the trailer, I'd noticed the Maine number plate on the back. Black-capped chickadee. Pine cone. The word *Vacationland*.

A jumble of pictures flashed through my mind. An old house. Twinkling, star-shaped lights. The sound of laughter. As I tried to grasp the fragments they retreated into the corners of my mind, disappearing from reach. Had I remembered something from my past?

More bewildered than before, I stumbled around the side of the trailer. With shaky fingers I reached for the handle, my mouth dropping in surprise when the door opened. I climbed in, groaning as I got out of the wind at last, until the pungent smell of a lemon air freshener dangling next to the window smuggled its way up my nose, making me retch. I looked around the compact space, took in the kitchenette, fully made-up bed, white bathroom complete with toilet, sink and shower, and the small seating area that had a padded bench and cat-print cushions. My legs wanted to walk the rest of my body to the bed and make it collapse there, but I refused. Drink. Clothes. Shoes. Those were what I'd come for.

I grabbed a glass from the cupboard and filled it with water, gulped as much of it down in one go as I could as the rest dribbled down my chin. Two more glasses followed and, once satisfied, I pulled open the small wardrobe next to the bathroom, yanked a green flannel shirt from a hanger and reached for a pair of jeans. They were so long and baggy they pooled at the bottom of my ankles, but they were warm, and as I hoisted them over my board shorts I heard loud voices outside, two people in a heated argument. I ducked, leaving a sliver of space for me to see out of the window. A man, his shoulders almost as broad as his legs were long, strode ahead of a petite blonde woman. She took twice as many steps to keep up with him, almost running by his side, and both yelled at each other as they approached, their words gaining enough clarity for me to hear.

"No, Rita," the man shouted. "I'm not going to calm the fu—"

"Don't you swear at me, Sal," Rita yelled back, her face pinched. "I apologized. I told you it didn't mean anything. And let's be real. It's not like you've never—"

"Don't put this on me." Sal stopped, turned and pointed a finger. "We weren't married."

Rita let out a piercing laugh. "You're a hypocrite."

"Get in the car."

"I'm not driving home with you in this mood."

Sal the giant didn't move, and when Rita refused to budge, he said, "Suit yourself."

He opened the driver's door, disappeared inside and started the engine. I wondered if he would leave his wife stranded there, but after a moment's hesitation, Rita scuttled over and got in the car.

This had been my cue, time to get out of the trailer and hope they were too distracted by their arguing to see me, but the vague shreds of recognition I'd experienced when I'd spotted the Maine number plate stopped me from moving. The air filled with the scent of lemon air freshener, and when the trailer lurched forward, I'd made no attempt to escape because something inside me gently whispered that Maine was home.

4

LILY

A little more than six hours had passed since we'd located Jack's truck at the beach, but it felt as if it had been years. Sam had taken over my call to the police as we'd stood next to the old Ford, our bodies lashed by the wind and rain. He'd had no choice because after I'd dialed 911, I'd panicked, shouting into the phone, spouting words in no particular order like *gone* and *boyfriend* and *beach*. When I'd become angry because the dispatcher couldn't string my nonsensical ramblings together, I'd told her, in no uncertain terms, to *fucking* listen. That's when Sam gently lifted the phone from my fingers, put his arm around my shoulders and guided me to his car. He opened the door and ushered me inside, all the while explaining the situation to the emergency services, his words making it through my ears and inside my head, where they swirled around in an erratic, confused mess.

I'm not sure how long it took for the police to arrive. Minutes, probably, but it could've been hours. Sam and I sat in his car as I called whomever I could think of—Jack's boss, our few friends and acquaintances—but nobody had seen or heard from him, and by the time I hung up I was no closer to solving the urgent mystery of his whereabouts. I brought my knees to my chest and wrapped my arms around them as Sam talked about his upcoming business trip, and how his daughter had broken her finger rock-climbing. Part of my brain acknowledged he was doing so to keep me from losing it, and so I listened and nodded, listened some more and nodded again, incapable of uttering a single word, but increasingly grateful for his.

When the police car arrived and parked across from us, a male officer in uniform and a woman dressed in a drab gray suit got out. They moved at a brisk pace, and although Sam had managed to keep me calm up to this point, I now scrambled for the door handle, jumped into the rain and ran toward them. The concerned expression on their faces reignited the panic bubbling inside me, everything I'd tried to push down by telling myself Jack was okay, we'd find him, and all this would be over soon. One glance at them made my stomach contract, threatening to empty my guts all over the parking lot. I clenched my fists, willing my food to stay down.

"And your boyfriend swims here regularly?" This came from the male policeman, who'd introduced himself as Officer Stevens before we'd given them the facts as swiftly and succinctly as possible. Stevens was about my age, maybe a year or two older, with four moles on his neck, arranged in a perfect square as if it were a connect-the-dots game for toddlers. As he talked, I caught the sweet scent of maple syrup. It made me think of pancakes, and how Jack and I were supposed to be at my apartment, making love again before lunch, or snuggled up watching Netflix. Where was he? Where *was* he? I took a breath, and another, then a third, fast and shallow, my head spinning.

"Lily?" Sam put a hand on my shoulder. "Does he swim here often?"

"Yes," I whispered, repeating the word twice to make sure I'd said it out loud. I exhaled, trying to keep the tremble from my voice. It didn't work. "H-he swims most days. Here, and other beaches. It…it depends."

The woman, who'd told us she was Detective Heron, and whose tone and handshake had already asserted she was senior to her colleague in rank, raised an eyebrow. "On what?"

"On the day. How busy the beach is. He likes swimming in peace. He says it lets him leave anything bad behind." I shrugged, looked at my sand-covered sneakers, mumbled, "He says the water makes all his worries sink to the bottom of the ocean."

"Would you say he has a lot of worries?" Heron said gently.

"No. Not at all." Anger surged at the question. What was she doing, trying to twist my words around and imply something that wasn't there? They had to call for backup. Start looking for Jack, now, not ask me a bunch of stupid questions. I wanted to say all of this, shout at them as loud as I could, but my history with cops made me stay quiet, tongue-tied.

Stevens rubbed his goatee with his thumb, and I noticed a shiny gold wedding ring on his finger. I wondered if his spouse had ever gone missing. If he or she had disappeared the way Jack had. Did Stevens understand what was happening any more than I did?

"So, he usually swims alone?" he said.

I nodded at first, stopped and brushed the sopping strands of hair from my face. Last time I'd mentioned I was getting it trimmed, Jack begged me not to, insisted the longer, the sexier. I'd told him in that case he was welcome to let *his* hair grow past his chest and deal with all the knots, the bird's-nest bedhead and ultra-bad hair days, before instructing the stylist to lop off a good three inches. Jack had loved it all the same, but in that moment, standing with Sam, Stevens and Heron near the beach,

I made a silent, desperate promise. If Jack reappeared here and now, I'd never cut my hair again. When Sam squeezed my arm, I saw them watching me, and he had to repeat the question.

"Does he usually swim alone?"

"Not always," I said. "Sometimes I go with him."

"Why not yesterday?" Stevens said.

"I told you." I raised my voice this time, I couldn't help it, and it had the same effect on Heron's and Stevens's eyebrows. I lowered my eyes, mumbled, "He was supposed to go for a quick swim before heading back to work."

"To the place he got laid off from," Heron said.

"Yes, but—"

Stevens jumped in. "You said Jake's thirty-three?"

"Jack." I pinched the bridge of my nose, fought hard to keep the anger inside because if I let it out, there was no telling what I might do, or if I'd get it back under control. They were wasting my time. Jack's time.

"His name's *Jack* Smith," Sam said, his voice firm with more than a touch of authority, and I was grateful for his gravitas to counterbalance my near hysteria. "And Lily clearly stated he's *almost* thirty-three. Shouldn't you be taking this more seriously?"

"Sir, we are, I promise," Detective Heron said before turning to me. "Have you called *Jack's* friends?" The emphasis on the name wasn't lost on anyone but she still shot her colleague an unmistakable *get it right next time, you idiot* look, which made him wither for no more than a split second.

"Of course I did," I whispered.

"Miss Reid—"

"Lily."

"Lily," Heron repeated, her tone still even. "Could Jack have had car trouble and called someone to pick him up? A friend or family member, maybe? Perhaps he—"

"*No.* I told you. I called everyone. Besides…what about those?" I pointed to the keys and wallet in her hand, the items

I'd given to her within moments of their arrival at the beach. "Anyway, Jack would've called *me*. He doesn't have family here. His, well, *ex*-boss is away for the weekend somewhere, and as for other people…" I let the rest of the sentence die, didn't want to admit Jack hadn't any close friends in the area, had chosen not to develop those relationships since he'd arrived in town two years prior because he'd been let down by people too often before. Telling them would invite too many questions I couldn't answer. Things I'd never pressed Jack about because I'd recognized his need to leave history behind, and because we were focusing on a future together, not our separate pasts.

The minutes ticked by, dragging us from Saturday morning to afternoon, and the rain had finally slowed to a steady trickle. At some point, more police vehicles arrived, and Jack's truck had been searched. When Heron had played the increasingly desperate voice mails I'd left for him on his phone, I turned away, not wanting to hear the terror in my voice.

A while later the local press interviewed me, but I couldn't remember what the immaculately made-up journalist had asked, or what I'd said. I felt like I'd gone numb from the inside out. The coast guard was alerted, something I became aware of through snippets of conversations overheard on the police radio, and well before Heron or Stevens filled us in. All this time, Sam stayed on the beach with me, dressed in his pajamas, listening, watching, hoping. I didn't want to leave. If I went home it meant abandoning Jack, but Sam insisted there was nothing we could do, I needed to at least try to get some rest.

"You'll be the first to know of any developments," Heron assured me in her calm yet efficient manner, and so I'd reluctantly agreed to Sam driving me back to his place to pick up my car. I declined his offer of going inside his house and him making something to eat. I wasn't hungry and needed to be alone. I made it half a mile before having to pull over by the side of the road so I could let out the cries of frustration, anger and fear, which had all mixed together into a ball of raw emotion I could no longer contain.

An hour later I'd paced my apartment a thousand times, and there was still no news. I'd lost count of how many times I'd checked my cell, how often I'd willed, ordered and begged it to ring, or for the screen to light up with a text message, but it remained silent and dark, useless. If it hadn't represented a life-line to Jack, I'd have snapped it in half and stamped on the broken remains until they were dust beneath my feet.

As I reached for my phone again to make sure I hadn't missed anything since the last time I'd looked, a sharp knock made me jump. I raced across the room, almost upending the coffee table in my haste, and yanked the front door open. It was Stevens and Heron, the bags under their eyes making them seem as tired, drawn and washed-out as I felt.

"Have you found him?" I said, my heart thumping hard. "Have you found Jack?"

"Can we come in?" Heron said gently.

No, I wanted to shout. *No, you can't come in because I don't want to hear what you have to say. I'm terrified. Please don't tell me. Don't say it. Don't you dare say it.*

I stepped aside. Once I'd closed the door behind them and, ever so politely, offered them a seat (which they accepted) and a glass of water (which they declined), I couldn't help asking again, my voice resembling a frightened child's who'd woken up from a nightmare. "Have you found him?"

They looked at each other, jaws clenched. No doubt Heron had already decided who'd do the talking: her as the seasoned detective, or rookie Stevens. Either way, whoever was set to deliver the bad news, I wanted them to hesitate or have a long, drawn-out argument about something with each other, anything to delay the message I knew was coming. I took a step back, trying to put more distance between us as I pulled at the neck of my shirt, which seemed to be strangling me.

"No, we haven't found him," Heron said.

Air rushed into my lungs, filling me with hope, making my head spin with the possibility of finding Jack alive. I resumed my pacing, fiddled with the heart-shaped charm on the bracelet he'd given me on our first Valentine's Day. He'd tucked it into a box of candy, and I hadn't seen it at first, felt a tinge of disappointment as I thanked him for the chocolates. Despite our shared and somewhat negative opinions of the kitschy, commercial pseudo-forced romantic day, I'd hoped for...*more*. It wasn't only the fact this was our first Valentine's Day as a couple, but also the first time I'd seen the point of celebrating it with someone. Consequently, and embarrassingly, when he'd turned the lid of the box upside down to reveal the hidden jewelry, the fact he felt the same had made me cry.

"He's still out there," I whispered, looking up. "Are they searching—"

"The coast guard is doing its job," Stevens said, holding up a bony hand, and his nonchalance made me want to grab his fingers and twist them backward until they snapped.

"The search isn't why we're here," Heron added.

I stopped pacing, and my eyes darted from her to Stevens and back again as I tried to fathom what other reason might have brought them to my door. What could be more important right now than being out there, looking for Jack?

"We came because we want some information about, uh, *Jack*," Stevens said.

"Okay." I reached for my phone. "If you need another photo, I can—"

"Perhaps you should sit." Heron gestured to the sofa, and something in her gentle tone told me to follow her command. I obediently walked over and sat down, perched on the edge of the seat, probably looking like I might make a run for it. Depending on what she told me, maybe I would.

"What's this about?" I touched my bracelet again, wishing

it were a portal to the past so I could tell Jack not to go swimming, or that it would transform itself into a magic lamp containing a genie who'd grant me three wishes. Or just one. One wish would be plenty.

"How well do you know Jack?" Heron said, and my forehead crinkled as I tried to focus enough to understand her question. "You mentioned you've been together for about a year and a half, is that correct?"

"Yes." The air around me had become thick again, making it hard to breathe.

"And in that time," Stevens took over, "have you met any of his family? Any old friends or acquaintances from before he arrived in Brookmount?"

"No. His parents are dead, and he has no siblings. Why?"

Heron rested her elbows on her knees. "The driver's license in his wallet is a fake."

"Huh?"

"A forgery," Stevens said. "A good one, but not perfect. They rarely are."

I tried to make sense of his words. The suggestion was ridiculous. Jack was in his thirties; he didn't need bogus identification to buy booze. If they were right, which they weren't, what would Jack be doing with a fake ID? I tried to imagine other possibilities. Had he got into trouble, been caught speeding, or running a red light? Had his license been revoked and he'd continued driving with a forged one? Had he never taken his driver's test in the first place? I'd read about a similar case once. A man had driven for almost ten years before being found out at a random traffic stop.

"Why?" I said. It was the only word my brain allowed my mouth to articulate.

"We don't know yet," Heron said, still leaning forward, close enough for me to see the yellow flecks in her deep brown eyes. "This Jack Smith doesn't exist, and by that, I mean the details on his license don't match any records. Lily, it may not even be his real name."

I wanted to rewind what I'd heard and listen again at quarter speed. If I did, maybe something, *anything*, would make sense. Their words sounded like gibberish, an alien language I couldn't understand. "You've made a mistake, I—"

"What kind of problems was Jack having?" Stevens said.

"Problems?" I whipped my head up and looked at him, searching my brain for any concerns Jack might have shared with me of late. I wondered if I should mention he'd seemed a little agitated a few times. He worried about money a lot, I knew that, and he was always careful about not overspending. On more than one occasion he'd said he wished he could spoil me with lavish gifts, and I'd laughed and said it wasn't the 1950s, thank you very much, I was perfectly capable of treating myself. Jack had countered that wasn't the point, but I'd waved him off and told him to stop being silly.

Then there had been another occasion just last week in the shopping mall parking lot. It had been uncharacteristically busy because of a big sale, and a teenager in a shiny black Audi had taken the spot Jack had patiently been waiting for. Jack had yelled at him, called him a "pretentious git for nicking my place." Once we'd parked elsewhere, and I'd suppressed a laugh after Jack translated *git* (jerk) and *nicking* (stealing), I said, "You never get bent out of shape for stuff like that. For a moment there I thought you'd go all Kathy Bates on him, like in *Fried Green Tomatoes*. What's up?"

"Nothing, it's fine," he'd said, before apologizing and leaning over to kiss me. "I hate showy knob-heads. Next time remind me to call the idiot a spunk bubble." At that point I'd collapsed in a fit of giggles, and we'd walked to the shop arm-in-arm, the mini confrontation already forgotten.

Looking at Stevens now, I decided neither of the incidents were worth mentioning. They were trivial. Irrelevant. What would I gain by bringing them up when I knew they meant nothing? "He didn't have any problems."

"Was he depressed?" Heron said softly. "About losing his job?"

The inference became clear as their heads tilted to one side, sympathetic expressions at the ready. "He didn't kill himself," I said, and as they exchanged an almost imperceptible glance, I wondered if I'd put the idea into their heads by somehow misrepresenting who Jack was. "He wouldn't do that. He *wouldn't*."

"We have to consider all possibilities," Heron said.

"Not that one," I fired off, straightening my back. "Because you're wrong."

As she opened her mouth to respond, her phone rang. She answered it swiftly, asked, "When? Where?" and finished with a curt "Uh-huh, fine," before hanging up and turning to me. "They found some clothes farther down the beach. It may be nothing, but they're sending—" Her phone beeped, and she held it up, screen pointed at me.

I let out a sharp gasp. There it was. The dark green American Eagle shirt I'd given Jack for Christmas, the one I'd chosen because it complemented his amber eyes, and which was so soft, I couldn't resist hugging him whenever he wore it. It was my favorite as much as his.

"They found this hoodie." Heron brought up another photo, and my hands flew to my mouth as I closed my eyes.

"Ask them if it has a hole in the left pocket," I whispered. "Half an inch long."

Heron fired off a text and I stayed silent as we waited for the reply, but when Stevens's phone rang, I jumped. As he moved to the kitchen to take the call, I struggled to comprehend what was happening. First, I refused to accept Jack may have harmed himself, and I didn't believe Heron's tale of his identity being fake, either. She'd made a mistake, or there was a glitch in the system. Someone, somewhere had made a clerical error, mixed up Jack's records with somebody else's. Jack Smith was a common name, and there had to be a thousand possible things that could have happened to create a mishap like this, and the ensuing confusion.

Still…doubts tried to wriggle their way in through the cracks of my mind, nibbling and distorting what I knew to be true. Jack hadn't shared much about his past. As I'd informed the police, his parents had died, and he had no siblings, only a few distant family members in England he never saw or stayed in touch with after moving to the US as a teenager. What if only part, or none, of that was true? *No.* I wouldn't doubt the man I loved, and with whom I wanted to spend the rest of my life. The man who'd said he had the same feelings for me.

The beep of Heron's phone ripped me out of the jumble of thoughts that had turned themselves into a minefield, making me incapable of taking a single step without the risk of blowing what I believed to be the truth wide open. She exhaled slowly, and said, "There's a hole in the hoodie. Left pocket. About half an inch."

Before I could process the information, collapse or let out a scream, Stevens walked back in with a dark look on his face. "Another round of storms is coming in, worse than the first. The coast guard has to suspend—"

"But Jack's still out there," I said, finding my voice. "They can't stop looking."

"The search will resume as soon as it's safe to go back out," Heron said, getting up and walking over, her palms facing me in a *calm down* gesture that did nothing to settle the crescendo of panic. "I promise you, they'll start looking as quickly as they can."

I closed my eyes again, tears spilling over my cheeks as my new reality set in. With Jack missing since last night, come tomorrow there'd be no more talk about a rescue mission.

It would be a recovery operation.

5

THE MAN FROM THE BEACH

A little while after the trailer had set off, I'd gone back to the wardrobe and searched through the bottom, where I located a pair of socks and running shoes. The sneakers were two sizes too big, but I pulled them on anyway, wincing when the insoles pressed against my shredded feet. As I closed the door a T-shirt caught my eye. It had the words *The White Stripes* on it, along with a picture of a guy in a top hat, and a woman with long brown hair, wearing a red dress. Snippets of a music video went through my mind. Images of red, black and white triangles. A woman… M…something. M… Yes, that was it, *Meg.*

I had to stop myself from punching the air with a whoop because I'd *remembered*. Things were coming back. If I could recall something so obscure, surely the more important stuff would return because the image of Meg White—*Jesus*, I knew her last name now—was so clear, it was almost as if I were watching the video on TV. As suddenly as it arrived, the image faded, replaced by one of a young girl. Her hair was shorter than Meg's, and instead of drumsticks she smacked a pair of chopsticks together so hard I thought they'd break, but then that picture blurred and faded, too, and after that…nothing. What did it mean? What did *anything* mean? I didn't know, and both my brain and body were so exhausted from the effort of trying to place things, I crawled to the bed and lay down, vowing I'd only let myself close my eyes for a second.

I didn't wake up until the trailer went over a bump, and I glanced at my watch, struggling to believe an hour had passed. The pain in my head had subsided, and when my fingers gently reached for the cut on my skull, I felt a mass of hair stuck together with dried, stiffened blood. Once again, I tried to force my mind to remember something—anything—but it was as if my existence only began on the beach. I looked out of the back window, squinting as the gray light hit me in the face. The winds had lessened but the rain held steady, bouncing across the asphalt in translucent beads.

As I sank back down on the bed, I noticed the corner of a brochure wedged between the mattress and the wall. I pulled it out. It was a take-out menu for an Indian restaurant, and the names of the dishes and the pictures of aloo gobi, samosas and malai kofta made my mouth water. Until now I'd been able to ignore the gurgling of my empty stomach, let the hunger pains transform themselves into a dull ache, but at the sight of food my gut contracted hard. I pushed myself up and headed for the kitchenette cupboards, where I found half a loaf of bread and strawberry jam. I fumbled with the lid and didn't bother opening the drawer for a knife, but shoved a piece of bread deep into the jar, groaning as I pushed the food into my mouth.

I was rummaging around the fridge and had gulped down half a pint of milk when the trailer slowed and came to a standstill. My heart raced as I heard the car door open and close, and heavy footsteps making their way in my direction. The driver, the big man called Sal, would immediately spot me when he opened the door. My body reacted in the same way as when I'd seen the police car, signaling an acute urge to run, but I wouldn't make it out of the back window in time and I had nowhere else to go.

The door opened, and as I was about to put my hands up and reassure Sal I wasn't any kind of threat, I heard his wife, Rita, yell something from the car. "I found them," she screeched. "They're in here, you moron. Come on. I want to get home already."

"You left the trailer unlocked again," Sal shouted back before slamming the door shut. I heard him turn the key before he meandered to the car at a glacial pace, not in any apparent hurry to do as Rita commanded. As the air rushed from my lungs I collapsed on the bed, vowing the next time the trailer stopped I'd be ready to push open the back window and run. Sal didn't appear or sound like the kind of person you messed with. Come to think of it, Rita didn't, either.

With the jam safely stowed in the cupboard, I forced myself to leave the rest of the bread, making sure I wiped away any crumbs from the counter to remove all signs of my intrusion. As I went to put the take-out menu back where I'd found it, I caught sight of the restaurant's phone number, which began with 207. A sequence flashed in front of my eyes. Two, zero, seven, followed by six other digits, a combination that came over and over, drowning out everything else trying to make its way into my head. It became a steady pattern that made no sense until I realized it was a phone number, I was sure of it, except I was missing a digit. But which one? The first, last, or another somewhere in the middle? Trying to figure out how many possible combinations that represented made my headache start up again, so I jotted down the numbers on a piece of paper in case I forgot them, and stuffed the note in my pocket. Exhaustion invaded me once more, and I headed back to the bed, falling asleep before I'd stretched out my legs.

Sal stopped briefly at another service station, and I watched him and Rita, who were no longer on speaking terms, and stayed close to the back window in case I had to jump out. They didn't approach the trailer again, and I settled in for the ride, incapable of staying awake.

The sun had started its descent when I woke up again, and as we drove over a bridge, I noticed a green-and-white sign announcing our arrival in Maine. I expected a rush of excitement, a massive influx of memories. Instead, a sinking sensation pulled at the pit of my stomach. What would I do now? Where would I go once I got out of the trailer? Coming to Maine had been a stupid, rash decision. Somebody in Maryland had to know me. Someone had to be wondering where I was. What had I been thinking? I spent the next hour trying to come up with a plan but failed, because, as it turned out, without a memory or history, there weren't many avenues to explore.

When the trailer slowed down again a while later, I decided it was time for me to go. I grabbed a black rain jacket and a blue baseball hat from the wardrobe, hoping Sal and Rita would blame one another for leaving them behind, and pushed the back window open. Even before we'd come to a complete stop I slid out, my legs buckling as they hit the ground.

I took in my surroundings. The trailer had pulled into a small plaza with an Irving Oil, a convenience store and a couple of fast-food places. I put on the jacket and hat, and headed away from the plaza, ducking my head. As I shoved my hands into the coat's pockets, my fingers closed over a piece of paper, which turned out to be a twenty-dollar bill. I whispered a thank-you to the rain-cloud-filled skies, and hid behind a couple of parked cars, watching Sal fill up his car as Rita periodically shouted at him to hurry the hell up. When they finally drove away I waited another few minutes in case they returned, and when I decided it was safe, went to the store.

The brass bell above my head jangled as I entered. The guy

behind the counter threw an uninspired glance my way before returning to the phone in his hand. I headed for the fridge, grabbed the biggest bottle of water I could find and picked up pretzels and chocolate. I ran my tongue over the fuzziness of my gums, for the first time realizing how rancid my breath must be. How long since I'd brushed my teeth? What brand of toothpaste did I use? Mundane questions, perhaps, but, damn it, I wanted the answers.

"What am I going to do?" I muttered as I walked up the aisle, adding a small toothbrush kit to my supplies, hoping the twenty dollars would cover it all. I set the items on the counter, and after the cashier handed over five bucks in change, I asked for the key to the bathroom.

He passed me a grubby tennis ball with a single key attached to it and pointed outside. "Around the back. Close the door when you're done."

The stale air in the bathroom smelled of shit, the toilet seat lay broken and abandoned on the floor, and someone had drawn an impressive array of boobs and dicks of every shape and size all over the piss-colored walls. The words *Peter sucks* and *for free* along with a phone number, all in three different sets of handwriting, had been scrawled above the hazy, scratch-covered mirror. I cupped my hands under the water and splashed some on my face, gazing at myself as I observed my short brown hair and the dark circles under my eyes.

I didn't know my name, didn't know how old I was, either, and if asked to guess, I'd have said somewhere in my thirties. Looking at myself in the mirror was as if I were meeting an old acquaintance—someone from my past I may have known well once, but who I no longer quite recognized. I lowered my gaze, splashed more water onto my hands and ran damp paper towels under my armpits, over my chest and the back of my neck, wishing for a hot shower. Barely any cleaner, and not feeling much better, I walked back to the store. I was about to pull the door open when I noticed the pay phone, and as I stared at it, the sequence of numbers I'd remembered in the trailer flashed through my mind again.

At the counter, I handed over the bathroom key, and pulled the rest of my money from my pocket. "Can I have some change for the pay phone?"

"Cool accent," the cashier said as he handed me the coins. "Australian? Or English?"

I stared at him and opened my mouth but didn't know how to answer. Up to that point my nationality hadn't crossed my mind. I was in the US. Didn't that make me American? And if not, why the hell did I feel such a strong connection to Maine? Without offering a reply I went back outside, where I piled the money in neat stacks on top of the phone box. Taking a deep breath, I pulled the note from my pocket, picked up the receiver and dialed the combination. Fingers unsteady, I hesitated before adding a one.

"Hello?" It was a man's voice I didn't recognize, which meant precisely bugger all.

"Hello." I hesitated, unsure what to say next. I hadn't thought this through.

"Who's this?"

"Uh…do you, ah, recognize my voice?"

"What? Who *is* this?"

"Are you sure you don't know who I am?"

The line went dead, and I couldn't blame him. I tried another few combinations, added a two, a three, a four and a five to the end of each new sequence. One woman answered in a language I didn't understand, another told me to piss off, one call had an automated message stating the number had been disconnected, and the last one went to a voice mail belonging to someone whose name didn't elicit the smallest flicker of recognition.

I hung up. And gave up. This was stupid. The possibilities were endless, and soon not only would my patience run out, but my money, too. I forced myself to keep going, added a six and a seven, both unsuccessful, but when I punched in an eight, a woman picked up.

"Hello?" she said, and my lips froze together, making me incapable of saying anything, even when she repeated herself twice over. "All right, dipshit." There was more than a little irritation in her voice now. "I'm sick of these stupid-ass robocalls. Get lost."

The tone. The voice. The combination stirred something inside me, faint and wispy like morning mist you could no longer see, but which had been there moments ago. "Hello?" I whispered. "I know this'll sound strange, but—"

"Ash?"

My heart sank to my stolen shoes. "No. My name is—"

"Where are you?" Her voice went up three notches, making her sound on the verge of panic and almost as desperate as I felt. "Ash? Ash! Talk to me."

My head buzzed with so much noise I could barely hear. Why was she calling me that? My name was Brad. It said so on my watch.

"Ash," she said, her voice a little quieter this time, and I could have sworn she was fighting to hold back tears. "*Please*, tell me where you are."

This was hopeless. The woman was confused. She'd mistaken me for someone else. My name was Brad. *Brad*. When she spoke again, demanding to know for a third time where I was, I decided if I couldn't handle my own problems, there was no way I could deal with hers, too. Hand shaking, I let the receiver dangle before making up my mind and thrusting it into the cradle.

I paused for a second. The woman had sounded so certain about my name, but it couldn't be. It said Brad on my watch, and for the past day, this had been my one anchor in a world full of crazy. I wouldn't let her mistake unmoor me; if I did, I'd have nothing left. Coming to Maine hadn't yet produced the epiphany I'd hoped for. If anything, it had made me more confused.

As I walked away from the service station and up the road, trying to find some clarity and a way forward, I spotted a derelict house with boarded-up windows. Its heavy wooden door was padlocked, and the place appeared empty, so I decided it would be my refuge for the night. It was getting late, the air had cooled, and I was too exhausted to formulate a better plan. Come morning I'd figure out what to do next. Maybe find a hospital—no, they might call the cops—a shelter of some sort then, somewhere they wouldn't ask too many questions.

After glancing over my shoulder to make sure nobody was watching, I sneaked around the side of the house, pushed open a creaky, rusted iron gate and found myself in an overgrown backyard that long hadn't been on anybody's to-do list. I got to work on the board covering a window on the left, and part of the rotting wood crumbled under my fingers as I wiggled the nails loose. Not long after, the broken board lay on the ground. I took off my jacket, wrapped it over my hand and gave the brittle pane a good punch. It shattered with a crunch, and after removing the rest of the shards, I hoisted myself up and over the windowsill, cursing when a piece of glass I'd missed cut into my thumb.

Once inside I stood still, listening for the noise of other unwanted guests, human or otherwise, but the musty air, which smelled of damp, rot and mold, remained silent. The light from the broken window behind me barely made it past my feet, and I put my hands out in front of me to feel my way, taking small, uncertain steps, hoping I wouldn't crash through the floorboards.

A couple of plywood panels had fallen away from the windows in the front room, letting in enough light for me to make out it was empty. There was no furniture, not even a crate or an abandoned cardboard box. A giant stone fireplace covered almost half of the left wall, but when I examined it, hoping to find wood and matches or a lighter to warm the place up a bit, I found nothing.

I stretched out on the floor, the scent of dirt and dust creeping up my nostrils, earthy and familiar. A flash of something went through my mind. A faint giggle, a girl calling out, "…nineteen, twenty. Ready or not, here I come!" Footsteps thudding, a trapdoor opening above me, someone peering down, their face obscured by the shadows.

I scrunched my eyes shut, willing the images to stay, to mean something, but they faded, and I was left in the old house, lying on the floor alone in the darkness, no closer to my truth.

6

LILY

When Sam came to my apartment to check on me Saturday evening, he brought a veggie sub with extra cheese and lettuce because it was my favorite—and because he didn't know what else to do. Nobody did, least of all me, and I pushed the food away, saying I wasn't hungry, but when I let slip I hadn't eaten since breakfast that morning, Sam insisted and cajoled. I gave in only because I half expected him to wave the sandwich in front of my face and make airplane noises if I didn't. After I was done, I reclaimed what had become my permanent spot on the sofa. I pulled the moose-pattern blanket to my chest—a relic from my days in upstate New York—making sure my phone was fully charged and close by, with the volume turned up all the way, the screen facing me.

Meanwhile, Sam rubbed his face and tapped his foot on the

floor, his nervous energy having nowhere else to go. "Uh, Lily, I need to tell you something."

"What?" My voice went up a few notches as I put my mug down for fear I'd spill hot coffee all over myself. "What is it? What's wrong?"

He held up both hands, waving them around. "Don't panic, it's nothing, really. Well, except I had to change my trip around. I'm leaving for Chicago tomorrow."

I exhaled, wondering if this was how I'd be from now on: jumpy and on edge, always expecting bad news. I chastised myself for thinking like that. Jack was alive. He was *definitely* alive. The search would start again soon, which had to count for something. "Don't worry, I—"

"I *am* worried. I'll be gone almost two weeks and I don't want to leave you alone. It's not fair. Are you sure you can't call someone to come and stay with you?"

Tears prickled the backs of my eyes. I blinked them away, forcing my face into a grimacing smile worthy of a contortionist act in the circus. I'd known Sam for almost as long as I'd known Jack, but we weren't close enough for me to share the details about my family. Hell, I hadn't told Jack everything. I wondered if now was the time to inform Sam that Jack might not be who he'd said he was, but I couldn't. I still didn't want to believe I was in love with a liar, and besides, what was the point in sullying Jack's reputation if it all turned out to be a stupid case of mistaken identity?

"I'll be fine, Sam. I promise."

"This isn't the kind of situation you want to deal with alone."

"I'm perfectly capable—"

"I know you're *capable*, but my point is you shouldn't *have* to." He paused, hesitated for a while before saying, "What's the next step?"

The anger I'd somehow suppressed thus far became stronger, and I tried hard to tamp it down. Subtle as they were, the comments the police and Sam had made all implied Jack wouldn't be coming home. How could they think that way when there was still hope? It was an insult, a punch in the face, and I wouldn't stand for it. If Sam wanted to convince me to give up on Jack, he'd have to be direct about it. I raised my chin.

"What do you mean, 'next step'?" I said.

"Uh, well, what are you going to do?"

"I'm going to wait," I whispered, jaw clenched. "He'll come back. I know he will."

Sam smiled faintly but said nothing. Jack would've called him a coward. Jack would've... *Jack*. How could that not be his name? If Heron and Stevens were right, then who the hell was he? Why had he lied? How could he have told me I was the most important person in the world and listened to me saying I felt the same about him? Our relationship had been the one thing in my life I'd been sure of. As corny as it sounded, when I'd met Jack it had been like coming home. I'd spent the years before drifting from job to job, city to town to village, with no clear plan on what I wanted to do, where I wanted to be, let alone with whom I wanted to share my life. I hadn't always been like that, so lost and unprepared. My family was *respectable*, as my parents had often reminded my brother, Quentin, and me. My mother was a family doctor, my father an executive banker. Well-to-do people, career people, *stable*. They'd tolerated what they'd identified as my "flaky phase," during which I'd been drawn to music and art before adding boys and makeup to the list. For quite some time, both Mom and Dad had been convinced I'd grow into the academic daughter they wanted, a carbon copy of Quentin, who was fourteen months my senior, yet light-years ahead in terms of meeting the life goals they'd assigned him. He was a sure bet, the thoroughbred my parents paraded in front of their friends. In contrast, I was the stable girl best kept in the back, lest she cause embarrassment.

If the annual round-robin announcements my mother sent at

Christmas were to be believed, Quentin was on the fast track to becoming an internationally renowned neurosurgeon. The thick, floral-white letter tucked into the padded, lavender-scented envelope rarely contained a mention of me, and I was certain they sent me the annual update merely as a reminder of what I'd messed up and lost, and as an overt signal to not bother visiting them anytime soon unless I met their exacting standards. Jack knew most of this, but I'd justified withholding some of the details about my past because we were all guilty of hiding things when we met someone we liked, I mean *really* liked, a person with whom we could imagine spending the rest of our life, but who might not feel the same if they knew all our ugly little secrets up front. Except I hadn't only withheld the information at the beginning, I'd never shared it at all.

"Lily?" Sam's voice tore me away from the memories of my dysfunctional family. "Do you want to spend the night at my place? The spare room—"

"No. I have to prepare a few things for work."

"You're going in tomorrow? Are you serious?"

Sliding my empty mug across the coffee table with my toes so I could stretch out my legs, I noticed the gray tinge on top of my white sock, reminding me I should've showered or at least changed my clothes. "I can't sit here all day. I'll go mad."

Sam nodded, watched me for another few seconds before standing up. "I have to pack. You've got my cell number. Call me as soon as you hear anything. And even if you don't. Okay?"

"I will, I promise."

I accompanied him to the front door, where he gave me a hug and a fatherly kiss on the top of my head. "I can't believe this is happening, Lily. You know how much I think of Jack."

"Thank you," I whispered, grateful he hadn't spoken about him in past tense. I closed the door behind him, relieved to be alone again, yet scared because it meant I had too much time for my mind to wander the desolate roads I didn't want to travel.

Sinking back down on the sofa, I allowed myself to wonder if I'd ever know the truth about Jack if he failed to come home. And then I wondered if it might be better if I didn't.

I woke up bathed in sweat after dreaming I couldn't breathe. The pain in my lungs, hot and searing, made me open my eyes and mouth wide as I sucked in air before coughing and struggling to get a grip. I reached out my arm, but the realization I was on the sofa, not my bed, and Jack was still missing, all sucker punched me right in the throat. Squinting at the clock I saw it was barely after 9:30 p.m., but I was wide awake and there was little point trying to get back to sleep for a few hours at least. I stood up, slipped on my shoes, grabbed my jacket and headed outside.

The winds and rain hadn't stopped, and the air was laden with moisture, all of it dulling the crunching noise the gravel made beneath my feet. I got in my car and drove, unsure of my destination until my instincts took me to the beach. The cops had removed Jack's truck, and there were no other vehicles in the lot, but I parked, got out and walked to the water, the wet sand squelching up into my shoes.

"Jack!" I screamed.

The waves crashed on the beach. Was he out there? Had he long slipped beneath the surface, his lungs filling with water, dragging him farther and farther to the depths and beyond? Stevens and Heron implied Jack might have taken his own life, but I couldn't believe it, I *wouldn't*. I knew him.

Do you? a little voice in my head sneered. *Maybe you don't know him at all.*

I couldn't stay at the beach with these terrible thoughts, alone and in the dark, and so I decided to go to Jack's place to search for him, comfort, or anything to relieve the pain inside me. Sam's Porsche sat in the driveway, but all the lights in his house were off, so I climbed the steps to Jack's apartment without making a sound. Heron and Stevens had already checked the place for "clues," which I'd interpreted as "suicide note," but they'd found nothing, and while I hadn't thought I'd be strong enough to come here, all I wanted now was to be surrounded by Jack's things.

Using the flashlight on my phone, I searched for the spare key he left in an old flowerpot, but it wasn't there, and when I lifted the mat, the space underneath was empty. Sam would understand if I rang his doorbell and asked him to let me into Jack's, but as well-intentioned as he was, I couldn't take another round of sympathetic looks and mother-hen clucking. I needed to be alone.

The lock on Jack's kitchen window had been loose for a while, something he'd intended on fixing for days. I hoped he hadn't got around to making the repair, and, sure enough, when I jimmied the pane it opened far enough for me to climb in. I left the lights off in case they alerted Sam to my presence, took off my shoes and walked down the hallway to Jack's bedroom. I knew the place was empty, but still had to fight back the tears as I pushed open the door and saw his neatly made bed with the dark blue duvet cover. After stripping down to my underwear, I pulled on a pair of Jack's pajama bottoms and an old T-shirt, clutching the latter to my chest as I finally let myself go, sobbing and begging.

"Jack," I whispered. "Please come home."

The sound of footsteps on the stairs outside made my breath catch in my throat and I leaped up and ran down the hall shouting, "Jack? *Jack!*" I pulled the front door open and looked down the stairs, ready to jump into his arms, but immediately froze. Even without seeing his face I instinctively knew this wasn't Jack. The man was tall and wiry, wore a black hoodie he'd pulled down over his forehead, obscuring most of his features. White skin, a beard perhaps, or maybe it was a shadow, but I definitely couldn't make out his eyes as they were hidden behind dark sunglasses nobody needed to wear at this time of night.

"Who are you?" I said, my voice sounding a lot firmer than I felt on the inside.

He glanced at me, took a slow, deliberate step forward and opened his mouth to respond when another car I'd never seen before pulled into the driveway behind us. Sam got out, and as soon as I called out to him, the man on the stairs backed off and disappeared around the side of the garage.

"Who was that?" Sam said, frowning as he walked over. "A friend of yours?"

"I don't know." I wrapped my arms around my middle. "One of Jack's maybe? Someone who wanted to check up on him?" I tried to make myself believe the words, but they wouldn't stick. Who would come looking for Jack in the dead of night? And whoever it was, why didn't he say anything, not even to ask if Jack had been found?

Why would he run away when Sam pulled up?

"I thought you were home," I said quickly. "I saw your car."

"I was out for dinner. Got an Uber." He paused for a second. "How did you get into Jack's place? I took the spare key earlier."

"The window." I shrugged. "I wanted to be...you know... close to him."

Sam gave me a small smile, nodded his understanding. "Here, use this next time." He pulled out a bunch of keys from his pocket and took one off the ring before handing it to me. "I'll fix the window first thing in the morning. Make sure nobody else can get in that way."

"Thanks, Sam," I said, trying not to shudder. Up to that point I'd considered spending the night in Jack's bed, but now the thought made my skin prickle.

7

THE MAN FROM THE BEACH

When I woke up again a couple of hours later it was dark outside, and it took a while for my eyes to adjust, even longer to remember where I was. My entire body had gone numb from lying on the floor of the house, and my back popped as I sat up. The winds outside had increased, whistling an ecrie tune through the walls, whooshing down the chimney and blowing an uncomfortable breeze onto my neck. I needed to get warm, and when I peered between the cracks of the boarded-up window, I saw the convenience store was still open.

Once I'd climbed back out the way I'd come in, I crossed the street and went inside the shop, sighing as the comforting warm air blanketed itself around me. As I stood in line behind another customer, waiting for him to pay, I glanced at the clock on the wall. Almost half past ten at night. The cashier wasn't the man who'd given me the bathroom key earlier, and this woman had pink streaks in her short blond hair, her lips the color of cherries. When she looked at me, she narrowed her baby blue eyes and a shadow of a frown crossed her face, disappearing so quickly I decided I must have imagined it.

"How much for a coffee?" I said, curling my chilly fingertips into my palms. The woman didn't move, and I pointed to the machine behind her. "Uh, a coffee, please?"

"Oh, yeah. Sure. It's on special. Any size for a dollar."

"Great. I'll have the biggest. Can I have the bathroom key first?"

After another attempt at washing the grime off myself, I handed back the scuzzy key and headed to the snack aisle on the hunt for something cheap, the chocolate and pretzels I'd scarfed down earlier not satisfying me in the least. The only other person in the shop was a short, red-haired woman who stood in front of the fridge, a chicken sandwich in one hand, an egg salad in the other, looking like she couldn't make up her mind. I looked at the basket on the floor behind her feet, filled with bread and packets of peanuts, and there, on the top, sat a phone. If I had a cell phone, I could search for clues about Brad and Rosalie. I could combine those with the name Ash, in case the woman I'd called earlier hadn't made a mistake, in which case I could try to speak to her again.

I glanced at the cashier, who'd turned her back to us and was talking into her own phone. Sandwich lady had gone for egg salad, and now debated her choices of a pot of fresh fruit vs. veggie sticks. As I walked past her, I casually bent over, snatched the phone from the basket and slid it into my pocket.

"Hey!"

I kept walking.

"Excuse me! You took my phone."

I froze. Could I make it to the front door without the woman tackling me to the ground or the cashier blocking my exit? Even if I made it outside, where would I go? They'd spot me running to the derelict house in an instant. They'd call the cops, and I didn't know where else to hide. Besides, I was too exhausted to make it far. Perhaps honesty was the best option. Give the phone back, apologize and leave. I turned, took in the woman's face. She had smooth, porcelain skin and she'd opened her big green eyes so wide, I thought they might pop out and skitter across the floor like marbles.

"Is something wrong, Fiona?" the cashier called over.

The woman called Fiona said nothing as she stared at me, her jaw dropping. "Ash?"

"No. That's not my—"

"It's really you! When did you get back?"

The jingling bells on the front door, and the man walking into the shop, spared me from having to answer. "Hey, sis," he called over to Fiona once he'd spotted her. "Are you coming, or what? Did you grab some beer?"

"Oh, boy," she whispered under her breath. "I didn't want him to see you."

When the guy looked more closely at us, he narrowed his eyes and walked over, his head perched on a neck larger than my thighs. He had to be close to two hundred and fifty pounds, most of it muscle, and as he approached I saw he had the same eyes as his sister's. His hair was the identical color, too, although his had been cut short and bristly, emphasizing the enormity of his skull. He ambled up to us, arms swinging by his thick sides, his jaw making sinewy movements as he observed me.

"What are you doing back in town?" he said, more of a snarl than a proper sentence. Who was this guy? And what did he want from me?

I held up my hands. "I don't know who you are."

He howled with laughter, and nothing like the genuine kind. "You think you can pretend not to recognize me? It hasn't been long enough, Asher *fucking* Bennett."

"Keenan," Fiona said before I could answer. "Knock it off. Ash, what's going on?"

I took off my baseball hat, as if that might lessen their confusion. "My name's Brad."

"Cut the crap." Keenan came closer, making me take a step back and butt up against the packets of popcorn and tortilla chips, which crinkled as they squished against my stolen jacket.

"Really," I said, feeling trapped and getting ready to take a swing at him if he came any closer. One punch would have to suffice, and better make it a big one so he couldn't get up quickly enough to retaliate. "I don't know who you are. I don't know who *I* am."

Keenan opened his mouth to say something, but Fiona got there first, holding out her hand. "Give me my phone, I'm calling Maya."

"She was here earlier." The cashier walked up to us with a curious expression on her face as I handed the phone to Fiona, not knowing what else to do. "Asked if I'd seen him."

"Who's Maya?" I said.

"Maya's your sister." Fiona patted my arm. "She's your sister, Ash."

"She showed me your photo," the cashier continued. "Gave me her number and twenty bucks. Said I should call right away if you showed up, so I did when you were in the bathroom. What's going on?"

"You remember Maya, don't you?" Fiona said, ignoring the question as I shook my head.

"This is bull," Keenan barked, his voice loud and forceful, making the three of us flinch in unison. "You're so full of it, Ash. You always were, even before Celine—"

"Stop it, Keenan," Fiona snapped. "Can't you see something's wrong with him?"

"Something's wrong, all right. He's back, and I told you if—"

The door opened again, and another woman rushed in, her

head on a swivel, panicked eyes darting around the place. As soon as she saw me, her hands flew to her mouth, and her face crumbled. She ran over and threw her arms around my waist as her head thudded into my chest.

"Ash!" she said, trembling as she squeezed tight. "Oh, God, Ash. I can't believe it!"

I wanted to argue my name was Brad, but with it now being four against one, the effort seemed pointless. Besides, I had no idea how else to respond to her emotional outburst, and so I didn't speak. Instead, I gently pushed her away and stepped back, taking in her jaw-length raven hair, and watery, piercing gray eyes she now searched my face with, making me feel like she was somehow peering into my soul. This was Maya? And she was my sister? Christ, how I wanted to remember her. I scoured every part of my brain for the slightest trace, but found only a deep, dark void where everything about my past should have been.

"Talk to me," she whispered, and her husky tones were definitely the ones I'd heard earlier on the phone. No question. This was the woman I'd spoken to.

"I think there's something wrong with him," Fiona said quietly. "Why doesn't he recognize any of us? It's like he has amnesia or something."

"Amnesia?" Maya said, turning her head but keeping her eyes on me. "Ash, what happened to you?"

"I don't know who I am," I said, my newly found voice rising along with the alarm growing inside me. All these people surrounding me, telling me my name was Ash, not Brad, and that Maya and I were related... It made me feel cornered. Hands and voice shaking, I said, "I don't know who I am. I don't know who you are. I don't know—"

"I'm still calling bullshit," Keenan said. "It's an act."

"Why are you even here?" Maya threw him a disgusted look before turning her attention back to me, her face softening. "Tell me what's going on."

"I don't remember." It came out way more forcefully than I'd intended, and she recoiled a little, making me want to kick myself. If she knew me, maybe she could help. Her and Fiona's concern felt genuine, not like Keenan, who stared at me now as if he'd be happy to set me on fire, providing he'd doused me with an accelerant first to make sure he finished the job.

"But you called me," Maya said. "You dialed my cell."

"The numbers kept running through my mind," I said quietly. "I didn't know why."

"Go to a hospital," Fiona said. "Seriously, he needs to get checked out."

"I will. I'll get him to a doctor." Maya grabbed my hand, her skin soft and warm. As I mumbled a thank-you to her she handed the cashier what looked like a few bucks before pushing me to the exit.

"Let me know how it goes," Fiona called over, at the same time as Keenan shouted, "It's still a pile of bullshit."

The door slammed shut behind us. Maya looked at me, took two steps, turned around again and pointed a finger at me, her concern changing to something else, but I couldn't quite tell what it was. Anger? Disappointment?

"Are you faking it?" she said. "Pretending not to know who you are? Who I am?"

"No—"

"Is this because of Keenan or something? Or because I found you, and you're going to leave again? If so, you can stop now, because it's not funny."

I had zero clue what she was talking about. What did she mean when she said she'd found me, and why did she think I'd leave when I'd just arrived? "I'm not faking it. I promise."

Maya threw a glance over my shoulder and pulled a face. "We'd better go."

"Go where?"

"Home. To our house."

I stepped away from her. "But I don't know you. And why did you give the cashier money?"

"Because I asked her to call me if you went back to the store. I was desperate," Maya said, pulling her phone from her pocket. "And you do know me. I'll prove it to you. I've got photos of us, right here, see?" She held up the screen, and I leaned forward, staring at the picture of this woman named Maya, and me. Her hair had been cut since the picture had been taken, and mine had grown, but it was definitely us, sitting on a porch of some kind, a couple of beers raised at the camera. "That was taken at the house. In Newdale. Where you lived for over half your life. Please, Ash. Come with me so I can show you, and before Keenan comes outside and starts up again. We can do without his stupidity."

I glanced through the window. He and Fiona stood by the row of fridges, and Keenan had what looked like two six-packs of beer under one arm. From what I could tell, they were in the middle of an argument, Fiona shaking her head and gesticulating with her hands. Maya was right, it probably wouldn't be long before they stepped outside, and he'd be in my face again.

"He doesn't like me very much, does he?" I said.

Maya's face softened. "Not exactly. You have a history. I lost count how many times you two got into dustups at school over the years. You really don't remember?"

"No, I really don't," I snapped.

"What do you recall?" she asked gently.

I tried to steady my voice long enough to explain how I'd woken up on the beach in Maryland the night before and found my way to Maine without understanding the need to be here. "I thought my name was Brad, because—" I pointed to my wrist, already knowing how pathetic I'd sound "—because it says so on my watch."

Her face fell and she put her hand on my arm, her touch soft. "It was your dad's."

"Brad's my father?"

"Yes. Your mom, Rosalie, gave it to him."

"Brad and Rosalie are our parents?"

"No. I'm your stepsister. My mom, Ophelia, and Brad met when we were teenagers. You and Brad moved to the US from England after your mom...after she..." Maya's eyes went wide and she swore softly under her breath before continuing, "After she died."

"My mum's...*dead*?" I said, and Maya bit her lip as she looked away. "What about my dad, and your mum? Do they live close? Can we see them? Maybe it would help, if—"

"Oh, Ash," Maya said. "They're gone, too."

"Gone as in...*dead*?" My feet stopped cooperating and I stumbled as Maya's hand went around my waist, propping me up. "*All* of them?"

She rubbed my shoulder. "It's been the two of us, you and me, for years."

I waited for this information to do more to me, make me feel something, *anything*—grief, anger, despair. Whatever I'd hoped for didn't hit, and instead, emptiness expanded inside my heart. My parents were both dead, Maya's mother, too, people I must have loved and mourned, but no longer remembered. All of my memories, history, identity...*gone*.

"I can't deal with this," I said, fight-or-flight instincts kicking in, making me want to run. Except I couldn't run from the person I wanted to leave behind, the most terrifying one of all: me. "I can't do this," I whispered again. "I don't know how to—"

"I'm here, Ash, I'm here." Maya wrapped her arm around my middle as she guided me to her car. "I'll help you. Let's go to the hospital—"

"*No.*"

"You need to get checked out. You're hurt."

I took a step back, escaping her grip. "I said no."

"Okay, okay. We'll go home. Get you cleaned up, and afterward we'll take our time and figure out what to do. It'll be okay, I promise. You can trust me."

My other choice was to return to the old house I'd broken into, and once she'd opened the door to a dusty Nissan Pathfinder and brushed off the passenger seat, I got inside. It smelled of sand and bubble gum, somehow familiar and comforting. She settled into her seat and as she was about to start the engine, I noticed her key chain, a shiny oval piece of wood with a single word burned into it in italics: *Hope.*

"Do you really think you can help me?" I said.

"Of course I can." She reached for my hand and gave it a firm squeeze. "We have a pact. A long time ago we promised we'd always watch out for one another, no matter what. Nothing's changed. Let me help you. I'll take care of you, okay? You can lean on me."

As we drove in silence, Maya kept glancing at me, as if to make sure I was still in the car. I had no recollection of who she was, yet something told me I was in the right place, and from now on, everything would be okay. She seemed to have no qualms about inviting a stranger into her vehicle, which meant either she was as crazy as I felt, or I was who she and the others said I was. I put my head back, looked out of the window into the darkness, saying nothing until we drove up to a house. I saw the lights first, a string of silver stars hanging in the window. I peered at them, the fog shifting inside my head as a sliver of my past tried to get my attention, but it wasn't enough for me to comprehend. Maya followed my gaze.

"You gave me those," she said, pointing to the lights. "A few days after Mom and I moved in, because I was scared of the dark." She gave me a small smile. "I never admitted it, but you sensed it anyway. After school you biked all the way to the hardware store and hung them over my dresser as a surprise for when I came home."

"Home," I said, staring up at the two-story building at the

end of a long, dark road, hoping for a memory jolt, but none came. The house appeared to have exhaled a long, languid sigh before giving up and slightly folding into itself. There were no neighbors close by; we'd passed the nearest place about a mile ago. I searched my mind for an indication of my being here before. Nothing. What if it was a lie? For all I knew, she was an ax-murderer.

"How long did you say I lived here?" I said.

"Ever since you moved here from the UK with Brad when you were fourteen," Maya said. "About a year before our parents married."

I nodded at the knowledge I was British but had lived in Maine for years, instinctively certain Maya was telling the truth, not a doubt in my empty mind. No wonder I'd recognized the number plate on the trailer and figured it was home. "But I left? When?"

"Two years ago."

"Where did I go?"

"I don't know."

"Why did I leave?"

"I don't know that, either." She glanced at the house again, and somehow, this time I wasn't quite sure I believed her.

8

MAYA

I couldn't believe Ash was here, or that the girl from the gas station had actually called. I'd found him. I'd finally *found* him. Ash was home.

When he'd first phoned me, I'd been asleep on the sofa, felt groggy when I'd answered my cell, but as soon as he'd said "hello" there had been no doubt it was Ash. I'd have recognized his voice if he'd whispered the single word from ten miles away in a hurricane.

Ash hadn't used his old cell to make the call, and I knew this because he'd left it on the kitchen table the day he'd walked out, along with a scribbled note saying, *Take care of yourself, Maya,* on the back of a receipt from the hardware store, and an envelope with over a grand inside. Ash had never been officially declared missing by the police. As he'd taken a suitcase full of clothes, his wallet, his truck, and there was no evidence of foul play or anything suspicious about his departure, I was told there was nothing they could do. That hasn't stopped me from searching as often and desperately as I could without ever finding anything. And now, two years later, he'd contacted me.

After we'd been disconnected, I'd frantically dialed back the number he'd called from, listened to the line ring and ring on the other end. When it stopped, I'd tried again, and a third time, but it remained unanswered until, finally, someone picked up. It wasn't a man I recognized, and when he'd told me he was standing at a pay phone in Falmouth, and had given me the address, I'd jumped in my car, breaking every traffic law to get there. Except I hadn't found Ash. I'd walked around the gas station, shouting his name, harassing passersby with photos on my phone I thrust into their faces, demanding *have you seen this man*, before doing the same with the store clerk, who shrugged and said she hadn't seen him, either.

"My shift just started but trust me," she added with a smirk, looking at the photo of Ash far longer than she needed to, "I'd remember a guy like him."

"Will you call me if he comes here? Right away? I'll give you my name and number."

She looked at me, cocked her head. "What if you're his crazy ex, or a psycho stalker?"

"I'm not. He's my brother."

"Didn't you say he has an English accent?"

"Stepbrother, it's complicated. Look…" I reminded myself of what Mom used to say about catching more flies with honey than vinegar, and softened my approach, forcing a happy expression and fishing a twenty from my wallet. "I'll give you another when you call. Deal?"

"Deal," she'd said, snatching the cash and sliding it into the pocket of her jeans.

I hadn't been hopeful. Actually I'd assumed I was twenty bucks poorer, which I couldn't quite afford, but then she'd called, whispering into her phone the man I was looking for was in the store, that I should hurry up and not forget her money. I made a second trip to the gas station, once again breaking multiple laws in the process, fully intent on making the cops chase me all the way if I had to, because until I arrived and found Ash, nothing would make me stop.

And now he was here. For the entire drive back to the house I kept glancing at him, wondering if he was a figment of my imagination and would disappear if I didn't have one eye on him at all times. Maybe the silver star lights I'd moved to the front room, hoping they'd somehow help him find his way home, had worked after all.

We continued to sit in the car in silence, both of us staring up at the old Victorian house. It had always been considered "quirky" by the locals, including us, but once morning came, Ash would get a better look at the place. Part of me was glad he didn't remember because he'd realize I hadn't managed so well with the upkeep, and the house had suffered for it. The siding, once a bright olive green, now resembled an ill-looking gray, like the face of someone about to vomit. The state of the shingles was no better, the candle-snuffer turret no longer proudly sat front and center, and while the multiple layers of paint on the wooden stairs leading to the front porch had been chipped away by our feet for years, they looked worse than ever. I kept telling myself I'd fix the place up, but after Ash had left, the motivation to pick up hammer and nails deserted me as swiftly as he had.

He wasn't the only one who'd gone. First it had been my mother, my stepfather and, finally, Ash. All of them abandoning me one by one. It had been a lot to cope with. I hadn't managed well. For goodness' sake, I still worked at the Cliff's Head, and the restaurant was almost my second home now that I'd spent fourteen years there in some capacity or another. Half of my life. A somehow comforting yet equally depressing thought, and after Ash had left, I'd assumed I'd be there until the end of it, an old waitress hobbling about, full of regret.

"Let's go inside," I said, pushing the thoughts away. There were more pressing things to worry about. Ash was home now, that was what mattered. "We'll figure things out, okay?"

Ash followed me as I unlocked the front door and stepped inside the house. I expected a sudden rush of memories to hit him, like I'd seen happen in the movies, but instead, Ash wandered around in bewilderment. He picked up a driftwood bowl I'd made, seemingly without having any idea it was one of my first-ever projects, and one he'd once fished out of the garbage, insisting it was great and I should keep honing my skills. Next, he glanced at the pictures on the walls, and still—nothing.

"Where did you get your clothes and shoes?" I said, pointing to his enormous sneakers and baggy jeans.

"I, uh, stole them from the trailer."

"Did the trailer belong to a clown?" I said with a smirk and Ash half smiled.

"I feel like a ruddy clown. The last clown out of the clown car."

"Ash," I whispered, trying not to gasp. "Your dad used to say that all the time."

A confused expression slid over his face, as if he were digging deep into the back of his mind but coming up empty. Fiona was right, he had some kind of memory loss, and I decided once he'd gone to bed, I'd research the possible causes until dawn, and then convince him to see a doctor, too. My brain knew this was Ash, there wasn't a single doubt. The way he moved, talked, and his appearance. The beauty spot on the side of his nose was confirmation enough on its own and yet, the way he looked at me, he may as well have been a stranger. I worked hard to contain my excitement about him being home again, knew if I came on too strong, he might feel claustrophobic and overwhelmed. I had to pace myself, or better still, follow his lead.

I took him to the kitchen, where I got us both some water. We sat at the table, where I watched him drink deeply, his fingers shaking as he set the glass down. When he turned to look at the pictures on the wall, I caught a glimpse of the side of his head.

"You're hurt," I said, leaning forward. "What happened?"

He moved back, out of reach. "I don't know. It's nothing. Just a cut."

"Let me see." I got up and gently pushed his hair to one side with my fingers, apologizing when he winced. "It looks nasty. We really need to get you to a doctor." He shook his head. "*Yes.* It's the weekend but…do you remember Dr. Golding?"

"I don't remember anyone."

"Crap. Of course." I sat down again, making sure I gave him enough physical and mental space. "Well, anyway, he was our family doc but when he retired, Dr. Adler took over his practice. He—"

"I told you, I don't want to see anyone." Ash jumped up, his left hip hitting the table so hard, the glasses went flying, spinning across the wooden surface, leaving a trail of water in their wake. His expression made me think he was going to run out of the room and into the darkness of the night without looking back. I could see his frustration mounting, and it was my job to stay cool and be reassuring. I knew Ash, he had a temper sometimes.

"It's okay, it's okay," I said gently, trying to keep him calm, keep him *here*, and gestured for him to sit as I wiped the spills with a napkin. "We don't have to decide now."

He complied, sinking back into his seat. "I *have* decided. I'm not seeing a doctor. This is all too confusing. I don't know who I am, or what's happened. He'll ask things I don't know the answers to."

"But maybe—"

"*No.* I can't. Not yet. I need some time to…I don't know, figure stuff out." Ash was about to jump up again, I could see the signs: jaw clenched, heels pushed into the floor. I put my hand on his knee, his muscles tensing beneath my touch.

"All right," I said. "No doctor. First, we'll get you settled back here at home."

"Home…" Shaking his head, he looked around. "Is my name really Asher Bennett?" When I nodded, he continued, "And I'm your stepbrother, and from England?"

"That's right, from Portsmouth."

"What do I do for a living?"

"You worked in construction. Carpentry, mainly. You have a knack for it."

"And you?"

"Officially I waitress at a place called the Cliff's Head. Unofficially I practically run the place. That's what my boss, Patrick, says, anyway. I can't wait to tell him you're back."

"Except I don't remember him, or anyone. Not you, Brad or Rosalie. Or your mom. You said her name was…?"

"Ophelia."

"Ophelia." He shook his head again, closing his eyes. "It's as if they never existed."

"They did, I promise."

"You said you had photos. I want to see them."

I hesitated. I didn't know what was wrong with him, had no idea what might or might not trigger a memory, and what could happen to him if it did. I wanted to protect him, make sure he was safe, but how could I do that if I didn't know what was going on?

"Maya?" He put his hand on my arm. "I need you to show me."

I got up and went to the old dresser that stood to the left of the fireplace in the living room, and slid open the top drawer. Ash had brought the piece of furniture home one day, a few months after he'd started working for the local carpenter to make a bit of cash while in high school. The pine dresser had been old and dusty, an unloved, dilapidated piece of furniture someone had put by the side of the road with a *FREE* sign stuck to it. Without hesitation Ash had hoisted it onto the back of Brad's truck and brought it home. I'd laughed at the state of the chipped, sky blue paint and the broken handles, the split wood in each of the five full-length drawers.

"What are you going to do with this piece of trash?" I said when I got home from school and found Ash in the garage, sander in hand, his brow glistening with sweat.

"Fix it," he said. "It has so much potential."

I'd given a dismissive *whatever* wave, and when I opened the bottom drawer and found a dried-up mouse inside, threatened to set fire to his new project if he as much as put it on our porch. A month later I came home to find the dresser standing next to the fireplace. Ash had stained it dark brown, given it new, shiny silver handles, and had somehow filled all the cracks in the wood, making them blend in and disappear. He'd sanded and treated the insides of the drawers, made them silky smooth to the touch, and I'd gawped with my mouth wide open as he walked in.

"Still want that flamethrower?" he'd said with a wink.

It was the first time I truly understood what a talented woodworker Ash was, and told him so, but he had other plans. He'd worked two jobs for over a year after graduating from high school to save up, got himself a generous scholarship and left to study economics in Denver. I'd cried every day for months, but then Brad died, and with Mom already gone, Ash insisted on leaving college and coming home to take care of me. This was something else he no doubt couldn't recall, more details from his life that had disappeared. Memories he'd left me to mourn.

"Maya?" Ash called out, his voice sounding uncertain now. "Is everything okay?"

No, I wanted to shout. *Do you have any idea what you put me through?*

Of course he didn't. He wouldn't know since he'd left two years ago that my life had been hell. How, at least three times a day, every single day, I'd opened the browser and plugged in *Asher Bennett*, crossing my fingers. My heart rate would accelerate, as it did whenever I searched for my stepbrother. I'd wonder if today might be the day I found something, hoped it would be good news but was always terrified I'd stumble across an obituary instead.

I'd never found anything pertaining to the Asher Bennett I knew. A man with the same name had been nominated for a music award in New York, but I hadn't needed to click on the link to know it wasn't my Ash, who'd always maintained he had no musical talent whatsoever, and would've preferred making an instrument to the torture of learning how to play one. He'd taken my school recorder as a joke once, and performed a mangled version of "Happy Birthday," and I swear no mice had come within a hundred yards of the house since.

Every time I continued my searches, playing with the parameters, a little voice would sneak into my head, whispering all the terrible things that could have happened to Ash, conjuring up images of the different ways he might have died in an accident, his decomposing body lying in a ditch somewhere, yet to be discovered. I'd never believed it. I'd have known if he were gone, felt it deep inside my heart.

I'd been right.

I grabbed the photo albums and walked back to the kitchen. "Let's see if these help," I said, settling next to him.

Ash turned the pages, his fingers touching the photographs, lingering as I pointed out who was who. "These are my parents?" he said, touching the picture. Rosalie stood behind Brad, her arms wrapped around his waist, both of them smiling. Her hair was as dark as Ash's, but he had his father's eyes, the perfect combination of his parents. "What happened to them?"

"Are you sure you want to know? It might be easier—"

"Of course I want to know," he snapped. "Tell me."

I chose my next words as carefully as I could, not knowing how to break the news. He'd gone through so much already. Would it be so bad if he didn't remember? "Not long after this photo was taken, when you were thirteen, your mom...oh, Ash, she...she committed suicide." I exhaled, wiped my damp hands on my pants as I waited for his reaction, but he continued to stare at me, and so I went on. "You and Brad came to Maine, where he met my mom, and they got married a year after."

"But now they're both dead?" he said, and while he sounded cold and detached, I knew it was because he didn't remember, not because he didn't care. He'd loved Brad and Mom very much, had been devastated after they'd died. We both had.

"My mom passed a short while later, when I was thirteen. She had a brain tumor." I touched the side of my head, trying not to remember how Mom had gone from vivacious and bubbly to a gray skin-and-bone skeleton of a human being in a couple of months. I didn't want Ash to recall it, either. Why would he want to?

He blinked. "We were the same age when our mothers...?"

"Yes," I whispered. The coincidence had never been lost on us. It had been something else to bring us together, our mutual loss and grief, which only the two of us seemed to understand.

"And my dad?"

I wanted to stop answering his questions. Didn't want to relive it, or be the one causing Ash to, but he asked me again and so I complied. "He was a foreman, and one day the load fell off a crane at the building site... It was thirteen years ago, when you were almost twenty." I didn't want to elaborate. Unless Ash remembered it himself, I wouldn't mention he'd been the one who'd gone to formally identify Brad at the morgue, that the only way had been the tattoo on his father's forearm because his skull and torso had been so badly crushed. Ash had broken down that day and it wasn't something I wanted him to remember. In fact, I'd do anything to make sure he didn't.

Oblivious to the dark memories swirling in the air between us, Ash said, "Thirteen really is an unlucky number for us, isn't it?" He shut his eyes and whispered, "Brad, Rosalie, Ophelia. Brad, Rosalie, Ophelia…"

"Do you remember them?" I said, reaching for his hand.

Startled, he pulled away, back out of reach. "Fragments, maybe. Bits and pieces I might be able to connect if I could grab hold of them long enough. What else can you show me? I need to see everything."

We kept on going through the photographs, the ones where we rented a trailer and went camping as a family, and when we got to his high-school graduation pictures, he managed a smile. "Christ, I was such a baby. Now I'm an old man."

"You're thirty-two, you're not old."

"What about you? You're younger than me, aren't you?"

"By three years. You always teased me about it, even though the difference doesn't count." He'd pulled his chair over and sat so close to me now I could smell the sea salt, sand and sweat. I wanted to touch his cheek, run my fingers over his skin in an attempt to make sure he really was sitting here in the kitchen, but I wasn't sure how he'd react. Before I had a chance to lift my hand, his stomach let out a piercing squeal, and I raised an eyebrow.

"Why didn't you say you were hungry?" I said.

"I'm hungry."

There it was, his wry, quirky sense of humor. I hadn't understood it when we'd first met, but when he left town, it was one of the things I missed the most. As always, he was trying hard to pretend everything was fine, and I decided I'd let him because it was what he needed right now. "What can I get you?"

"What kind of food do I like?" His shoulders dropped, another smile forming on his lips. "Shit, that's such a dumb question."

"No, it isn't." I swallowed. "You know, maybe it's an opportunity."

"How so?" Ash crossed his arms, both eyebrows raised as he expected more of an explanation. Right then, he looked exactly how I remembered his father and it made my heart swell. Brad had been a good man, fantastic both to Mom and me. He'd never tried to overtly muscle in and assume the role of my dad, but I'd wanted him to anyway. Growing up knowing my biological one hadn't loved me enough to stay had hurt a lot more than I'd ever wanted to admit.

"It could be a kind of blank slate," I said, and shrugged. "Maybe you'll develop a taste for things you didn't like before."

"That's one way of looking at it, I suppose. Are you always this optimistic?"

Pushing my seat back, I said, "You relax, I've got frozen lasagna."

Ash reached over and touched my fingers. "Thank you for helping me…Maya."

The way he said my name, so guarded and with such caution, broke my heart in two and I turned away, trying to hide. Ash didn't notice, and as he filled our glasses with water, I dug the pasta out of the freezer, unboxed it and shoved it in the microwave. "We can go shopping tomorrow," I said over my shoulder. "I need to get more stuff anyway. I'll show you your favorites." He didn't answer, and when I looked up, I caught him gaping at the window, his brow furrowed.

"Where are the chickens?"

"What chick—" My eyes widened. "You remember the *chickens*?"

"Were they in the garden?" he said, rubbing his temples with his fingers as if he were trying to massage the knowledge back into his head.

"They weren't real. We had blinds with a chicken pattern."

"Red and orange," Ash said. "Big, fat, red-and-orange hens."

"On a green background." My voice went up a notch. "Brad thought they were absolutely hideous and swore us to secrecy because Mom bought the fabric and spent ages sewing them. She loved them so much, but he said they drove him clucking crazy."

Ash actually laughed, his shoulders dropping. "*This* is crazy. How can I remember these bloody red-and-orange chickens but not remember you or our parents?"

"It's a start," I said, giving his arm a squeeze. "Baby steps, right? You don't want to become overwhelmed."

A while later the two of us sat at the table, Ash's belly full while I stuck with my glass of water. My appetite hadn't been the same since he'd left and most of the time I hadn't seen the point in cooking for one. Ash pushed the rest of his food around his plate, and I could almost hear his mind whirring, trying, and failing, to get traction as he covered a yawn with one hand.

"It's late, Ash. Why don't you go clean up and try to get some rest? We'll talk more in the morning. The clothes you left are still upstairs in your room, and your bed's made." I wondered if he'd ask why I'd regularly laundered his sheets and made up his bed again when I hadn't heard from him in two years, but he didn't.

"Could you show me?" he said quietly instead.

"Of course. Come."

I led him across the black-and-white diamond-tiled foyer and up the creaky, dark-stained wooden stairs that used to have a dollar-bill-green runner with golden stair rods. The carpet had bunched so badly we'd ripped it out. Replacing it was another renovation project I'd put on hold. Motivation, not time, had been lacking. Not to mention the cash.

At the top of the landing I pointed to each of the doors as we walked by. "This is mine, the one on the left is the spare. That's the bathroom, and this one's the main bedroom. You took it after...after...Brad died."

Ash didn't reply, and I couldn't tell what he was thinking as he flicked on the light and stepped inside the room. It was exactly as it had been the day he'd left. A double bed with a blue-and-white-striped duvet cover. A wooden clock he'd made and a cluster of family photos on the wall, my favorite a selfie of the two of us he'd taken when we'd gone snowtubing one winter, our cheeks and noses pink from the cold. Ash had never been one for clutter, and his bedside table was bare, save for a digital alarm clock, a blue lamp and a deck of cards. The only other items were his refurbished wooden desk and the empty chair standing in front of it. I walked to the closet and pulled it open, revealing a few pairs of folded pants, T-shirts and sweaters.

"You'll find something in here. They'll still fit you, I'm sure. I'll set a towel and a toothbrush out in the bathroom for you. Your old razor is in the cabinet."

When Ash didn't reply I couldn't stop myself from closing the distance between us and wrapping my arms around him, planting a gentle kiss on his cheek. I'd have hugged him forever if he'd let me. "I'm glad you're home," I whispered. "I've missed you."

"Good night," he said, taking a step back as he extricated himself from my grip, looking at me as if he might give my hand a neighborly shake. "And, uh, thank you. For everything."

I retreated downstairs, listening to the water running as I cleared the table, washed the dishes and wiped the counter. When the shower turned off, I waited awhile before creeping back upstairs, hovering at the top of the landing, out of sight as Ash walked out of the bathroom with a towel wrapped around his waist. I watched as he headed down the hallway, droplets of water glistening on his smooth, naked back. He'd always been handsome, and he hadn't changed much, not physically at least. If anything, he'd gained muscle, particularly on his arms and shoulders, which, I noticed as I craned my neck to get a better glimpse, were even broader now. As he disappeared into his room I wondered again where he'd been the past two years, and with whom. Now he was back, what would happen next?

9

MAYA

Back in the kitchen I opened my laptop and switched on the kettle, planning on making an industrial-size vat of coffee to fuel a research-filled night. I'd investigate all causes for memory loss, hopefully finding enough to convince Ash to see a doctor in the morning. As I waited for the water to boil, my mind wandered, thoughts traveling back to when Ash and I had first met.

I'd been twelve going on trouble, a sulky, sullen tween my mother couldn't work out what to do with. "We were such good friends, little Bee," she said, using the nickname she'd given me because she'd watched a cartoon called *Maya the Bee* with her German mother when she was a kid. "Don't you want us to still be friends?"

I hadn't bothered answering. On this particular day, the argument had been about my meeting her boyfriend, a word that made me shudder. Mom was supposed to be exactly that, my mom. She shouldn't be dating, it was gross, but she'd met an English guy named Brad at the eye specialist's office where she worked as an assistant. For weeks she'd gushed whenever she mentioned him, her face lighting up so bright, we could've used it to power the entire state. I'd said I didn't want to meet him, too stubborn to admit I was afraid of losing her, instead insisting it was because I didn't care. For once, she'd put her foot down.

"He's important to me," she said, hands on hips, her long brown hair flowing over her narrow shoulders as we stared each other down at the kitchen table, and from her tone I knew she'd already won, but I wasn't yet ready to concede. She'd never talked that way about a man before. As far as I was aware, she hadn't had any kind of relationship with a guy since my father walked out seven years prior, after unceremoniously announcing he didn't want the responsibility of the family he'd helped create. "I want you to meet Brad," Mom continued, her tone gentle again. "I really, really like him, and I know you will, too."

"I don't need a dad," I'd said as I scowled at Mom, crossing my arms over my chest in an attempt to amplify the stubbornness effect, except the only thing it did was remind me I still hadn't developed breasts as the other girls in my class had. "We're fine on our own."

Mom sighed, pulled out a chair and sat down. "Brad won't try to be your dad, Maya."

"He will. It always happens in books and movies, and—"

"This isn't one of your fairy tales."

"I don't read those anymore, they're stupid."

"But you used to love—"

"No, they're dumb," I insisted, launching into my reasoning without letting her stop me. "First, Snow White should've known the old hag was bad news. Sleeping Beauty could've had the prince arrested for sexual assault. Maybe Cinderella's sisters weren't ugly but it's what she wanted us to believe. Oh, and if I'd been Rapunzel, I'd have chopped my hair off when the witch was in midclimb, so she'd have plunged to her death."

Mom giggled. "Okay, so they're a bit outdated—"

"Outdated?" I was on a roll. With any luck we'd continue this debate and she'd forget all about introducing me to Brad. "What about the 'Someday My Prince Will Come' song? Ugh. It's never going to happen, and why hang around for a boy, anyway?"

"Honey, I understand what you're saying and while I agree with most of it, you must see I'm lonely." This was typical Mom. Always up-front and direct, never one to hide away her feelings. It was at least partially true what they said about apples and trees. I'd acquired my directness—something teachers called me out on daily—from her and my dad, had received a double dose of the bluntness gene while still in the womb.

"I'm tired of being alone," Mom continued. "I want to be happy."

"You're not happy with me?"

"Maya..." She reached for my arm but I shook her off, stood up so quickly I knocked my chair back, and before she could stop me I fled to my room, locked the door and put on my headphones, ignoring her pleas for me to come out and talk. Still, as I turned up my music and grabbed a pair of chopsticks, slapping them on my desk and pretending I was a real drummer, I couldn't drown out the fact I didn't want Mom to be unhappy or lonely. I knew how it felt.

I gave in a day later, and much to Mom's delighted hand-clapping, agreed to meet Brad and his son, Asher, for breakfast at a diner in Newdale, the town where they lived, which was on the coast about a twenty-minute drive south of us, and fifteen from Portland.

We arrived early. Mom hadn't shown me any photos so I wouldn't start what she already called *our relationship* with pre-conceptions, except I had them anyway. I pictured Brad bald and fat, unfair considering Mom could've been a model. I imagined Asher as a gangly fifteen-year-old, resembling the boys at school whose growth spurts had been too much, too fast, and left them stretched out like bubble gum. We'd have nothing in common, I decided, and even less to say to each other. I'd be stuck at the stupid diner until I could make some excuse about having a stomachache and get us to leave early.

I sighed as I wriggled in my seat, the teal pleather already gluing itself to the backs of my bare legs, and promised myself I'd try to be good—civil, at least—for Mom. It wouldn't be easy, but I was a good actress, so pretending for an hour wouldn't be too hard. I looked around, saw three teenage girls with perfect, straight white teeth and killer cheekbones. If I was as old as them, if I was as beautiful as them, would Mom make me sit here? Would I feel as threatened by her having a *boyfriend*—ugh—as I did now?

Five minutes later the diner door opened, and Mom's face lit up. I followed her gaze to the two people who'd walked in, realizing I'd got it completely wrong. Brad stood around six feet, had a full head of salt-and-pepper hair, and a sculpted beard. He wore a pair of trendy jeans, and his blue T-shirt skimmed his flat stomach. He held up a muscular arm as he waved at us, and when my eyes moved to the boy behind him, my heart almost stopped.

Asher Bennett was the most beautiful thing I'd ever seen. He was a little taller than his father. His shock of dark brown hair—longer on top, shorter on the sides—had been swept back, revealing a face belonging on the cover of a magazine. Full, heart-shaped lips, a beauty spot to the right of his nose, which was neither too big, nor too small, but Goldilocks. I couldn't stop watching the way he walked to us, self-assured and grown-up, his back straight. Mom had mentioned Asher ran track and wrestled in high school, and you could tell. His arms were toned, his chest broad. When he caught me staring at him, mouth agape, I blushed and dropped my gaze, hoping I'd die on the spot.

I forced myself to look at Brad, who gave Mom a chaste kiss on the cheek before shaking my hand and introducing himself, his words a garbled sound swirling around my ears. Asher's presence made me will the floor to open beneath me. I wished I'd worn something other than my denim shorts, blue Mary Janes and the mint-green shirt Mom had bought me for my birthday that said *√144 YEARS OLD* in big white letters. Until then, I'd thought it was the coolest thing, except now it screamed *nerd alert* louder than anyone did at school.

"Nice to see you again, Ms. Scott." Asher took Mom's hand before reaching for mine, and I was convinced I'd burn up when our fingers touched. When it didn't happen, my face continued to glow as a trickle of sweat rolled down my spine and seeped into the waistband of my shorts.

"Hi, Maya," he said when I finally let go of his hand. "I'm Ash."

Ash, not Asher, Mom, I'd have said, if only I retained the ability to speak.

She nudged me with her shoulder. "What do you say, Maya? Where are your manners?"

I couldn't manage a single word. Ash lowered himself into the chair opposite me, while Mom fussed over him and Brad, handing out menus and rattling off the specials as if we'd been here a million times before. I couldn't tell which one of us was more nervous.

"It's nice to meet you," Ash said to me, his voice deep, his English accent as pronounced as his dad's, only way, *way* cooler. As he perused his menu, I stole another glance, noticed his eyes were an orangey-gold color I'd only ever seen on the top of the old man's walking stick in *Jurassic Park*, the original one Mom insisted I watch before the newer movies because she considered it a classic.

I still hadn't spoken, and tried hard to come up with something that wouldn't sound utterly lame. Impossible, so I kept quiet, focusing on getting a new bouncy sensation in my heart under control instead. I wondered if Mom might come to my rescue, but she and Brad were already engrossed in conversation, chatting about something they'd seen on the news.

Ash gestured to my shirt. "I'm guessing you're twelve and a math fan?"

I looked up at him, swallowed hard and nodded once.

"Me, too." He let out a small laugh, so lush and thick, I could almost taste it, like hot chocolate sauce poured over a banana split. "Well, I'm fifteen, not twelve," he continued, "but math is my favorite subject."

I took my first breath in what had to have been a year. "Not sports?"

"Sure, I love sports, too. But math is cool. If you ever need any help—"

"Hey, Ash, how are you?" One of the girls from the other table stood next to us, the prettiest one with the big, deep blue eyes, a blond mane, which almost reached her tiny waist, and glossy pink *kiss me* lips. She twirled a thick lock around her finger and shifted her head to one side as she waited for his reply.

"Hi, Sydney." Ash sat back in his chair but wasn't smiling. His face had gone into neutral—indifference, almost. He obviously had superpowers because I'd seen boys like him fall under the spell of girls like her in less than a nanosecond.

"We're going to the beach," she said, still twirling and leaning toward him, the tops of her breasts dangerously close to spilling from her shirt. "Come with? I have a new bikini."

"No, thanks."

Sydney put her hand on his shoulder, her fingers kneading the skin beneath his shirt. She seemingly noticed my presence for the first time, her eyes sweeping from my head to my stupid Mary-Jane-clad feet, which I swiftly tucked under the seat. When her eyes came to rest on the big white letters sprawled across my flat chest, she raised an eyebrow and smirked. "Nice shirt."

More heat shot to my face, burning me. "It's math. The square root of a hundred and—"

"Shall we go?" Sydney walked her long, slim and perfectly French-manicured fingers across Ash's chest and up toward his neck.

He put his hand over hers, and I expected him to stand up, make his excuses and take off, but instead he removed her fingers and let them drop by her side. "I said no, thanks."

She flashed him another smile, not quite as bright this time, and tossed her hair over her shoulder. "Come on, it'll be fun."

"I'm having fun here. With Maya."

Sydney blinked three times in quick succession. Something told me she was used to getting her own way, be it at home, school or with her friends. "But—"

"Later, Sydney." Ash looked at me, grinning as he leaned in. "Okay, Maya, can you explain that math concept again because I'm not sure I understand it completely."

Sydney turned and marched to her table, where she spoke with her friends in a clipped tone. From what I could gather, she insisted they were leaving, *now*, and they stormed out of the diner in a collective bad mood, each of them throwing looks of disgust our way.

Mom and Brad hadn't paid attention to the exchange, they were too busy chatting about a movie they wanted to see, and when Brad reached over to wipe a spot of ketchup from Mom's cheek with his napkin, I promised myself I'd be much nicer to her about him.

"Thank you," I said to Ash, the words coming out as a whisper.

"Anytime." He gestured to our parents with his thumb. "I don't know about you, but I suspect we'll be spending quite a lot of time together. Maybe I should call you Little Sis?"

I giggled, soda spilling from between my lips. "Or Bee."

"Bee?"

"It's what Mom calls me. Maya the Bee."

"Cute. Okay, Bee it is."

I needed to say something else, anything to keep him talking so I didn't have to. "Do you know why you were named Asher?"

"I'm not sure," he said, looking down, his smile fading, his lips falling silent.

Scrambling to change the subject, I asked about school and the wrestling team, and when his smile returned it made my chest swell as I sat back to listen. After half an hour, Mom leaned over and whispered in my ear, asking if I wanted to leave. I shook my head, and she gently squeezed my knee.

The afternoon turned into a lazy supper at Brad and Ash's house, an old Victorian place at the end of a road, perched near some cliffs, which I thought was the coolest thing I'd ever seen. Once the dishes were done, and we'd played cards together (kids vs. adults—we won by ten miles thanks to Ash), Mom and Brad sat out on the porch while Ash showed me his old school photos from England, laughing as I made fun of his uniform and choppy hair.

"Why did you come to Maine? Your dad's work?"

"Not exactly. We needed a change."

I swallowed, unsure how to ask the question and decided on, "What about your mom?"

After a moment's hesitation Ash said, "She was depressed. She died."

My mouth dropped open. How could I have been so forgetful, so crass and careless? I'd only half listened when Mom had told me his mother was no longer alive, and there I was, bringing it up. He seemed so sad, so lost. I'd hurt him, and I couldn't bear to see the look on his face, or knowing I'd put it there. I decided there and then I'd do anything to make it up to him. It was a promise I'd never forgotten.

The noise of the boiling kettle pulled me out of the memories. As I was pouring the water into my mug, a noise behind me made me jump and I spun around. Ash walked into the kitchen, dressed in his favorite pajamas and the soft New York Giants T-shirt I'd given him for his twenty-fifth birthday, a shirt he'd left behind.

"I'm sorry," he said, holding up his hands. "I didn't mean to startle you."

"It's all right. Are you okay?"

He pointed to his temple and pulled a face. "Headache. Do you have any pills?"

"Of course. They're in my bag."

Once I'd given him some aspirin and he'd headed back to bed, I opened my laptop and was about to focus on researching amnesia when another thought hit me. On the way home from the gas station, Ash had told me a little more about the trailer he'd hidden in. I frowned, typed "Asher Bennett Maryland" into the search bar. Nothing. What had he been doing down there? Traveling through or living there longer term? I drummed my fingers on the table before widening the parameters, covering New Jersey to Florida, Delaware to Kentucky, but the only Asher Bennetts I found were under the age of ten, or over fifty. I'd almost given up when I went back to basics, and the headline of a small article on *Ocean-CityToday* caught my eye.

HOPE FADING FOR MISSING BRITISH SWIMMER

I leaned in, heart beating fast, palms sweating, my fingers unsteady as I clicked on the link and began to read.

10

LILY

I had every intention of going to work Sunday morning, but by eight thirty I hadn't even showered, let alone bothered to put on clothes and makeup. Everything seemed an impossible effort and the thought of leaving the temporary cocoon I'd built myself filled me with dread.

It wasn't that I didn't like work. I'd held the position of office manager at a garage called Beach Body Auto for three years, although my job title sounded more glamorous than the reality, not that I cared. My daily routine consisted of answering the phones, booking appointments and issuing invoices, and the latter had dwindled considerably since a big franchise opened its doors a couple of blocks away, luring people in with bargain prices and a shiny coffee machine churning out custom-made drinks faster, and, if rumors were to be believed, way tastier than Starbucks. My boss, Mike, the sixty-five-year-old owner of Beach Body who still maintained it was the best garage name ever, remained convinced his shop would survive because of its decades-long history, customer loyalty and quality of service. The empty hoists, dwindling profits and the fact we'd lost another mechanic to our competitor all told a different story, which Mike had thus far chosen to ignore, except for us now opening on Sundays. I'd tried talking to him about it, offered to bump up our presence on social media, but Mike was old-fashioned and, other than a website, wanted nothing to do with "that stuff" because he "didn't see the point."

"Things will be fine, Lily," he'd said before telling me he'd been through recessions before and come out the other side. I didn't have the heart to keep arguing, tabling the conversation for another day instead. Mike had been good to me, given me a job after we'd struck up a conversation one morning when I'd gone to the beach to watch the sunrise, which still had me in awe every single time. We'd sat on the same bench in silence before introducing ourselves and chatting about where we were from and finding out we'd both been born on the same day in Buffalo, thirty-five years apart. He hadn't asked for a reference, or probed much into my past, but offered me a week's trial, after which I could tell him if I wanted the job permanently. It never seemed to occur to him he might want to let me go. As far as he was concerned, we were a perfect professional fit.

As much as I liked working for Mike and respected him as my boss, the prospect of going to the garage now and sitting at reception, smiling and forcing myself to be friendly when all I wanted to do was scream, made my skin crawl. I grabbed my phone, sent Mike a text saying I wasn't well. Not long after he replied, hoping I'd feel better soon. Instead of his message giving me relief, it made me feel like a selfish jerk because I knew he'd end up doing my work for me. I'd explain everything to him tomorrow, I decided, knowing he'd understand and offer a comforting shoulder once he found out about Jack, but right now I couldn't face telling him.

I soon knew I'd made a mistake. Without work, the entire day stretched out ahead of me, time I didn't know how to fill. I headed to the kitchen for a cup of coffee, but when I opened the fridge and saw a plastic container with the leftovers of the last meal Jack and I had shared—butter chicken, his favorite—I burst into tears. How could he be gone? Disappeared without a trace from one moment to the next, leaving nothing behind but clothes on a beach?

Although I tried to push the disbelief, anger and fear away, it all slipped through nonetheless, burrowing deep into my heart. Perhaps going back to Jack's apartment would ease the pain somehow, because not doing so and avoiding the place altogether would make me feel as if I were abandoning him all over again. I pulled on some clothes, tied up my hair and put on my shoes, forgoing the shower and makeup because what did it matter?

I sighed with relief when I got to Jack's apartment and saw that Sam, good as his word, had fixed the broken kitchen window. I fired off a quick text, not expecting a reply because he was on his way to Chicago, but within a few seconds the three telltale dots appeared and he replied Call me if you need me, to which I responded with a simple thumbs-up. I wandered through to Jack's bedroom, where I stared out the window. From my vantage point I saw a blue Dodge Charger crawl down the road and up to Sam's driveway. I couldn't see the number plate, but as I watched it sit there for a good minute, something started to feel off. I snapped a couple of pictures with my phone and waited until the car took off again. The windows were heavily tinted, and I hadn't been able to spot who was in the vehicle, but coupled with the guy showing up at the house the night before, a feeling of unease dug into my stomach.

Needing to restore some sense of calm, I went back to the kitchen, where I filled the kettle and fetched a mug from the cupboard, into which I dropped a spoonful of instant coffee. My stomach let out a long, high-pitched wail, and I admitted defeat, deciding a piece of toast might keep it quiet for a while. When I opened the bread box, my eyes landed on the stack of mail on top of it, the one I'd teased Jack about a few weeks ago, as we were cooking pasta.

"You do know it's the only thing in your entire apartment that's untidy?" I'd said with a laugh. "I mean, everything's pristine, your dishes are always done."

"Why would you leave them lying around for the flies to get to?"

"Your bed's always made."

"The advantage of having a duvet, not sheets."

"I like my sheets. Anyway, I thought you were trying to impress me at first, but I've never seen you leave as much as a dirty sock lying on the floor."

Jack pulled me close, kissed my neck, murmuring, "I never knew dirty socks turned you on. I'll leave a trail of them leading to the bed…" He pressed his lips to mine, making a delicious shiver of excitement, the one I always felt when he kissed me that way, travel to my belly where it set me on fire.

"I don't need any help," I whispered. "And I don't need a bed." He'd groaned as I'd unbuckled his belt, proving my point on the kitchen table, and we'd eaten overcooked pasta and burned Bolognese sauce for dinner.

Another surge of anger bubbled up inside me as I tried to cling to the memories of Jack, of his lips, his hands, his voice. I wanted to keep them vivid and alive—because he *was* alive—and I couldn't let them ebb away, have them replaced by the agonizing uncertainty of what had happened to him, or of who he truly was. I grabbed the stack of papers and threw them into the recycling bin, before changing my mind and fishing them back out, spreading everything over the table. There was nothing of interest in the restaurant flyers and take-out menus, offers for better cable TV or pool supplies, but as I went through the mail again, what *wasn't* there settled on my chest with the weight of the entire United States Postal Service.

None of the letters were personalized. Every single one, without exception, was addressed to *Resident*. Jack preferred to pay cash for everything, had said it kept him on budget, something I'd admired him for, but flicking through the mail, there wasn't a single bill from an insurance company, or an official letter, and no bank or credit card statements, either. Not even a check or pay stub from his ex-boss.

Another uncomfortable sensation grew in my stomach as I wondered if the reason Jack didn't have a truck of his own but had talked Sam into letting him borrow his was because the arrangement suited them both, or because Jack was unable to get insurance. Did he not have a credit card because of his self-imposed financial constraints, or because he hadn't been able to provide proper identification to apply for one? If so, why? The answers I played in my head ranged from Jack being a serial killer to an international spy, or in witness protection, and everything in between. The insatiable desire to know the truth about the Jack Smith I'd fallen in love with grabbed me by the throat, the knowledge of his lies combined with the mystery of what they meant, and what *we'd* meant, transforming into a raging war inside me. I had to know his secrets. I needed information. Details. *Something.*

My pursuit of the truth began in the bedroom, where I riffled through his clothes, trying to quash the memories they represented so they didn't distract me from my purpose. The blue shirt Jack had worn the day we'd met, the black one he'd loaned me when I'd splattered pancake mix all over mine—almost every item held some significance. I pushed them away as I emptied his closet, searching the pockets of every damn pair of shorts and pants, shaking out shirts and underwear before unfolding his balled-up socks and examining them, too.

The bedside table was next. Two books, a box of condoms, the lip balm I'd left here because he never had any, something else I'd teased him about as his mouth was always so soft. "All the better to kiss you with," he'd whispered, and the memory of his voice made me gasp.

"Figure this out," I urged, abandoning the bedroom, and heading for the bathroom to continue my mission. It didn't take long to inspect the open shelves, or the medicine cabinet above the sink. When I examined the toilet, I told myself I was being stupid, but couldn't stop the relief from coming when I didn't find a gun, or a stack of drugs and fake passports duct-taped to the tank.

Only the living room, kitchen and hallway closet were left. I plowed through the first with an equal amount of fervor, my rage billowing when my rampage yielded nothing, not until I grabbed a chair to reach the top kitchen cupboard, where I found a dented Christmas cookie tin I'd never seen before, stowed away at the back, hidden behind a set of mugs we never used.

I opened the tin, my heart thumping, pulse tap-tapping in my temples. The cookies had been replaced by packs of batteries, books of matches and appliance warranties. I dug deeper, inhaling sharply when I found a wad of cash, a stack of folded twenties, fifties and hundreds sandwiched inside a brochure and secured with a blue elastic band. At least a couple grand. I lowered myself onto the chair in case my legs gave way, clutching the tin in my hands as I examined it from every angle, taking in the scene of a jolly Santa and his rosy-cheeked elves. I tried hard to justify the discovery. Yes, Jack preferred using cash, but why leave this much lying around, especially with a broken window he hadn't repaired? Why hadn't he put it in his bank account? I shuddered. What if he didn't have one? And, once again, *why* wouldn't he have one? I looked more closely at the brochure. It was from a jewelry store, and one of the pages had been dog-eared. Not only that, but an item had been clearly circled three times with red pen. A white-gold and sapphire engagement ring. *Sapphire.* My birthstone.

With a lump in my throat I shoved the flyers to one side and turned the cookie tin upside down, frowning when I noticed a box the shape and size of a deck of cards among the debris. It was wrapped in shiny red paper with golden swirls, rattled when I shook it, and as I turned it over, I spotted a tiny folded note attached to the top with tape. I took it off, and opened it, recognizing Jack's neat penmanship.

Dear Lily,

Stay tonight & every night after.
I love you.

Jack x

I tore into the paper and ripped open the box, but instead of the ring in the brochure it was a house key, one I instinctively knew was for his apartment. Jack had planned on asking me to move in, maybe even propose, and I'd have said yes to all of it if he hadn't disappeared. If I hadn't found out he was a liar. As the future we'd had together crumbled between my fingers, I pressed the box and brochure to my chest, trying not to scream. Scream for Jack to come home. For him to tell me the truth, and, most of all, for this nightmare to be over.

11

MAYA

I barely slept all night, and early Sunday morning, at what Ash and I had long ago baptized *stupid o'clock*, meaning the sun had scarcely graced the bottom of the skies, I gave up and got out of bed. Once I'd made sure Ash was in his room, and everything that had happened the night before wasn't a dream or my overactive imagination, I paced the kitchen for a while before going for a run to clear my mind.

Exercise wasn't something I'd done much of since Ash had left. I hadn't had the desire or energy, preferring to stay home and work on my driftwood art in the garage. It wasn't just for the badly needed extra cash my pieces brought in, but also the feeling of satisfaction the work gave me, and the illusion I was doing more with my life than simply letting it pass me by. Barbara, who ran a store in town called Drift and who was charged with selling my pieces, often said she thought I could have a much broader reach if I set up online. Maybe I would now that Ash was back. But first I needed to figure out what was going on with him.

While the rain had stopped, the gray, low-hanging clouds appeared to be in no hurry to make way for the sun, and the crisp air was cooler than I'd anticipated. I went to the back of the yard to the path at the top of the cliffs and turned left, upping the pace, my legs already protesting from the lack of care and attention. I slowed down, deciding on a walk so my lungs wouldn't collapse, and found a steady rhythm, my feet barely making a sound as they hit the earthy path.

Forcing myself to push some of what I'd seen online the night before from my mind, I focused on what I'd found out about Ash's potential condition, and the mental notes I'd made. Complete memory loss could have multiple causes, including Alzheimer's (far too young?), a stroke (no other symptoms?), drugs or alcohol withdrawal (he'd always been antidrugs and drank responsibly), mental health issues (genetic predisposition?), and what Fiona had mentioned, amnesia, which seemed the most feasible but opened up a plethora of possibilities.

Anterograde amnesia was the inability to form new memories, but Ash had mentioned falling asleep in both the trailer and the old house he'd broken into, and when he'd woken up, he'd recalled being at the beach. Transient global amnesia meant forgetting pretty much everything, so it was a contender. However, retrograde amnesia was also the inability to recall past events, and could be caused by a head injury, which Ash had definitely suffered judging by the gash I'd seen last night. I'd read through site after site until the pages blurred and I'd gone cross-eyed. In my mind, if he had amnesia, I ruled out anterograde because the part of his brain that made new memories seemed to be working, but what did I know other than reading up on Dr. Google?

Walking a little faster, I stumbled and tripped when the tip of my shoe caught on a root because I was too busy thinking about what would happen if Ash had one of the other types of amnesia, I got home and he no longer recognized me. Or if he'd had a stroke after all, a precursor to a bigger, more damaging and potentially fatal one. Getting outside was supposed to help my focus. Instead it was turning my brain to mush, making it a soupy mess of terrifying questions, with not nearly enough answers.

When the first raindrop smacked me on the forehead, I cursed myself for coming out in the first place. Ash had been sound asleep, but what if he woke up while I was gone, and ran off again? I was freaking out now, cutting through the forest before bursting out onto the main road, running full throttle, my lungs burning. It took me another few minutes to get back to the house, and well before I ran up the driveway, I saw Keenan's bright red Subaru WRX parked askew.

"Oh, hell, no," I wheezed, leaping up the porch steps, and as my fingers touched the door handle, I could already hear the shouting.

"...because you sure as shit should crawl back underneath it," Keenan yelled. Ash must have said something in reply because Keenan raised his voice again. "Should I take that as a confession, you goddamn piece of—"

I rushed through the door and into the kitchen, where Ash was dressed in jeans and an old sweater, his hair sticking out at different angles. He stood behind the kitchen table as a red-faced Keenan, who held his car keys tightly in his fist, moved in on him.

"What the fuck are you doing here?" I roared, and both of them spun around.

"I want answers," Keenan said, turning back to Ash. "And you're going to give—"

"I told you already, I don't know what you're talking about." Ash reached for the back of a chair, looking like he might collapse, his eyes darting from Keenan to me and back again.

"Get out." I walked over and grabbed Keenan's arm, but he

shook me off. "I said get *out*. Leave. Now. I mean it. You don't get to come here and mess with my brother."

"Stepbrother. And I'll do whatever the hell I want, Maya."

"Not in my house. Why can't you understand he's lost his memory? Besides, Ash is—"

"Innocent?" He led out a pseudo-laugh. "Yeah, yeah. He had nothing to do with Celine or Kate, blah, blah, blah. It's a load of horseshit. You know it, I know it, and—" he pointed to Ash "—so does he."

I narrowed my eyes, took a step closer. "For the last time, the police cleared him. They never found anything implicating him in any way. Nothing. Nada. Zip. Because he's inno—"

"Them finding nothing means fuck all," Keenan said. "I sure as hell don't believe Kate slipped. And Celine—"

"Who are Kate and Celine?" Ash said.

Keenan whipped his head around, taking a step in Ash's direction, his balled fists moving up to his chest, locked and loaded. "You don't get to say their names, asshole."

"Enough." I pushed Keenan toward the door, an almost impossible feat given our size difference. "Get out and don't come back. Stay away or I'll have a restraining order slapped on your sorry ass."

Keenan's jaw made tiny sinewy movements, and I was about to order him out of the house once more when he glared at the both of us and marched to the front door. I followed, slamming it shut and locking it behind him, and moments later heard the tires of his prized possession spinning on the gravel as he sped off down the road. When I walked back into the kitchen, Ash had slumped down at the table. I went to him and put my hands on his shoulders.

"You shouldn't have let him in," I said.

"He kept banging on the door, I figured I could calm him down." Ash looked up at me. "Who was he talking about? Celine, and…Kate? What happened to them? Where are they?"

"Listen, Ash, I really think we should go to the doctor—"

He smacked his palm on the table, bellowed, "I'm not a child. Tell me. *Now.*"

I took a step back, blinked hard and tried to keep my face neutral as the harshness of his voice rang in my ears. My hopes he'd left his temper somewhere in Maryland along with his memory faded a little. I'd hated how angry he'd become in the run-up to his abrupt departure from Newdale. I didn't want that Ash back, but the one from before, the one who was always gentle and kind, the one who always made me feel I was at home.

"It's all right, I'll tell you," I said, slowly pulling out a chair, observing Ash for the smallest of reactions, wondering if any of it might act as a trigger, as my research had indicated things could, and trying to plan how I'd handle the situation if it did. "Celine lived in a house farther up the street. The first on the right, the run-down one with the red shutters. Keenan lives there alone now."

Ash raised his eyebrows. "That dickhead's our neighbor?"

"Technically, yeah. But he's almost a mile away." I didn't want to continue, but could tell Ash wouldn't let this go, and I couldn't blame him. He had no recollection of Celine or Kate, and Keenan had rattled him twice. If I didn't give Ash something, he'd try to get information elsewhere and, depending on the source, it would do more harm than good.

"Celine's a year younger than you," I continued. "Keenan's her older brother, and Fiona, the redhead—"

"I remember. I tried to steal her phone."

"Right, well, she's Keenan's twin. Their mom left a few years back, after their dad died. I don't think they've seen her since. Fiona runs the Harbor Inn motel in town, and Keenan works at the mill. He—"

"I don't care about them. What does their sister have to do with anything? Why is Keenan so pissed off at me?"

I tried to determine how much of Pandora's box I should

open. Celine had always been the bona fide Sunshine Girl everybody loved, and both my mom and Brad were delighted when she and Ash grew close. Ash was sixteen back then, and despite the fact I'd grown up in the year since Mom and I had moved in with Brad and Ash, I knew he still saw me as the little kid with the nerdy math shirt and boring Mary Janes.

"You're spending a lot of time with Celine," Mom said one night as we sat at the family dinner table. She handed Ash the mashed potatoes before exchanging a glance with Brad, a bemused smile playing on her lips. In return, Brad made wide eyes at her, signaling he wanted her to stop talking, which, of course, she didn't. "Tell me, are you two—"

"*Friends*," Ash replied, dumping another spoonful of mash on his plate, which was already piled high with roast beef, carrots and Yorkshire puddings, a Sunday dinner both Ash and Brad had taken great delight in introducing us to. I couldn't believe how much Ash could get away with eating, or how much he'd grown in height and muscle over the past year. In comparison to the guys in his grade, he looked like he'd finished high school, especially since he'd taken up carpentry. The other boys were pubescent, and acted as if they were little kids, but not Ash. He had the body of a man, like the ones on TV or in magazines.

Earlier in the afternoon I'd stood at the kitchen window, peeling potatoes, and watching him cut the grass without his shirt on, beads of sweat gathering across his back and flat stomach. The sight made my belly flutter, a strange sensation I'd never felt before, as if I'd swallowed a hundred fireflies. Mom had to ask me to pass the milk three times before I heard her, and then I handed her the juice.

"*Friends?*" Mom raised her eyebrows at him. "Are you sure that's all it is?"

"Ophelia," Brad said. "Leave the lad alone. A man needs his secrets."

"Ash doesn't keep secrets from me." I hadn't meant to say it out loud, hadn't meant for it to sound so childish, either, and when Mom laughed, my scowl deepened.

"Oh, little Bee," she said. "I bet Ash doesn't tell you everything he gets up to."

"Of course I do." Ash winked at me, but I couldn't say for sure it was the truth.

Mom changed the subject and patted my head as if I were five, not—at last—a *teenager*. How I'd longed to call myself that, a teenager, only to learn the word held no superpowers at all. When I looked in the mirror, I still saw an awkward *thing* staring back at me. Shaggy black hair and an angular face with huge eyes, which might have been fine if I'd lived in an anime comic book. I wondered if it was what everybody else saw when they looked at me, including Ash.

"Hang out with me this afternoon?" I'd said to him three weekends ago, as we'd sat on the porch eating ham sandwiches and drinking Mom's delicious homemade lemonade. "I want to get some more wood at the beach and make necklaces and bracelets."

"Maybe tomorrow," Ash replied, which sounded much the way Mom talked to me when she'd already decided I wouldn't get what I'd asked for.

"Why not today?" I sounded whiny, but I couldn't help it. We hardly spent any time together anymore, and I missed him.

He lowered his voice and leaned in, his whisper tickling my ear. "Can you keep a secret?" After I'd given him my most sincere nod, and crossed my heart, he'd continued. "Celine's having some trouble. She needs someone to talk to."

"What kind of trouble?" I whispered back, leaning in, and throwing a glance over my shoulder to demonstrate my utmost levels of discretion.

"I can't tell you. I promised, and it's important to keep your promises. Always."

I'd insisted I wouldn't share with anyone, I was excellent at keeping secrets, but he'd still refused to elaborate, maintained it wasn't his place to tell, he couldn't betray her. I didn't like him excluding me from parts of his life, and stomped up to my bedroom, ignoring Mom's pleas to be quiet because she had another headache.

Ash saw Celine more and more often, hanging out with her after school, sometimes at her house, or at ours as they worked on math and biology because she was, quote, "smart, and a grade level ahead." His voice had gone soft when he'd made that comment, and I'd winced as it pinched my heart like a crab's claws.

"Are you okay, Bee?" Ash had asked, bringing me back to the Sunday dinner table. I'd nodded but picked at the rest of my food in silence, not saying another word, even when Ash asked again if something was wrong. Once Brad's homemade sticky toffee pudding had been devoured, the dishes cleared, and Mom had told us we were free to leave, I turned to Ash, my cold shoulder already thawing.

"Want to shoot some hoops?" I said.

"Not now. Maybe when I get back."

My scowl returned. Ash hadn't said anything about going out. Usually we spent Sunday evenings watching a movie or playing basketball or baseball outside. "Where are you going?"

"Out for a little while. I'll see you later." He gave me one of his big smiles and turned to Brad, who'd already collapsed on the sofa and buried his nose in the newspaper. "Dad, can I take the car?"

Brad lowered his paper, glancing at Ash over the top of it. "Rules?"

Ash grinned and counted on his fingers. "Drive safely. Don't drink. Call if I do."

"You got it, kid. Keys are in my jacket pocket. Have fun."

I watched Ash leave, uncertainty mixing with curiosity and anger, an unpleasant concoction bubbling away inside me as I heard him drive away. "Tell Mom I went outside," I said to

Brad, adding a hasty *please* so he wouldn't call me back to correct me on my manners.

"Be home by seven thirty," he said through a yawn.

I ran to the garage to get my bicycle, a green-and-yellow racer Ash had helped me repair. We'd spent ages on it together, fixing the gears, getting new tires Ash had paid for out of the money he'd made doing carpentry. He'd even saved up and bought me a new seat because I'd complained the old one hurt my butt.

A mile later I got to Celine's house. Brad's car stood in the driveway and I hit the brakes on my bike, making sure I stayed hidden behind the leafy trees. Ash leaned with his back against the driver's door, his thumbs hooked into the front pockets of his jeans. Celine stood about a foot away from him. Unlike Keenan and Fiona, who'd inherited their father's Irish looks, Celine had taken after her Italian mother—or her mom's lover, if the rumors were to be believed. Whatever her parentage, she had long dark hair, which shone in the sunlight, a mix of dark brown and mahogany, and she'd showcased the tan skin on her arms with a fitted pink T-shirt. She had the perfect round breasts I wanted, hips I'd have killed for and a tiny waist accentuating the curve of her bottom, which was framed in a pair of black shorts. No wonder Ash wanted to spend time with Celine. Everyone in school did.

I tried to hear snippets of their conversation but was too far away. As I watched, Celine shook her head before covering her face with her hands. Ash put his arms around her, pulling her against his chest, the way he did with me when I had a nightmare. I knew how Celine felt in those arms, as if nothing in the world could ever hurt her again. A powerful shot of envy like nothing I'd ever experienced before traveled from the top of my head and down to my toes. That was the moment I realized I *hated* her for taking Ash away from me. The more time he spent with her, the less he had for me.

I watched, waiting for their embrace to end, willing it to

be over. They were only friends. He'd said so. But Ash put his index finger under Celine's chin, gently tilting her head toward his. I gasped when their lips touched, stood frozen to the spot when her arms went around his neck, and his hands traveled underneath the back of her shirt. My head spun, turning my vision blurry as Celine took Ash's hand and led him inside the house. I wasn't a stupid little kid. I knew *exactly* what they were doing. There were no other cars in the driveway, which meant her parents weren't home—no surprise there, apparently they'd left Celine, Keenan and Fiona alone for weekends ever since the latter two turned double digits—but it didn't seem as if the twins were home, either. I couldn't stand the thought of Celine and Ash being together, doing *that*. If he fell in love with her, he'd never hang out with me again.

I waited for a while, hoping I was wrong, and Ash hadn't lied when he'd said they weren't a couple, and they'd soon come back outside. When another few minutes passed and they still hadn't shown, I grabbed the biggest rock I could find, crept as close to the house as I dared, and hurled the thing straight through the window.

I ran, jumped on my bicycle and pedaled home, where I locked myself in my bedroom, refusing to come out until it was time to get the school bus the next morning. Ash didn't sit with me that day, or the one after, and I suspected he knew who'd launched a rock at his *girlfriend's* house, but I never admitted it.

It wasn't long after that the whispers started at school. Ash and I had had a falling-out, a "lover's quarrel." People stared at me when I walked down the hallway, laughing and cupping their hands to each other's ears as they quietly but not nearly discreetly enough talked about me. I'd ignored the name-calling, *freak* and *weirdo* were nothing new, but then my notebook had fallen out of my bag and *brotherfucker* had been added to the ever-growing list, filling me with so much shame I'd wished myself dead. Back then I hadn't told Ash about my new nickname for months, and now that he was home again and couldn't remember any of it, I certainly wasn't about to bring it up.

He looked at me as we sat at the kitchen table, his expectant expression transforming to frustration. How long had I silently reminisced? I gave him some succinct details about Celine, just enough of the truth to satiate his curiosity, finishing with, "You were close. Boyfriend and girlfriend for a while but a little before your seventeenth birthday, she left."

"Where did she go?"

I closed my eyes for a moment, told Ash how I remembered the sharp knock on the door one morning. It had come a few months after the rock-meets-window incident. Mom had answered and Celine's mother, smelling of stale booze and cigarettes, ranted and raved about how Celine had left a note, saying she was running away. After Mom assured her Celine wasn't at our house, and Ash was working, she'd left, but the next evening the cops showed up.

"They asked all of us questions about Celine," I said. "And they spent ages asking you when you'd last seen her, and where you'd been."

"They think I had something to do with her leaving?" he said.

"Not really. With the note she left about running away, and when you told them her father beat her, and Keenan and Fiona confirmed it, things changed."

"How?"

"Her parents had to accept the truth. She ran away because of them. Her father was an alcoholic, a heavy-handed prick, and her mom had done nothing to stop him. She was usually too off her face to try."

"Did Celine come back? Did they find her?" Ash asked, and I shook my head. "And Keenan still thinks I had something to do with her going away after all this time? Why?"

"Because he's an asshole and you shouldn't listen to him. It took him a while to stop throwing accusations around, then he left town for a few years and when he came back we thought he'd accepted you had nothing to do with Celine leaving, but then Kate..."

Ash looked at me. "Who is she?"

I got up, walked over to the drawer with the photo albums, where I pulled out a bundle of loose pictures, and flicked through them until I found what I needed, pictures that always surprised me because Kate looked so much like Celine, and with their dark hair and big eyes, they both resembled me, too. I set the photos on the table, slid them toward Ash with my index finger. "This is Celine, and this was Kate."

He was about to touch the photographs but retracted his hand as if the pictures had the potential to scorch him. "*Was?* What do you mean?"

"Kate was your girlfriend, and she...she died. Almost two and a half years ago, a couple of months before you left town."

"Kate's *dead*?" Ash's eyes went wide, and he jumped up, running his hands through his hair. "For Christ's sake, why do all the people around me keep dying? What the hell happened to her?" When I remained silent, he asked again, louder, urging and insisting I tell him because he needed to know, he wanted the truth.

I blew the air from my lungs in a shaky stream as I worked up the nerve, my insides feeling as if they were on fire, burning me from the inside out. "She had an accident by the cliffs on the path behind the house."

"*This* house?"

"Yes. She was an avid runner, come rain, shine or snow. She even got me to join her, would you believe?" I knew I was babbling and forced myself to get to the point. "It was a few miles from her place along the cliff path to ours, and she used to run it all the time. Called it a shortcut. We think she was on her way here one night, when it was raining, and she slipped..."

Ash stared at me, the color in his face gone. "Why can't I remember any of this?"

"I don't *want* you to remember," I said, trying hard not to raise my voice but barely able to contain it. "You were a mess, both times. Celine was your first crush, and you told me you had plans to propose to Kate."

"Why does Keenan think I had something to do with Kate's death?" When I looked away, Ash took a step toward me and grabbed my hand. "Tell me. *Now.* I want to know if—"

"What?" I shouted, snatching my hand away as my anger erupted. "What do you want me to tell you? That Keenan dated Kate before you did? That he blames you for stealing her away and consequently for her death, because if she'd stayed with him, she'd have had no reason to come here?"

"Woah, I—"

"Or that the police investigated you when she fell? Came to the house? Asked us questions?"

"Maya, slow down—"

"Of course they did, it's their job. But you were with me all evening. We went out for a drive and weren't even here. Kate slipped and *fell*, Ash. It was an accident."

"Keenan doesn't think so."

"Of course not. He's hated you from day one. Kate's accident was just an excuse to reignite his obsession with blaming you for everything, including Celine's disappearance. But we all know you had nothing to do with it. *Any* of it."

"Then why did I leave town?" Ash fired back, his tone and temper almost matching mine.

"Don't you think I've asked myself the same thing? Don't you think I've wondered every single day? And now that you know about Celine and Kate, I'm terrified you'll leave again."

"Maya—"

"I lost you once. I can't go through it again. I won't. First my dad, then Mom, and Brad. We thought that was it. We promised each other we'd stick together, you and me, because it's all we had, but you left. You *abandoned* me. I came home to a god-damn note on the kitchen table and the cops wouldn't even let me declare you as a missing person because you chose to leave." Unable to stop myself I grabbed the saltshaker from the table and threw it at the wall, where it punched a half-moon-shaped dent before skidding across the floor, leaving a thin white trail behind. "You hurt me, Ash. You have no idea how much."

"I've no idea about anything," Ash shouted back, and I realized I'd pushed him too far, I'd let my frustrations out and this was the result. Anger begets anger. How could I have been so stupid?

"For God's sake, Maya," Ash continued, his voice rising further still. "People think I hurt those women? I can't deal with this. I don't know how to..." He looked at me for a moment, his chest heaving, and before he said anything else, he stormed past me and out of the kitchen.

I flinched as I heard the front door slam shut behind him and, heart racing, I reached for my bag, for the clonazepam in the side pocket that I hadn't needed for months. I dropped what was supposed to be my last pill ever into my palm before rolling it between my thumb and index finger. If I swallowed it my anxiety levels would immediately wane, but the consequence was my brain would feel fuzzy as cotton wool for the rest of the day. I stared at the medicine, cocking my head to one side, thinking things through before biting off half the pill and swallowing it dry.

Sometimes we all needed a little bit of help.

12

ASH

Standing outside clutching the wobbly railing of the old, rickety porch, I took deep breaths, attempting to steady my head, which whirred and spun from my sister's revelations about the two women I couldn't remember, but had been involved with. Celine had run away when we were teenagers. Kate had *died*. And then, a couple of months later, I'd disappeared from Newdale overnight. If that wasn't the sign of a guilty conscience, I didn't know what was.

Maybe Keenan's suspicions were valid, but Maya had been adamant I'd had nothing to do with Celine leaving, or Kate's death. My sister's reassurances were welcome, because, without any firsthand knowledge of what I had or hadn't done, her comfort was all I had.

Last night Maya had pushed pretty hard for me to see a doctor, and perhaps she was right, except…what if I saw someone, got my memory back and found out she was wrong about my lack of involvement? What if the doctor told me my condition was permanent, that I'd never remember anything about my past or know who I truly was? I couldn't figure out which was worse. When I'd woken up on the beach in Maryland I'd felt lost and confused, scared even. Since my arrival in Newdale those feelings seemed to be turning into anger, a sensation buried deep inside my chest and which I was unable to explain. I could almost feel it expanding and growing, a snarling beast I wasn't sure I could get under control. Had I always felt this way? This tightly wound? So close to exploding?

After another few minutes of deep breaths, ruminating and trying to force my brain to work properly, I went back inside. Maya sat on the stairs, and when I saw her, my anger dissipated some more. She hadn't done anything wrong. From the moment she'd heard me on the other end of the phone at the petrol station, she'd bent over backward to help me.

"You don't have to worry about me leaving town," I said gently. "You're my sister. I may not remember it, but I'm going to do whatever I can to make everything come back."

She nodded, pressing her lips together, looking like she might cry. "But I don't want you to remember everything. I mean, I wish I could forget the pain of losing Mom and Brad. You don't have any of that anymore, why would you want it back?"

"I don't think it works that way. How can I leave who I am behind?"

She looked at me with her big, unblinking eyes, and gave me a small nod before getting up. "I'll be back in a minute," she said, and headed upstairs where I heard her close her bedroom door softly behind her. It seemed she needed to retreat and regroup as much as I had.

I turned and stared at myself in the hallway mirror, still feeling like I was looking at a stranger. My face seemed to have regained some of its color, and after a good shave I no longer appeared quite so disheveled, but as I examined my features in the reflection, I couldn't stop my brain from wandering back into dangerous territory.

Was this the face of someone who'd harmed two women? Keenan believed I was responsible for something, but Celine had run away—she'd even left a letter for her family—and the police had ruled Kate's death an accident. Maya had said I'd been cleared of all suspicion, but no wonder the authorities had wanted to speak to me on both occasions. Had that been why I'd freaked out when I'd seen the cruiser near the beach? Was my anxiety because I'd been subjected to their questioning twice already? I looked away, not wanting to see my expression change as I silently admitted it wasn't anxiety I'd experienced when I'd come across the police vehicle as much as it had been blind terror.

"Because you felt so messed up," I whispered, my head snapping up, gazing into my own eyes as I tried to convince myself. "That's why you panicked, there's nothing more to it."

My mind continued to torment me. What if Maya was wrong and I was a bad person, an evil one? Right now, I felt like there was a stranger within, but what would happen if I discovered a monster instead? Surely if I'd hurt Celine in some way to make her leave town or had something to do with Kate's death, I'd know. Then again, I didn't remember either of them. Not their names, faces or the sounds of their voices, so how could I be sure? I could tell my anger wanted to resurface so I forced it down.

A little while later I joined Maya in the kitchen, hoping she'd tell me more about Celine and Kate now that we'd both had the opportunity to calm down. She had her back to me, and as she poured something into a sizzling pan, I heard her humming a tune. A song I instantly recognized.

"That's the White Stripes," I said, and saw her back stiffen for a second. "'Seven Nation Army,'" I added, her eyes widening as she turned around, and I felt the need to explain. "There was a T-shirt in the trailer. I remembered the band, but this image of a younger girl kept coming to me… I think…I think it was *you*."

Her face lit up, her apparent confusion transforming into a broad smile. "Ash, this is incredible. You remembered something from our past. You remembered *me*. Meg White was my hero. I dressed up as her three Halloweens in a row."

The relief I felt from retrieving a memory, something clear but unthreatening, sent a rush of adrenaline through my body. Before I had time to think about it again or change my mind, I said, "You're right, I should see a doctor. I need to know what's going on."

She gasped, put a hand to her throat. "Really? You'll go see Dr. Adler?"

My initial excitement waned a little but held firm. There was no backing out of this now. "Yeah. Things are coming back and maybe he can help make it happen faster."

"I'll come with you. I'll call him now."

"No, I'll do it. If I want to get back to normal, I should start by advocating for myself."

Maya pulled out her cell, swiped her finger across the screen and handed it to me. As it was the weekend, I didn't expect Dr. Adler to answer, was preparing to leave a message, but he picked up the phone with a baritone *hello*.

"Good morning," I said quickly. "My name is, uh, Asher Bennett."

"Good morning to you, Mr. Bennett." His voice rumbled a little, his words neat and precise, measured, and in direct contrast to mine. "How may I help?"

"I need an appointment. I…I'm having trouble with my memory."

He paused. "What makes you say that?"

"I can't remember anything before yesterday."

"Oh, goodness. In that case you'd better come to my practice today."

We agreed to meet as soon as I could get there and he gave me the address, which I scribbled down before realizing Maya probably didn't need it. After we hung up, I turned to her, hoping she wouldn't see how anxious I felt. "We can go now," I said, "but remember I told you how I felt when I saw the police cruiser? I don't know why that happened, but…I don't want to tell Dr. Adler I was in Maryland. Let's keep that to ourselves for now."

"Of course. Whatever you say."

"And when we get back, I want to search for myself online."

She hesitated, playing with the wooden, seahorse-shaped pendant hanging on a leather strap around her neck. "I spent hours last night doing exactly that when I couldn't sleep."

My pulse throbbed in my neck as my throat ran dry. "Did you find anything?"

"No, I'd have told you. Are you sure you came up from Maryland?"

"Yes, that's where I got in the trailer. Why?"

"Because I ran searches from there to Delaware and New Jersey. Then I added Virginia and the Carolinas, and still nothing. No missing persons, no reports mentioning you and no phone listings, either. It's as if you're a ghost."

"Are you sure? Let me—"

"A hundred percent certain. There's nothing about you anywhere. Trust me, I've been searching for two years. If there was anything, I'd know."

"How is that possible?" I said, fists clenched. "Somebody must be wondering where I am. A partner—"

"You're not wearing a ring—"

"Maybe not a wife then, but a girlfriend? A friend? My boss? Don't I have a job?"

Maya sat down, put her hands flat on the table. "I have a

theory. It might sound a bit out-there, but what if you were in Maryland somewhere on vacation?"

"On my own?" I shot back. "What do you think I was doing, taking a spiritual trip to find myself or something?" I almost laughed at the irony, but given the circumstances, it wasn't remotely funny.

"Maybe you were traveling solo," Maya said, her voice calm, making me wonder how hard she had to try to stop herself from telling me I was acting like a jerk. "It's possible, plenty of people do. Perhaps you were meeting someone there. What if you lived, I don't know, in South Dakota or Wyoming or somewhere? For all we know you were staying in Alaska. To your point of having a boss and friends, they might not even realize you're missing yet."

"But why would I—"

"Hear me out. If you were on a beach on the first day of a week's solo vacation, nobody would know you're gone yet, especially if you were renting a place and not staying in a hotel, and—" Maya let out a yelp and rushed to the stove, where she pulled the pan off the burner. "Balls, the eggs are ruined." She turned to me, heaving a sigh. "God, I feel so useless, and now I'm coming up with all these ridiculous theories, confusing you even more." She took a few breaths, pinched the bridge of her nose between her fingers. "After we've seen the doctor I'll go and pick up a few things at the grocery store. Give you some space."

"I'll come with you. It'll be good to get into town and have a look around. Maybe you could show me my old haunts, see if anything comes rushing back." I forced a grin that didn't fit my face all too well, but I made it stay there all the same. "You know, fingers crossed and all that."

"Maybe that's not a good idea until Dr. Adler has cleared you. You shouldn't be overexerting yourself. I'll drop you off, grab some food, and when I come back you can help with my driftwood pieces in the garage. I have a couple of candleholders to varnish. You used to help me with my projects all the time."

"Did I?"

"Yeah. We'd go to the beach and collect stuff together. Maybe we could go tomorrow if the doc says it's okay. You know, start small, local to the house."

I looked at her, a row of virtual pennies dropping one after the other, a metallic crescendo resounding in my head. "Hold on a sec. This is about Keenan, isn't it? You don't want me going to town in case I run into him."

"*Yes*, that, too." She turned away, put the pan in the sink and filled it with water as she continued talking over her shoulder. "But I'm more worried you'll get overwhelmed and it'll make things worse."

"What if I—"

She whirled around. "No, Ash, please. This is hard for me, too, you know. I hate not knowing what happened to you. I thought...I thought you were *dead*. I'd almost accepted it. I *mourned* you."

I saw her big gray eyes fill with tears as she bit her bottom lip to stop it from trembling. All this time I'd been focused on myself, how frustrated and angry I was at my memory being wiped clean. I hadn't considered Maya for more than a few seconds. I tried to justify my selfishness somehow but couldn't. I'd been treating her, the person who could provide me with many of the answers I was searching for, like utter shit. Seeing the dark shadows under her eyes now and hearing the edge in her voice...she probably hadn't had a good night's sleep in years, and that was all on me. I'd left. Abandoned her. Whoever I was in the past, I'd been an egotistical prick. I got up, and after hesitating a little, kissed the top of her head, noticing how her hair smelled of pine cones. "I wish I could explain everything that's happened, but I can't. Not yet."

"I know," she whispered, squeezing me hard.

Maya went upstairs to get ready for our trip to the doctor's while I cleaned up the kitchen of a house in which I should've known every nook, cranny and squeaky floorboard, but where all felt unfamiliar and strange.

When I saw her laptop on the kitchen table, I decided to run a quick search of my own and lifted the lid, squinting at the bright light. When the password prompt appeared, I closed it again. I wouldn't have been able to guess my own security settings, let alone take a stab at my sister's. As I leaned back in my chair, I thought about her theory of me being on holiday alone, decided it was plausible, even if it meant nobody would be searching for me yet.

"Are you ready?" Maya said as she came downstairs, and when she pulled the car keys from her pocket, a piece of paper fluttered to the floor. As she moved ahead of me I picked it up, turned it over and saw it was a receipt from a pharmacy for a bottle of Benadryl.

"Do you have hay fever?" I said, unsure how I knew that's what the medicine was for, but grateful for the random fact leaping from the depths of my brain nonetheless.

"It's been awful this year," she said as she opened the door, before spinning around and almost bumping into me, her face filled with excitement. "Oh, my God, you remember?"

"Uh, yeah." I nodded and made all the right noises as she beamed, saying she couldn't believe it. She'd had terrible hay fever ever since she was a teen, and practically guzzled Benadryl by the gallon to get some relief. I didn't want to let on I'd had no idea, or see her expression change to disappointment, and so I crushed the pharmacy receipt up into a ball, and a while later threw it in the trash.

Sweat pooled under my arms as we drove to Dr. Adler's, my head twisting left and right as I tried to get a good look around. Maya pointed out Keenan's house, which had a rusty swing-set in the front garden, the broken yellow plastic seats gently moving in the wind. After that we continued in silence for a while. I soon noticed our house was at the end of a long road flanked only by a few other dwellings, and all of them were spaced at least a quarter of a mile apart.

"Do you know why Dad chose the house?" I said. "It's so remote."

"It was your grandfather's," Maya said. "He left it to Brad when he died. Your pops was American, got your English grandmother pregnant when he was working over there, married her but couldn't stick it, apparently. He came back here a year after Brad was born, basically abandoned his wife and your dad in the UK. They never had much of a relationship after that, and I think you only met your grandfather once, when you were small. Brad always said he got the house out of guilt."

It was probably a story my father had shared with me, one we'd maybe talked about over a drink. The impact of another lost memory hit me squarely in the chest, and it renewed my determination to do whatever I could to unlock my mind, no matter the truth. I couldn't pick and choose. I either wanted all of my past, or none of it.

"...and I never thought it was that remote," Maya was saying. "Not with the path behind the house along the cliffs. If you turn left, it splits and there's another one leading down to the beach. Turn right and walk for about two and a half miles and you get to the other side of town."

"That's where Kate fell, though? Along the path?"

Maya nodded, and I didn't say anything else but stared out of the window as she brought us closer to Newdale. It seemed a handsome town, and the large wrought iron sign in the shape of a wave with the words *Welcome to Newdale,* as well as the immaculate multicolored flowerbeds on either side, all indicated a certain level of prosperity and charm. Main Street appeared to contain the heart of the place, both sides peppered with bijou clothes boutiques, a bookshop, antiques dealers, a jeweler, an arts and crafts store, as well as multiple cafés and restaurants.

As we waited at a red light, I knew Maya's eyes were on me and I turned my head, caught her observing. "Nothing's coming back," I said. "I don't remember any of this."

She reached out and put a hand on my arm. "Don't worry. We're almost there."

Sure enough, she turned left and took a few side streets with tall, leafy oak trees on either side. Dr. Adler's office was in an annex next to his Victorian house similar in style to Maya's, but twice the size, and it seemed freshly painted. After we parked the car, we headed to the right side of the building, the sun warming my skin, the scent of something flowery—sweet and heavy—in the air. Before I had a chance to knock, heavy footsteps approached from the other side of the door, and an older gentleman dressed in a tartan shirt and brown corduroy trousers opened up.

"Mr. Bennett?" He peered at me over the top of his round spectacles and, when he saw Maya behind me, smiled. "I'm delighted to see you found your stepbrother."

"Not as much as me," she replied happily as we walked inside.

Dr. Adler ushered us past a little reception area with half a dozen orange plastic chairs, and into the first consultation room on the left. Its walls were slate gray, and he'd adorned them with pictures and self-portraits of what I assumed were his younger patients. They had toothy grins, bandaged arms, stitches in their knees and speech bubbles with words of thanks written inside. He gestured for us to take a seat, before following suit, and placing his hands in his lap.

"You mentioned memory trouble on the phone," he said. "Shall we start from the beginning, so to speak? Tell me what you remember."

With Maya's help, I explained most of what had happened, including the various flashbacks I'd experienced so far, but staying sufficiently vague about the location I'd woken up in, as Dr. Adler made notes.

"And the first time you realized you couldn't remember anything about yourself was when you woke up somewhere on a beach yesterday morning?" he said.

"God, I can't believe it was only yesterday, it feels like years," I said. "And I can't explain it. I know there's stuff inside my head, but I can't access it. It's as if there's a roadblock, or a big gaping hole. Does...does that make any sense?"

"Perfect sense," Dr. Adler said.

"If it's amnesia I'd say it's retrograde, not anterograde—" Maya shrugged when I raised my eyebrows in surprise "—because he's perfectly capable of forming new memories."

"Somebody's been doing research," Dr. Adler said with a smile. "But it's a little early to jump to conclusions. Your memory loss could be related to many things, Ash, such as an injury, or disease."

"*Disease?*" I said. "You think I'm ill?"

"Not necessarily. You mentioned a head wound. May I?" When I nodded, he pulled on a pair of latex gloves and gently touched my scalp, tilting my head to one side. "This had to be quite the blow. You could've done with a few stitches."

"To be honest, it didn't feel like a priority."

Dr. Adler smiled. "Understandable. Do you know how it happened?" When I shook my head, he added, "Head injuries can trigger memory loss. Maybe this has brought us a step closer to figuring out what's going on." He made sure the cut was clean and continued to examine me, listening to my heart and lungs, checking my reflexes, shining a light in my eyes, and evaluating my balance before taking my blood pressure. "It's a little on the high side," he said, making another note. "However, that's also understandable."

"Can you help him?" Maya said.

Dr. Adler leaned forward, put his fingers in a steeple under his chin. "I'd like to send you to the ER for more thorough testing. They'll no doubt order an MRI or a CT scan, and blood tests. We need to be thorough. Rule out as many reasons for your memory loss as we can."

"Dr. Adler," Maya said quietly. "We've no clue if Ash has insurance. Neither of us ever have."

"I understand," he said, drumming his fingers. "Let me see what I can do."

Hours later, after a visit Dr. Adler had arranged at a free clinic, and which involved me being poked, prodded and tested repeatedly, we now sat opposite the ER doctor, a tall, wide-shouldered woman called Gwen Soares. She read over the notes that had been compiled as I'd undergone a CT scan, too many blood tests to count, a psychiatric evaluation and an in-depth discussion about family history. I had to bite my tongue and swallow my frustrations as Maya helped me with almost all of the questions, clarifying there were no strokes, aneurysms or brain tumors on my side of the family. She gave my hand a squeeze as she told them about my mother's suicide, which she concluded with, "But Ash has never been depressed. Never."

Dr. Soares nodded once, looked up at us and smiled. "How are you feeling, Ash?"

"One hundred percent arsed off," I wanted to say, but settled for, "Bushed."

"I understand," she said. "Here's the good news. All your blood work was clear. No signs of drugs, alcohol or any kind of infection in your system. Not only that, but your semantic memory is in good working order."

"What's that?" Maya said.

"The part of your brain that understands things such as words, colors, places and so forth," Dr. Soares said. "Things not necessarily drawn from personal experience but which are common, as well as general knowledge you've accumulated throughout your life."

"And that's a good thing?" I said.

"Exceedingly. You're functioning normally: walking, talking. You know how to eat, for example, and what you're eating. You know how to take care of your personal hygiene. I'd say, along with the other symptoms you're presenting, it's possible your memory condition is temporary."

"It'll come back?" Maya said, her voice going up. "All of it? When?"

"It could be days, weeks, perhaps more," Dr. Soares said. "And I'm afraid it's impossible to say if everything will return. There are signs of concussion, more than likely from the blow to your head, but there's no bleeding in your brain."

"But it won't stay like this," I said. "Thank Christ."

"Let's not get ahead of ourselves just yet, Ash," Dr. Soares said. "The mind can be a tricky thing, and I need to caution you about false memories caused by confabulation."

"Confabu...what?" I said.

"It's a phenomenon where a person with a brain injury constructs false memories," she said. "They can experience extremely vivid recollections of things that never happened at all or may recall events differently from true reality, yet be a hundred percent convinced they're accurate. It's a brain's way of coping, you see, filling in the blanks."

"Even if it's not real?" Maya said.

Dr. Soares nodded. "On a smaller scale, false memories happen to people without amnesia or brain injuries, too. If you think about it, most of us believe our memories are accurate. In general, we see our minds as video recorders, with everything memorized exactly as it happened. However, if you ask the police about eyewitnesses—"

"They'll say they're notoriously unreliable," Maya said.

"Exactly," Dr. Soares replied. "Even if a person isn't suffering from amnesia, their memory is prone to fallacy. For example, houses burn to the ground because the owner was certain they'd switched off the stove, and in extreme cases, people create entirely fictitious memories about things they're certain happened, but never took place."

I held up a hand. "Wait a sec. You're saying stuff might come back but I could have made it all up because of…what did you call it again?"

"Confabulation," Dr. Soares and Maya said at the same time.

"Like the chickens last night?" Maya turned back to the doctor. "Ash was convinced we had chickens in the garden at home, but they were actually on the fabric of the kitchen blinds. We never had real ones."

"The condition may resolve itself over time as the brain heals," Dr. Soares said. "But I need you to be patient with yourself, and each other, as you navigate your way through this. Maya, it'll be a delicate balance of knowing Ash's recollection is incorrect but not needing to convince him otherwise because that particular memory or detail doesn't matter when it comes to the big picture of his life. Most of all, Ash, you need to rest as much as you can. Do you work?"

"Not at the moment," I said, still trying to wrap my head around the false-memory concept, adding it to my ever-growing list of things about my life that were pissing me off. "I'm staying with my sister in the old family home."

"That's a good thing. Concussions take time to heal. You need to listen to your body, and don't overdo it. No sports or vigorous movements, another blow to your head could have dire consequences, and stay off screens as much as possible. Other than that—" she gave a small shrug "—I'm afraid a strong dose of patience is required while you get better."

"So, was I right?" Maya said. "It's retrograde amnesia?"

Dr. Soares hesitated. "It's a strong possibility, yes."

"There must be something else you can do, surely?" I said. "Can't you give me anything? Can you *do* something?"

"There's no magic pill, unfortunately," Dr. Soares said. "It's excellent you're staying with Maya in your old home. Familiar people and surroundings tend to help, as does trying to relax, which sounds ridiculous, I know. Sometimes smell or touch can be powerful triggers."

"Basically, it's a waiting game," Maya said.

"I'll send my notes to Dr. Adler," Dr. Soares said. "I recommend you see him in a week. If anything changes before then, call him immediately, and if you have violent headaches, nausea or blurred vision, dial 911 without delay. It could be serious."

Maya had more questions about what may or may not spark memories, but I zoned out when she wanted to go over how confabulation worked a third time. While I hadn't expected anyone to produce a "magic pill," as Dr. Soares had called it, I'd expected…*more*. A better approach than *wait and see*. I wanted them to fix this, now, or give me the tools to fix myself.

"I'm so glad they figured out you're not sick," Maya said as we walked back to the car. "Although it bugs me they won't commit to a diagnosis, it's pretty obvious from what I read what's going on. I mean, I understand they're not miracle workers, but still…" She put her hand on my shoulder and I shrugged her off. "Hey, Ash," she said. "It's going to be all right."

"Is it?" I tried tamping my anger back down before it made its way up my throat, but only managed to swallow it about halfway. "It's not good enough. What am I supposed to do? Just wait and see what comes back? Not know if it's real?" I dug my nails into my palms, hard, as I fought to regain control before I put a fist through the car window.

"I'm sure they did their best," Maya said quietly. "We'll get there. I know we will. All in good time, okay? And I'll help you. Tell you if whatever you're remembering is real or confabulation. You'll get through this. *We'll* get through this."

I almost let out a laugh. Jesus, she really didn't understand a thing, did she? I wanted to yell at her, shout I shouldn't have to ask her to verify my memories, that what I needed was to feel human again, whole, not a broken shell of a man. Letting out a breath, jaw still clenched and heart pounding, I muttered, "Yeah, yeah. All in good time."

13

LILY

It was Thursday, and somehow five days had passed since Jack had disappeared. I'd stopped counting the minutes, but only because they'd morphed into hours, and the hours into days. Although I wanted time to stand still, or better yet, be reversed, it kept going, relentless and cruel. I hadn't yet found the courage to return to Jack's apartment but I contacted Heron and Stevens every day, twice a day, and we'd reached the point where they no longer knew what to say other than, "We're collaborating with all the different counties on missing persons but we're afraid there's still no news."

Mike had insisted I take some paid leave from the garage, an offer I'd ungraciously refused. "What am I supposed to do all day if I'm not here?" I'd snapped, throwing my hands in the air as he gave me a pained expression, no doubt unsure how to handle my misplaced anger and volatile mood swings. I'd stayed late at the garage that night, reorganized the files, archiving the old client records and making sure the new ones were color-coded and alphabetized—things I'd wanted to get around to eventually, but which took on a sudden and immediate urgency.

I knew it was an attempt to keep at least one part of my life under control. I needed to be busy, it helped me avoid sleeping. The night before I'd dreamt I was in the ocean, the skies blue, the sun hot, a perfect summer day until the clouds darkened and the waves picked up. I'd seen Jack's bloated body floating beneath the surface, his face a mass of rotting, half-eaten flesh, his beautiful features almost unrecognizable. He'd held out a putrid arm as his blue lips mouthed, "Help me, Lily." I'd woken up screaming and shivering, unable to get back to sleep.

It was lunchtime now, and after Mike shooed me out the door, insisting I take the afternoon off because the bags under my eyes were as big and black as the tires he sold, I headed to the grocery store for a few supplies. As I wandered around, picking up milk that would turn sour and food I swore I'd eat but which would mostly end up in the garbage, my cell rang.

"Lily," Sam said. "How are you doing? Do you have any news?"

He'd called daily, and this was the way each of our conversations started. I sighed, rested my elbows on the handlebar of my shopping cart. "Nothing."

"God, this is so stressful, and I can only imagine what you're going through. It's so unfair, Jack was…uh…I mean, *is*, such a great guy."

Ignoring the slip, I forced the lump in my throat back down, and exhaled quietly, counting to three. "I know… How are things with you? Where are you?"

"Company HQ in Chicago. That's the other reason for my call. I got a promotion."

My heart ached. Sam's life was moving forward, and while I was happy for him, all it did was illustrate how much mine would never be the same again. I ordered my lips to move into a smile, hoped it would be enough for Sam to hear the gesture in my voice. "How fantastic. Congratulations."

"Yeah, thanks. VP of national business development. I can't quite believe it even though it's been in the works for a month. I would've mentioned it before, but it was top secret."

"This is good news, isn't it? You don't sound very happy."

"Oh, yes, I'm thrilled. More than that, but, uh, the job's here, in Chicago."

"Don't tell me they've turned you into a Cubs fan?"

He chuckled. "You know my heart will forever belong to the Orioles, but this is a once-in-a-lifetime chance, that's for sure. Actually, before I came here for the final negotiations I'd already decided if I got the job it would mean a permanent move for me."

It took a while to reach the depths of my messy brain, but Sam's message finally got there. "You're selling your house? But you love this area. It's where you grew up."

"I know, but things...well, they change. I'm getting older, the amount of travel really is insane. Between us, there's talk of our HQ relocating to California, in which case I'll be closer to my daughter. There's no point keeping a place on the East Coast I'll never get to anymore."

I closed my eyes, pressed the phone to my ear. "I guess you've made up your mind then, haven't you? And I suppose you need me to clear out Jack's things?"

"There's no rush," he said quickly. "I'll put it on the market within the next month or so and have the place staged professionally. The apartment above the garage is a huge selling feature, apparently."

"But what about Jack?"

"Like I said, there's no rush—"

"But he's not going to be very happy when he comes back and finds you've sold the place, is he?"

"Oh, sweetheart..."

The sympathy in his voice made the hair on the back of my neck stand on end. I knew that tone, the veterinarian had used it when I was eight, and our dog, a fluffy, happy-go-lucky Collie we'd named Pebbles had got run over. I'd insisted she'd be fine, the vet should operate. Neither the doctor nor my parents had agreed.

"You don't think he's coming home," I said, my voice a few degrees cooler.

Sam let out a breath. "I want to believe it, truly, but it's been almost a week..."

"Fine. I'll get his things. Make the place all nice and tidy so you get the maximum amount of dough seeing as that's what's most important to you." My words were glacial now, and I hoped they cut him as deep as I meant them to.

"Please, Lily, you don't need to do anything yet, I—"

"Don't worry about it. It's fine. I'll take everything to my place and when Jack gets back, he'll stay with me. And, Sam?"

"Yes?" he whispered.

"Fuck you for giving up on him."

I silenced his protests by hanging up, and when he called back, I switched off my phone. Fueled by anger, I abandoned my quest for pointless food, picked up a roll of packing tape and asked the store clerk for their entire collection of empty boxes.

Once I got to Jack's apartment my anger and frustrations had subsided a little, but not enough for me to change my mind about collecting his things. If I didn't do it now, and as more and more days passed, I wasn't sure when I'd find the nerve.

As I walked up the stairs with a few boxes in my hands, I stopped midway. Jack's front door was ajar.

I threw the boxes over the banister, ignoring them as they crashed to the ground, and took the rest of the steps two at a time.

"Jack," I shouted, bursting into the apartment.

I was met with complete silence, and it took my brain a while to click into gear and process what my eyes were seeing as I walked through the hallway. Jack's things strewn across the floor. Clothes and shoes, pillows and bedding, utensils and broken glass. It looked like a tornado had torn through the place. *Get out*, my brain screamed at me. *Get out now!*

I backed away, my feet sliding across the floorboards as they tried to gain traction. Someone had been in here, gone through all of Jack's things. Had they already left? What if they were behind me, coming back up the stairs? There was no noise aside from the beating of my heart, but that didn't mean I was alone. I retreated to the front door. Once outside, I leaped down the stairs and pulled out my phone, dialing Heron and whispering a silent thank-you when she picked up after one ring.

"Someone broke into Jack's apartment," I blurted before she had a chance to say more than hello, and as I relayed what I'd seen upstairs, she told me to make sure I was safe, and they'd be right over. A car arrived within a few minutes, lights flashing, sirens blaring, and Heron ordered me in no uncertain terms to stay outside while she, Stevens and the team secured the area. I stayed on the sidelines, watching the officers from a distance, shivering. It didn't take long for them to confirm there was nobody in the apartment. Whoever had broken in was gone.

"Could you follow me, please?" Stevens said, approaching me after what felt like hours. "It would be helpful to know if anything's missing."

I nodded and silently followed him back up the stairs, my throat running dry, my pulse beating in my neck from the mere thought a stranger had been here not long ago. Jack's possessions were still in total disarray, and as my fear changed to anger, I had to work hard to keep it in check as we moved from room to room and I took in the carnage. I knew the cash from the cookie tin hadn't been stolen because I'd taken it home with me, and from what I could tell, Jack's clothes were all accounted for, and there wasn't anything missing from his bedroom or the kitchen. The bathroom never had much in it anyway, and the small TV he'd bought secondhand had been left untouched on the cabinet in the living room.

I looked around, almost as if it were the first time I'd visited, a tingling sensation settling somewhere in the middle of my spine. If I'd noticed it before, I hadn't paid much attention, or perhaps brushed the thought off as inconsequential, but Jack didn't have many personal things. No devices other than his pay-as-you-go phone, and apart from a few magazines and books, and the photograph of us we'd snapped one day at the beach, and which I'd framed, there wasn't much else in the living room, or the others. For someone who'd lived in an apartment for close to two years, the decor was decidedly sparse.

"I don't think anything's missing," I said quietly.

"When were you last here?" Stevens said, making notes as I answered. "Do you have any idea who might have broken in?"

I was about to open my mouth to say no when I remembered the man who'd come up the stairs to Jack's place the other night, and the blue Dodge Charger that had creeped me out. Stevens made more notes as I showed him the photos and recounted what had happened, and I couldn't help feeling he wasn't taking it very seriously. "I told Sam I'd remove Jack's things," I said after he asked me what I'd come here for, and had to try hard to keep the irritation from my voice as I explained about Sam's intentions to sell.

Stevens shook his head. "You'll have to wait until we finish processing the place. I'll let you know when we're done."

I was being dismissed, and so I muttered a goodbye and stepped into the hallway. The door to the closet was open. There had been nothing of value in there, sentimental or otherwise. It was where Jack kept an ironing board I'd seen him use once, along with a multitude of cleaning supplies and a box filled with shoe polish and old rags. I was about to walk by when I spotted a book on the floor, a dusty copy of a novel called *Creep* by Jennifer Hillier. At first, I assumed it belonged to Sam, something he'd forgotten, and which Jack either hadn't seen in the closet, or hadn't passed along. Except when I bent over, picked up the book and opened the front cover, right there, stamped on the first page, was a rectangular black-and-white bookplate with the words *Yarmouth Public Library, Maine.*

My palms turned clammy as I recalled Jack telling me how he'd moved from England to the States when he was a teenager, not long after his mother committed suicide. He'd also told me he'd lived in Maine for a while, somewhere near Portland. When I'd shared this information with Heron and Stevens, they'd said they'd "look into it" but as far as I could tell they'd done nothing, concentrating their investigation on the surrounding counties instead. It wasn't surprising. There had to be a thousand men named Jack living in Maine, we still had no clue if it was his real name or when he'd left that state, and besides, police manpower was limited.

I hesitated, wondered if I should give the book to Stevens, but didn't trust him enough to actually follow up, decided I could do a little research of my own before sharing all the info with Heron, with whom at least I had a bit of a rapport. Feeling like a thief, I stuffed the novel under my jacket and walked back to my car before driving straight home. Once behind closed doors I grabbed my phone, ran a search for Yarmouth and discovered it was a town in Cumberland County about twelve miles north of Portland.

I could barely stop the excitement as I dared to imagine the tiniest of cracks in the door that led to Jack's identity opening before me. If the library could tell me who had borrowed the book, I might have his real name. I'd know more about him. I found the number for the library, my finger hovering over the screen, my brain fighting my heart on whether to make the call and take a step closer to uncovering the truth or turn my back and walk away. My brain won the battle, and I hit the call button, pressing the phone against my ear and keeping my left hand by my side in case it developed a will of its own and tried to hang up.

"Yarmouth Public Library, this is Mary speaking."

My words tumbled out. "Hello, I have one of your books. I think it's overdue."

"Let me help you," Mary said. "What's your library card number?"

"Uh, I'm not sure."

"Not to worry. What's your name?"

I opened my mouth, almost blurted *Lily Reid* but my brain took charge, warning me if I told Mary I didn't have an account, she'd cite some privacy laws and shut me down. I went with a different angle and let out a sob without having to try very hard. "The book's called *Creep*. It was my brother's favorite. He must have borrowed it before he passed away…"

"Oh, my Lord," Mary said, clicking away on her keyboard. "You poor thing."

Another sob escaped my lips. I was an utter piece of shit for manipulating a kindly librarian, but with the possibility of a detail about who Jack was dangling in front of me, I wouldn't let one little lie stop me. It wasn't hurting anyone.

"Here we go, yes, there it is," Mary said. "We only had one copy and, my goodness, it *was* overdue. Maya Scott borrowed it over two years ago, and…" Her voice shifted, became hesitant. "Didn't you say it was your brother's?"

I hung up before she had the opportunity to call me out any further on my lies, and blocked the library's number in case she phoned back. Excitement traveled from my toes to my fingertips, and everywhere in between. I had a name. Maya Scott.

Who was she? Jack's previous girlfriend, perhaps? Unless…no. *No.* Did he have a wife and kids in Maine? He'd told me he'd never married, but was it true? What if he'd abandoned them to get out of alimony payments? As the last few days had passed, I'd figured in time—lots of time, and then some—I might accept I'd been going out with a liar, but with a cheater and a deadbeat dad? He'd seemed so sincere, faithful and committed. Had my rose-tinted glasses been Coke-bottle thick?

I clutched the library book to my chest, understanding the damn thing hadn't provided me with answers. If anything, I had more questions than before. I couldn't tell Heron or Stevens about this, couldn't stomach her looks of sympathy and his thinly veiled amusement at how I'd been played.

My heart sank. I wanted to go back to the apartment, get all of Jack's belongings and set them on fire, watch them burn. He'd lied to me. About *everything*. I'd never know who he truly was because—and this time I allowed myself to finish the thought— he wasn't coming back. Jack had drowned. He was gone. I'd never, ever see him again, and in that moment, I hated him. Detested him for putting me through this. If he'd trusted me enough to share his secrets, if he'd told me the truth about who he was, I'd either have walked away when we met, or stuck with him, leaving me free to mourn the man I'd loved. Sam had been right about one thing: it was unfair, it was all so completely unfair, and, damn it, I wanted and deserved to find some answers.

In no time at all I was on social media, hunting for profiles, and after another while I'd found two women in Maine named Maya Scott. As I had no idea what the person I was searching for looked like, I selected the first profile. I scrolled through her posts, from which I determined she was around forty, had a profound dislike for cottage cheese and loved to bake anything with chocolate. I watched videos of her three cats called Skippy, Zippy and Boo, fast-forwarded through her daughter's multiple piano recitals because they only showed her hands, and made a start on the photos. I took my time, zooming in on each one, trying to determine if the back of a head or a half-cropped-out arm belonged to Jack. An hour went by, and still nothing.

The first profile exhausted, I selected the next, soon realizing this one wouldn't take nearly as long. This Maya Scott enjoyed her privacy, and most of what she shared wasn't set to public. She hadn't posted for quite some time, either. Then again, neither had I.

I flicked through her limited posts and clicked on the link to her photo albums. Again, most of them weren't accessible, but when I scrolled down, a picture she'd added a few years ago made me gasp. I slid a finger across the screen and zoomed in. It was a photo of a dark-haired girl, wide-eyed and slim, dressed in a black-and-yellow-striped bikini, and with a huge grin on her face. The man next to her wore dark sunglasses, and had slicked his wet hair off his forehead, but the shape of his chin, his nose, and the beauty spot next to it, were unmistakable. I'd know him anywhere. Jack.

Heart pounding, I went back to her profile, searching for clues about where she lived, where she worked, but found none. I almost threw my phone against the wall in frustration, but as I scrolled back through the pictures and posts, a more recent one caught my eye. She'd been tagged in a photo with a group of people, all dressed in black pants and wine-red shirts, standing in front of a modern building by the ocean. Their bodies obscured the sign behind them, and the unhelpful caption read *Best Resto Crew!* Undeterred, I focused on the top left part of Maya's shirt and zoomed in enough to make out the silver writing.

The Cliff's Head.

In comparison to Maya Scott, the restaurant was easy to locate. I found it nestled away in a coastal town called Newdale, up the coast from Portland, not far from Yarmouth. Not far from the library. Fingers crossed and heart pounding harder than I ever thought possible, I dialed.

"The Cliff's Head," a woman said.

"Hello, I'm looking for Maya Scott."

"This is she."

Her voice was deep, a little husky, and I couldn't speak—didn't want to—in case it turned out to be a dead end, a mistake, a misunderstanding. I cleared my throat in an effort to psych myself up for the conversation, but she spoke first, an audible smile in her voice.

"Hello? Can I help you make a reservation?"

"No, thanks. I, uh, my name's Lily Reid. I—I'm looking for Jack Smith."

A long pause, then, "We don't have anyone who works here named Jack."

"No, uh, that's not what I meant. I…I think you know him."

"Me?"

"Yes."

"I'm afraid you're mistaken." Her pleasantness had disappeared, her voice now sounding wary and firm. "I don't know a Jack Smith."

"Are you sure? He's my boyfriend, and he went missing almost a week ago. I…I know this'll sound strange, but I found you on Facebook. I was going through your posts—"

"*Excuse* me?"

"—and I came across one of your photos. You're in a black-and-yellow bikini, and you're with a man. Brown hair, beauty spot on—"

"Hold up. Did you say you went through my Facebook photos?"

Shit. "I know how crazy this sounds, believe me, but I need to know if this man—"

"You really shouldn't be snooping."

"But if you could take a quick look at the photo—"

"I can't help you." The phone went dead.

"No!" I yelled. "No, no, *no!*"

I'd found one lead—*one*—since Jack disappeared, and I'd blown it. Maya Scott thought I was a psycho, and who could blame her after I'd told her I'd gone through her photos? I considered my options, decided the best one was to take a screenshot of the picture, send her a groveling message and explain what I needed, and why. But as I swiped back to her photographs, my phone rang. The number was blocked, but I answered anyway.

"Hello, Lily? It's Maya Scott. You just called me."

"Oh, thank God," I said, my voice breathless as I sank into my seat. "Thank you for calling back, I'm sorry—"

"No, I am," she said. "I didn't mean to be rude. You took me a little by surprise."

"I shouldn't have invaded your privacy..."

Maya laughed, warm and kind, a hundred and eighty degrees difference from moments before, and I felt my shoulders melt away from my ears. "Well," she said, "it was a little strange, to be honest, but in your defense, whatever someone puts on the web becomes public domain. I overreacted. I apologize."

"You're very gracious," I said quietly.

"Not at all. But I'm curious, why exactly did you call me?"

I told her about how Jack had disappeared, how I'd found a book, called the library and got her name before working my way through Facebook to locate her at the Cliff's Head. She listened without saying a word, which I found admirable considering how insane it sounded. "Can you tell me the name of the man in the photo?" I pleaded as I got to the end of my story, holding my breath as I waited for her answer.

"I'm confused," she said. "I thought you said your boyfriend's name is Jack?"

"I don't know," I whispered. "I think he gave me a false name."

"You're kidding? What a piece of...well, it's none of my business. I shouldn't—"

"It's okay, it's fine. Please, tell me what you know about the man in the photo."

"Well, it's not much," she said, and I let out a little groan. I'd been hoping for a miracle and I wasn't about to get one after all.

"I'm pretty sure his name's Gordon Jones, or Gordon James or something. I can't quite remember, it was so long ago."

"Where was Gordon from?"

"Hmmm… Australia, maybe? I'm terrible with accents," Maya said. "I met him at our local beach one day, that's when the picture was taken, actually." She laughed in a *what a funny coincidence* way that made me bite the inside of my cheek. "You know, I'd always wondered what happened to my damn library book. He must've picked it up by mistake. I never saw him again."

"Do you know where he was living?"

"No idea. Somewhere in Maine, I think, but he said something about a new job in Connecticut, or New York, maybe? I can't remember. Perhaps you'll find him on social media, the way you found me. I don't think I connected with him, though."

"Gordon Jones…or James," I repeated. "Thank you, you've been really helpful."

"My pleasure. Best of luck. I hope you find him, although if he gave you a fake name, who knows what he's been up to. Tell him he owes me two bucks for the library fine."

"I'll be sure to let him know." As soon as we hung up, I returned to her Facebook profile, intending on saving a copy of the image so I could share it with the cops. But as soon as I got to her photo albums, my brow knitted together tighter than before.

The picture was gone.

14

ASH

A few days had passed since my visit to Dr. Adler and the free clinic, but it would've been a lie if I said things had improved much. My brain was as muddled as ever, except for the time when Maya and I had played cards one evening. On a whim, I'd grabbed the deck from my bedroom, walked into the kitchen, slapped it down on the table in front of Maya and said, "Wanna play?"

My sister had grinned and rubbed her hands together, declared I'd better get ready for a serious thrashing. She'd been wrong, cursing me to hell and back as I instinctively remembered how to play poker, recalling all the rules, even calling her out on a few of them. By the end of the game she was shaking her head, laughing and begging for mercy.

"Brad taught you," she said as I shuffled the cards, a feeling of contentment from the fact I'd remembered something spreading throughout my body, even though it was insignificant in the grand scheme of things. "He was an expert at the game, but you were twenty times better. And you never confessed, but we all thought you were playing for money in school. Secretly I think Brad was a bit proud of that, not that he'd ever have admitted as much to my mom."

I'd fallen asleep on the sofa afterward and when I'd woken up Maya had teased me, saying it was something else I'd got from my father because he'd always dozed off before finishing the newspaper. Despite her good humor I could tell she was worried I'd overdone it, and she was unhappy about having gone back to work at the Cliff's Head. She didn't feel comfortable leaving me alone, despite my reassurances I was fine, and the next morning, when she'd dropped off what she called her "side gig"—key rings, bowls and other wooden trinkets she made— at the shop in town called Drift, she'd insisted I go with her, and I'd complied.

Today, though, after sleeping another nine hours straight, I was woken up by the phone. Somehow, I managed to recall Maya telling me she'd be at the restaurant, so I stumbled out of my room and got downstairs before the ringing stopped. It was Dr. Adler calling to reschedule our appointment because of an emergency, and once he'd confirmed the details and we'd hung up, I groaned and stretched, forced myself back upstairs and walked across the landing to the bathroom. Before I got there, sudden flashes of images hit me. In them, I was opening a door, not one of the oak ones in this house, but one that had been painted dark blue, with a brass handle rather than a silver knob. The picture faded and I took a step forward, but then the next image came, and it was so strong, so vivid, it almost brought me to my knees. Red-tinged water splashing onto a white tile floor. The shadow of a body lying in the tub behind the half-open shower curtain. My feet scrambled backward as my hands groped for the banister. I didn't know what I'd seen, or what it meant, only that I had to get away. *Now.*

"Maya?" I called out, retreating from the bathroom door, holding on to the railing so hard, I thought it might snap between my fingers. "*Maya?* Are you home?"

The house remained quiet, not a single noise save for the tick-ticking of the clock on my bedroom wall, and the air only carried the faint smell of coffee. My panic lessened as I went downstairs and checked each room for my sister before putting on my sneakers and going outside. The door to the garage was open, and when I saw Maya moving around, I headed over. The temperatures had risen during the past few days, bringing with them the promise of a long summer, and the air was filled with the smell of sea salt and the sound of rustling leaves. All of it seemed so normal, and what had just happened in the house began to fade into the background.

Maya was at the back of the garage, dressed in her standard outfit of black jeans and T-shirt, standing over a piece of driftwood the size of my leg. Purple earbuds firmly in place, she swayed to whatever she was listening to, running her hands over the wood, her lips moving without making a sound. Because I wasn't paying enough attention, my foot caught on a frayed, faded orange rug and I stumbled, almost crashing into the shelf full of neatly arranged tools and supplies. Maya looked up and pulled out an earbud, her face breaking into a smile.

"Hey, sleepyhead." Her grin faded a little. "You okay? You're really pale."

The red bathwater images pushed and shoved, once again making sure they were the only thing I could think of. "I remembered something…at least I believe so. I'm not sure."

I ran a damp palm over my hair. This was impossible, trying to sort out reality from dreams, fact from fiction, truth from confabulation. How could I live like this? Weren't we humans, at least in part, the sum of our experiences? Without a firm grasp on my history, how was I supposed to move on? How could I know, or have any kind of trust in who I was?

Maya walked over and put a hand on my shoulder. "Tell me what you saw."

"A blue door with a brass handle. I think it was a…"

"Bathroom." Maya exhaled deeply. "Wow, of all the things to come back…" She grabbed my hand and led me to a green bench at the back of the room near some open framing, where she made me sit down and gently said, "You're remembering what happened to your mom."

"Rosalie?" I said, the name still strange and unfamiliar on my tongue.

"Yes. When she committed suicide…you found her. In the bath at home. Her wrists…"

"Christ," I whispered. I'd found my mother, veins slashed, bleeding out in the family bathroom. It must have been terrifying, life-defining, something I'd surely wanted to forget. "That's one thing I wish my brain had made up."

"Me, too." Maya rubbed my hand as she looked at me with her huge eyes. "You never talked about it much, you found it too distressing. God, I wish you could leave it behind."

I shook my head. "I've already told you. I've got to take the good with the bad, and at least real memories are coming, bits and pieces of them, anyway. I mean, this thing with my mum… obviously it's horrendous, but it's also significant, surely, even if the entire memory didn't come back."

"Thank God. But you have to be patient. And you need to rest."

"I *am* resting. I've barely been out of bed for more than five minutes. How the hell am I supposed to ever get back to work, feeling like this?" I looked at her. "Speaking of, aren't you supposed to be at the restaurant?"

"This afternoon."

"Are you sure? I could've sworn you told me last night you'd be working this morning."

"Maybe you got mixed up? I've got to go back to Drift in a while, drop more stuff off before the weekend rush." She smiled. "Come with me. It might help take your mind off things."

I thought of going back to the house, where I'd no doubt do nothing other than wrestle with the revelation about finding my mother. It was an easy decision. "You're on," I said. "Lead the way."

A while later, Maya had parked on Main Street and disappeared into Drift with a box of her pieces. When she'd asked if I wanted to join her, I'd passed, preferring to spend the time alone to mull things over. Barbara was on the nosy side, and last time she'd let slip she was penning her debut novel, and I had no intention of letting her use me as a character study.

The sun beat in through the window, warming my chest, and as I closed my eyes someone tapped on the glass. I turned my head. The redhead whose phone I'd attempted to steal at the petrol station stood a few feet away, smiling at me. I searched my brain for her name, remembered it was Fiona and opened the door to get out.

"Hi, Ash," she said, her smile broadening still. "How are you?"

"I'm all right, thanks," I said with a nod, adding, "I'm doing okay."

"That's great. What about your memory? Any better? Did you see the doctor?"

I sighed, leaned back against the car and shoved my hands in my front pockets as I told her about the different tests and suspicions of retrograde amnesia. "Not much has come back, I'm afraid. The odd flash here and there."

"Well, that's something, though. It might not be perfection, but at least it's progress."

I looked at her. She seemed nice, gentle and concerned, the

exact opposite of her brother, Keenan, who thankfully hadn't made another appearance at the house. Weighing my options, I decided to take a gamble on her empathy. "Maya told me about Celine and Kate."

Her eyes widened. "That must have been…a shock for you," she said carefully.

"Yes, honestly it was, because I don't remember either of them."

Fiona winced but recovered quickly. "I'm sorry, Ash. This must be incredibly difficult. Did Maya…did she tell you about them?"

"A little," I said. "She showed me some pictures, too. I'm sorry Celine left town. You must miss her."

"Every single day. But she's out there somewhere, no doubt still stubborn as a mule." She shook her head. "Mom used to say, 'That girl can do anything if she puts her mind to it,' and it looks like she was right. There's no way I'd have had the courage to walk away from my father the way she did. She was very brave. But I still wish things had turned out different. You two would have been great together, although you and Kate were, too."

"You knew Kate?"

"Of course," Fiona said, nodding enthusiastically. "We met when she was out running and I was, well, trying to. Getting fit was a New Year's resolution, except it was June by then, and I could barely walk up the stairs without needing an oxygen mask. But in all seriousness, we got talking and the next thing I knew, she'd taken me from couch potato to running five miles without breaking a sweat." Her eyes glistened and she dabbed at them quickly. "She was an amazing person. Kind, funny, generous… for whatever reason her favorite thing was knock-knock jokes."

"I wish I could remember. I've only seen a couple of pictures."

"This might help." She grabbed her phone, fingers flicking across the screen. "I took this on Kate's birthday a few years before…"

She didn't finish her sentence and I leaned in as Fiona brought up a video. In it, Kate sat at a table with a sparkly pink birthday hat on her head, grinning from ear to ear, her long brown hair swishing as she clapped her hands, oohing and aahing as a giant, sprinkle-covered chocolate cake complete with lit candles was set down on the table in front of her. I stared at the screen, hoping for this one thing to make everything else fall back into place but, once again, nothing happened.

As I tried to get a better look, a familiar voice said, "Happy birthday, babe," and cake bearer Keenan bent over and kissed Kate on the lips.

"Shit," Fiona said, pulling the phone away, her face reddening. "I forgot about that part."

"It's all right, Maya mentioned they dated," I said as she grimaced some more, giving me an apologetic shrug, and I decided to push for a bit more information. "She didn't mention how long for, though."

"About a year, on and off, when she first moved to town." Fiona slid her phone back into her pocket. "But she left him, and a few months after that she started seeing you. She really cared for you, and you seemed to, I don't know, *click*, I suppose, way more than she and my brother ever had. Don't get me wrong, I love Keenan and all, but you saw how he acted at the gas station. Sorry about that again."

I wondered if I should mention his house call, decided not to. "Not your fault."

"Thank you. Anyway, sometimes you can tell when a relationship will work just by looking at the people, and you and Kate had that *je ne sais quoi*, if you'll pardon my lousy accent." She laughed, a warm sound that made me smile. "Look, I'd better get going. Stop by the Harbor Inn anytime if you need to talk? Maybe I can help fill you in on things."

After she'd left, I felt I had a better, at least partial understanding of why Keenan hated my guts and some of the tension I'd been holding on to evaporated. His girlfriend had dumped him, but instead of having the insight to dissect what he might have done for her to leave, he blamed me. I frowned. Was it possible he'd hurt Kate in retaliation for her leaving him? Was his attempt to put her death on me his way of throwing off people's suspicions about himself? I wanted to run after Fiona and ask her opinion, but it would be a step too far. Blood was thicker than the proverbial water, and I had no intention of testing that particular theory on the streets of Newdale in the middle of the afternoon. But if Keenan showed up at the house again, this time I'd have some of my own ammunition to fire back.

15

LILY

This had not been a good few days. First, the cops had released Jack's apartment, and had told me that Sam, to whom I hadn't had the guts to speak since I swore at him on the phone, had called someone in to change the locks. That meant it was time for me to get Jack's things, and when I'd finally summoned the courage to return to his place for what would likely be the last time, I'd tried to wrap my heart in a thick layer of self-preservation because without it, I'd never have made it up the first few stairs.

I worked swiftly, picking Jack's belongings up from the floor and stuffing them into his backpack, suitcase and boxes, and as I did so, I allowed myself to mull over the conversation with Maya again, as I'd been doing ever since we'd hung up. The more I thought about it, the more anomalies there were. Maybe it was wishful thinking or me clutching at an entire straw factory, but

I was certain there'd been a slight waver in her voice, a tremor when she'd said the man in the photo was called Gordon Jones or James, some random guy she'd met once and who lived in a different state. Her delivery had almost been too slick, too convenient, and she'd either set the photo to private or deleted it from Facebook altogether. Whichever, she'd done so while we were still talking. If it—*he*—meant nothing to her, why the rush? Why bother at all? Adding all these details together, my gut feeling and instincts all whispered Maya Scott was hiding something.

Calling her again was pointless. I'd have bet all my money, a paltry sum unless I gave her Jack's stash, she'd spin another tale. Trouble was, I wouldn't be there to see it. Maybe she'd cooperate with Heron and Stevens, but the only proof I had linking her to Jack was a library book he'd taken by mistake, and a picture that no longer existed. The memory of the latter faded a little more with every passing day, to the point where I couldn't be sure it had actually been him.

Maya wasn't my only problem. Once I'd loaded Jack's things into my car and got home, I realized I couldn't keep them there. My space was limited, and unless I wanted to stumble over his stuff stacked on my living room floor every night, which I didn't think my heart would withstand, I had to find another solution. I'd dug through the boxes and removed two of Jack's favorite shirts and the framed photo of us, and driven across town to the cheapest storage facility I could find, where I rented the smallest space available on a rolling monthly basis.

Things only got worse the next day. I salted my dinner with sugar and forgot to pick up toilet paper, and as I was about to step out to the store, the doorbell rang.

"I'm glad you're home," Heron said after I'd let her and Stevens in, and they'd sat down on the sofa. She threw a glance at Stevens and gave him a slight nod as if to say, "Your turn."

"We need to talk about a few things." With the gruff delivery of his words there was an acute shift in the atmosphere. Jack had been missing for over a week now, but Stevens's sympathy had turned into something else. He was so stoic and guarded, I couldn't tell what it was. He spoke again. "How often have you used a motorboat?"

The question threw me, and I stumbled to reply. "What? Uh...never."

"What about the night Jack disappeared?" Stevens said, raising his voice, and as I shook my head, Heron put a hand on his arm, which I interpreted as code for the rookie to take it easy.

"Did you rent or borrow a boat the night Jack went missing?" Heron said softly, sympathetically, as if she were talking to a friend. I knew that ruse. I'd seen it before.

"No, I was here, I told you. What's this about?"

Stevens tapped his notepad with the tip of his pen. "Someone saw a boat out on the water the evening Jack went missing, down by the beach where we found his truck." Tap. Tap. Tap-tap-tap. The noise became louder and louder as the implication of his words landed on top of my shoulders.

"You think it was *me*?"

Heron shook her head. "That's not what we said."

"But now that you've brought it up, was it you?" Stevens said.

"No." A tingly shiver ran down my spine and all the way back up again. "Of course not."

Heron studied me, her expression still neutral. She slid a finger across her phone and turned it toward me, revealing a mug shot of a thirtysomething man with watery-blue eyes, blond spiky hair, and an L-shaped scar above his left eyebrow. "Do you know him?"

I leaned closer, examined the shape of his jaw, the way his lips curled into a half smirk... I put a hand to my throat. "It looks like the man who was at Jack's place. I'm not a hundred percent certain..."

"This is Jason Whitmarsh," Heron said. "His car matches the

description you gave us." She waited a few beats. "Lily, did you and Jack like playing cards?"

"Sure," I said. "The two of us played together a lot. Jack always wins, though. He's really good."

"Do you play for money?" she continued.

"Hardly." I let out a small laugh. "Jack always says my 'tells' are so obvious I might as well scrawl them over my face. I'm so bad, I'd never even win at Go Fish. Besides, we don't have cash to lose and it would be weird betting against one another."

"What about with others?" Stevens said impatiently. "Did Jack gamble with anyone?"

"No," I said as I remembered the money hidden in the cookie tin. Could Jack have won it playing poker? Had he been gambling when he'd told me he was working late? How much more didn't I know about him?

"No," I said again, slowly shaking my head. "Not that I'm aware of. Why? Who's Jason Whitmarsh?"

Heron leaned in and smiled but said nothing as she continued to observe me. When I thought I couldn't take the silence any longer, she said, "Can you tell us about Dominic Martel?"

The air left my lungs as my body seemed to fold into itself, and I knew there was zero sense insisting I didn't know who they were talking about. As much as I'd tried to run from my past, hide from it, forget about it, here it was, my dirtiest secret ready to be exposed.

"It was a long time ago," I said. "And I really can't see how it's relevant."

"Humor us." Stevens sat back, arms crossed, digging in for the long run. Heron nodded at me, sending a polite but firm message they weren't going anywhere until I explained what they probably already knew. If I said nothing, they'd continue focusing on me, which meant they weren't doing anything to find Jack. If I refused to cooperate, their wasted time was my fault.

"I was eighteen," I said, "and I was broke because I'd moved out from home."

Moved out was the polite way of saying *unceremoniously kicked out.* It happened three months after I'd declared I still had no intention of following in my parents' medical or banking footsteps but wanted to pursue an art degree instead. After spending a number of weeks trying to convince me otherwise, my parents sat me down at the dining table.

"An art degree won't pay the bills," my mother said, and Dad grunted his agreement. "We feel you should experience what not having any money is like as soon as possible. You've been privileged, sheltered—"

"Didn't both of you have trust funds?" I said, folding my arms over my chest.

"That's neither here nor there," Dad said. "We're prepared to pay for your education as long as you pursue something worthwhile—"

"You mean something you approve of."

"—but if you insist on an art degree, you need to finance it yourself."

"Basically, if I don't do your bidding, I'm on my own."

"Correct." My mother gave me a curt nod and shot my father a victorious look.

They were right. I was privileged and sheltered, but that didn't mean I wanted to turn out like them, let them mold me into something I didn't want to be. Our relationship had been difficult for years and it was time for me to do something about it. Join the real world. See if I could hack it on my own.

I stood up, put my hands on my hips and said, "I'd better go pack my stuff."

Knowing how the minds of the infallible Ronan and Suzanna Hetherington worked, I suspected they had a bet going as to how long it would take me to fold and come back, homemade ceramic begging bowl in hand, compliance at the ready.

Quentin had probably taken that bet, as well. But they all lost because I hadn't returned. I'd remained stubborn, moved into a crappy little apartment, worked three jobs six days a week— often seven—to make rent and save for my art degree every single month. I knew what people would think if I told them about my background: poor little rich girl, waah, waah—and so I never told anyone. There were millions of individuals trying to make ends meet, my situation was hardly a rarity or special.

Had it been hard? Excruciatingly. Had I become disillusioned? Of course. I'd worked in so many different places I'd lost count. My most regular gig was bartending, but I'd also been a store clerk, a dog walker, and given car detailing a go. The things people left in their vehicles had astounded me: full wallets, cell phones, dirty underwear, even used condoms—nothing was off-limits to some—and, although it had been gross at times, it had been fun, right up until a customer grabbed me between my legs and asked if it was where he could leave me a tip. I was pretty sure he left with a cracked rib from where I'd elbowed him. The next day I'd been fired for not being a, quote, "team player."

Working at the bar had paid the most, and I'd been good at it, knew how to charm the customers without flirting, and calm the rowdy ones before things got out of hand. I was employed at an upscale hotel bar in Buffalo when I met Dominic Martel, a smooth-talking Frenchman who'd immediately spotted my potential—his words, not mine. He'd whispered them in my ear as we were lying in bed on our fourth date, after we'd gone back to his huge, loft-style apartment. My potential wasn't the only thing he'd seen, because the next thing he told me was, from the glimpse he'd had of the location and size of my tiny studio when he'd picked me up, he'd also gathered I was broke.

"I have a way to get you into some money." Dominic traced a finger down my arm. "And I know you'll be really good at it. You'll get all dressed up and go to a bar…"

"A bar?" I froze for a second as I realized where this was heading. "What the hell? You want me to be a hooker?" I shoved him away and leaped out of bed, reaching for my jeans. "Why don't you go f—"

"That's not what I meant," he'd replied, holding up his hands. "Not at all. Are you kidding? You're an amazing person, Lily. Beautiful, smart, funny—"

"Yeah? Is this the part where you tell me I'll meet one of your friends for a quiet drink, or maybe someone who wants to buy me dinner? Only dinner, of course, nothing more?" I grabbed my shoes. "I thought you said I'm smart."

"Let me tell you about my idea," he said, his voice calm, and damn it, his French accent, and the memories of the sex we'd had, all making my resolve crumble. "It's an easy way to make money. No sex, no strings, nobody gets hurt."

I put down my shoes and gave him two minutes to explain before cutting him off after one. No way would I get involved in his illegal bullshit. I left his apartment, cursing him all the way home, but when I lost another of my jobs three days later, and my landlord refused to give me an extension on my rent, I changed my mind. It would be easy, Dominic said when we met for coffee. I'd go to a bar and have a drink. When someone Dominic had preidentified as the owner of an expensive car walked in, I'd get a signal and distract the mark by spilling a cocktail over them. By way of apology I'd proceed to buy them drinks until they were past the point of being able to drive. Dominic, a seasoned pickpocket, would lift their car keys and, a while later, I'd send the drunken mark home in an Uber.

"By the time they've recovered from their hangover and notice their car has been stolen, it'll be in a shipping container," Dominic said. "And you get a ten percent cut."

"Fifty," I answered. "I want fifty. Equal partners."

Dominic shook my hand on twenty-five before taking me back to his place again. I'd known what we were doing was bad, but reasoned the only victim was the insurance company.

Not a watertight argument—I knew that, too—but I was desperate, and the prospect of having to crawl home to my mother and father was a lot worse by far.

The scam worked—so well, we did it again before moving on to other locations around the city so the cops wouldn't see a pattern. I continued to accidentally-on-purpose spill a drink on unsuspecting men, mainly, or tripped into them so they'd spill theirs. I invested in a set of wigs and fancy new clothes—paid for out of my cut—to conceal my identity, and used a different name and accent each time. At the rate I was going, I'd be able to pay for my entire art course in one go and have money to spare.

Dominic called me a natural, and I got greedy, cocky and careless. My demise was swift. The last mark he chose turned out to be an undercover cop working the case, and I was arrested, and all my money was seized before you could say *Mercedes*. I was in danger of doing some serious time until my parents stepped in. Because of their high-priced lawyer, long-standing connections with the District Attorney and regular rounds of golf with a number of judges, I was offered a heavily reduced sentence—twelve months—providing I gave up whoever I was working with. I did, and when I found out Dominic, who'd professed his undying love for me, had at least three other girls in different cities with whom he ran the same ruse, I didn't regret selling him out one bit.

I shuddered at the memory of my father's voice the last time I spoke to him after I'd been released. "Don't forget our agreement," he said, sliding an envelope containing fifteen hundred dollars across the table before listing his conditions on his fingers. "Leave town, always provide us with your contact details and, most of all, stay out of trouble. Follow through, and we may consider putting you back in our will."

"Can't I come home?" I said, my voice small. "I want to come home."

"You've brought so much shame on us, Lily. Your mother

may never recover. As far as everyone else is concerned you're studying law in the UK. You'll probably love it so much you'll stay, permanently. We'll visit you from time to time, of course." When he put air quotes on the word *visit*, I knew this was the last time I'd see him, the exact moment I'd lost my family, whether I now wanted to or not.

"Can I speak to Mom and Quentin before I go? Please? I want to apologize."

Dad tapped the money-filled envelope with his index finger. "Goodbye, Lily."

I'd been lucky, in the end. After half a decade and a slew of jobs, which took me from Syracuse to Philadelphia, Baltimore to Washington, an old school friend who owned a sports shop in Ocean City offered me a job. When she'd sold the place, I'd met Mike while watching the sunrise, and joined Beach Body. Not long after, I'd moved to Brookmount, putting more distance between me and the hordes of tourists, and changed my last name to Reid, which had been my grandmother's. I never got my art degree, but I had met Jack. The irony that it had been in a bar and he'd given me a false name wasn't lost on me, and maybe it was penance, not only for my past, but also because I'd never shared my secrets with him. If I had, perhaps things would've turned out differently. Maybe he'd have had the courage to confide in me.

As I finished my story, Heron said, "And Jack knew nothing of this?"

"No," I whispered. "I was too ashamed."

"Maybe you were running another scam together," Stevens said, flipping to bad-cop mode, which was starting to seriously piss me off. "Maybe Whitmarsh was involved, too. Perhaps it wasn't working for you anymore and you decided you could do it on your own, or at least without Jack. Make more money that way."

"*Enough,*" I shouted, and they raised their eyebrows in unison. "I don't know anyone called Whitmarsh, Jack and I weren't running any kind of scam and I'd never hurt him."

"You need to calm down," Stevens said. "You're not doing yourself any favors here."

My jaw clenched. When they'd arrived, I'd considered telling them about the library book and my conversation with Maya. No way would I do so now. They'd turn things around, they couldn't be trusted, and I'd be damned if I'd let them do to Jack what they were trying to do to me, especially when he wasn't here to defend himself.

"I did my time," I said. "I don't know what you want me to say. I didn't know him then."

Heron nodded, smiled that sympathetic smile of hers again, thinking she'd get me to open up that way. Not a chance in hell. "Lily, perhaps—"

I cut her off by raising my voice again. "Tell me about the boat."

"We can't comment at this point," Stevens said.

"Why?" I snapped. "Because of your ridiculous theory it was me?"

Heron quietly said, "You do understand if you ran into Jack—"

"I *didn't*, I already told you," I said, trying hard not to yell. I knew how this worked, I had to be calm and give them the facts. "I wouldn't even know how to drive a motorboat. Besides, I was here Friday evening, and all Friday night, right up until I went to Sam's."

"Alone." Stevens seemed to make a point of saying this as a statement, not a question, and one I was certain he didn't believe.

"Yes, *alone*. Talk to the people in the building. Ask my landlord downstairs. I got here at four on Friday, stopped by to pick up some cookies she'd made and came right up. I was on the phone with the cable company for ages, and had a pizza delivered at six. I'll give you the receipt and you can see for yourselves.

My car never moved, neither did my cell. Check them. Check it all. I've got nothing to hide." Neither Heron nor Stevens responded, and when the silence became unbearable again, this time I got up and gestured to the door. "I didn't hurt him, so unless you're going to arrest me, I'd like you to leave and start searching for him again."

They both stood slowly, and when they got to the front door, Heron turned around. "I'm here if you need to talk," she said, and I bit down hard on my tongue to stop myself from screaming, "No thanks, you two-faced bitch."

Once they'd driven off, my fury turned to despair as any remaining hope disintegrated around me. Jack, Gordon or whatever his name was, was never coming back. Not only was I left holding a mess of grief and rage, not only would my questions remain unanswered and gnawing away at my core, but now the cops thought I had something to do with Jack's disappearance. I didn't have my parents' financial backing now, couldn't afford to lawyer up if they arrested me for something that, this time, I hadn't done.

I couldn't live this way. I wouldn't. I needed to know the truth. All of it. Who Jack was, why he'd lied and, most of all, if any of what we'd had was real.

I grabbed my phone and plugged in Newdale, Maine. It was the only clue, never mind how small, and it was a little over a nine-hour drive from Brookmount, more if I hit traffic. No way would my temperamental Chevrolet make it that far, and the last thing I needed was to break down and end up stranded by the side of the road. I could fly, but that wasn't cheap, and I wanted to travel without leaving a trail for the cops to follow in case it raised their absurd suspicions.

I dialed Mike's number. Without hesitation he agreed to give me more time off, let me borrow one of the garage's trusty runaround cars, a sprightly orange Ford Fiesta, and said it would be dropped off within the hour. After thanking him a million times, I took a duffel from the closet in the hallway and marched to my bedroom, where I pulled out pants, shirts and underwear, stuffing them into the bag. I'd use some of the cash I'd found in Jack's apartment to pay for my trip to Newdale, I decided, and find a way to return it.

As I finished packing, I asked myself if I was being impulsive and irrational, stupid even. Most certainly, I decided. Maya might have told the truth. Maybe she wouldn't talk to me and would throw me out of the Cliff's Head, or call the local cops. Regardless, I was done sitting at home, wallowing and waiting. If I wanted answers, I had to damn well go after them myself.

Once I had the keys to the car, I tried to rest for a while, but sleep wanted nothing to do with me. I spent a few hours tossing and turning, half of my brain trying to talk me out of going to Newdale, while the other half ordered me to get up and move. I complied with the latter and set off a few minutes after 1:00 a.m., settling in for the long drive ahead.

Hours passed, the sun came up, and I still wondered what the hell I was doing, and what I'd say when I found Maya. When I stopped at a gas station to fill the car and use the bathroom, I made sure to pay for everything with cash. Heron and Stevens hadn't said anything about having to stay in town, but until they checked out my alibi and cleared me, driving off—no matter the reason—was surely ill-advised.

I continued, so lost in thought I barely registered when the GPS indicated Newdale was a mere hour away. Not a lot of opportunity for me to calm my nerves, but plenty of time to try and talk myself into taking the next exit, turning back and scurrying home.

I wasn't sure why the thought of meeting Maya made me break out into a cold sweat. Something in how her tone had switched from guarded and annoyed to sweetness and light. My mind went into overdrive, cataloging the gazillion different ways our face-to-face encounter could go, and in almost no time at all, I'd arrived at the Cliff's Head right in time for lunch.

I parked the car and got out, gazing up at the restaurant. I'd read online it had once been run-down and tired, serving the same old lobster rolls, which had become so bland, rubbery and boring, even the number of tourists dwindled thanks to the shitty online reviews. Everything changed when the place had sold a few years ago and a wealthy retiree from Bangor gutted and fully renovated the building before putting his son in charge. As well as turning into a gourmet hot spot boasting an acclaimed new head chef, the Cliff's Head had gone from weathered shack to modern, two-story brick-and-steel combo, complete with glass-sided balconies, all perched on the New-dale Bluffs, overlooking the Atlantic Ocean and affording the best views in town.

As the smell of the salty ocean breeze and the sound of seagulls filled the air, I wondered how long Maya had worked here. Was she in there right now? Only one way to find out.

I walked to the front door and pushed it open. Light streamed in through the massive windows, making the place bright and airy. A server was setting up the wooden tables for the upcoming service, arranging heavy-looking silverware, white china plates, glinting crystal glasses and cloth napkins folded into lover's knots. The high-backed black leather chairs and gleaming maple floors added to the restaurant's classy feel. No doubt it was a popular choice for first dates, birthday celebrations and anniversaries.

A few guests sat at the tables closest to the floor-to-ceiling windows and I realized the photos hadn't done the place justice because the breathtaking view stretched out for miles. The host walked over, dressed in black pants and a burgundy shirt with the silver logo—the same outfit I'd seen in the photo of Maya.

"Welcome to the Cliff's Head," he said. "May I get you a table?"

I wanted to blurt out I was looking for Maya Scott, but from my experience of living in Brookmount, I knew how small communities worked. They protected their own. Being too direct might not get me what I needed. Besides, Maya could be in the back somewhere, or maybe her shift hadn't started yet. Either way, she didn't know my face. When she saw me, she'd have no reason to suspect I was anything other than a paying customer, a tourist traveling the coast.

"A table for one would be great," I said.

"Of course. You chose a lovely day to stop by. I'm Patrick, by the way," he said as he guided me over to a table for two by the window. "Let me get you some water and the menu."

After he'd brought both, I wiped my hands on my pants, acutely aware of how clammy and damp my palms had become. I sipped my drink, staring out over the ocean, my stomach lurching as the images of another dream I'd had about Jack took over: his body limp, bloodied and bruised, tossed around in the waves like a rag doll, smashed and cut against the rocks. I moved farther back, away from the view.

When Patrick returned to take my order, I muttered something about being chilly next to the window, and then asked for the daily special. When he walked over with a sweet-smelling lobster quiche and a colorful side salad, the mere sight of them made my stomach growl. I hadn't bothered eating much again and was glad I'd brought a belt with me to stop my pants from slipping.

"Are you visiting the area?" Patrick said as he put the plate down.

"Yes, I've never been to Maine before. Are you local?"

"Waterville, originally, but my boyfriend's from here. It's a great place—I love it."

I wanted to keep our conversation going, but I didn't seem able to string another sentence together. I was about to make a pathetic comment about the weather when a huge man with short red hair walked into the restaurant.

"Hey, Patrick," he called over. "Maya in today?"

"Excuse me," Patrick said, and as he walked to the entrance, I heard him say, "She's got the day off."

"Probably at Drift then," the other man said, and Patrick gave a noncommittal shrug.

I wondered what Drift was, and quickly searched it up on my phone, finding a local store selling knickknacks made from driftwood, including mobiles and a number of impressive animal sculptures. I didn't notice Patrick until he stood next to me, inquiring if I was enjoying the food. Replying it was delicious, I hoped he hadn't noticed my screen, the sweat above my lip or how badly my fingers shook as I slid my phone back into my pocket.

16

MAYA

As I was about to head out to work in the garage in the morning, Ash practically bounded down the stairs, his face freshly shaved, the dark circles under his eyes almost gone. "What are you up to?" he said with a small yawn as he rubbed the back of his neck. "You're not at the restaurant today?"

"No, I'm covering for Barbara at Drift over lunch."

Ash frowned. "Did you tell me that?"

"Yes," I said, keeping my gaze even. "Last night."

"Are you sure?"

"She's taking her grandson to the dentist, remember?"

"Right, right." He let out a sigh. "Actually, no, I don't remember you telling me."

"I did... Look, maybe mention how you're forgetting stuff like this to Dr. Adler today?"

He looked at me, and I could practically see his brain trying to make the connection as he narrowed his eyes, gave his head a small shake. "Hell's bells, I'd almost forgotten about that. Did you say you'd take me or am I messing that up, too?"

"No, you're right. It's at two, so you can come to town with me and hang out at the store until your appointment."

Ash sighed again. "Thanks. I've decided I'll ask the doc about when he thinks I'll be ready to find a job and go back to work, at least part-time or something."

"Hold on," I said, raising a hand. "I really think we should discuss—"

"There's nothing to discuss," he snapped. "Don't baby me, Maya. I've got to get into a proper routine, have something to get up for in the morning, and if I need more checkups or whatever, I'll need cash to pay for them. I'm not mooching off you forever, it's not right."

"Don't worry about the money. I've got some savings."

"They're *your* savings," he said. "And it makes me feel uncomfortable. I want to find work as soon as I can. Maybe get back to carpentry."

"But you don't remember being a carpenter."

"What does that matter when I feel like one in here?" He tapped the side of his head. "I'm sure I can do it. Maybe it's muscle memory or something. Whatever it is, I'm asking him about it." He raised a hand when I opened my mouth. "Can you give me the password for your laptop so I can see what work might be available?"

"Dr. Soares said you should stay off screens. You have a concussion, and—"

"That's *enough*, Maya," he said, his voice sharp, a clear warning I should back off, and although I shut my mouth again he continued anyway. "You really need to stop trying to protect me from everything."

"You know the old bathroom in the garage?" I said, deciding to change tack and waiting until he nodded. "A few weeks before Brad died, you two put in the plumbing for a shower."

"In the garage?" he said, pulling a face, his frustration turning to curiosity. "Why would we do that?"

"Because there were three of us here and we couldn't add another to the house. Anyway, the plumbing's all there. Actually, before you left, we talked about finishing it. It makes sense, considering how much time I spend in there."

His face softened. "That's a good point. It's practically your second home."

"Right, and I started making another part of the garage into a proper storage room but didn't have time to finish. You know the rough framing? I need to insulate it properly and add a subfloor and heat to keep the temperature stable so I can work on my pieces all year."

"Want me to take a look?" Ash said, his eyes lighting up, exactly how I knew they would.

I smiled. Ash had always been the first one to offer assistance, never wanted to let anyone down. "Would you? I've thought about selling my stuff online for years, and I'm excited to make a proper website, but I need to be able to keep up with demand."

"I'd love to help, and it'll be great practice for when I get a job."

I smiled tightly, hoping he wouldn't notice. "Sure, sure," I said, stopping when my phone buzzed and I looked at the screen, immediately recognizing the number. My stomach tightened. I held up a finger to Ash in a *give me a minute* gesture before turning away and answering. "Hi, Barbara, is everything okay?"

"Barbara?" Dave laughed. "Okay, I'll roll with it."

I knew he would. Dave Decato was a chameleon of the highest order, capable of adapting to any situation he was thrown into. The fastest liar in Maine, he liked to say, probably the entire East Coast. I'd met him a few months after Brad died and I'd tried to cope with the loss by drinking too much and partying too hard. I'd gone out with some friends one night, ended up at a bar thanks to my fake ID. Everyone else admitted defeat and went home while I was intent on ending the night as drunk as possible. Enter Dave, who liked to pretend he was a NYC drug lord instead of the country bumblefuck he truly was. He'd bought me another drink and struck up a conversation before slipping me a little bag of weed, what he called a "teaser," and writing his phone number on my arm in case I wanted access to a more regular supply. I had, and often, until Ash caught me smoking in my bedroom one night and had gone ape.

"It's just *weed*," I'd said. "Jeez, lighten up, grandpa, what's your problem?"

I'd protested as he'd insisted I flush the rest down the toilet, and promise—cross my heart and hope to die—I'd never bring drugs into the house again. Although I'd crossed my fingers behind my back, too, I'd mostly kept my word. Even after Ash left Newdale and I was losing my mind, I only partook on the odd occasion when a joint happened to be going around after a shift at the Cliff's Head. I tried Molly once and vowed I'd never do it again because I hated not being in control. It was why I never got drunk anymore. Most people developed a loose tongue when they had too much booze. God only knew I'd seen it often enough at work. But the clonazepam I'd got from Dealer Dave after Dr. Adler stopped prescribing me benzos helped me relax whenever I couldn't deal with not knowing where Ash was. I'd done a good job slowly weaning myself off them, hadn't called Dave in over six months, but with Ash home and my anxiety levels rising, I needed a refill, and Dave had been more than happy to oblige.

"Earth to Maya." Dave's voice snapped me out of my thoughts. "You high or what? I said I'll be at the usual spot in ten. If you can't make it, it'll be next week."

"I'll be there."

I hung up and walked to the kitchen, where Ash sat at the

table with some paper and a pencil. As I got closer, I saw he'd sketched out the rough shape of the garage, and when he looked up, he smiled. "I'm working on your fancy-shmancy bathroom. Figuring out where the claw-foot tub and walk-in steam shower will go."

I laughed. "My check might bounce, but by all means, you carry on. I have to run an errand. Won't be long. Can you be ready to leave for Drift in about forty-five?"

"Uh-huh," Ash replied, barely glancing up as he continued drawing.

See, I thought, *I know what's best for us*. Of course I did. I always had.

When I got to the old Newdale cemetery, I parked the car. As usual, the place looked deserted and no other vehicles were in the lot. Nobody would ask, but if they did, it also had great walking trails for the less morbid, and I'd changed into my sneakers before leaving the house in case I needed a plausible excuse for being there. As I walked down the path to the spot where my exchanges with Dave always took place, the grave of a family called Snow—which he thought was "poetic destiny"—I noticed the woman coming toward me in the distance. Too late to turn back, she'd already seen me and was waving now, her red curls bouncing as she picked up the pace.

Ash had told me about his chat with Fiona outside Drift, and I was in no mood to speak to her. When she got talking, she barely knew when to stop.

"Hey," Fiona said. "Sorry I haven't been to see you. How are you and Ash?"

"We're okay," I said, hoping she'd leave it at that. When she raised an expectant eyebrow and smiled, I gave her as succinct an overview as possible about the last few days.

"I only just found out about Keenan causing trouble at your house," she said. "He's been on a hunting trip this past week."

I let out a grunt. "That's why he hasn't been around. I'd hoped he'd come to his senses. Wishful thinking, I suppose."

"Yeah, well, he told me about how he laid into Ash." She rolled her eyes, pushed her hair out of her face. "Christ, my brother can be such a hotheaded dipshit, particularly when he's been enjoying his beer. What a prick."

"No argument there."

"The cops know Ash's back," Fiona said, and I shrugged. "No, it wasn't a question. I know Keenan told Ricky, hoping he'd do something now that he's been promoted, but you and I both know none of the officers ever bought into my brother's ramblings, including Ricky."

I blinked. "Still no news from Celine?"

She sighed, her breath escaping in a slow and steady stream. "No. Quite honestly I don't think we'll get any. I can't see why Celine would ever forgive us. I know my dad beat us, too, but she was the youngest, and she took the brunt of it. It was our duty to help her, and we failed."

"It wasn't your fault. Anyway, I should—"

"I disagree, and we both feel responsible. Between us, I believe that's Keenan's real problem. He feels guilty and needs someone to blame because he can't cope with the truth."

"Maybe you can remind him it's not Ash's fault," I muttered, and her face fell.

"I do, Maya, on a regular basis, I promise." She smiled tightly. "I'd better get back to the motel. I went to tidy Dad's grave because it's his birthday. I'd like to say God rest his soul, although I'm not sure he had one, but I'm glad I ran into you. Don't be a stranger, okay? Stop by sometime. And bring Ash."

We said our goodbyes and I watched as she walked back up the hill, my stomach tightening as another person appeared at the top of the path. Dave. Shit. I watched for signs of them knowing each other, let out a sigh of relief when there weren't any, but as I was about to walk on ahead, I saw Fiona turn. I raised my hand in a wave, but she was staring at Dave. I had no choice but to press on, stuffing my hand in my pockets, my fingers closing over the money I owed him for the benzos. I was supposed to have dropped it graveside already, tucked the neatly folded bills inside the crack on the left and gone for a walk—a long one because Dave was typically late—and pick up the goods on my way back. His one rule was money never exchanged hands directly, and I hoped I hadn't blown it and he'd leave.

With a quick glance I made sure Fiona had really gone and nobody else was around. I deftly slipped the cash inside the broken headstone and walked away without a sideways glance. Five minutes later the exchange was done, and I headed back to my car, a little baggie of pills shoved inside my pocket.

When I got back to the house I sat in my car, examining the meds one by one to make sure they were all the same and Dave hadn't slipped something else in there just to fuck with me. He'd given me fewer tablets than we'd agreed—again, typical Dave—and I decided, moving forward, I'd look for a reliable dealer, an oxymoron if I'd ever heard one.

I headed inside. Ash was still in the kitchen, and when I heard him whistling softly, I recognized the familiar tune of the Portsmouth Football Club chant immediately. Brad had been an avid supporter and had passed the love of his hometown soccer club down to Ash. "Play Up Pompey" was something the two of them sang on a regular basis if the team did well, and even when it didn't, and they often watched games together, wearing matching shirts, something Mom and I shook our heads at. "It's in the genes." Brad had winked at Ash. "Isn't it, mush?"

Ash looked up at me now, stopping midwhistle, and then he actually sang the entire chant. "I remembered my dad's favorite soccer team."

It took me less than a split second to decide which path I had to take on this. I didn't *want* to lie to him, but I *had* to, and my plans had already been set in motion. Some of the little things I'd pretended I'd mentioned and insisted he'd forgotten were only the beginning. My work schedule, covering for Barbara—he'd seen those as tiny, seemingly innocent slipups, but it wouldn't be enough. That's why I'd told him the plumbing for the bathroom in the garage had been his and Brad's work, when it had been Ash and mine. If or when he thought he remembered us working in there together, I'd insist he was mistaken. It would make him doubt himself, and the reliability of any recollection he had. Did I want to lie to him now about the love of soccer he shared with his dad? No, of course not, but I had no choice. I needed to make sure he'd believe me when I explained away any significant memory that resurfaced, and told him it was pure confabulation, something that had happened differently, or not at all. I had to be careful, make sure I only ever lied about something nobody else could contradict. It had to be done.

I let an empathetic look slide across my face, walked over to Ash and gave him a hug.

"What was that for?" he said, his body tensing under my touch, making my breath catch.

"Oh, Ash," I said, holding him tighter still. "I'm so sorry, but Brad hated soccer."

17

LILY

After I finished my lunch, had two coffees and worked up the courage, I got back in the car, plugged in the address for Drift and headed to the center of Newdale. My belly contracted as I thought about a possible encounter with Maya, almost hoped it wouldn't happen so I'd have more time to prepare. I'd find a place to stay for the night and go back to the Cliff's Head tomorrow, or the day after... No. This wasn't the time to be a coward. Maya potentially held information about Jack. There was no way I'd return to Brookmount without seeing her face-to-face, and the sooner I could engineer a meeting, the better.

Drift was located on Main Street, and a large, polished wooden sign with the store's name carved in italics hung over the bright green door. The lights inside were on, and after I dumped the car a hundred yards down the street because all the other parking spots were taken, I got out and stood on the side-walk, trying to make my feet move.

The town was bustling, and I took my time as I walked back to the store, running through what I'd say to Maya. I couldn't decide if I should use shock and surprise as a method of getting what I needed, or show her a recent photograph of Jack and de-mand she tell me everything, minus the bull. Maybe I should take a gentler approach, explain my situation in more detail and hope for empathy, or perhaps I'd have to gauge her reaction and take it from there.

I was about forty feet from the store, and still undecided, when the front door opened. I recognized Maya from her Facebook profile immediately. Her dark hair was cut in a shorter, choppy chin-length bob, and it made her eyes seem even bigger. She was tall, had a good couple of inches on me, and the heels of her black leather lace-up boots were a direct contrast to my canvas flats, making her tower over me even more. She was beautiful, edgy, the kind of person who didn't take any crap from anyone, someone my parents would've glanced at and labeled *trouble*. I was about to call out her name, but my heart almost stopped when another person walked out behind her. A man.

Jack.

They turned in the opposite direction, and I wanted to go after them, but my legs buckled and I stumbled, losing my bal-ance, landing on my hands and knees, the asphalt piercing my skin. Was it really him? Were my mind and the lack of sleep play-ing tricks on me? My vision seemed to blur and when a passerby stopped to ask if I was okay, I told them I was fine and pushed myself up. "Jack!" I cried, but my voice came out so strained, I barely made a sound. "Jack!"

I couldn't take my eyes off him, but he didn't turn around, didn't notice or hear me as he continued down the street along-side Maya. I watched, hopeless and pathetic, as he kept walking away. Away from *me*. I went after them, ignored the stinging in my palms and knees as I ran across the road, narrowly avoiding two cars before finally catching up to them. I reached for his arm. *"Jack."*

In the time it took him to turn around I wondered if I'd gone insane, somehow become delusional. I imagined the embarrassment of being mistaken, grabbing hold of Maya's boyfriend or husband. Perhaps my desperation had projected what I'd wanted to see, what I'd needed to see, but the split second passed, and he turned around.

It was him.

Jack. *My* Jack.

A combination of emotions I hadn't known possible, or could be this intense, flooded my body, swelling up from my heart and spreading across every square inch of me, growing, ballooning, expanding to the point where I thought I'd burst. Fear followed by relief, and then anger, which turned into elation, but that transformed itself into hatred before, finally, settling on love. Jumbled waves of conflicting feelings washed over me, all of them coupled with the knowledge, the absolute certainty Jack was alive. He was *alive*. He hadn't drowned. He wasn't dead. I'd found him.

My joy shifted back to terror as I panicked. This was all a dream. I'd wake up in my bed in Brookmount, the space next to me empty and cold. If this *was* a dream, if I was imagining any of this, I never, ever wanted to wake up.

I reached out to touch Jack's face, searching for confirmation he was real, but when I stared into his eyes, the smile that had taken over my face faded, and I lowered my arm. He was different somehow. It was him, no question, but something had changed. With the small frown on his face, I almost expected him to reprimand me for being here.

"Jack," I said again, a whisper this time. "It's you. It's really you."

I couldn't wait any longer, and flung my arms around him,

pulled him close, burying my head in his chest. His clothes smelled of a different kind of laundry detergent, but the scent of his skin, the warmth of his neck, were exactly as I remembered. We'd been apart a little over a week but standing in the middle of the sidewalk on Newdale's Main Street, I realized how my memories had begun to fade no matter how hard I'd tried to cling to them. I wanted to hold him forever, felt his hands on my arms, expected him to pull me closer and whisper my name, but instead he gently pushed me away and took a step back, creating a chasm between us.

"Why didn't you come home?" I said, and before he was able to say a word, another surge of anger rose from within. Unable to tame or get it back under control, I yelled at him. "How could you do this? How could you disappear? Why did you say your name was Jack? Who are you? What are you doing *here*?"

"Hey," Maya said, putting a hand on my arm.

I shook her off, my chest heaving. "Why did you leave? Do you have any idea what you put me through?"

He stared at me. "I don't know—"

"What the hell do you mean, you don't know?"

"Enough," Maya said. "You need to back the hell off, lady. Now."

"And *you*," I snapped, finally turning my attention to her. "You *lied*. You told me his name was Gordon, and—"

"Wait…are you the woman who called the other day?" She looked at me, eyebrows raised.

"Maya," Jack said, sounding uncertain. "What the hell is going on?"

"Listen, I don't know what you think you saw," Maya said to me. "I already told you—"

"I know what I saw. It was Jack—" I turned to him "—or whoever the hell you are."

"I'm sorry," he whispered. "But I don't know you."

His words stopped me dead, but then I let out a cold, sharp

laugh, taking a step back. "Is that honestly the best you can do? I'm Lily Reid, in case you've forgotten. What is this? I caught you in a massive lie and now you think you can spin an even bigger one in front of your wife to get out of it?"

"Maya's not my wife," he said, shaking his head, and I laughed again, but it came out as a shrill, practically neurotic sound.

"He's telling the truth," Maya said. "My brother—"

"Your *brother*?" I stared at Jack. "You never told me you had a sister."

"Stepsister, technically," he said. "And I don't know why you keep calling me Jack. My name's Ash. Asher Bennett."

Undeterred and unconvinced, yet confused and angry about what he was doing, and why, I pulled out my phone and swiped through the photos. "You told me your name was Jack Smith. See?" I pushed the screen into his face, flicking through photo after photo. "This is us. Here. In this one. And this one. And this one. You and me. Jack and Lily. We live in Brookmount, in Maryland."

Jack looked at Maya. "I got into the trailer in Maryland."

"Ash…"

He ignored her, touched the screen with a fingertip before whispering, "Lily. *Lily*."

The renewed uncertainty in his voice glued my lips together and I looked at him, I mean *properly* looked at him for the first time since I'd started my rant. His furrowed brow, his lost expression—it was as if he'd never seen me before. This wasn't right, this wasn't an act. Something was terribly wrong. I wanted to reach for him again and pull him close, but an invisible wall had now gone up between us, keeping me at even more of a distance, making me feel as if we were strangers.

"What happened to you?" I whispered.

"I woke up on a beach in Maryland," he said.

"Yes, you went swimming one night after work. You never came back."

"I didn't know where I was," he continued. "Or who I was. Only that I had to get to Maine. They think I have retrograde amnesia—"

"*What?* Oh, my God."

"—and ever since I arrived here, Maya has helped me."

I glanced at her. "You remembered your stepsister?"

"No…" he said quietly. "Someone called her, and Maya brought me home."

"But your home is in Brookmount. With me," I said.

Ash grimaced, face flushing with embarrassment. "I don't recall anything from before. I want to believe you, and the photos must mean we knew each other."

"Knew?" I let out a laugh. "We took them last month." Tears stung the backs of my eyes and I opened and closed my mouth, unsure what to say. This wasn't how I'd pictured our reunion in my fantasies. There was crying, yes, but tears of joy, not this, anything but this.

Maya stepped in front of him. "Ash has been under a lot of stress with his condition and you showing up is making things worse. We need to go."

"G-go?" I stammered. "You can't leave. I need to understand. I want to know why—"

"Can't you see you're upsetting him?" She looped her arm around his.

"Maya, she *knows* me," Jack said, his voice raised. "I need to talk to her."

"Ash—"

"*No.* Lily, maybe you can help me figure out what I was doing in Maryland." He didn't spot Maya glaring at me, but I didn't care. The only thing that mattered was not losing him again.

"You have a doctor's appointment," Maya said.

"Who cares about Dr. Adler?" Jack snapped in a tone I'd never heard him use before.

"I do," Maya said, her voice firm, nonnegotiating. "It's important, and he's going on vacation as of tonight. You have to see him. Today. *Now*."

"I know, I know, you're right," Jack said with a grimace and I fought back more tears. I didn't want him to leave, couldn't bear us being apart any longer. He was *alive*.

He lifted his hand a little as if he might reach for mine, but instead of touching me, his gaze dropped to the bracelet on my wrist, the one with the heart-shaped charm he'd given me for our first Valentine's Day, a look of concentration taking over his face. "We live at...uh..."

"Twenty-two forty-nine Birch Road," Maya said. "Come at seven."

"I'll be there," I whispered, wanting to shove a hand into my chest and cradle my heart as I watched them walk away.

18

ASH

Lily had long disappeared from view, but until she had, I'd watched her stand on the same spot, arms by her sides, as if she were a statue. The image of her—cat-shaped sapphire eyes, bow lips, and long blond hair gently blowing in the breeze—still hadn't left me. As I thought about her sudden arrival in New-dale, panic rose. What if her departure was just as abrupt? What if this was just too plain crazy for her and I never saw her again? I needed to know what she knew, including why she'd insisted my name was Jack. From the sincerity in her voice and on her face, I had no reason not to believe her, but unless Maya, Fiona, Dr. Adler and even Keenan were a bunch of liars, my name was Asher Bennett. I wanted to tell Maya to turn around, go back so I could talk to Lily properly, but my head felt as if I'd shoved it into a vise and squeezed it for days because the confusion about my identity could only mean one thing.

"I lied to her," I said. "Why the hell did I tell Lily my name was Jack Smith?"

"I don't know." Maya stared ahead, her eyes focused on the road, unblinking.

As I replayed the conversation with Lily in my head, I turned to Maya. "What did she mean when she said you told her my name was Gordon?"

"Shit." She exhaled deeply, her knuckles whitening as she clenched the steering wheel. "She called me a few days ago, asked if I knew a Jack Smith because she'd found a photo of me with another guy on my old Facebook profile. It wasn't you. But I should've listened to her. I should've realized..."

"Did she tell you she was in Maryland?"

"I don't remember."

Without warning, my anger erupted, all of it directed at my sister. I turned to her, felt my face contort itself into an ugly mask as I shouted, "Why the fuck wouldn't you tell me about this? Why didn't you think it was important? Are you kidding me?"

Maya swallowed hard and blinked three times and, in that moment, I hated myself for making her look so scared, but I couldn't help it. It was as if she'd pushed a button I didn't even know I had.

"Listen," she said quietly. "I had no idea she was looking for *you*. With everything going on it didn't seem relevant and it must've slipped my mind. I'm having a hard enough time dealing with you remembering things that aren't true and forgetting things I've told you."

So was I, but right now, mixing up the times of her shifts or incorrectly remembering my father's favorite sport, which according to Maya he'd pretended to like only for my benefit, both paled in comparison. "You should have told me Lily called," I said, struggling to keep my voice even. "I can't believe I was living in Maryland, had a girlfriend but said my name was Jack. Why did I lie? What did I *do*?"

"You didn't *do* anything, Ash."

I wanted to ask how she could possibly know what I had or hadn't done in the time since I'd been away from Newdale, and even before. Maybe I *had* done something to drive Celine away. Perhaps I'd hurt Kate somehow, too. If I had, I wouldn't have told Maya, would I? There was no way she'd have stuck by me if I'd harmed someone. I'd disappeared from town and moved south where I'd given Lily—my new *girlfriend*, apparently—a false name. Nobody did that unless they were trying to escape from something, not unless they had something to hide. I sat in silence, wrestling with it all, forcing my anger back into a box and shoving it down my throat. "Have you told me everything, Maya?" I said, turning to her. "Did you leave anything out because you're trying to protect me?"

"No."

"Because if you are—"

"I'm *not*."

"Are you sure? I need you to level with me, because I can't go on this way."

She reached for my shoulder and gave it a squeeze, her touch feeling like a red-hot poker. "Maybe we can ask Dr. Adler to give you something to help you cope with all this stress."

"That's a hard no," I said, shrugging her off. "I'm not taking anything. My head's already fuzzy enough, you said so yourself. Some days I feel like I'm going backward."

We drove on in silence until we arrived at Dr. Adler's, where he ushered us into the same consultation room. When he asked how I was doing, I snapped, "I'm sure I've had better days, but I can't remember them." I knew I was being a complete dick but really didn't care. I wanted him to take the bait so I had an excuse to be an even bigger one.

He sat back in his chair and crossed his legs, revealing a pair of Scooby-Doo socks. When he followed my gaze, he smiled. "Christmas gift from my wife. She does it every year without fail. I have quite the cartoon collection. But back to you, Ash. Your frustration is normal."

"Sure, I get that," I said, "but it doesn't help much, does it?"

"Ash," Maya said, "we're not the enemy."

I exhaled, apologized, and with some gentle prodding from Maya, explained about the new flashbacks, the general state of my memory and, most importantly, Lily arriving in Newdale.

"Well, the confusion you're experiencing sounds completely normal given the circumstances," Dr. Adler said. "But if you're concerned, we can run some more blood tests to be sure."

"I'm fine," I said, waving a hand. "You already did some."

"Do you think we should, Dr. Adler?" Maya said, ignoring me, and I suppressed a sigh. "Can we make sure no underlying issue has cropped up since last time? I really think we should, just in case. I can pay, it's no problem."

"Absolutely, we can, if you're in agreement, Ash?"

I was about to protest again when I took in the dark circles under Maya's eyes and reminded myself how difficult this situation was for her. She'd become a glorified babysitter since she'd been called to the petrol station. Whether she was working in the garage, running errands or at the restaurant, she always worried what I was doing, where I was and if I'd still be there when she came back. With no job and no money, I'd put a financial burden on her, too. The least I could do was let them run some more tests to make sure I really wasn't sick. I rolled up my sleeve.

"Have at it," I said.

As Maya excused herself and went to the bathroom, Dr. Adler set about half emptying me as he filled multiple vials with blood. "Try to relax," he said quietly.

"Maybe you could tell Maya to relax," I said before holding up my hand. "Sorry. I think my, uh, girlfriend turning up spooked her."

Dr. Adler swapped out a full vial for another. "I'd imagine you're a little spooked, too."

I listened for Maya's footsteps, and when I heard none, said, "Not exactly. I'm more excited. Anxious. Bewildered. I don't remember Lily, at least I don't think so." I pressed my eyes shut and recalled the bracelet with a heart-shaped charm on her wrist, almost certain I'd seen it before. "I can't figure out if the bits I remember are real or if it's because I'm desperate."

As he withdrew the needle and pressed a cotton ball into the crease of my arm, he said, "I saw in the notes Dr. Soares talked to you about confabulation."

"The false memory thing? Yeah, she did, and the way I see it, whatever I remember might be my brain making its own epic blockbuster movie."

He chuckled. "Not necessarily, and again, as a family doctor this isn't my area of expertise, but from what I've read, I suspect Lily being here is an opportunity. She may be able to help you reconstruct your more recent history and be instrumental in unlocking your past. I'd advise you to spend time with her, if you feel comfortable doing so, and if it doesn't cause you stress. It could be of great benefit."

I nodded, more excitement building in my chest. "I think I'd like that," I said, and as I pictured Lily, a sense of calm seemed to gradually wrap itself around me, making my heart rate slow. "And I've been thinking about working, too, doing some projects around the house."

"I can imagine boredom is beginning to set in, but you have to take your time and listen to your body. Your accident wasn't long ago, and you still need plenty of rest. You can do the odd job here or there, but build up slowly, and if any of your symptoms get worse, ease off immediately."

I was about to argue I'd be fine when I heard a creak outside the door. I closed my mouth, didn't want Maya to hear Dr. Adler repeat the fact he thought I should take it easy. She was protective...and a little intense if I was being completely honest. Sometimes I'd find her standing in the doorway observing me, and more than once her doing so had weirded me out. I knew it was strange for her, having me—most of me—back here, and it couldn't be easy for her. One moment I was vulnerable yet angry, the next apologetic yet ungrateful, and consistently argumentative when she told me my recollections were off. Not a fantastic combination for her to put up with. Plus, I was her older brother. As far as I was concerned, and old-fashioned as it sounded, I was supposed to look after her, not the other way around, even if Maya was perfectly capable of taking care of the both of us.

I looked up as she stepped into the room. She smiled and pointed at the neatly aligned row of blood-filled vials. "Jeez, Ash, you're completely hollow."

I forced a laugh that sounded false even to me, and after finishing up with Dr. Adler, who promised he'd call me with the results in a few days despite his going to Mexico on holiday, we thanked him and left. It was almost three by the time we'd stopped off at the grocery store and got back home, but ever since we'd left the doctor's office, Maya had hardly said a word.

"Are you all right?" I said as we finished unpacking the groceries.

"I've been thinking," she said. "I was a bit shocked when Lily turned up. I don't trust people at the best of times, and certainly not someone you don't recall. A person I've never met, and who claims she's your girlfriend, but to whom you gave a fake name." She sighed. "I don't like it. Maybe you lied because you never trusted her to begin with. We invited her to our home. What if she's a psycho?"

I threw my hands in the air. "I've no idea, but it seems unlikely, doesn't it? Going to all that effort to find me? Coming all this way? I need to see her. She has information about me, information I badly need. It's a huge breakthrough."

Maya stared at me. "Did Dr. Adler say anything else about her being here?"

I knew she wouldn't approve of him suggesting I spend time with Lily, so I said, "He was too busy playing vampire, the bloodthirsty bastard." When Maya didn't laugh, I added, "I'm going to do some research online before Lily comes over. And before you say I shouldn't be on a screen—"

"I won't."

I frowned. "I thought you were adamant about me staying off them?"

She shrugged and grabbed a pen and piece of paper, writing down a sequence of letters and numbers. "Here's my password. Want me to help you?"

I shook my head. "This is something I need to do alone."

Maya looked at me for a second before giving me a nod. After she'd left the kitchen and headed upstairs, I reached for the laptop. Taking a deep breath, I took my time as I opened the lid and typed in Maya's password, all the while trying to convince myself I was ready to find out the truth about who Jack Smith really was.

19

LILY

I'm not entirely sure how I made it back to my car, or when I realized I had to find a place to stay for the night. It was as if the logical part of my brain was still functioning somehow, and it took over, forcing me to drive through town. The choice of accommodation was between a hotel, which looked way out of my price range, and two more budget-friendly motels. After I'd gone past both twice, I pulled up in front of the Harbor Inn, which wasn't anywhere close to the harbor, but was the only place with a vacancy sign. I parked the car and sat in the lot for a while, trying to come to terms with what had happened.

Jack—Ash, he said he was *Ash*—was alive. Finding him had been something I'd barely dared dream of, something I'd played out only in my wildest imagination. The discovery had also brought home how much I'd given up on him, and while I hadn't wanted to admit it, I'd resigned myself to the fact that

Jack—damn it, *Ash*—was gone. Regardless of his name, it made me feel like a traitor, and I wondered if he'd sensed my abandonment somehow. Was that why he hadn't come home? It was a stupid theory. He had amnesia. He'd had no idea who I was, had looked at me as if I were a complete stranger. A tightness wrapped itself around my heart and squeezed hard.

Sitting in my car I put my head back and closed my eyes, trying to untangle my emotions, but every way I turned, a new, stronger and more confusing one jumped out. I was overjoyed Jack was alive. Pissed he'd come to Maine (how ridiculous, he'd lost his memory, for God's sake). Frustrated he hadn't recognized me. Frightened of the answers I'd come here for. Terrified that I might lose him all over again, but...he'd lied to me. Perhaps cutting him loose was the best thing for both of us. I took a deep breath. I hadn't thought it possible for me to have so much going on inside my head without it exploding.

"Imagine how he's feeling," I whispered. "Imagine what it's like for him."

I needed to share the news about Jack being alive with someone, and reached for my phone, about to call Sam, deciding to alert Heron afterward. Before pressing Sam's number, I played out the calls in my mind. Any relief and elation would soon switch to bewilderment and doubt as soon as I explained Jack Smith was really Asher Bennett, and he was suffering from retrograde amnesia. How could I tell them anything when I didn't know the full story? Besides, what if Heron arranged for someone from the local police department to interview him? He'd been so confused when I found him, I didn't have the right to put him through more.

I dropped my phone into my bag. I'd wait until after I'd spoken to him, and no doubt Maya could help with more information.

Maya. Why hadn't he told me about her? Shared the fact he had a sister—stepsister—with me? He'd led me to believe he was an only child, that his mother had committed suicide and he and his father had moved to the US shortly after because they needed a fresh start. He'd never mentioned Brad remarrying, never talked about having a stepsister, not even after I'd told him about Quentin and my childhood. Why had he left out such a significant part of his life?

As I pictured Maya standing on the sidewalk, observing me, unease slithered around my feet, crawled up my legs and settled along with all the other emotions in my stomach. Had I made a mistake with the Facebook photo after all? It was possible. I'd been so desperate to find clues. Maybe I'd seen what I wanted to see. The guy in the picture had worn sunglasses. Perhaps Gordon was Ash's doppelgänger or something, and somehow Ash had ended up with Maya's library book when she thought it was Gordon. It would mean my coming here was a lucky coincidence, and sometimes things worked out for a reason…or fate.

I grabbed my duffel from the trunk and headed inside. While the outside of the motel seemed lackluster and windswept, somebody had taken great care and obvious joy while decorating the reception area. A wood-paneled desk with a sparkling, white quartz counter, and soft recessed lighting gave it an inviting cozy feel. Black-and-white photographs of the ocean and awe-inspiring cliffs adorned the pale walls. A mobile, the kind I'd seen on Drift's website, with shiny pieces of polished wood cut into stars and hearts, and engraved with inspirational words such as *Peace*, *Trust* and *Happiness* hung in a corner, turning gently midair.

Kitchen noises and the smell of gravy wafted through the saloon doors on the right, but as nobody was behind the desk, I put my duffel down, letting my eyes wander. They settled on the rows of flyers to the left of the counter, all arranged by color, advertising an array of attractions in the area. Before I could learn more about zip-lining, local breweries or whale-watching tours, a young woman in ripped jeans and a sailor-style shirt strolled in through the saloon doors, her face bursting into a smile when she saw me. She'd pinned her curly red hair into an elaborate swirl on top of her head, turning it into a ginormous cinnamon bun, and her green eyes had the longest natural lashes I'd ever seen. Her name tag said *Fiona*.

"Hello and welcome." Her smile broadened further. "How can I help you?"

"Do you have any rooms available?"

"We sure do," Fiona said. "How many nights are you looking to stay?"

"I'm not exactly sure…two or three, maybe more?"

"No problem. Why don't I put you down for four and I'll ask you the day after tomorrow if you want to extend. That way you'll be sure to have a room. What do you think?"

I sighed. "Sounds great."

"Perfect. It's seventy-nine a night, which includes breakfast, served from six thirty until ten in the dining room through there." She pointed to the doors. "I'm Fiona. Ask for me if you need anything." She took my information and credit card, and handed me a key, which was attached to another piece of polished wood like the ones on the mobile, except instead of an inspiring word engraved in it, it was the number *12*. I thanked Fiona, and once she'd given me directions, parked my car around the left side of the L-shaped building.

My room was small, but fresh and clean, with soft gray walls and a queen-size bed, which had two thick pillows on either side. More black-and-white photographs hung on the walls, as dramatic as those at reception, and a large flat-screen TV covered most of the opposite side.

While I was exhausted from getting up early, traveling and the day's events, there was no way I could rest. I grabbed my phone, and after trying to talk myself out of it for fear of what I might find, ran a search for *Asher Bennett, Newdale*.

It quickly became clear he didn't have a social media profile

I could work my way through, and I reframed the parameters. There was a small article about an Asher Bennett winning a high-school wrestling championship, but it was years ago and didn't have any photos, so I couldn't be sure it was him. A few swipes later an obituary for Brad Bennett caught my eye, and I skimmed through the piece. Brad had died in a freak workplace accident, and was survived by his son, Asher, and his stepdaughter, Maya Scott. This was definitely my Jack, but while he'd told me his father's name, he'd said Brad had died in a car crash. As I sat there staring at my phone, I realized if Heron and Stevens had followed up on the information I'd given them about Jack Smith living in Maine, it would surely have been near impossible to put things together and identify him as Asher Bennett. What had made him lie about his father's death, never mention Maya or his stepmother, and give himself a fake name? What had happened to him? I shuddered. Maybe the real question was: What did *he* do?

After a few more unsuccessful searches, I set my phone down and watched TV, hoping to find something I could concentrate on long enough until it was time to meet *Ash*, but I couldn't focus, I was too wired, so I gave up and headed to the tiny white bathroom, cursing as I unpacked my toiletries and discovered I'd left my toothpaste at home.

"Hi, Fiona, it's Lily in room twelve," I said when I dialed reception. "I forgot my toothpaste. Do you have some?"

"Of course, I'll be right over."

"No, don't worry. I'll stop by now."

I hung up and walked back to the front entrance, grateful for the distraction my forgotten toothpaste was offering. Fiona stood talking on the phone, and as I waited, my eyes were drawn back to the photographs on the wall. I couldn't help it. There was something so majestic and foreboding about the way the rugged cliffs plunged deep into the ocean below.

"Impressive, aren't they?" Fiona said as she put the phone

down and set two miniature tubes of toothpaste on the counter. "Dangerous, too."

"Are they the Newdale Bluffs?"

"Yes. If you go for a walk along them, make sure you have proper footwear, and stick to the marked paths. Even the locals have been known to get into trouble." A shadow crossed her face, but it quickly disappeared, replaced with a smile. "Need anything else? How's the room?"

"It's perfect, the bed's super comfortable."

"Fabulous, glad to hear it. We replaced them last fall and the guests seem to approve."

She looked like she was about to wish me a pleasant evening, but I couldn't stand being alone in my room again. "Have you worked here long?"

"You could say that," she said with a grin. "Born and raised in town, and this place belongs to my aunt, but I run it now. My brother helps out a bit, too. Where are you from?"

"Buffalo, originally."

"Do you have family here or are you just visiting?"

Her question made my face crumble. I thought I'd done well, almost congratulated myself on how I'd held it together since I'd arrived in town, but the mere kindness in her voice made my eyes well up. Before I could stop them, hot tears spilled over my face.

"Oh, no," she said, rushing from the counter and putting an arm around me. "Oh, crap."

"I'm s-sorry…"

"No, I am, poking my nose into your business. Come with me, let's get you a drink." She guided me into a dining area, with pastel beach paintings on the dark blue walls, whitewashed tables and sky blue chairs. There were a few other guests at the far end of the room, and Fiona got us settled at the table farthest away.

"What can I get you?" she said. "On the house."

"A water, please."

"Are you sure?" When I said yes, she hurried off to get my drink. Upon her return, she waited until I'd taken a few large gulps before saying, "I feel terrible for upsetting you."

"It's not your fault. It's been a weird day and...I just found out my boyfriend lives in town and has amnesia."

"Wow, wait. You're not *Ash's* girlfriend, are you?" she gasped, eyebrows shooting up, and mine did the same.

"You know him?"

"Oh, we go way back," she said. "But why are you staying at the motel? No, wait, that's none of my business, either, so don't—"

"He can't remember me." My lips wobbled and I pressed them together.

"I'm so sorry, that's awful." She reached forward and patted my hand. "I can't imagine how you're feeling. The first time I ran into Ash after he got back, he kept insisting his name was Brad. He was so confused."

"Did he recognize you?"

"Not even slightly. Not Maya, either, when she arrived." She shook her head. "I was surprised to see him at all, to be honest. I mean, he'd been gone two years, and nobody had heard a peep. I don't blame him for leaving, considering what happened."

I didn't dare reply as she leaned in, lowering her voice to a whisper.

"For the record, I never believed any of the rumors. I know some people were glad Ash left, including my brother. I'm sure Ash told you all about him, but in his defense, Keenan really was a mess when Celine left, and when Kate had the accident..." She shook her head as my mouth dropped open, and before I could ask her who all these people were and what she meant, she added, "I don't blame Ash for wanting to get away. No wonder you two never visited—"

A bell rang at the front desk. "Shoot, that's my cue." She pushed her chair back and stood up. "Feeling better?"

"Yes…yes, thank you," I lied, wishing I had the courage to ask her to sit down and explain everything she'd said, but I couldn't get my brain or my mouth to work properly.

"Great. Come and chat anytime, and don't forget to stop in for breakfast in the morning. Our bacon's divine. You'll never want to leave." She took a step before turning back. "Tell Ash I said hello when you see him. I hope things work out for you. He's a good guy. After everything he's been through, he deserves to be happy."

Before I could answer, she turned and left, and after I finished my water, I walked to my room, head spinning. Who were Celine and Kate? Why had Fiona's brother been happy to see Ash leave? What the hell had happened here? I sank onto the bed, grabbed my phone and ran more searches. There was nothing about a Celine, but a little over two years ago, a young woman called Kate Jansen had accidentally fallen off some local cliffs while out running and had died. I wanted to go back to reception, demand Fiona tell me if this was the Kate she'd mentioned, but I didn't have the nerve in case she said yes.

Still, I needed someone to talk to, someone who could help me figure stuff out. I flicked through my contacts and dialed Sam's number, hoping he'd forgiven me for swearing at him.

"Lily," he said, answering right away. "How are things?"

"I found him," I said, still unable to believe what I was saying. My words tumbled out as I told him everything. The library book, locating Maya and my trip to Maine.

Sam couldn't believe it, and after asking a million times if I was sure this man called Ash really was Jack, he let out a long whistle. "This is unbelievable. You've called Heron, right?" I hesitated a beat too long. "Lily? What's going on?"

"Before I left Brookmount they told me they thought Jack, I mean, Ash, might have been involved with some shady guy. Something to do with illegal gambling."

"What? That's impossible."

"That's what I told them. I mean, we both know he liked playing cards and was super competitive at it. But gambling? It's nuts."

"I agree, he's not the type," Sam said. "He's always been timely with his rent, never asked for an extension of any kind. Maybe they were mistaken?"

"I'm sure," I replied, trying to believe it as I pictured the cookie-tin cash tucked away in my duffel. "But I'm not calling them. Not before I see Ash again. Don't mention any of this to them, please. If he did owe someone money, or stole from them, they can't know he's alive and living in Maine."

Sam went quiet for a while, before saying, "All right, but be careful, please?"

"There's nothing to worry about," I said, ignoring the whispers in my head saying Sam had a point, I had to be wary, not because of the guy who'd been at the apartment, or the break-in, but because, although he was alive, the Jack Smith I knew and loved might no longer exist.

20

MAYA

After working in the garage for a while I wondered if Ash might be asleep on the sofa following today's events, but when I peered through the kitchen window, I saw he was still wide awake. Frowning, I walked to the front door, not daring to open it until my pulse settled. I'd forced myself to the garage earlier, feared if I didn't, I'd give in to my frustrations, shout at Ash, demanding to know all about Lily. Who she was, how they'd met, if she'd been the real reason he hadn't come home. I knew he wouldn't have been able to answer, and so I'd retreated, left him alone with my laptop, his brow furrowed, fingers darting over the keys as he tried to uncover the last two years of his history.

Now, balling my fists by my sides, I forced my nails deeper into my palms. Lily arriving in town was unexpected. I thought I'd thrown her with my cover story, most definitely hadn't expected her to show up in Newdale. Her arrival was something

I'd have to handle swiftly, before she wheedled her way back into Ash's life. Before he *remembered* her or she could contradict any of the fibs I'd told him already.

I'd overheard Ash's conversation with Dr. Adler about Lily. Maybe "deliberately eavesdropped" was a more accurate description. Finding out what Ash really thought about his supposed girlfriend being here had been my entire reason for pretending to go to the bathroom, but Dr. Adler suggesting Ash spend time with her hadn't been something I'd bargained on. Ash was conflicted, yes, and by the sound of it considering my feelings, but I had to make sure it stayed that way. I didn't have much time. In a little over two hours Lily would show up here, at the house, and I hadn't yet come up with a proper plan of how to get rid of her. I pushed the front door open, let an innocent look settle over my face and headed to the kitchen.

"Hey," Ash said, as soon as I walked in.

I gestured to the pages of scrunched-up paper strewn across the table, the laptop he'd pushed to one side and the empty soda bottle. "Did you find anything?"

"Jack Smith from Brookmount, Maryland," he said, almost in a daze, his left leg bouncing up and down, fingers drumming the table. I tried not to blanch as I wondered if his nerves weren't because of what he'd found, but because I hadn't performed a good enough purge of my search history and he'd realized he was telling me something I'd known for days.

"Come and read this," he said, waving me over, and when I looked at the screen, saw the same article I'd found on *Ocean-CityToday* over a week before.

HOPE FADING FOR MISSING BRITISH SWIMMER

The U.S. Coast Guard's search for British man Jack Smith is unofficially being called a recovery operation. 32-year-old Smith went missing while swimming off the coast of Brookmount (MD) Friday evening. His partner, Lily Reid, raised the alarm the next morning. Efforts to locate Smith have remained unsuccessful. Owing to violent storms and heavy rainfall, the search efforts have been postponed. A source from the Coast Guard said if Smith was in distress, they had to give him the best possible chance for rescue, but the weather conditions meant the likelihood of finding Smith alive at sea was now "basically nil."

"What's on the video?" I said, as if I hadn't watched it multiple times. Ash clicked on the link titled *Girlfriend of Missing Swimmer's DESPERATE Plea* and I watched the screen fill with the already familiar image of two women. The one on the right, the reporter, had immaculate hair and makeup, her ruby-red lips poised to ask a question, the creases in her crisp white shirt sharp as a knife's edge. The woman on the left was Lily. The first time I'd watched the clip, I'd immediately identified her as a "surfer chick," with her slight but muscular frame and long, blond, windswept hair. Her features were perfectly proportioned, and although her delicate nose, cat eyes and pink lips didn't have a trace of foundation, blush or mascara, she was undeniably and effortlessly beautiful, on camera, and even more so in real life. When Ash pressed Play, Lily's expression turned from helpless to terrified.

"Lily, thank you for talking to us," the reporter said, her voice gentle and coaxing, the exact mix to get anyone to spill their guts. "I understand your boyfriend, Jack Smith, went missing yesterday evening while swimming at this very beach."

Lily nodded, swallowing hard before quietly saying, "He was supposed to come to my place, but I assumed he was working late." Her voice was soft as a lullaby, and she swallowed again, her lips trembling. "When he didn't show up this morning, I knew...I knew..."

"What did you know, Lily?" the reporter nudged. "Can you share with our viewers?"

"I knew he was in trouble." Lily put a fist to her mouth and bowed her head, pressing her eyes shut, trying to contain her sobs.

"You told me earlier Jack's a strong swimmer?"

Lily's voice filled with hope. "Yes, very. He swims almost every day."

The reporter leaned in, a pained and no doubt meticulously rehearsed expression on her face. "What would you like to say to everybody who's watching? How can they help?"

"If you're out on the water, please, *please* look for him. Help me bring Jack home."

The camera zoomed in on the reporter's face. "Such a devastating story of this missing man, Jack Smith. We'll, of course, bring you the latest developments, and…" Her voice trailed off as I stopped listening, because a picture of Ash appeared on the screen, the one that had made me gasp. I'd never seen this particular photo before, and while he looked the same—his grin, the way his hair fell to one side—he also appeared different. Relaxed and happy. Free.

Ash paused the video and looked up at me. "Lily's telling the truth. I was living under the name Jack Smith in Maryland. And guess what? There's a more recent update. Apparently, there was a boat out on the water around the time I went missing." He gave his head a shake, tapped his temple with an index finger. "This whole amnesia thing might be because someone ran into me. Oh, and I'm presumed dead, by the way. Can you believe it?" He didn't wait for my answer and continued, "You should've told me about her calling you—"

"I didn't make the connection."

"Fine, but I need to contact the police down there, tell them I'm okay."

"What? You can't."

"I have to. They think I'm dead."

"Have they arrested anyone?"

"Not that I'm aware of, but—"

"Then leave it." I held up a hand as he opened his mouth to respond, and my mind sped up. "You were living there under a fake name. They'll have figured that out by now. What if they want to bring you in for questioning? Or worse, get the local police involved? With your history surrounding Celine and Kate, what if they think it's suspicious?"

"Why would anything be suspicious?" He raised his voice, the veins in his neck pulsating. "You said I was cleared. When I left Newdale, nobody suspected me of anything."

"Officially, no," I said, which was the truth. "But who knows what some idiot cop might be thinking, especially with Keenan shooting his mouth off. Him and Ricky—"

"Ricky?"

"The local cop. He's good friends with Keenan."

"For crying out loud," Ash shouted, his face turning red. "What the hell am I supposed to do with all this? How am I supposed to *live*? And what about Lily? What if she told the cops about finding me already?"

"She's coming over soon, we'll ask her then."

"Providing it's not too late and they're not on their way already."

"We'll figure it out."

He let out a half laugh, his teeth clenched. "How can I if I don't remember anything, and the little I do is mostly a pile of crap? Doesn't it freak you out, sharing a house with me? I'm clearly a liar, Maya, and an angry one at that. Doesn't that worry you, at all?"

I stared at him. "No. Not in the least. I know you. You're angry because of the situation, because of your memory. That's all. This isn't who you are."

"Isn't it?" he snapped. "Then why do I feel like it is?" He

shook his head, his shoulders falling. "I need to get out for a bit before Lily arrives. Get my head straight so I can figure out what to say to her, and what she might say to me. I can't believe I didn't ask her to come with us to see Dr. Adler. I can't believe I left her there in the middle of the street. What was I thinking?"

"You probably weren't. We were all in shock."

"Yeah, no kidding," he said, and after putting on his shoes he came over and stood in front of me, looking uncertain about what to do next. I pulled him in for a hug, felt him hesitate before he tentatively put his arms around me, making me want to hug him harder, and when I rested my cheek on his chest, I could hear the beating of his heart.

"Stay away from the cliffs," I murmured.

Ash took a step back and nodded. "I'll be home in an hour."

Once he'd gone, it took me all of ninety seconds to figure out Lily was staying at the Harbor Inn. The girl at the front desk, thankfully not Fiona, offered to connect me to her room, but I declined because I didn't want to talk to Lily, I just wanted to know what she was up to. Seemed she had a similar idea, because as I hung up, the doorbell rang. It was *her.*

"Maya," Lily said, and I noticed how her hands trembled by her sides, her smile tight, her gaze darting behind me and into the house. "Can I come in? Is…uh, is *Ash* here?"

"He stepped out," I said. "I'm not quite sure when he'll be back."

Her face fell and she bit her lip for a second. "Oh. I know I'm early but I…I couldn't wait, I…" She covered her mouth with a hand as tears leaked down her perfect cheeks.

I opened the door and stood aside, chose my next words carefully, my voice soft and coaxing, like the one the reporter had used. "Are you okay? God, what a stupid question. Why don't you come in?"

Her face caved again. "Th-thank you so much."

"Not at all." I led her to the kitchen and gestured for her to sit as I busied myself with getting her a glass of water, which she downed in four gulps.

"Thank you." Lily let out a sigh. "Maya, can I please ask you something?"

"Of course," I said, smiling and nodding, making sure she felt comfortable.

"Was it Ash in the Facebook photo?"

"No." I shook my head as I wracked my brain to remember what I'd told her on the phone. I'd given her a different name to throw her off. Fuck. What was it again? Gavin? George? Graham? *Gordon*. I gave her a sympathetic smile, my mind racing ahead. "I can understand why you thought it was Ash, he and Gordon looked so alike it was uncanny. When I first saw him on the beach I thought it was Ash and waved to him. That's how we met."

Her shoulders sagged, her entire body almost collapsing in onto itself. "It wasn't him."

"No, and I feel so bad for not realizing you were talking about my brother, but I had no idea. I was so preoccupied with his condition, I didn't connect the dots. I feel so guilty."

"But then why did you delete the picture?"

The directness of her question caught me a little off guard, but it didn't take me long to recover. I shrugged. "It weirded me out, you calling like that. I reacted."

At the realization she was to blame, Lily's shoulders sagged some more, and her voice became soft again. "Why do you think he lied to me about his name?"

"Oh, wow... I really don't know."

"You have no idea why he left town and pretended to be someone else?" Her left eye began to twitch, and she pressed a finger over it. The dusky circles under her eyes told me she was exhausted, and upon closer inspection I saw she had sallow skin, too. She looked like a once-pretty princess who'd lost her sheen, and I wasn't about to allow her to get it back.

"No, I really don't. I'd tell you otherwise, I promise."

"Does it have anything to do with Kate or Celine?" she said, and I felt my eyes widen. "Who are they?"

"It doesn't matter, Lily. They're in the past."

"It *does* matter," she said, looking me up and down, and I wondered if her tears had been a ploy to get into the house. "It matters a lot and if you don't tell me, I'm sure someone else in town will. Fiona, or her brother, Keenan, for example. I hear he and Ash don't exactly get along."

The intensity of her voice and her newly found backbone surprised me. I'd expected neither, had pegged Lily as being a bit of a pushover and a little weak, realized I'd have to be more careful around her than I'd first thought.

I told her about Fiona, Keenan and Celine being siblings, and that Celine had been Ash's high-school sweetheart. Once done, I took a dramatic pause before finishing with, "Celine disappeared when she was sixteen."

"What do you mean, disappeared?"

"She left town. Ran away."

"And who was Kate?"

From the way she said it I could already tell she didn't want the answer. Ash hadn't told her about either of them, and now that she had the opportunity to find out, Lily didn't want the truth. She was scared. "Kate was Ash's girlfriend. She died a little over two years ago."

"Did she fall off a cliff?" Lily whispered.

"Yes, she did, it was horrible." This time, as I recounted the story of Kate's death, she let out a little gasp. "God, it was awful," I said. "He loved her so much. He was going to propose."

Lily's face turned white, all the color sliding from her cheeks. "He never told me about either of them. Why wouldn't he share something so important?"

I pretended to consider her question, leaned in and whispered, "Ash is a complicated man with a difficult past. Talking about exes is difficult enough, but with Kate dying... I don't know, maybe he didn't want to tell you because the police suspected him of foul play."

"What did you say?"

I sat back, put a hand to my chest, talking fast. "Oh, well... he was a suspect for a while, and that's a lot to admit to someone, don't you think? But don't worry. They couldn't prove anything."

She blinked three times, and I could tell she was working hard to process what I'd implied. That was strike one. "I can't believe it," she said. "Why wouldn't he... Why didn't he..."

"I imagine this is a huge shock for you, and really hard to hear, especially with the amnesia and him not remembering you. At all." I sighed heavily and crossed my arms, shaking my head. "I wish he'd told you about them. He really should have."

"I...I thought I knew him. I thought he loved..." She stopped but I knew she wanted to say *me*. That was strike two. Another blow to her already crushed heart.

"It's not easy for any of us...but can I ask, have you told the police about finding Ash?"

She shifted in her seat. "No, not yet."

"I'd say it's best if we don't," I said. "At least until he's feeling a bit better."

"I'm not sure—"

"Just for a while, please. What my brother needs right now is space and rest, not to be hauled in for questioning about why he was living under a false identity. Let's not do that to him. I'm sure you understand he's completely overwhelmed. Before he went out, he told me he needs a break."

Her eyes flashed. "From me?"

I paused for a while before answering. "I'm sure that's not what he meant..."

"*I* need some time," she said, getting up, her voice filling with panic as she took a step toward the door. "Coming here early wasn't a good idea after all. I need to think things through before I speak to him. I—I'd like to come back tomorrow morning instead. Around nine? I'll give you my number in case that doesn't work for...*Ash*."

Was that strike three? Was she hoping it *wouldn't* work for him, and this was her way out? Would she even come tomorrow? The seeds of doubt had been planted and were already taking root, getting ready to bloom. I could see it in her demeanor, the way she looked like she couldn't wait to turn and bolt out the door. With any luck she'd drive straight to Maryland without looking back, leaving Ash here, where he belonged. With me.

After Lily scribbled down her details, she left without saying a proper goodbye. I closed the door and rested my back against it, let the relief of my actions seep in. When I caught a glance of myself in the hallway mirror, I smiled. Ever since I was a kid, I'd known what people saw when they looked at me: long, lanky legs, skeletal frame, black fluffy hair and enormous eyes. *Waifish* and *elfin* were two words often used to describe me. I'd loathed and detested them for their synonymy with *weak*. Except I knew now they'd always been to my advantage. They were why people underestimated me.

21

LILY

Not long after I'd left Ash and Maya's place—was that how I'd have to refer to it as of now, *their* place?—my mood flipped from despondent to enraged. I was relieved Maya had agreed to my returning in the morning because if I saw Ash now, there was no telling what I might say or do to him. He'd been considered a suspect in Kate's death? How could he have kept something like that from me? No, I'd never told him about my sordid past, but I'd been convicted, he hadn't. I'd had more to hide...hadn't I?

My feelings shifted again, my heart pounding as I pulled over, rested my head on the steering wheel and shut my eyes, willing myself to wake up from this incessant freak show and go back to my normal life where Ash was Jack and we were happy, and I was blissfully ignorant.

I didn't move until a short *pap-pap* of a horn sounded in my ears. A red Subaru WRX had pulled up next to me, and the huge red-haired guy I'd seen at the Cliff's Head earlier, now sporting a pair of shiny aviator sunglasses, had rolled down his window, and gestured for me to do the same. "Are you okay?" he said when I'd complied.

"Y-yes, I'm fine." I tried a smile, which probably looked like a hideous grimace.

"You sure? Need directions or anything?"

My smile felt a little more natural this time, the amiability of small towns warming my heart. "No, thanks. I know where I'm going." At least geographically speaking, I wanted to add.

"All right then." He gave me a grin and a small salute as he set off again.

The random act of kindness stirred up my emotions, releasing another wave of feelings I didn't know what to do with. "Jack lied to me," I whispered. "Damn it. I mean Ash. Ash. *Ash.*" I was shouting now, bellowing in my car, and pounding my steering wheel with my palms. Once my nerves and anger all subsided enough for me to drive without crashing into a utility pole, I started up the engine. As I headed for the motel, I tried convincing myself I hated my boyfriend—ex-boyfriend?—and should pack up and leave town, but my desire to understand who he was and somehow come to terms with why he'd lied, triumphed.

Did I still love him, though? *Could* I? The potential answers terrified me, so I turned my thoughts to Maya. Despite the lies and half-truths I'd uncovered about Ash, I could feel a large part of me was jealous of his stepsister. Resentful he'd found his way back here to her and not to me. Hurt he had no recollection of who I was. It was unreasonable and churlish, and there was no time for any of it. I decided to ignore the part of my brain screaming at me to flee Maine and pretend none of this was happening. Not an option. I had to help him, which meant I couldn't go home, not yet. I'd only found Ash again today, and we'd barely spoken. There were too many open questions, so much I needed to know, even more so after what I'd learned from Fiona and Maya.

Besides, Ash would now be expecting me in the morning and that gave me enough time to sort through my seemingly endless thoughts. No, running away wasn't an option. Not when I still had some kind of feelings for him, and not until I discovered the truth. Staying was the only way to know for sure if we had any kind of future—and if I wanted one—or if our relationship had died in the ocean on the night everyone thought he'd perished, too. One way or another, I needed closure, and the only people who could help with that were Ash and his sister.

I tried not to shudder when I remembered how Maya had stared at me, as if she could somehow see into my soul. I figured we were about the same age, but she seemed older, wiser and way more self-assured. Being assertive like that didn't come naturally to me, something Dominic Martel had picked up on easily, and used to his full advantage. I'd noticed how Maya spoke, too, always direct and with certainty, and in the few encounters we'd had, I'd never heard her use a single filler word—not an *uh*, or an *um*, not even a misplaced *like*. She knew exactly what she wanted to say, and expressed herself so precisely, it was as if she'd rehearsed for weeks. *Charismatic, interesting, sexy* and *seductive* were words to describe Maya. Where did that leave me? Intimidated, that's where.

I grabbed a sandwich from a small store in town and added a bottle of white wine on a whim. Back at the motel I sat on the plastic chair outside my room, absentmindedly eating food I didn't want, and leaving the alcohol to cool in the fridge. My belt would need another hole soon if I didn't eat properly and on a regular basis. Had Ash been the Jack I knew, and he'd noticed my shrinking frame, he'd have burst in with a giant, cheese-laden pizza, and a stack of Patti's blueberry pancakes bigger than my head.

My face fell, replaced by the fear he'd never know me again, wouldn't remember anything we'd ever shared. All our inside jokes and all our memories were now mine and mine alone. Losing him once had been hard enough, but a second time, especially when he was in front of me, so close yet out of reach... I didn't think I was made to withstand those levels of heartache. I'd loved Ash more than anyone. We'd had a future together. He was the first man who didn't make me doubt myself, who let me be me, and loved me for who I was. A good man, Fiona had said. Except he'd lied. And because of that I now doubted everything.

I sat back, pulled out my phone and was about to dive into research about amnesia before changing my mind and searching for local doctors instead, scrolling down the short list until I found the name Ash had mentioned: Dr. Adler. "No time like the present," I said, putting my sandwich down and dialing his number, explaining who I was, and why I was calling, in ten seconds flat.

Dr. Adler cut me off as soon as I mentioned Ash's name. "I'm afraid I can't discuss—"

"I understand. Confidentiality and all that. But could I come and talk to you about amnesia in general? Please? I'm so lost and I don't know what to do."

"I'm sorry, Ms. Reid, but I'm about to go on vacation."

"On the phone then?" I said. "I don't know much about amnesia, but I've heard of the retrograde kind before. I believe it's what Ash has, where he's lost his past?" His silence reminded me he wouldn't discuss his patients, so I tried again. "I don't know much about it, but is it true it may only last awhile?"

"Each case is unique," Dr. Adler said, "but as I mentioned, I can't go into specifics."

"Yes, yes, of course, but I'm wondering if my being here is a good idea."

"You have to understand I'm a family physician, not a neurospecialist. However, theoretically speaking, in the case of retrograde amnesia I'd advise the patient to be in familiar surroundings as much as possible, and to try and get back to their normal routine."

"But in Ash's case…?" I stopped. "I mean, what would the best scenario be for a person who's been living elsewhere? Where would it make the most sense for them to try to get their memory back? The place they've been living for the past few years, or the town they grew up in?"

"Well, depending on the type of amnesia, often older memories are recovered first, so I suppose the argument could be made the person might benefit from being in their childhood surroundings."

"Oh…"

"On the other hand, someone who spent a lot of time with the patient in recent years may well jolt the memories of their more recent past. Frankly, it's difficult to say. Each brain is wired a little differently, and each case of amnesia is unique. There are no hard-and-fast rules."

"Could my… I mean—" I blew out my cheeks "—I want to know if my being here might harm him or hamper his progress."

Dr. Adler took a deep breath. "In this *theoretical* case I'd advise you to watch for the patient's reactions. If he seems distressed or angry when he sees you, my advice would be to back off and try again later. Less might be more. Does that make sense?"

"Yes, thank you. Could Ash—"

"Ms. Reid, I can't go into more detail. If you want to discuss this case specifically, please come back with Mr. Bennett. I'm afraid it's the best I can do. Be patient with him," he added softly. "And with yourself. I can only imagine how difficult it must be, but he's lucky to have people who care so deeply for him. It'll definitely help with his recovery. You can come see me again anytime after I get back, together, or for matters pertaining to your own health, of course, or should you need a referral to a specialist to help you deal with this situation."

"Of course. Thank you," I whispered, not wanting to hang up, but knowing I had to.

As I sat outside on my plastic chair, I wondered what to do for the rest of the evening. I debated sightseeing, taking a drive up the coast or down to Portland, but with everything weighing on my mind, playing tourist felt ridiculous. I still hadn't decided what to do when I saw Fiona walking to the room a few doors down, a stack of folded towels in her arms. She waved at me as she knocked on the door, and once she'd delivered the laundry, came over.

"Hey, Lily. How's everything?"

I was going to reply everything was great, but couldn't get my mouth to utter the lie, and so instead I said, "I'm supposed to see Ash tomorrow and I don't know how to deal with it." I looked up at her and wrinkled my nose. "Oh, you meant the room, didn't you?"

She shook her head. "No, I didn't. I meant you."

"I don't know how I am. This whole situation is so…*weird*. I went to see Ash at the house, but he was out and after talking to Maya I'm not sure I want to go back."

"Maya's always been very…*intense* when it comes to her brother, he must have mentioned that," she said, her words and delivery cautious.

I'd actually meant I might not want to return to the house because of what I'd discovered about her sister and Kate, but while Fiona's interpretation of my words was different, it wasn't entirely wrong, either.

"Intense?" I said. "You mean protective?"

"Sure, that, too." She hesitated again before saying, "I'm sure he told you she had a major crush on him when they first met."

"Oh, yeah, sure." I tried to keep my voice light so she wouldn't realize I didn't have the slightest idea, or that it sounded a little creepy. "But at that age, I mean, he was…?"

"Fifteen. She was twelve. Everybody knew from the start,

but Maya thought it wasn't obvious. Did he tell you about the notebook?"

"Uh, I don't think so."

"She carried it with her everywhere, used to scribble in it incessantly, like a journal, I suppose. Anyway, she dropped it on the bus. Apparently, one of the high-school mean girls found it, you know the type."

"Too well, unfortunately."

"Yeah, well, this girl, Sydney, passes the notebook around and everyone's in hysterics because it's covered in hearts and scribbles of 'Maya and Ash forever.' They called her a—" she lowered her voice to a whisper "—*brotherfucker*. It went on for months and months. Ash didn't know for ages. Celine didn't want to be the one to tell him."

"That must've been horrible for Maya."

"No doubt, and it explained why mean girl's favorite possession, a two-hundred-and-fifty-buck designer jacket, went missing and ended up in tatters, flying on the school's flagpole."

"Maya did that?"

"Nobody knows for sure, but we all assumed she did. And who could blame her, really?"

"What about Ash? What did he do?"

"I don't think she told him, either, not at first. I don't know why, because Ash was immediately popular when he arrived from England. He would have put a stop to it right away, and people would have listened. He was untouchable, in a way. A leader. Before Ash arrived, Keenan thought *he* was the king of the castle, and then Ash dated the most popular girl in high school…"

"You mean Celine?"

"Yes. Keenan went bananas, tried to make her stop seeing Ash, but of course she wouldn't listen. Why would she? Ash is a great guy. But then Celine left, and Keenan blamed him. Things seemed to settle down for a while, at least on the surface, but then Keenan went out with Kate before Ash 'stole' her, as my brother still puts it. Honestly, I've told him a hundred times it was because he drank too much and didn't care enough about her, but the animosity between him and Ash runs way too deep for him to listen." She wrinkled her nose. "Doesn't this weird you out, talking about Ash's exes?"

I let out a half laugh. "A little."

"Only a little? You're a better woman than me. So, what do you think you'll do now?"

I flicked through the options in my mind. Go back to Brookmount, call Heron and Stevens and let them figure stuff out, or... "Stay a couple more days, at least until I speak to him properly. I can't leave before that happens."

"Good decision. And don't worry about your room. We'll go on a day-by-day basis, it's yours for however long you need it."

Ten minutes later I still sat outside alone, soaking up the last of the sun, and debating whether I'd made the right decision, when my phone rang. When I saw Mike's number, I picked up immediately. "Hey," I said. "How are you? You don't need the car, do you? I took a little trip."

"Ah, in that case this really isn't the best time for my call..." He let out a long sigh. "Lily, I apologize, but the garage... I'm afraid we've got no choice. We're closing. End of the month."

"Closing?"

"It's been looming large for a while, but I didn't want to say anything last week, not with everything that happened to you. Basically...well, the truth is I can't keep the business going. I thought I had someone lined up to take it over, but the deal fell through. I'm sorry, Lily, but I have to shut things down. Time to retire."

"Oh, Mike, that's awful."

"I feel sick to my stomach. You were the last one on my list to call. Not because you were the least important, but because

I kept hoping for a miracle. I don't want to lose you. But it's official, and I didn't want to tell you while you're on leave, but…"

"Don't worry, it's okay, I understand. What can I do to help?"

"Nothing, but thank you. You're the first person to ask. I've been called all kinds of names in the past twenty-four hours, none of them pretty. I'll do everything I can to pay your two weeks' severance."

"What about the car?"

"You said you're on a trip?"

"Yeah, I'm not exactly in town."

"Screw it," he said. "Bring it back whenever you're ready, it's the least I can do."

After we hung up my mind wouldn't stop churning. Not only did I have multiple reasons to stay in Newdale, but losing my job meant I now had the time, too. The one thing I didn't have a lot of was money. A week, I told myself. I'd give myself a week to find all the answers I needed and decide, one way or another, what I'd do next.

22

ASH

The walk I'd hoped would clear my head hadn't worked, and by the time I got back to the house I'd been anxious and wired with the anticipation of seeing Lily. When Maya told me she'd come and gone, I exploded. "What do you mean, she *left*?" I yelled. "How could you let her go?"

"Calm down, Ash," Maya said. "She needs time to get her head straight. She'll be back in the morning."

"Are you kidding me?" I said, my voice increasing in both volume and intensity. "You should've made her stay. Told her to wait until I got back." I felt my fists clench into tight balls, the muscles in my neck straining. It was at that point I noticed Maya's wide eyes, the way she'd taken a step back, as if she was scared of me. And who could blame her? What kind of a person acted this way, yelling and screaming at someone who'd done nothing but help? I thought back to what Maya had said, that my increasingly irate behavior was because of the situation, and my amnesia, and hoped she was right. I could barely keep my frustrations at a simmer and not only did it make me hate myself right then, but also I felt ashamed.

"Can you please tell me what you two talked about?" I said gently.

Maya relayed their conversation, ending with, "Surely you can see how this has to be really hard for her?"

"Yes, I can," I said, my anger dissipating some more.

"Anyway," Maya continued, "you'll talk to her tomorrow. It'll be fine, I'm sure."

"Maybe I should go and see her now."

She shook her head. "I'm not sure that's a good idea. You don't know how she'll react. You could end up pushing her away. Look, let's try to relax and talk things through some more. I need a drink. Want a beer?"

Given the circumstances, I would've happily downed an entire keg. As Maya got our drinks I headed to the bathroom, where I reminded myself to get a grip. Lily needed some more time to think things through. Understandable and no big deal. Except it was a big deal because I wanted to see her.

Back in the living room Maya handed me a bottle of beer, some unfiltered stuff with licorice or something. I'd examined it earlier and put it straight back in the fridge in favor of a soda. When she saw my raised eyebrow she said, "You love this brand. It's local stuff, you can only get it around here."

I shrugged and took a sip. It tasted bitter and smelled worse than dog crap, so when Maya turned her back I poured most of it into the only houseplant we had, hoping I wouldn't kill it.

After dinner we watched some television, but I could feel Maya observing me, so I feigned heavy yawning and headed upstairs only to toss and turn in bed as my nerves built.

A few hours until Lily would arrive, and I was expected to hold a proper conversation with her, my *partner*. Thinking of her that way felt odd. What would I do when she arrived? Give her a hug? A kiss? If it was the latter, on the cheek or the lips? Or should I be formal and shake her hand? Her not coming until the morning was a good thing after all because I needed more time, too. The situation was bizarre enough, but what compounded it further was the fact I found Lily attractive. Exceedingly so. It shouldn't have come as a surprise seeing as we were a couple, but realizing we'd been together—including intimately—and I had no recollection of her, made me feel a combination of angry and helpless, anxious and sad. I wondered what she'd seen in me when we met, what I'd been like as a boyfriend. Had I been as foul-tempered with her as I was with Maya? The thought made me shudder and I added the question to my growing list and included another: Why did she want to have anything to do with me now, considering my lies?

I wondered if I should've been writing this stuff down in case my memory morphed into even more of an unpredictable animal. I clenched my jaw tight, squeezed my eyes shut. Dr. Adler would give me the results of the second batch of blood tests soon, and it would've been a lie to say I wasn't worried. What if there really was something more wrong with me? What if my amnesia had less to do with whatever happened on the beach that night and more with a cancerous tumor eating away at my brain? I flopped around in bed for another while before giving up, but trying to ignore everything wrong with the inside of my head became impossible.

The house was quiet—I'd heard Maya go to bed a while ago—and I sneaked past her bedroom and down the stairs, avoiding the third one from the top because I now knew it creaked. Maya had told me how she'd figured it out the first time she and Ophelia stayed in the house, when she'd sneaked down to the kitchen for a midnight snack. My dad had heard footfalls, and when he'd found Maya with her nose buried in the fridge, he'd made her a giant hot chocolate complete with sprinkles and marshmallows, and two slices of peanut butter toast.

"I loved your dad," she'd said. "He was the dad I'd dreamed about when I was a kid. Our family was perfect. It was everything I'd ever wanted."

I'd made some excuse about having something in my eye because the thought of my father being such a good man, of whom I only had filaments of memories, made me choke up. I wanted to remember him, my mum, Ophelia and Maya, properly. I wanted to remember the place I grew up in, where I went to school. I wanted to remember Celine, Kate and Lily, even my history with Keenan so it all made sense.

Maya's car keys hung on the fish-shaped hook in the kitchen, so I grabbed them, pressing the set into my palm. I hoped driving was part of what Dr. Soares had referred to as my semantic memory and I wouldn't end up in a ditch. Now was the time to find out.

As I reached the front door, I doubled back to the kitchen. I took a couple of twenties from Maya's wallet, wrote an *I Owe You* note and popped it inside before deciding to scribble another message to leave on the table in case Maya woke up to find the house empty.

Gone out for a drive. Back soon. Don't worry.

Not quite satisfied, I underlined the last two words three times and added four exclamation marks to convey the message properly.

The air outside was cool with a hint of a salty breeze, and I hurried to the car, glancing over my shoulder as if I were a teenager whose parents might bust me as soon as I turned on the engine. I headed out of the driveway, enjoying the sudden sense of control, the certainty I knew what I was doing and the freedom that came with it. I accelerated up the street and glanced at Keenan's house, where the lights were off, and no car was parked outside. I kept going, taking my time as I got into town, looking around for nighttime clues or hints, places I'd been or people I knew—anything I might recall from the years I'd spent here. Still, nothing.

Maya had mentioned how Newdale's population grew over the summer months, filled with campers, beachgoers and other tourists passing through. The balmy evening had kept the masses outside, many of the bars and restaurant terraces still at least half-full, the quiet din of late-night chatter filling the air.

I recognized the turnoff to Dr. Adler's office. If it hadn't been so late and he wasn't on vacation, maybe I'd have considered stopping by for someone to talk to, although I knew he'd reiterate Dr. Soares's statement about there being no magic pill. "Give yourself time to heal," he'd say. "Be patient." Fine, but how much bloody time and patience was I supposed to have?

I kept going, past Drift and the few other stores, coffee shops and restaurants, and farther still. It was the first time since I'd arrived that I'd explored this side of town and, with the confidence in my abilities bolstered, I kept going. I passed a bar and grill called the Place Down the Road, and a blue neon sign above the barn-style door flickered sporadically, proclaiming it to be open. It looked almost full inside, and I craned my neck to see the terrace on the side, which was lit up with twinkling fairy lights, and looked just as crowded. The smell of fish and chips wafted through the air, making my stomach rumble.

I nabbed a free parking spot a little farther down and doubled back on foot, not yet certain I could face that much hubbub. When I got a little closer, I looked across the street and saw one of the only people I recognized—Lily. She sat on a bench alone, her head bent. As I looked at her, she lifted her chin, and when she saw me her mouth dropped open. She slowly raised her hand in a tentative wave, and when I returned the gesture, she smiled.

Hoping my feet wouldn't betray me and make me trip, I crossed the road and walked up to her, the warmth of a blush creeping over my face. Once again, I felt as if I were a teenager—

although I had no recollection of what I'd been like, but if my dry mouth and the way my stomach had turned itself into knots were anything to go by, I must've been an awkward, tongue-tied fool.

"Hi," I muttered when I got there, before trying again. "Hello, Lily."

Her face lit up, a small dimple forming on her left cheek. "Couldn't sleep, either?" she said, and I shook my head. "Are you and Maya out for a walk, too?"

"No, it's just me."

"Oh, well, uh, do you want to…?" She gestured to the empty spot next to her.

I sat down and the silence settled between us. I wasn't sure how to act. This was a woman I'd cared for, maybe loved, even. We'd no doubt been together countless times, yet, here I was, searching for something to say. I stole a sideways glance at her. She'd swept her hair into a loose ponytail, which had come a little undone, a few soft strands framing her face, reaching down to her neck. Her deep blue eyes, straight nose and high-set cheekbones—each feature beautiful in its own right—combined, made her stunning.

She turned her head, and when she caught my stalker-in-the-headlights gaze, she laughed. "You're staring. Stop it or you'll make me feel *really* self-conscious."

I pulled a face, relieved she'd been the one to break the tension. "I'm glad you're still in town. I was worried you might leave before I got to see you again."

She looked away, her face turning serious. "I thought about it. Leaving, I mean."

"Did you?"

"Yeah… I'm confused. I'm angry. And it's all so…*weird*."

"I'm not sure the word is strong enough."

"Let me know when you come up with a better one."

I smiled. "But…you decided to stay. Why?"

She took a deep breath before counting on her fingers. "Be-

cause I have questions, because I want to help, but most of all...
because—" she shook her head "—because I need to know how
much I still care about you." Her eyes met mine, deep and intense. "I can't believe I found you. Or that you're alive. My life
has been hell."

"I'm not even going to pretend to understand," I whispered,
almost reaching for her hand. "I keep reminding myself I'm not
the only one trying to figure it out, but I owe you whatever
explanation I can give." After taking a deep breath, I told her
about the beach and the trailer, and what had happened since I'd
got to Newdale. She sat, nodding and listening, taking in every
word. The more I talked, the more I realized something about
her presence seemed to have a calming effect on me, making my
pulse rate and breathing slow down for the first time in days.

"I get you have amnesia," she said when I'd finished. "I get
you don't remember me. I mean, I don't *understand* but...you
know. What I don't get is why you lied about who you are."

"I wish I knew," I said. "I honestly wish I had all the answers
we're looking for... After we saw you in the street earlier, Maya
told me how you found me with an old Facebook photo."

"*After* you saw me in the street?" Lily said, her eyebrows darting upward. "She didn't tell you before?"

"She didn't connect the dots," I said.

Lily looked like she was going to argue the point but instead
she paused and changed the subject. I listened as she talked
about her trip to Newdale, took in how she gesticulated with
her hands for emphasis, tucked the same lock of stray hair behind her ear, her heart-pendant bracelet twinkling in the moonlight as she did so.

"I need to ask you something," she said. "And I want you to
be honest. Promise?"

"I promise I will if I know the answer."

"That's fair... All right, here goes. You need time to work

things through, so do you think it's a good idea for me to stay in Newdale?"

I looked at her and hesitated, not because I didn't know what to say, but because I wanted it to be the answer she was hoping for. Maya had said Lily seemed glad I was out when she came to the house this afternoon. Did that mean she was wishing for a get-out-of-jail-free card, a way to absolve herself from our relationship so she could go home, put all this behind her and continue with a less complicated life? Or did she want to stay?

"Ash? Can you please tell me what you think?"

"Selfishly, yes, I want you to stay. Unless you don't want to, or they need you at work—"

"Actually, I got laid off earlier." She shrugged. "Life can really suck, can't it?"

"Was it because of me? Because you came here?"

Lily gave a dismissive wave. "Mike knew—" She must've caught my clueless expression because she stopped and said, "Mike's my boss. I work at a garage. The place folded."

"I'm sorry to hear that."

"Two weeks ago, I'd have been devastated. Now, the only thing that matters—" she gave a small shrug "—is you."

I was about to answer when a man across the street caught my eye. Tall, wide, red hair. Keenan. Jesus Christ, the last thing I needed was for a fight to erupt on the genteel streets of Newdale, or for Lily to see me get into fisticuffs with my neighbor. Thankfully, he disappeared into the bar, but when I turned my head, Lily was eyeing me, frowning.

"Someone you know?" she said.

"A guy called Keenan and let's just say he's not my number one fan."

"*That's* Keenan?"

"You know him?"

"*Of* him. I met his sister Fiona. She runs the motel where

I'm staying. The Harbor Inn? She mentioned you two don't get along. Something to do with their sister?"

"Celine," I said, and when she nodded, I let out a breath. I must have told Lily about my high-school sweetheart, which had to count for something, surely, but then she continued.

"Fiona said it's also because he dated your girlfriend Kate before you got together." She lowered her voice. "You never mentioned them in all the time I've known you. Just like you never told me about Maya, either."

My head felt as if I'd stuck it inside a wind tunnel, all the words flying past at warp speed, none of them making it into my brain properly. I tried to process what she'd said. The music from the bar seemed to have increased tenfold, my messed-up brain incapable of separating or dealing with all the sounds and words and meanings. Lily must have made a mistake. Maybe she'd forgotten I'd ever mentioned Celine or Kate. Besides, wasn't it normal for most people to keep relatively schtum about their exes? Except Celine had left, Kate had died, Keenan blamed me for both and I'd told Lily exactly zip about it all. And all that on top of never mentioning my stepsister. What the hell was wrong with me?

I felt my pulse racing in the side of my head, blood thundering in my ears. I'd gone out searching for answers but ended up worse off than before. It was late, I was tired, exhausted, actually, as the entire weight of the situation sank onto my shoulders like a couple of giant boulders.

"I should go," I said.

"Shit. I've upset you—"

"No, it's fine, but I should get back. Get some rest."

"Can I still come by tomorrow morning?" she said quickly. "If you need to rearrange you can call the motel, or I gave Maya my number…"

Her voice sounded desperate, but as rude and cowardly as it was, I didn't have the mental bandwidth to deal with it. That wasn't the only thing, I realized, as I stood up. Another reason for leaving Lily there on the bench was because I didn't want to have one of my angry outbursts in front of her. I didn't want to disappoint her. "Of course. I'll see you then," I said, giving her a brief wave before walking away, back to the relative safety of the car.

The drive home took a lot less time than it should have, and when I got back to the house, I prepared to creep back upstairs. Impossible, because the lights were on, and when I got close enough to see in through the windows, I spotted Maya pacing the living room. As soon as I opened the front door, her hands went to her hips.

"Where the hell were you?" she shouted.

"I went for a drive. There's a note in—"

"I saw. What the hell, Ash? I thought you'd crashed the car, or—"

"Obviously, I didn't. I saw Lily and we had a chat."

Her mouth was still open, but her words seemed to have dried up. She walked over, yanked the car keys from my hand and said, "And what did you two *chat* about?"

"I don't believe that's any of your business," I said, about to brush past her and go upstairs but she grabbed hold of my arm.

"Of course it is. I want to make sure you're safe."

Once again, Maya had pushed that invisible button, making all my anger rush up my throat in one go. "Jesus Christ, stop treating me like a child, would you?" I shouted, removing her hand as my voice bounced off the walls. "Stop breathing down my neck all the time. Just back off, will you?"

"But—"

"*No.* That's enough." I forced my rage back inside myself, moved toward the stairs before I said or did something I might regret. I threw a glance at her over my shoulder, expecting to see a look of hurt and confusion on her face, and which I'd apologize for in the morning. Except there was none. Her expression was one of outright fury far greater than mine. She stood in the middle of the hallway, car keys clutched tight to her chest, knuckles white, her eyes like daggers, piercing my skin all the way to the bone.

23
LILY

I'd been in my motel room for two hours, walking back and forth, left to right, right to left, wearing down the carpet as I went over the events of the evening. My visit with Maya had made me question if my leaving town would be better for Ash, and myself, but Dr. Adler had said it might help, and Ash wanted me to stay. As I thought about how Maya hadn't told him I'd called, two details hit me, and made me stop pacing. First, during our initial conversation I'd told Maya I was looking for a man called Jack Smith, and second, despite his amnesia, Ash had known he'd traveled up from Maryland. Surely, he'd have told Maya that when he'd arrived here the day after he went missing, which would mean she'd have known *before* I'd called and asked about the photo.

I pulled out my phone, plugged in *Jack Smith Maryland* and hit Search. The first six results were the articles about him going missing off the coast, the next two detailing how the search had been abandoned. Not only did the links include the video of me pleading for help on the beach, but also photos of him. How could Maya not have seen them? How had she not made the connection? Hadn't she been curious after I'd called? Ash was right, she must have been overwhelmed by his return, I decided, because otherwise it would imply she didn't want me to find him and that made no sense at all. She clearly cared for him. She wouldn't do anything to hurt him. There had to be another reason, although whatever it was, nothing yet explained why Ash had never mentioned Maya once in eighteen months. Hadn't he been in touch with her at all while he'd lived in Brookmount? That seemed so odd—then again, I couldn't remember the last time I'd spoken to my brother, and Quentin seemed to prefer pretending I didn't exist.

A tingle crept down my spine as I wondered again why he'd been living his life as Jack Smith—such a common name—off the radar, quite possibly without a bank account and definitely without a credit card or a car, and with a fake ID. He had cash stowed away in his apartment, and the place had been ransacked. Heron and Stevens thought he was involved in gambling trouble, and while they suspected he'd been playing for a while, I wondered if it was a more recent thing and had something to do with the engagement ring brochure I'd found. All that aside, could it be he hadn't wanted to be found by Maya? Had he been hiding from her all this time? I grimaced at the ridiculousness of it, but the thought kept bugging me, and as I was about to go around in circles again, someone knocked on the door.

"Who is it?" I called out, wondering if I'd disturbed the people in the next room with my incessant pacing, until I heard a familiar voice.

"It's Ash."

I almost tripped over the corner of the bed in my haste to get to the door, which I tried to yank open only to find I'd put on the chain. "Crap," I muttered, my heart speeding up as I fumbled with the lock, my fingers refusing to do as they were told. When I finally got the damn door open, Ash stood in front of me, his face pale.

"Can I come in?" he said, the remaining color sliding from his face. "Please?"

I took a step closer and put my arms around him, pulling him toward me and inside the room at the same time. With the length of his body pressed against mine, and his arms wrapped around me tight, I took in the scent and heat of his skin. It was almost too much—an emotional tsunami I'd fought hard to keep back, all of it spilling forth now, no matter how hard I tried to stop it.

"I have to ask you something," he murmured as he put his hands on my shoulders, gently creating a little distance between us, which I immediately wanted to close again.

"Anything. Whatever you need." I watched him hesitate, run a hand through his hair as he turned away, shaking his head. "What's wrong? Has something happened?"

"No, it's not...it's..." He turned to face me, his eyes pleading. "Have I... Did I... Christ. Okay, I'm just going to say it." He took a breath and held it, eyes closed. With an emphatic *whoosh* he exhaled, looked at me and said, "Have I ever hurt you?"

"Hurt me? I mean, we've argued a few times..."

"I mean really hurt you. Verbally, or...physically?" He winced. "Did I ever lay a hand on you? Have I ever hit you?"

"God, *no*. Absolutely not. Why would you think that?"

"Because...because I've been so angry all the time, and I don't know what to do with it, how to handle it. Maya says it's probably because of the amnesia, the stress of the situation."

"That seems like a fair observation," I offered gently, but when I looked at him I realized he didn't quite believe it. He seemed terrified. Frightened of himself and what he was capable of. Scared he might hurt someone, and...

"Hold on," I said. "Does this have something to do with Kate and Celine?"

"Yes," he whispered. "Why didn't I tell you about them when we met? Why not mention it, unless… What if…what if I hurt them somehow? What if that's why I abandoned everyone here?"

"I don't believe that for one second." The certainty in my voice surprised me until I realized it was exactly how I felt. Deep down, I knew he'd never do such a thing. "Were you in contact with Maya when you lived in Maryland?" I asked, and when he shook his head, I led him to the chair by the desk, where I made him sit down before I took a spot on the edge of the bed, our knees almost touching. "What if you left Newdale because you were overcome with grief? Maybe you needed to get away to stay sane."

"That doesn't explain cutting ties with Maya or my fake name."

I hesitated, trying to decide if I should tell him the theory I'd dismissed about his stepsister's jealousy, but what was there to tell? I risked alienating him from her, and from me—and I wanted neither. "I don't know what to make of that, Ash. I wish I could help, but for what it's worth, I can't imagine you ever hurting anyone."

A beat passed, and another. I thought he might get up and leave again, but he gently reached for my hand, and said, "Tell me what I was like when we met."

Despite everything, I couldn't help but smile. "Very clumsy."

His shoulders dropped away from his ears as he pulled a bemused face. "Clumsy, huh? In that case, maybe it's a good thing I have zero recollection of making a total arse of myself."

"You didn't," I said, grinning some more as I thought about the moment I'd first set eyes on him. "In fact, you were extremely gentlemanly."

It had been a Thursday evening, the week after Thanksgiving. Monica, one of my colleagues from Beach Body, had in-

sisted on dragging me out for a drink when I'd let slip I hadn't
set foot in a bar since the summer, and it had been twice as long
since I'd been on a date.

"That's it, sweets," she'd scoffed in her thick, Texan drawl.
"I'm takin' y'all out tonight."

I'd laughed when we'd arrived at what she described as her
favorite place on earth. The Charlie Horse was an old, dusty
shack, a relic plucked straight from a Spaghetti Western. As we
sat down, I half expected a young Clint Eastwood to stride across
the beer-stained, wooden floors and demand a shot of whiskey
from the waistcoat-clad barman. Instead, Monica, who'd been
named salesperson of the month every month for the past year,
flashed me a smile as she pushed a pint of beer toward me.

"Drink up, now. There's plenty more where that came from."
We clinked glasses and she leaned in. "Cute guy at the bar's been
checking you out."

I'd noticed him, too. Tall, dark hair, a smile that made me
want to get up, walk over and ask him for his number. If I had
the guts. As I sneaked a glance at the stranger, he looked at me
and grinned. Not long after, I made my excuses and went to
the bathroom, and when I got back, Monica was surrounded
by three guys, arguing the merits of standard transmission vs.
paddle shift, and which was better for street racing, all of them
googly-eyed at her expertise.

"She's quite the gearhead, isn't she?" It was the guy who'd
been standing at the bar, his eyes twinkling as his lips curved
into another smile that drew me in, his English accent charming and sexy as hell.

"Would you believe it if I told you she was born in a car?" I
said with a laugh.

"You're pulling my leg."

"It's true, I swear."

He smiled again, a lock of hair falling over his left eye, making me want to reach out and brush it away, but he held out a hand. "I'm Jack," he said.

"Lily," I answered, and before I could say anything else, someone bumped Jack from behind and half a pint of cold beer sloshed straight down my shirt.

"Oh, fuck it," he said, which made me burst out laughing because with his accent, he made the word sound so formal and posh, it was downright delightful. "I'm so sorry," he continued as he reached for a few napkins and pressed them into my hand. "Here, take these."

I dabbed at my sopping shirt as he offered his apologies again and I waved him off with an *it's fine* gesture. "I never liked this shirt much anyway."

His turn to laugh, and, amid another thousand apologies, he offered to buy me a drink. I decided on a Diet Coke, and when he returned, we squeezed into the space at Monica's table, where she was still deep in conversation about her near-death experience with nitrous oxide. As Jack and I chatted, I barely noticed the first hour go by, didn't pay attention to the second one, either. That was how easily the conversation flowed between us, as if we'd known each other for years, and there was no way I'd end the evening without getting his number. And I had, but it was his house number because I'd gone home with him, and we'd been together since.

Ash looked at me now, his eyebrows knitting together. "Beach…body…" he whispered.

"That's the name of the garage," I said. "You remember."

"'We'll give you a better body at Beach Body.'" He hummed the tune of the ancient advertisement Mike had made for radio years ago, and never updated, and I let out a laugh as I covered my eyes with one hand.

"That's not my handiwork. We used to make fun of that damn thing all the time. This is amazing, Ash. I can't believe that came back."

"Neither can I," he said. "I wish there was more, things about *us*."

I hesitated for a moment. "We could go back to Maryland, see if it helps."

He shook his head, his expression changing to one of concern. "No, I can't. I promised Maya I wouldn't leave again. Besides, a large part of my memories is here. I have to try to find those first. Figure out who I am, not to mention why I left. I owe it to Maya, and to myself, and you."

"Then let me help," I said. "Because I'm not giving up on you."

"I lied, gave you a false name, and you still want to help me. Why?"

"Because I want you to find the person you truly are." I looked at him, the doubts I'd had lessening. "You must've had a good reason for what you did. Let me help you figure out what it was. I know you. You're not a bad person. You're incapable of hurting anyone."

"Are you sure?"

"A thousand percent." I took in the contours of his face, the edge of his chin, the amber in his eyes. My belly fluttered. "I'm still angry about what happened but...I fell in love with you the second I first saw you, and I can't let you go through this alone."

"Lily..." he whispered. "I don't know what I can offer in return."

"I know, and I understand, but it doesn't change how I feel."

The air between us shifted and crackled. It would've been so easy to give in to my longing, so simple to put my arms around him, kiss, touch and seduce him under the pretext of trying to get him to remember me, *us*. My body ached for his, and I wanted him, no question, but it wouldn't be right. It would make me unscrupulous, something I promised myself I'd never be again after I got out of prison. I moved my leg so it no longer touched his.

"I should go," Ash said. "Let you get some sleep."

"I'm not tired," I said, shaking my head, thinking I'd never been more awake. While my conscience wouldn't let me seduce him, there was nothing wrong with me spending as much time with him as I could. "I have some wine in the fridge. Unless you're driving?"

"I walked."

"That far at this time of night? Are you nuts?"

Ash let out a laugh. "There's a shortcut and I've got long legs, and to be honest, this is the first night in a while I've felt alive. Honest to God, sometimes it's been as if I was drowning." When he caught my expression, he closed his eyes. "Christ, that was as subtle as a brick, wasn't it?"

I burst out laughing and Ash joined in, the tension evaporating. As I collapsed on the bed in a ridiculous, giggling heap, for that short moment, it was us again—Jack and Lily—and I wanted it to last forever. I fished the bottle from the fridge and retrieved a couple of paper cups, and as I filled them both, Ash sat down next to me on the bed, which seemed both strange and intimate at the same time.

"A toast," I said. "To new beginnings."

"To new beginnings," Ash replied, taking a sip.

The wine flowed as easily as the conversation, and not long after, we both stretched out. Ash put his hands under his head, listening intently as I described our lives in Brookmount, how he'd worked as a carpenter, and my job at the garage. I talked and talked, told him everything about my history, my relationship with my parents and brother, but I still couldn't bring myself to share the sordid details about Dominic Martel, or my conviction. *Not yet*, I thought. *Don't give him a reason to leave.*

"But we weren't living together in Brookmount?" he said when I took a breath.

"Uh, no..."

"Why the hesitation?"

"Well, I went through your things because your landlord is

selling the place, which reminds me—" I sat up and reached for my keys "—I put it all in storage. This is the key. You should have it now. I'll give you their details and contact them to make sure they have your name in case you want to..." I waved a hand, not daring to finish the thought of him getting his stuff without me because our lives were no longer entwined.

Ash slipped the key in his pocket. "Thank you for doing that. And thank you for not giving up on me, for coming all the way to Newdale. It means...a lot."

I glanced at him and smiled. "You're welcome."

"So...back to our living arrangements..."

"Ah...well, at the risk of being completely wrong—"

"Which I wouldn't remember anyway."

"Har, har. I see you haven't lost your funny bone. Anyway, I found a gift you'd addressed to me."

"Please tell me I got you something good."

I laughed. "It was a key to your place. I think you were going to ask me to move in."

Ash's smile faded, the jovial banter popping like soap bubbles around our heads. "I wish I could remember *that*. Seriously, why the hell did I go swimming that evening? Who does that, anyway? Head into the ocean when a storm's coming? What an idiot."

"You swam almost every night, it wasn't unusual, but there's something else I have to tell you." I hesitated, didn't want him to think badly of me for going through his stuff even though I'd had little choice. There were so many things between us now, so much I wanted to say but to which I wasn't sure how he'd react.

"What is it?" He rolled onto his side, rested his chin in his palm.

"I found money, in a cookie tin in your kitchen. Over two thousand dollars."

He gave a low whistle. "Two grand? My emergency funds, maybe?"

I wanted to ask him if he knew a guy called Jason Whitmarsh, or if he'd ever gambled for money, but I couldn't, not tonight. I shrugged. "I'm not sure, but I used some of it to come here. I'll pay you back as soon as I can, I promise."

"I'd like you to keep the money," he said. "All of it."

"What? No way—"

"Yes, way. It's the least I can do for messing up your life."

"You don't have to pay me, it's—" I waved a hand "—weird."

He grunted and closed his eyes, taking a while before opening them again. "Keep the cash, okay? I don't want it back." He rubbed his eyes, pushed himself off the bed and stood up, swaying gently. "I'm wrecked. What was I saying about feeling alive? I should head back."

"You're not walking home now, are you? You can barely stand."

He stared down at me, blinked hard three times. "I'll get a cab or something."

"Stay here." The words tumbled out before I could stop them or had time to reconsider. I reached for his hand and pulled him back onto the bed, and as he stretched out again, I rested my head on his shoulder. I wanted to press my lips against his, feel his hands around my waist as I let mine slip underneath his shirt. His muscles would tense beneath my touch, as they always did when I ran my fingers over his flat stomach, and when I put my hand on his belt, he'd let out a low sigh. Working hard to stop myself from doing something he might regret, I raised my head, observing his soft lips, the intensity of his eyes. Part of me—all of me—wanted to make love to him, once, twice, three times in the hope the act would unlock the memories of us.

The voice of reason in the back of my mind chided me, insisting again if, or when, something happened between us, it had to be for the right reasons, but still, I couldn't bear for him to leave. "Stay," I whispered, putting my head down as he wrapped his arms around me, pulling me close. "Let's stay here for the night."

"It's a deal," he murmured, and within minutes, both of us were fast asleep.

24
MAYA

All was silent in Ash's room when I got up early the next morning. I forfeited having breakfast because I was still too angry with him to eat, and made a thermos of coffee as quietly as possible before heading to the garage to work.

Lily wasn't due to arrive for another two hours. I'd initially felt confident I'd done a good job of getting her to question who Ash really was and hoped she might leave town immediately because of it. Just in case, I'd come up with another plan, and before handing Ash the beer yesterday, I'd poured the rest of my bottle of Benadryl into it. With that amount of medicine, he'd sleep late, and when Lily arrived, I'd tell her he'd changed his mind and didn't want to see her again after all. I'd tell him the same thing about her. But then he'd slipped out, and after some light detective work, I figured out he'd poured his drink into my potted plant. Almost wishing I'd dosed him with my clonazepam instead, I knew I'd now have to improvise and find another way to get Lily to leave.

I still couldn't believe Ash had sneaked out like that, and then had the audacity to accuse me of suffocating him, when the only thing I'd done was care for him since he'd come home, put him first, as I always had. He deserved the iciest of shoulders for his actions, plus a reminder of how much he needed me. I'd make him grovel a little, but I already knew I'd forgive him. He wasn't himself, and I understood why, but I wouldn't have him hurt me like that again.

I unlocked the garage and went inside, taking in the familiar scent of polish and sawdust, all of it steadying my nerves. Most of the wood I'd found the last time I'd gone to the beach was twisted and gnarled, things I'd turn into fruit bowls and key rings, maybe a small sculpture or two, and a few of the pieces were ideal for candleholders. I'd transform another log by cutting it into discs and burning pictures of pine cones and trees into them. Once polished, they'd become sets of coasters, which always did well at Drift. Tourists were willing to pay as much as fifty bucks for a set, half of which Barbara gave me, and they took no time at all to make. My sculptures could fetch as much as four hundred, depending on size and intricacy. One of them, an eagle, had gone for double, and if I started selling online, I'd get all the cash.

Ash had always marveled at my ability to see things in the raw pieces others couldn't, how I transformed what would have otherwise been ignored detritus into works of art. He'd called it a gift, boasted about my skills to anyone who'd stand still long enough to listen. For a few months after he'd left, I hadn't worked on my art at all, and then it had become sporadic at best. I'd start a piece and throw it away only to try again. Things had improved over time, but since Ash's return, I saw the potential in every piece of wood, and felt the rush of excitement I'd thought might be lost forever. Ash had brought my magic touch back home with him. It was just another reason why I had to make sure he stayed in Newdale, and why Lily had to leave.

I lined up my tools and protective gear, deciding I'd push Ash to start the garage renovation. I'd insist he work slowly, but knowing him, he wouldn't. Either way, it would keep him close while I was working on my pieces. We'd spend more time together, not to mention the project would be a distraction from Lily's arrival and, hopefully, her equally swift departure.

I was about to switch on my band saw when I heard a car pull up in the driveway. Lily couldn't possibly be coming over this early. Maybe it was Keenan, drunk and on the prowl for more trouble. I wouldn't have put it past either of them, but whichever one it was, I'd had enough. They needed to get out of our lives.

I stomped to the garage door, ready to tell whomever to turn around and leave, but when I got there and pulled it open, my feet rooted themselves to the ground.

It *was* Lily. She stood in my driveway with another huge, sugar-sweet smile on her tanned face, and Ash was with her. With *her*. Not upstairs in the house where he was supposed to be. He was in the driveway, staring at Lily, neither of them noticing me behind them, openmouthed and in the doorway. How the *fuck* had this happened, and when? I'd hidden the car keys in my closet after he'd gone to bed. Besides, my Nissan was still where Ash had dumped it when he'd come home from his late-night escapade.

Transfixed, unable to move, I watched as he whispered something to her. She touched his chest and put her head back, laughing. The intimacy between them. The proximity. The way he stared at her. I knew that look, had seen it a thousand times. First with Celine, and again when he'd been with Kate. Entranced, mesmerized, whatever you wanted to call it, but I knew what it meant. She'd got to him. And he'd let her.

How could things be moving so quickly when until yesterday he hadn't remembered Lily existed? I knew the brain and heart could do strange things at times, and not always in conjunction, but she'd ensnared him overnight. The burning fury bubbling at the surface made me choke. He must have sneaked out again after our argument. They'd spent the night together, no question, but had he *been* with her? Ash had never seemed interested in one-night stands, had once told me he needed to feel a connection with someone to sleep with them. Did he feel something for Lily? Was he going to leave me again? Go back to Brookmount with *her*?

I wanted to shout at her to leave, scream at Ash, remind him *I'd* been the one whose number he'd remembered when he woke up on the beach, I'd been the one he'd called. Even through my rage I knew it wouldn't work. That kind of behavior would rally them against me. I had to be smart. Whatever was going on between them had only just begun, and Lily had instigated it. Ash was vulnerable. She'd taken advantage of him, and if the encounters between her and me thus far had been battles only I had known were being fought, as of now I'd wage an outright war. Wars meant collateral damage. But that was on Lily. It was *her* fault. She was the one who'd come here. She was the one who wouldn't leave things alone. Anything and everything I did would be her responsibility.

Ash and Lily disappeared into the house, walking close together, still chatting, not even throwing a backward glance. I counted slowly under my breath, forcing myself to get to at least thirty and to keep going until I couldn't stand it any longer. At fifty-two I strode to the house, repeating I had to keep my cool. Fake it 'til you make it. This was a long-term play.

I opened the front door and walked into the kitchen with a well-honed smile slinking across my face. Ash had his back turned and was in the process of digging two mugs out of the cupboard while Lily flicked on the kettle as if she'd been here, in *my* house, a million times. She must have heard me come in, and when she turned around, had a startled look on her face.

"Maya," she said, her grimace easing as she took in my relaxed expression. "We, uh—"

"I spent the night at the Harbor Inn," Ash said, matter-of-fact.

"I didn't hear you leave again. I thought you were still asleep." I congratulated myself on how calm I sounded, not aloof or indifferent, but curious. "Ash, can I talk to you?" I gestured to the hallway and as he followed me, I decided to change tack. Making him grovel with Lily around wasn't going to work. "About our argument last night," I said, bowing my head. "I was worried when I got up and you weren't home. I was scared."

"I understand," Ash said. "I shouldn't have shouted at you like that, it was wrong."

"So, we're okay?" I said, looking up at him.

"We're fine, I promise." He glanced toward Lily, smiling. And just like that, as he headed back into the kitchen with me following behind, I became the proverbial third wheel, exactly as I had when he'd started hanging out with Celine and then Kate. More anger bubbled beneath my cheery facade, threatening to crack it clean down the middle.

"I'll get back to work in a minute and I have a shift at the Cliff's Head later," I said, trying not to grit my teeth. "What are you doing, Ash?"

"Not sure," he said. "Out for a drive or a walk somewhere. Maybe check out the beach."

"The beach?" I said. "Considering what happened?"

"Yeah. I can't explain it, but Lily and I got talking and I realized I miss the water. Anyway, we haven't decided."

We. I needed to intervene before they made themselves a dainty little picnic and skipped toward sandy shores and blue skies as if we were in the middle of a vomit-inducing romantic comedy. "Oh, well, actually I was hoping you'd start working on the garage."

"We're building a proper storage room for Maya," Ash explained, as if Lily needed to know. She didn't, not when I'd make sure she wouldn't be sticking around town long enough to see its completion. "And we're adding a shower."

"Can I help?" she said, her voice eager and bubbly, like an annoying puppy bounding around, looking for attention. "I used to when you worked on the kitchens."

He opened his mouth to say something but when he looked at her, he frowned. He crossed his arms, a sly smile spreading over his face. "Only if you don't run a paint roller over my back again."

Lily stared at him, her lips forming a perfect O in surprise. "You remember that?"

"It's real? It happened?"

"Yes! I couldn't help it. You'd taken your shirt off. It was the perfect—"

"Blank canvas," they said at the same time. A beat passed before they burst out laughing, both of them babbling how exciting it was he'd remembered something new, something so recent, because the paint-meets-naked-back incident had been only a few months ago. I stared at him. His anger at me from the night before had long melted away, his happiness fully restored. By *her*.

"I'd love your help." Ash was beaming now. "We can get the supplies and—"

"You shouldn't trouble yourself with that stuff, Lily," I said, needing to remind them of my existence.

"Oh, no, it's no trouble," she said, smiling. "I'd be happy to help, make sure he doesn't do too much, too soon. He told me about the concussion. I know he has to be careful."

"Great, I'll show you the plans." Ash turned to her, the bubble of intimacy enveloping them again. I had to get out of there before I threw something. As I muttered about seeing them later and left the kitchen, the air behind me shifted. The relief they felt over my departure was palpable and so thick, I could have served them a slice of it for breakfast. They didn't want me here.

My heart pinched as I pretended to go upstairs before tiptoeing back, getting close enough to hear.

"See? There was nothing to worry about," Ash said. "She's overprotective, that's all. I'm sure once you get to know her, you'll really like her. Anyway, about the garage..."

As their conversation changed to the project and I crept away, I heard a soft *ding* coming from Lily's bag in the hallway. I leaned toward the kitchen, but she and Ash were talking about framing and plasterboard, and she hadn't heard her phone. I bent over and retrieved it, read the message twinkling on the screen from someone called Sam.

How are things? How's Jack?

I slid my finger across the phone, tut-tutting at Lily's lack of proper security as the screen lit up with apps. It quickly became clear she and Sam were nothing more than friends, which was a shame because if she'd been seeing someone else, it would've helped me. I scrolled up, reading through more of her messages, did a double take when I found one from her boss. He apologized for having to let her go, and in another, told her he'd have to delay paying her two weeks' severance. A third text was from her landlord, saying she could have an extra week to pay this month's rent. Lily had replied she'd get the money as quickly as possible, but when the landlord had inquired the day before if a payment was looking likely, Lily had left the message unanswered.

I flicked through her photos, the green-eyed monster inside me surging to epic proportions as I saw picture after picture of Lily and Ash. At the beach, a bar, a movie. At a restaurant, ax-throwing, celebrating his birthday. It seemed wherever they went, whatever they did, there was a picture of the two of them smooshed together, her looking up at him with those fucking puppy eyes. It made me sick to think of them spending all this time together when I was here at the house, fretting over Ash's well-being. This was her fault. He might have left Newdale, but she'd kept him in Maryland. If it hadn't been for her, he'd have come home.

Standing in the hallway clutching her cell, it took every ounce of willpower I had to not delete her photos or hurl the thing on the floor and watch it shatter into a hundred satisfying pieces. Fingers trembling, I tucked the device into her bag and went back to the garage, where I sat on my bench, picked up a knife and started cutting into a piece of wood, slicing deeper and deeper. As I worked, I thought about the fact Lily had lost her job. It was a strike against me; she no longer had time constraints forcing her back to Maryland. However, from her boss and landlord's messages it sounded as if she was broke. A point in my favor, something I could, and would, use. A plan of how to get rid of Lily formed in my mind. Her Newdale vacation wouldn't last. With what I had in mind she'd be gone within the week.

25

ASH

Before Maya left for her shift at the Cliff's Head, she came into the living room and hugged me first before giving Lily a hesitant embrace. "It's so nice to see you happy," she said to me, and I was glad we'd moved past last night's argument. Given the circumstances, I hadn't known what to expect when I'd shown up at the house with Lily. I knew Maya felt awkward about her arrival in town, and although I sympathized, I'd decided she'd just have to deal with it.

As I grabbed a fresh pair of jeans and a T-shirt upstairs, the thought of Lily being here in the house with me made me smile, and I headed back to the kitchen, where she stood by the sink with her back to me, staring out the window.

When I approached, she turned around and the light streaming in behind her lit up her hair like a golden halo. Man, she was beautiful. My belly clenched, which was ridiculous considering we'd dated for ages, but as heat rose to my cheeks I crossed over to the cupboard and pretended to look for something so she couldn't see my face. Spending the night with her had felt relaxed and comfortable, like being with a good friend I happened to also find very attractive. I'd wanted to kiss her on more than one occasion, but what would she have thought if a man who claimed to have no memory of her tried to get it on anyway? No clue how good or bad I'd been at relationships before, but either way, it would've been a crass move. Thankfully, Lily interrupted my thoughts of what kissing her might have led to by asking if I wanted to have a look at the garage so we could finalize the plans, and we headed outside.

It didn't take long for us to move Maya's workbench, band saw, sander and nail gun out of the way so I could get a proper look at the framing Maya had worked on a while ago. She told me she'd made a start after I'd left only to abandon the project midway, her motivation having disappeared. It gave me another reason to do this for her because I sensed my departure had affected her even more deeply than she cared to admit. I grabbed my tape measure and some chalk I'd found, ready to mark the outline for the new shower pan. As I looked at the cracked tiles an image hit me. Maya laughing at the old pattern as she removed them and threw them into a pile in the corner. I pressed my eyes shut. I'd worked in here with my father, not her. It had to be another false memory, another stupid confabulation, just like when I'd believed he'd loved soccer.

"What's this?" Lily said, pulling me out of the thoughts.

When I looked over, I saw her pointing to the floor where she'd rolled up the tatty orange rug I'd tripped over the other day. I frowned at the sight of a trapdoor in the floor. It was about three feet wide and had a large, rusty metal ring.

"Let's find out," I said, pulling the door open to reveal a thin wooden ladder propped against the top frame, and which disappeared into the darkness.

Lily pressed the switch on the inside of the trapdoor and within an instant the faint glow of a light bulb emanated from below. "I'm going to check it out," she said, her face full of excitement, and she clambered onto the rickety ladder with me following behind.

What turned out to be a kind of storage room underneath the garage was a little over a hundred square feet, and apart from a few dusty shelves, a broken lamp and some empty beer bottles in the corner, there was nothing inside.

"Well, this is a bit disappointing," Lily said. "I was hoping for treasure or an expensive wine collection or something. Oh, well..." She made her way up the first couple of rungs of the ladder before looking at me over her shoulder. "Are you coming? Ash...?"

Her voice faded away as the scent of the earthy ground filled my nose and lungs, the musty air taking me back to the decrepit house I'd hidden in next to the petrol station, and the flashback I'd had of someone playing hide-and-seek.

"Maya," I whispered. "It was Maya."

"What do you mean?" Lily stood next to me now, her hand on my arm.

"She wanted to play hide-and-seek with me all the time and I'd indulge her, even though I moaned and complained and said I was too old. I used to hide—" I pointed to the corner "—over there, so when she opened the trapdoor she couldn't see me."

"Ash, this is amazing."

"Providing it happened," I said, explaining what the doctors had told me about confabulation and false memories, which Lily had never heard of, either, and finishing with, "That's why I never know if what I'm experiencing is real."

"Do you remember anything else? Maybe I can help?"

"Blueberry pancakes," I said with a smile. "For whatever reason, you remind me of blueberry pancakes."

"From Patti's," she whispered. "It's a café in Brookmount.

We'd get blueberry pancakes whenever we went, or you'd bring them to my place, and we'd eat them in bed."

I scrunched my eyes shut again, trying to force an image, but nothing appeared. "This is almost worse than not remembering anything at all," I said. "Having stuff come back but not knowing if it really happened, having to verify everything with other people, almost having to ask *permission* to allow whatever images to stay in my brain. Jesus, it's so *frustrating*."

"But you've just experienced a few memories in a row, Ash, that's huge, and two of them—the paint and the pancakes—are definitely real. More will come if you give it time, they have to. I know it's stupid to say you should chill out, but…"

As I looked at her, I felt the same sense of calm I'd experienced when we'd sat outside the bar, and again at the motel. "You're right," I said, hoping it was the truth, and headed for the ladder. "How about we go to town and pick up the stuff for the garage? Maybe we'll find a new pancake place, too."

Lily smiled. "You sure know how to show a girl a good time."

An hour later we walked out of the hardware store with some of the supplies we needed, plus an order form for the larger items we couldn't fit in her car, and which would be delivered to the house in the morning. It had been another strange experience, going through the shelves in the store and knowing exactly what I needed, and how to work with it, yet not remembering how I knew. Lily was right. I needed to chill, and with her here, it felt surprisingly easy. Trying to force my brain to work so hard was counterproductive. Dr. Adler had said multiple times I should slow down, and while I knew it would be impossible for me to physically sit still, at least I could give my brain a rest.

"I appreciate your help with everything," I said to Lily as we loaded up the car, "and I know Maya will, too. She's really excited about having the garage done so she can work in there all year. She's hoping to make more sculptures and eventually cut her shifts at the Cliff's Head."

"I'm happy to help. Was Maya always into art? Do you know?"

"Apparently, she was all set to go to the Maine College of Art in Portland, but when my father died, she derailed a little." I didn't want to betray Maya's confidence about what she'd told me, how desperate she'd been, how happy and thankful when I'd given up studying economics, which had apparently been my lifelong dream, and came back here so she wasn't alone. She'd cried when she'd told me how she felt guilty about holding me back, how she thought it could be the reason why I'd left Newdale after all. Me already in my thirties and her not far behind, both of us still living together in the family home. And then I'd gone off on one last night and told her she was suffocating me. Good job, Ash.

Back at the house we unloaded the supplies. "What do you fancy doing now?" I said, hoping Lily wouldn't tell me she wanted to go back to the motel or had other plans.

"I'm happy to check out the beach if you're still game. Only, fair warning, I didn't exactly pack with that kind of trip in mind and I'd imagine it'll be freezing, but I'll go for a dip in my underwear if you will. Unless you think we'll freak out the locals?"

I grinned. "Either way, it's a deal."

We drove with the windows down, the radio playing softly in the background. If I tried hard enough, I could almost pretend it was a normal day, the first one in ages. I glanced at Lily, and when she caught me doing so, smiled broadly.

"You okay?" she said.

Was I okay? Things felt better, somehow. More new and distinctive memories had come back. I'd been able to plan the renovation for the garage without any trouble, put in an order without becoming confused, and now I was spending time with Lily.

"I'm okay," I said, reaching over to hold her hand.

We figured out the general direction of the coast before stopping to ask one of the locals for the nearest recommendation. He sent us to Sandy Point Bridge, where the tide wasn't quite in yet, and the beach a combination of pebbles, sandbanks, mud and grass, but hardly any people. Lily and I walked along the shore for a little while, the water squelching beneath our toes.

"This'll do," she said, unzipping her jeans. "Last one in's a loser." With a whoop she pulled off her shirt and ran to the water shouting something that sounded like, "Towanda!"

I let my gaze wander over her lithe legs, her turquoise boy-shorts and matching bra, her long hair swish-swishing behind her. Everything around me faded, took me back to somewhere in my past. An image of her at a different beach, the sound of her laughing and yelling at me to hurry, except she'd called me Jack. The picture faded only to be replaced by another of us on a squishy blue sofa, watching one of her favorite movies. As the images faded and I came back to reality, I heard Lily calling me again, using my real name.

"Wait," I shouted. "Lily, wait. Hold on."

"What's the matter?" she said, standing calf-deep in the water, her face falling.

"*Towanda,*" I said, wading in, ignoring the frigid temperatures and my anxiety about being back in the ocean. "Towanda," I repeated, softly this time as I touched the bracelet on her wrist, the one with the heart-shaped charm I'd carefully hidden inside a box of chocolates. "I remember this. And the film about those fried tomatoes. I remember...*you.*"

We stared at each other before I pulled her to my chest, held her close as her hands slid up my back, arms looping around my neck. I bent my head toward hers. Our kiss was soft, cautious, and although I didn't want to, I made myself pull away after a few seconds.

"That was wrong," I said. "I shouldn't have..."

She pulled me back in and kissed me again, with more intensity and urgency this time, her hands cupping my face, her mouth open, her tongue gently searching for mine. A voice somewhere in the distance shouted, "Get a room, you two."

Lily laughed and let me go. "That was...nice," she whispered.

I raised an eyebrow, putting a hand to my chest. "*Nice?* I'd better up my game."

She laughed again and grabbed my hand, pulling me deeper into the water, our arms wrapping around one another again. It wasn't warm enough for us to stay in long, and we soon headed back to our belongings, where we sat shoulder to shoulder on one of the rocks, watching the waves creep closer, her hand in mine.

"I haven't felt this happy since before you went missing," she said, pushing her wet hair out of her face, leaning in to me. "I didn't think I'd ever feel like this again."

I knew what she meant, except it wasn't only happiness, but excitement about the future, too. Although she and I had barely spent any time together it seemed Dr. Adler had been right, Lily could well hold the key to my memories, more than anything or anyone else. While I didn't want to put that kind of burden on her, I didn't want her to leave Newdale, either, and not only because of her potential to unlock my mind. I wanted to spend more time with her, get to know her again, but last night she'd said she'd have to go back to Brookmount soon because she was running out of cash. I couldn't go with her. Lily had told me I'd recently been made redundant from my job, and I wasn't about to take off for Maryland without any kind of income, or a place to stay. And then there was my being unable to abandon Maya again, but the thought of Lily leaving Newdale, and me being stuck here out of obligation more than anything else made my jaw clench.

Oblivious to everything that was going on inside my head, Lily pulled out her phone. "Let me take a picture of us," she said, pressing her cheek against mine, "so we can remember this day as a new beginning." I leaned in, feeling her soft skin against my stubble as she took a photo. "Crap, I blinked," she said, swiping her finger across the screen, and I put my hand over hers as I stared at the photo of a blue Dodge Charger.

"Is that yours?" I said, my heart racing, throat running dry.

She shook her head. "No. It kept driving past your apartment one day..."

Her voice trailed off as a new memory surged into the forefront of my mind. I was in a parking lot by a beach, sea salt filling the air, a steady breeze blowing. When I heard a yell, I turned around to see a man coming toward me. Tall and wiry with a scar above his eyebrow.

"You cheated, you motherfucker," he shouted.

"You lost, pal. Deal with it."

"I want a rematch. I need to win my money back."

"No chance. I told you from the beginning, one game only and I'm out."

He took another step toward me, snarled, "That's not how this works."

"It's exactly how this works. Take it up with the cops, see what they make of your side hustle. We're done here."

As I turned and took a step in the direction of the shore, his fist connected with the side of my head, and the surprise attack sent me to the ground. Before I could get up, he shoved his foot onto the middle of my back, and when he struck me in the head again, I felt a blinding pain, white stars blurring my vision. I heard a dull thud, squinted at the rock that had landed a foot away. When I managed to focus enough, I saw the rock was smeared with blood. My blood.

"We're not done, you asshole," the man said, his voice and everything else fading around me. "Not until I get my money."

"Ash?" Lily put a hand on my arm. "Ash? Are you all right?"

My heart continued to race and I opened my mouth to tell her, imagined saying I thought I'd remembered what had happened on the beach the night I'd gone missing. Some shady guy had struck me, possibly dragged my body into the water and left me to die. I couldn't tell her that. Not when I didn't know for sure if it was the truth or another montage my brain had made up. Besides, I didn't like what any of it said about the kind of person I'd been.

"Did you just remember something?" Lily said, her hand still on my arm.

"I thought so," I lied, "but no, nothing."

"Are you sure, you look—"

"Hey, you two." Neither of us had noticed Fiona approach. She now stood in front of us, an overstuffed yellow-and-white-striped beach bag in hand, a pair of large green sunglasses perched on her nose. With a wide smile dancing on her lips, she said, "Having fun?"

"Very much so," Lily answered. "How are you?"

"Excellent, thanks," Fiona said. "Enjoying my afternoon off. How's your memory?"

"A little better. A lot, actually."

"That's good." She hesitated. "Uh, I don't want to intrude, but could I talk to you in private for a minute, Ash? It won't take long."

"Yeah, sure." I got up, suddenly self-conscious of the fact I was wearing only a pair of boxer shorts. "I'll be right back," I said to Lily as I pulled on my jeans and followed Fiona, my mind buzzing with the memory of the man on the beach, and the possibilities about what else I was about to discover.

26

ASH

Fiona kept walking, and I presumed she wanted to get out of Lily's earshot, which didn't exactly fill me with confidence in what I was about to hear.

"What's going on?" I said as I caught up to her. "If this has anything to do with Lily or Keenan—"

Fiona stopped and turned. "Keenan? Jesus, he hasn't come back to see you, has he?"

"No. I haven't talked to him since he was at the house."

"Okay, good. There's something else I need to tell you." She hesitated, took a breath before continuing. "It might be nothing, and I don't want to be a tattletale, but...do you remember a guy called Dave Decato?" I didn't answer and she sighed. "It would've been easier if you did. Okay...when your dad passed, Maya went off the deep end..."

"She told me," I said, my familial defenses and protective

instincts rising. "I think it was completely understandable. She went through a lot back then."

"You both did," Fiona said quickly. "But this Dave guy? He's a dealer. A sneaky little son of a bitch who somehow manages to fly right by the cops' radar without ever getting caught. Anyway, I saw Maya with him the other day."

"Are you sure? Where?"

"The old cemetery. It could've been nothing, or a coincidence they were there at the same time, or… I just thought you should know. Listen, she was into weed back then and it's legal here now, but you may still want to have a talk with her, check if—"

Something came flying in our direction, and before I had time to react a soccer ball bounced off the back of Fiona's skull. She cried out and dropped her bag, spilling the contents across the ground. I crouched down, helped her pick up her things as the ball's owner, a little girl with a smattering of freckles and two missing front teeth, ran over.

"Sorry, ma'am," she said, turning deep red. "I really, really, *really* didn't mean to."

Fiona laughed. "It's okay, I'm fine. Quite the kick you've got there."

"Thanks," the girl said with a giggle, grabbing her ball and speeding away.

I turned to Fiona. "Look, I appreciate you telling me about Maya. I'll figure out what's going on."

She nodded. "I'll see you soon. Take care of yourself, and Lily. She's lovely, and I hope you don't mind my saying, but I'm rooting for you guys. You look happy together."

She gave me another nod, and as she walked away, something multicolored and sparkly by my feet caught my eye. It was a postcard, a glittery picture of a monarch butterfly. I picked it up and turned it over, saw the Boston postmark from years ago. I read the handwritten message, the letters full of loops and swirls.

DEAR FIONA AND KEENAN,

I'M IN BOSTON AND EVERYTHING'S FINE, BUT I DON'T THINK I'LL EVER COME BACK. TAKE CARE OF EACH OTHER.

LOVE,
CELINE XOXO

I reread the note again, the realization of what I held in my hands making my heart soar. This was the confirmation I'd needed to confront my darkest thoughts. Whether I remembered it or not, this was proof Celine had decided not to come home of her own accord. Maybe I'd encouraged her to leave, yes, but who wouldn't have, considering her father beat her on a regular basis and her mother did nothing to stop it? Keenan had it all wrong. It *wasn't* my fault.

As I read the words again, and then a third time seeking even more reassurance, an uncomfortable sinking feeling I couldn't place, nor understand, pulled at my stomach. I turned the card over to look at the front picture again and something darted through my mind. Butterflies. Butterflies of all shapes, sizes and colors, hundreds of them, so vivid it felt as if I could catch one with my bare hands.

I called out to Fiona, and when she turned around and saw what I held between my fingers, her face fell. She rushed back and I gave her the postcard, an inexplicable feeling of relief invading my soul as she took it from me.

She clasped it to her chest. "My bookmark! I don't know what I'd do if I lost it."

"It's from Celine," I said, my voice sounding shaky and uncertain.

"It arrived a year after she left," she said. "I showed you as soon as it arrived and... Of course, you can't remember. I should've thought to share it with you again. I'm an idiot."

"Did Celine ever send anything else?"

"No. She hasn't written or called since. This postcard is the last we heard from her."

I nodded. "Celine loved butterflies."

"Yes." Fiona smiled. "They were her favorite thing in the world, aside from you. You took her to the butterfly gardens once. She talked about it for weeks, before and after." She pulled out her phone, flicked through her photos, held out the screen. It was an old, grainy picture of Celine. In it she wore a light blue summer dress, her long dark hair tied up in a ponytail, her head tilted back, the delight of a full-on laugh captured on her face. She seemed so young, so carefree and happy. Fiona zoomed in on her sister's neck, and I watched as a silver-and-amethyst butterfly pendant filled the screen.

"You bought it for her that day," she said. "She loved that necklace. Never took it off. Not once. I bet you she still hasn't."

"You must miss her very much."

"Every day. I don't understand why she never contacted you again. We were all hoping she would, even if she didn't call us, but… I don't know… She was young, impressionable. Maybe she was too scared because she thought we'd find her through you. Perhaps she got mixed up with the wrong crowd." She let out a huge sigh before a smile settled on her face. "Or maybe she's sipping cocktails on a beach a lot farther south than this one. Believe me, I've googled and combed every social media platform for years without any luck. I do everything I can to imagine her sitting in the sunshine, deliriously happy, because the hardest thing is not knowing."

"I understand completely."

She patted my arm. "Of course. Anyway, I'd better get going."

After saying our goodbyes, I walked back to Lily, and when she asked me if everything was okay, I hesitated. It didn't feel right to tell her about Maya and this Dave character, not before I'd spoken to my sister about him. Fiona's suspicions could be unfounded, or a complete misunderstanding.

"She showed me a postcard," I said. "Celine sent it from Boston about a year after she left, saying she wouldn't be back. They haven't heard from her since."

Lily shook her head. "I can understand a little how she must feel, having someone they love disappear like that." She paused, reached over to touch my cheek as she smiled. "I got lucky. Maybe Fiona will, too, and Celine will come home one day."

Not long after, we gathered our things and walked back to the car, our arms brushing lightly until I reached for Lily's hand. "Thank you for this," I said. "For making today feel almost normal."

"You're welcome. I had a great time. That little girl with the ball could have given you a run for your money. I bet your dad would have joined in, too."

"Even though he hated it," I said with a laugh.

"What? No, that's not true. You told me you guys played all the time when you were in England. You'd go to the local park. You called them your 'Sunday Kickabouts.' And you always watched matches together."

"Yeah, until he finally confessed he hated everything to do with the sport and couldn't bear admitting it because I loved it so much."

Maya had grinned when she'd explained how Dad's revelation had turned into a standing joke at the house, with him groaning and moaning whenever I turned on a match. In the end he'd always sat down next to me for the whole thing anyway. I couldn't recall that part. The memory had been swallowed up by the abyss along with so many other things.

"You never shared that with me," Lily said, looking down.

"Right," I said, her words making me feel guilty for having withheld something else from her, and I quickly changed the subject by continuing with, "Want to join us at the house for dinner?"

"I'd love to. I'll grab a shower at the motel first. But you don't think Maya will mind?"

"Not at all," I said, hoping I was right but not caring if I wasn't. "Can you drop me off at the Cliff's Head? Her shift will be over soon, so I'll catch a ride home with her. Come to the house in an hour or so? If you get there before us, there's a spare key under the flowerpot on the left side of the door."

Lily grinned. "Some things never change."

When I walked into the Cliff's Head, Maya stood behind the host's desk, her face lighting up as soon as she saw me. "Hey, perfect timing. I'm almost done here and…" She frowned. "What's wrong? Did something happen with Lily?"

"Can we talk somewhere private?" I said, and after she'd led me to a small room at the back and closed the door behind us, I decided to be as direct as possible so I could gauge her immediate reaction. "Why are you buying drugs from Dave Decato?" I said, her startled face confirming Fiona's suspicions. "What the hell are you doing? What are you taking?"

"Nothing," she said, sticking out her chin. "It's none of your business."

"It is. What's going on?"

I watched her resolve falter. She glanced at the door before whispering, "Weed, okay?"

"But you can get it legally—"

"His stuff is way better."

"But why are you smoking—"

She threw her hands in the air. "Because your being back here has stressed me out. I'm so worried I'll wake up and you'll be gone. Or you'll never get your memory back… Or I won't be able to support us financially and we'll have to sell the house. It's a lot of pressure, Ash. I…I guess I needed something to help me relax."

"Jesus, Maya."

"It's no big deal—"

"Not the weed. The fact I put you in this situation." I ran my hands over my face, shook my head. "Who the hell do I think I am, striding in here, being such a sanctimonious shit?"

"You're not, and it's okay. I only got a little bit but please don't tell anyone. Especially not Lily. I want us to be friends and can't bear her thinking badly of me."

"I know what you mean," I said, sitting down on one of the chairs, gesturing for her to do the same. "I haven't told her yet, but I remembered something about the night I got hurt."

"*What? Are you sure?*"

"I think so, and I don't think it was an accident." As I told Maya about my flashback and the man hitting me with a rock, I decided it was good I couldn't remember more details about my assailant, like his name. With the look on Maya's face, if I *had* known, she'd jump in her car, drive to Brookmount and throttle him with her bare hands. I wouldn't have been far behind.

"What are you going to do?" she said. "Should we call the cops?"

I shook my head. "I think I should wait and see if I remember anything else so I can give them more details. It might not be too long because Lily being here is definitely helping. Way more stuff has come back since she arrived."

"Like what?" Maya said quickly, and I explained about the hide-and-seek memory, which she confirmed was accurate, the blueberry pancakes, the movie, and the butterflies I'd seen after finding Fiona's postcard. I left out the dragging feeling I'd experienced as I'd read the last words Celine had written to her family. I didn't know what to do with that bit yet.

"How could I have forgotten about the postcard?" Maya said. "Fiona was so excited when it arrived. We were all certain more would follow, but they never did..."

"She mentioned that. Oh, and Lily also thought Dad loved soccer."

Maya scrunched up her face. "Really? You mean you never told her about him going along with it because of you?"

"I guess not. But why wouldn't I—"

"Listen, we'll talk more but right now I'd better finish my shift before Patrick wonders if I've already left. Do you want a drink at the bar while you wait?"

"No, I'm fine. I'll go outside."

I headed for the front door, relieved my conversation about Dave had gone well with Maya. I couldn't blame her for wanting something to help her relax, although getting weed illegally was pretty stupid. Perhaps she'd feel less stressed with my memory returning some more, and again when I could help financially if I got a job as quickly as possible. Maya's funds had to be dwindling, and it wasn't fair for all that pressure to be on her, too. I sat down on a metal bench to the left of the door and leaned back, closing my eyes for a second as I tilted my face toward the sun, thinking.

"Hey, asshole."

My eyes flew open. Keenan stood over me, his jaw clenched. "Christ, not you again," I said. "What do you want?"

He leaned in closer, a waft of alcohol going up my nose. "The truth."

"Seriously?" I stood up, putting a little distance between us. "I keep telling you I—"

"Can't remember?" He let out a laugh. Cold, hard and full of hatred. "This amnesia stunt you're pulling? You may have everyone else fooled around here, but not me. You're a liar—"

"Maybe you're the one lying. I hear Kate dumped you. What happened? Couldn't handle the rejection? Decided to do something about it and blame me?"

"Nice try." He lowered his voice, took a step toward me, fists clenched by his sides. "The cops couldn't find evidence of what you did, but I'll never stop looking. Do you hear me? I won't stop until you've been shanked in prison and you're bleeding out all over the ground."

"Sounds like a threat."

"Nah. It's a fucking promise."

"I don't need this," I said quietly. "For the last time, I don't know—"

I didn't see the punch coming before Keenan's fist connected with my middle. I stumbled backward.

"Did that jog your memory?" he said before coming for me again.

This time I was ready. I took two steps back, weaving out of the way as his hand almost slammed into the wall of the restaurant. I wished it had. Maybe he'd have broken a few bones, although with the rage on his face, I didn't think some busted knuckles would've been enough to stop him. Keenan cursed and rushed at me, sending us flying. I pushed him off, both of us scrambling to make it to our feet before the other. A second passed, then two, and with a deafening roar, Keenan lunged for me again. As I stepped to the side and brought up my knee, hitting him squarely in the gut, he let out a grunt. He grabbed my arm and threw me backward. When I landed, something sharp dug into my shoulder and I jumped up, brushing a shard of glass from my skin, the remains of an old broken bottle I'd landed on. I ignored the steady gush of blood making its way to my fingers, and Keenan's smirk made me want to pound him into the ground. He wanted a fight. I'd give him one. He'd pissed me off one time too many.

"Plenty more where that came from, dipshit," he said. He was about to charge me again when the front door to the restaurant burst open and Maya stormed out, eyes ablaze.

"What the hell are you doing?" she shouted.

"Teaching him a lesson," Keenan said. "And he started it."

Maya laughed, indicating behind her with her thumb. "What

are you, five? Think our security cameras will back you up? Let's call Ricky, see if he believes your bullshit."

Keenan held up his hands and backed away.

"Good decision," Maya snarled as we watched him leave. "If you touch Ash again, he won't be the one coming for you—I will."

27
MAYA

Keenan took off, tires of his Subaru spinning. I opened my mouth to ask Ash what the hell had happened, what he'd been thinking, that with his concussion another blow to the head could be deadly. I was about to start berating him when my eyes dropped to his shoulder, and I gasped when I saw the blood.

"Ash, you cut yourself."

He waved me off. "I'm fine."

"You're not fine. We have to get you inside."

"It's a cut, I'm not losing an arm. I'll fix it when I get home."

I disagreed, but he didn't look like he was in the mood for another argument. Pushing him down on the bench, I said, "Fine. I'll get my stuff. Give me a minute."

Ash grunted but gave in, so I rushed inside and grabbed my things. That Keenan had gone after Ash was no surprise, with their history it had been a long time coming, but thankfully

I'd been here to put a stop to it. What was it with everyone today? Fiona had always been such a goody-goody blabbermouth (translation: nosy bitch), but she'd blindsided me by telling Ash about Dealer Dave and triggering more of his memories with that damn postcard. The latter was a problem I'd have to handle somehow, and good thing I'd come up with the weed story so fast. The expression on his face when I'd told him I'd needed it because of his return was exactly what I'd wanted, and the revelation made him back off immediately. Still, if I needed another supply of benzos, and so far I hadn't touched the stuff, I definitely needed to get them from someone else. Then there was Lily's soccer comment, but that, too, could be handled. It was my word against hers.

I had a more pressing problem in Lily, who'd obviously been sharpening her claws and was digging into Ash more quickly and deeply than I expected. My mind sped ahead, calculating twists, turns and outcomes. By the time I stepped outside the Cliff's Head to rejoin Ash, I'd reengineered my plan, and we were in my car, heading home. That's what sly people do, adjust and pivot seamlessly without anybody noticing what's going on until it's too late. Of course, the cleverest among us never let on we're doing anything in the first place.

As I drove us home, Ash pressed a clean damp cloth I'd taken from the kitchen over the gash in his shoulder. Goddamn it, my anger toward Lily and Keenan simmered right beneath the surface, ready to burst forth. A large part of me wanted to let it. See what would happen. But no, softly—softly would work far better in the longer run.

"Keenan's insane," I said, gripping the steering wheel. "I'm tired of his stupidity and random accusations. Someone's got to put a stop to this bullshit, once and for all."

"I would've punched him if you hadn't arrived, maybe that would've helped."

I scoffed, couldn't help taking some of my emotions out on

Ash. "And get a more busted head in the process? That would make him happy." I let out a wry laugh and drove on in silence, thinking how Keenan had calmed down after Ash had left Newdale. More than once I'd wondered if it was because he'd forced Ash to scribble the hasty goodbye note before taking him into the woods somewhere and leaving him to die. In my darkest moments, the thought had almost been easier to cope with than knowing Ash left of his own free will. But now that he was home, there was no way the pair of them would ever call a truce. Keenan wouldn't let this feud go, even if Ash whooped his ass multiple times over.

When we got home, Ash tried fobbing me off again as I insisted I look at his wound, but I didn't give in. Once in the bathroom he sat on the floor, leaning against the tub as I fetched bandages and first-aid supplies from the cabinet under the sink. I dabbed an antiseptic-soaked cotton bud on the gash, holding firm as he winced and cursed under his breath.

"It's a neat cut and there's nothing in it," I said. "Barely an inch and not as deep as I thought. You don't need stitches. I'll use these strips instead."

"Good, because I'm not going to the hospital. I've had enough people poking me with needles to last a lifetime."

I rolled my eyes. "Don't be so dramatic."

"Look who's talking. You fell off your bicycle and refused to see a doctor."

"My accident," I said with a gasp, willing him to go on, to recall everything.

"We were outside," he said slowly. "You skidded on the gravel and cut your leg when you crashed into Dad's garden shovel. It was my fault. I'd left it lying on the ground, and it made a really deep gash, right here." He leaned in, reached out and touched my calf with the tip of his finger, making my skin tingle. My breath became shallow as I watched him furrow his brow in concentration, almost as if doing so would make more memories flow from my body to his.

I remembered the day, of course I did. I'd watched *The Fast and the Furious* again and pretended to be Letty because she was the most badass character I'd ever seen. I still had the result of my bicycle-drifting mishap on my leg, exactly where Ash had touched me, a smooth scar he'd always said looked like Lake Erie.

"I made you promise not to tell Mom because I didn't want stitches," I whispered, the excitement of something about the two of us coming back so intense, it almost made me want to throw up. I couldn't lie, wouldn't pretend he was mistaken or it wasn't true. This memory was different. It was about him and me.

"Small things are coming back all the time," Ash said. "I'm getting little glimpses here and there. I don't tell you about all of them—"

"What?" I stared at him, blinking hard as my stomach lurched. "Why?"

"Because they might not be real. How many times have you told me I'm mistaken?"

"But you'll only know if you ask me."

"Or Lily," he added.

"Yes, her, too," I said, forcing a smile as the rest of my cheerfulness evaporated at the mention of her name. I couldn't be happy while she and Keenan kept disrupting our lives and messing with Ash's head. It was time to problem solve, tackle things full-on. "You'll be okay, right? I have to go out for a while, but I won't be long. You wash up and we can make dinner when we get back."

"About that," he said. "I invited Lily over."

"That's great," I said, and before he had a chance to answer or see the expression on my face, I headed for the door. Once outside I got in my car and made the short trip to Keenan's. He stood in the garage, his head bent over the engine of his car, a pack of tallboys by his feet, two discarded crumpled cans lying by an overflowing garbage can. When I got out of my car and he turned around, a smirk spread over his face.

"How's the patient?" he said. "Bled to death yet?"

"Stay away from him, Keenan."

"What is it with you women? First Fiona gives me a hard time, now you. He had it coming, he still does."

"Stay away from Ash or—"

"Or what?" He waved his hands around in mock terror. "You and Ms. Hetherington are going to gang up on me? Help me. I'm scared."

"Who?"

"Lily, your new BFF." He raised his eyebrows and let out a long whistle. "So, you had no idea she changed her name? I did wonder…and tell you what, with her dubious past she's the perfect match for your asshole of a stepbrother."

I stared at him, watched his grin widen. "What are you talking about?"

"I guess being friends with Ricky has more than one advantage, but why don't you google it. See what comes up." He smirked even harder as he reached for his beer, winking at me before taking a long swig and giving me a *wouldn't you like to know* grin, which made me want to stab him with his screwdriver. I ignored him and got back in my car, hands trembling as I shifted into Reverse. Before I got home, I pulled over and grabbed my phone, and as I plugged *Lily Hetherington* into the search engine, the anticipation of what I might find became almost unbearable.

It took a lot of digging, scrolling and patience, but after a few minutes, there it was—a mug shot from the night she'd been arrested, her mascara smudged in teary rivers down her translucent cheeks. I read article after article, my heart pounding with elation. Lily wasn't the innocent little Snow White she liked to portray. She had a sleazy past, a rotten history—one I could, and *would*, use. Getting rid of her was going to be so easy now, it almost wasn't fun.

Suppressing the urge to laugh out loud, I dialed the Cliff's Head and asked for Patrick.

28

LILY

It was almost surreal how quickly things had changed over the past few days. As soon as the renovation supplies arrived the morning after we'd been to the beach, Ash and I got started on the garage. As we worked, he'd told me about his altercation with Keenan outside the Cliff's Head, and showed me the cut on his shoulder, but reassured me he felt fine, I shouldn't worry. I did at first, until I realized there were more pressing issues at hand than Keenan's misplaced anger.

While Ash had initially felt the recovery of his memory was gaining traction since I'd arrived in Newdale, it led to him throwing himself into the garage project with vehemence. On the first evening, he'd fallen asleep on the sofa shortly after dinner, and according to Maya he'd stayed there until the next morning. The second night hadn't been much better and every day he seemed increasingly tired. Both Maya and I joined forces

in an effort to get him to slow down, congratulating one another on day three when he agreed to ease off.

I knew he loved the feeling that accomplishing something
gave him, and the rush he felt from being physically active, but
there seemed to be more to it than that. He wasn't just worn-out
from working, and when I pressed him, he let slip that sometimes his mind felt befuddled and cloudy, and he worried he'd
stopped progressing, or worse, was going backward. I reminded
him how Dr. Adler had phoned from vacation the day before to
say he'd received Ash's blood-work results, and everything was
fine. The news had done little to appease Ash's frustration. It
was understandable, he wanted his memories, and to feel normal again, but with the way things were going, he worried it
might never happen.

Things between Ash and me weren't tense, not exactly, but
in comparison to the day at the beach his mindset had definitely taken a more negative turn, and every evening when I
drove back to the motel, I wondered if my being there was really such a good thing after all. We'd kissed a few times, but I
hadn't pushed for things to go any further, and neither had he,
and I promised myself I'd take things slow despite wanting more.

At least Maya had been chirpy, pleasant even. We'd chatted
about our mutual passion for art, how we'd both had dreams
of studying it at college. When she'd told me how her ambi-
tions had evaporated after Brad had been killed and she'd lost
focus, I made up an excuse about the impossible cost of the tu-
ition being my biggest barrier. At that point she'd said degrees
were overrated in her opinion, led me to the garage and showed
me her sculptures, detailing all the ideas she had for the wood
she'd collected and stored. She asked me my opinion, listened
intently as I described how I'd wanted to revamp the website
for Beach Body, and told her I'd be happy to help with hers. I
no longer felt anxious when she was due to finish work, and
when she arrived at the house one evening, about a week after

I'd arrived in Newdale, she walked around the garage with a massive smile on her face.

"This is amazing, guys," she said, gesturing to the plasterboard we'd put up in her new room. "Really, it's fabulous. I can't believe how much you've done."

"I've got a cracking coworker," Ash said, wiping the sweat from his brow. "With her help we'll be finished in no time."

"Ah…" Maya pulled a face. "What if it took a little while longer…?"

"You're not adding more items to the list, are you?" Ash said curtly, and not for the first time I wondered why he always seemed more tense when Maya was around. From what I could see she was bending over backward to help him in any way she could, but I supposed sibling rivalry could get the best of us, no matter our age.

"Uh-oh," I joked, trying to get rid of the tension before it bloomed. "Sounds like you'll have to put in a change request with the boss."

"No, it's not more work in here," Maya said. "What you've done is fantastic, but the thing is, we both know Ash should take a break."

"No, I shouldn't," Ash said.

"Yeah, you should," Maya and I replied in unison.

She grinned. "Anyway, we could use your help at the restaurant."

"Me?" I said. "Really?"

"Yeah. I talked to Patrick and he's more than happy to give you a few shifts a week, maybe more. He knows our situation, we're short-staffed and I said I'd vouch for you. You could start tomorrow. I'll show you the ropes, but you'd be hosting, mainly, and the guests will love you. You've got that innocent, girl-next-door charm thing going on. You don't mind me stealing her away for a bit, do you, Ash?"

As he shook his head I could feel the heat in my cheeks. Maya had paid me multiple compliments since I'd arrived, from my complexion to my freckles, my toned arms and my tenacity to find Ash and not having given up on him. I'd worried it was fake at first, but she'd gone out of her way to make sure I was comfortable when visiting them. The initial vibe of jealousy I'd picked up from her had waned and disappeared. Maybe with my being in Newdale she didn't see me as a threat anymore, and in her mind, getting me to work at the Cliff's Head would lessen the worry about me trying to whisk Ash off to Maryland. Not that he had any intention of leaving, he'd made it quite clear, and the more time I spent here, the less I wanted to go back myself. Yes, there was still the confusion about Ash giving me a fake name, not to mention the cash, possible gambling and the break-in at his apartment, and yes, it all bothered me, but I wanted to keep my promise and help him figure things out. Until I knew for sure why he'd felt the need to mislead me about his identity, I wasn't willing to give up on him.

As tentative and temporary as it was, I could feel my world falling back into place here. Being away from Maryland, Heron and Stevens, meant I could do a little soul-searching of my own. Like Brookmount, Newdale was small, manageable, and not too far from a larger city so I could get my fill of hustle and bustle if I needed to, before retreating to the peace and quiet. I hadn't told Ash, but I'd scoured the internet for local office jobs. My search hadn't yielded much I could apply for in the immediate vicinity, and if I decided to stay on a more permanent basis, I'd have to widen the scope. While I was happy helping Ash part-time with the garage renovation, the money I had left from his emergency stash was almost gone. Mike had yet to pay me, I had enough for this month's rent but the one after would be due in no time… As I looked at Maya beaming at me with an expectant expression on her face, I decided a few shifts at the Cliff's Head was an opportunity I couldn't turn down.

"I'm in," I said. "Thank you so much for doing this for me."

She waved a hand. "Nothing to thank me for. It'll be fun working together and getting to know each other some more. We need to be there at eight thirty tomorrow morning. Fair warning, Patrick hates tardiness. He's got super strict rules about it, among other things. Trust is his number one issue, so make sure you never break it."

"Got it," I said, and Maya smiled. "Oh, before I forget, Ash mentioned you have some Benadryl? I think some of the dust or something in here is getting to me. Look." I pulled up the sleeve of my shirt to reveal a cluster of itchy red dots.

"Sorry, I used it up weeks ago," Maya said. "I forgot to get some more."

"Are you sure?" Ash said. "I could've sworn there was a bottle in the bathroom the other day, and I saw a receipt from the pharmacy."

Maya looked at him and frowned. "Must've been an old one. Or maybe you're remembering something from Brookmount?"

"Maybe," Ash said, his face a mixture of frustration and confusion. I hated seeing him this way, struggling to connect the pieces of his mind. It wasn't fair, and I didn't know how to help other than reassure him I used to buy Benadryl all the time, and Maya was right, it probably was a memory from something he'd seen months before.

"I'll get some on the way to the restaurant tomorrow," I said. "There's a pharmacy close to the motel."

"About that," Maya said, looking at Ash. "Have you asked her yet?" When he gave a slight shake of his head she laughed. "Oh, for God's sake."

"Asked me what?" I said.

Maya sighed. "Do it now or I will."

Ash grinned and he held up his hands in surrender. "Fine. I—"

"*We,*" Maya corrected him.

"Right, right. Ahem. Lily, *we* were wondering if you'd like to move into the house."

"Wh-what?" I said. "Move in here?"

"All right, you kids," Maya said before Ash could reply. "I'm going to make a start on dinner, so I'll leave you two to discuss logistics, but when you come to the house, Lily, I expect your answer to be yes." She headed for the door with a decided spring in her step, and gave me a wink before disappearing out of the door. After she'd gone, Ash put his arms around me and I sank against his chest, pulling him closer.

"Are you sure about this?" I said. "Me taking a job with Maya and moving into the house. I don't want to put pressure on you and it sounds like it might extend my stay."

"I think it's an excellent idea," he whispered. "We have the spare room—"

"The *spare* room?" I grinned, running my hands up his arms. "That doesn't sound like fun." I cupped his face with my hands and kissed him. When his fingers slid under my T-shirt, gliding across my back, I reciprocated. His embrace was harder now, hungrier, igniting the passion I'd stuffed away since I'd found him, and I responded, urging him to keep going. As his body reacted to mine, I pressed myself against him, before remembering the promise I'd made to myself about taking things slowly. I made myself pull away.

"I don't want—"

"Me?" he said softly, a sly smile on his lips.

"No, I mean, *yes*, but I want you to want me... Oh, shit, I'm a Marvin Gaye song."

I kissed him again. His lips slid over my neck, making me arch my back as a delectable shiver traveled the full length of my spine. In one swift movement I pulled his shirt over his head, revealing his flat stomach and the hair on his chest, which tapered into a sexy thin trail and disappeared into the top of his jeans. I'd imagined our first time together again in bed as romantic, gentle and tame, but as I fumbled to loosen his belt that was no longer what I wanted. What I wanted—*needed*—was for him to be inside me, as fast and deep and reckless as possible.

There was no time or need for foreplay. We were both ready. I clung to him as he pushed me against the workbench, cried out as he slid inside. His mouth and hands found my breasts, and when his fingers slipped between my legs it didn't take long for me to reach the point of no return. When he whispered my name, the way he said the single word made me pull him deeper still, dig my nails into his back, and propelled me over the edge, taking him with me.

Afterward, as I peered over his shoulder, our breath ragged and our hearts pounding, a slight movement by the garage door caught my eye. I blinked three times, unsure of what I was seeing, but when I looked again, she was still there. Maya. She stood in the doorway, her gaze squarely on my face. How long had she been there? How much had she seen? I folded myself into Ash, trying to hide, and pressed my eyes shut.

"Are you okay?" he whispered, kissing my neck, wrapping his arms around me.

I couldn't speak, couldn't utter a single word, and when I found the courage to peep over at the doorway again, Maya was gone.

She didn't say anything when we joined her in the house for dinner, and I didn't bring it up with her, or Ash, either. The atmosphere between her and I remained amicable and unchanged, especially when I told her I'd agreed to stay at the house, and by the time we were doing the dishes I began to wonder if I'd imagined her standing in the garage doorway somehow.

"Will you spend the night with me?" Ash asked after we'd gone to the motel to collect my things. Fiona had been so delighted when I told her I'd be staying with Ash she'd rushed around from behind the counter and given us both a hug.

"What about Maya?" I said, discomfort sneaking back into my gut.

"What about her?" Ash shrugged, a chill in his words. "We're adults. She's the one who suggested you move in."

It wasn't enough to convince me, and I didn't want to jeopardize my new job at the Cliff's Head, either. "I'll sleep in the other room for a while, then we can decide."

Ash grinned and kissed my fingertips. "All right. I don't mind sneaking about in the middle of the night. It's kind of...sexy."

Despite my reservations I crept to his bedroom later that night, hoping to make love to him slowly and gently this time, but he was fast asleep, and I couldn't bring myself to wake him. I curled up beside him instead, wishing I could rest as peacefully.

As I tossed and turned, I thought about how I should give Sam more of an update than "things are going well." Then there were Heron and Stevens, from whom I'd heard nothing since I'd left. Good, because I was still furious at them digging up my past, not to mention their unfounded accusations of me having anything to do with Ash's disappearance. I'd checked online, and so far, no arrests had been made in connection to the case, so I didn't feel compelled to contact them, not until Ash was okay with it.

When he'd first asked if I thought we should speak to the cops in Maryland, I'd balked. I'd secretly worried they'd either still think I had something to do with his accident, or bring up the whole Dominic Martel debacle, something I wasn't ready for. I'd tell him at some point, but all in good time. Instead, I'd gently fished for any recollection about him gambling for money, and casually mentioned the name Jason Whitmarsh, relieved when he didn't react at all.

I'd also insisted I agreed with Maya, and that we should wait until we'd figured out more about why he'd left Newdale, and why he'd lied about his name. The only tangible reason we'd come up with was Keenan. We'd speculated he'd threatened

Ash, or scared him into leaving, but if that was what had happened, why hadn't he told Maya where he was going, or contacted her once he'd settled in Maryland? Maybe Keenan had threatened to hurt her. Perhaps we'd never know and it would remain one of life's unexplained mysteries.

As I lay there, listening to Ash's rhythmic breathing, I asked myself once more if I was prepared to invest in a relationship with all these unknowns and complications, and the answer was an emphatic yes. He and I both had histories we wanted to leave behind. The only difference was I knew the full extent of my past. What mattered to me now was what we did with the future, and I wanted him to be in mine more than anything.

When I heard Maya downstairs shortly before eight, I stumbled out of bed. Ash was still asleep, lying on his side and snoring gently, so I quickly went to my room to get ready for work, and headed downstairs.

"I made you coffee," Maya said when I walked into the kitchen. "Cream and sugar."

Her generosity and attention to detail gave me the sudden urge to clear my conscience. "Thank you…and…uh, about yesterday, in the garage—"

"It's none of my business."

"I love him, Maya."

"I understand."

"I won't hurt him."

"I know." Her eyes narrowed. "Because it'll be the last thing you'll ever do."

I expected a smile, for her to make a joke about pretending to be a Newdale mafioso, but she remained serious and unflinching, the weight of her words hanging between us.

As I turned around to escape her gaze, a bleary-eyed Ash walked in, pulling a T-shirt over his head while stifling a yawn. "Man, I could sleep for another week," he said.

"We keep telling you you're working too hard," Maya said. "Stay in bed."

"I'll go back up in a bit," he snapped, before closing his eyes for a moment and adding, softly this time, "Didn't mean to jump down your throat there. Sorry, Bee." He frowned as Maya let out a cross between a gasp and a squeak. "Maya the Bee," he whispered. "That's what we used to call you when you were a kid. That's your nickname."

Maya rushed over and flung her arms around him. "Yes, yes, that's right."

"This is huge," I said, unable to contain my excitement. "Isn't that one of the oldest things that's come back so far? That's got to be significant."

"Let's not get ahead of ourselves," Ash said.

"But it could mean more of your memory's returning," I said. "Dr. Adler mentioned—"

"Dr. Adler?" Ash said. "When did you speak to him?"

"Oh, I, uh…I phoned him when I first arrived. We talked about amnesia in general."

"You never mentioned it…did you?" Ash said.

"No," I replied quickly. "With everything that's been happening, it slipped my mind."

He grinned. "I can relate."

"We'd better get going," Maya said, cutting him off with another hug. "This is amazing, so incredibly amazing. We'll talk later, okay? We really shouldn't be late. You take it easy today, you hear me?"

He held up his hands. "Fine, fine, I promise. In any case, you should be able to move the shelving units into your new room soon. Are you sure you don't want me to put a window on the back wall?"

"Way too much work." Maya gave him a peck on the cheek. "But thank you."

"You're welcome," he said before a frown crossed his face. "By the way, before you go, have either of you seen my dad's watch?"

Maya shook her head. "Have you lost it?"

"I don't know how," Ash replied. "I put it on my dresser. I'm sure I did."

"It'll show up," she said. "Come on, Lily, we'd better get going."

The day went by in a blur. Maya had filled me in on Patrick before we got to the restaurant and she was right: I liked him even more the second time we met. Maya had given him the details about my arrival in Newdale, and he hadn't pressed me for information about my first visit to the Cliff's Head, something I was grateful for. Patrick had a serenity about him. Even when one of the suppliers brought cilantro instead of mint Patrick never raised his voice, didn't once utter a cross word. In many ways he reminded me of a younger version of Mike. At the end of my shift he congratulated me on a job well done, and said he hoped to put me to work as close to full-time as possible, at least until the end of the summer, if I agreed. I told him I needed a day or so to think about it.

"You seem pleased," Maya said when we got in her car.

"Patrick asked me to stay longer term," I said, relaying his plans, to which she smiled broadly, insisting it was a great idea, that now I had no reason to leave Newdale. "I'll talk to Ash about it, but thanks for this, Maya. I know we kind of got off on the wrong foot."

She sighed, letting her hands fall into her lap. "I was a jerk. I was terrified I'd lose Ash again when you arrived here. To be honest, I was angry he'd never told you about me, jealous, too, but I realize I had nothing to worry about. It's all working out perfectly."

"Yes, it is, isn't it? That new flashback this morning was fantastic. I'm hoping it's just the beginning of a proper recovery. Maybe in no time at all, everything will come back."

"Maybe, but...look, the doctors were very clear about him possibly never getting back to normal, whatever normal is. I know I can live with that, but can you?"

"Yes," I whispered. "I told you I love him, and...well, I hope he still loves me."

"That's wonderful, I'm happy for you both," she said as she reversed out of the parking spot, but when I glanced at her, despite her joyful-sounding delivery, her smile was all teeth, and zero elation.

29

ASH

I hadn't expected my feelings for Lily to develop so fast, for me to care for her as much as I did already after her arrival not even two weeks ago. Now she was staying at the house, I found myself even more excited to see her in the morning and looking forward to her coming home after work. It was almost as if my subconscious had connected with her before the rest of me, leading the way, knowing exactly what I needed.

Our relationship strengthened daily, and when we were together, she made me believe I'd always been the person she saw when she looked at me. We hadn't yet alerted the cops in Maryland about my being alive, and I'd told Lily I wasn't ready. She'd agreed, but I hated lying by omission. I still hadn't said anything about the flashback of the man attacking me on the beach. No more details about the incident had returned, and with my level of exhaustion and the way my brain-fog had made a comeback,

I wasn't sure if they ever would. That was my justification for staying silent, waiting to see if I remembered more, not wanting to put anyone in danger in case my assailant was still after me. Besides, even if I'd remembered what had happened correctly and told the cops, surely the likelihood of a conviction would be remote. Maybe the best solution for everyone was to let people believe "Jack Smith" had drowned. Perhaps that was the only way to move forward without having to look back.

To take my mind off everything as much as possible, I pushed myself as hard as I dared on the garage project, trying to fit in as much work as I could while Lily and Maya were at work, lying about being unable to get out of bed before lunchtime most days. I was exhausted, but the alternative of sitting in the house all afternoon would've pushed me to a breaking point far sooner.

In between their shifts, Lily and Maya had helped with the new room's subflooring and plasterboard, and I'd doubled the insulation as per Maya's request. I didn't think it necessary, but she was adamant, and so I'd complied. The bathroom turned out to be an easier project than I'd initially thought because the plumbing my father and I had preinstalled years before was still in excellent shape. Another few days and I'd be done, and providing I could somehow clear the fuzziness in my mind, I wanted to get a proper job, try to figure out what my future would look like, and I hoped Lily would be in it.

That morning, she'd gone to the Cliff's Head for her shift, and Maya had taken the day off to help me clear up, move around the shelving units and her supplies.

"I should've asked you for air-conditioning," she said, fanning her face with her hands. "It's boiling in here."

It was the hottest day of the summer so far, although if the news was to be believed, relief was on its way in the form of multiple heavy storms traveling up the coast, and which threatened to join into one big humdinger. I pointed to the back wall. "There's still time to add that window."

"Maybe later. It's mainly for storage anyway, so it'll be fine." As she bent over to pick up another box, her phone rang, and when she pulled it from her pocket she sighed. "It's Patrick. I hope he doesn't need me to go in. There's so much to do here... Hey, boss, what's up?" Her face fell as she listened, shaking her head. "No way, I can't believe it. It must be a mistake."

"What's going on?" I whispered, but she held up a hand to silence me.

"Are you absolutely sure...? A million percent?" She went quiet again before apologizing profusely and hanging up. "Cash has gone missing from the register," she said. "Six hundred and eighty-three bucks."

"He doesn't think you took it, does he?"

"*Me?* No..."

"Then who?" My eyes went wide. "*Lily?* No way. She wouldn't."

"That's what I thought. But she was the last one there yesterday except for Patrick."

"Then he misplaced it. Lily wouldn't steal. She's not that kind of person."

"Are you sure?" she said gently.

"Yes, I'm bloody well sure," I said, the anger I hadn't felt for days making a sudden and fierce reappearance. "Why the hell would you ask that?"

Maya hesitated. "How often have you heard her say she's broke?"

I didn't answer. Last night Lily told me she was concerned about money, and we'd talked about her giving up her flat and moving to Newdale on a permanent basis. I'd kissed her when she said it was what she wanted, too, and as we'd tried to figure out how we could best pick up our things in Brookmount, our excitement had grown. She had to return her car to the garage, and we couldn't afford to buy another, so we'd planned on asking Maya if we could borrow hers for a couple of days while we made the trip.

"Brad's watch. Did you really misplace it?" my sister said to me now, scrunching up her face as if she couldn't believe she'd even thought it, let alone said the words out loud.

"Yes." Except while I may have been exhausted and confused, I knew I'd taken my father's watch off and set it on the dresser, as I did every night before I went to bed. I sighed. "Actually, no…not exactly."

"I didn't want to say anything." Maya's voice sounded increasingly uncomfortable, and she wrung her hands without meeting my eye. "A pair of my earrings has disappeared."

"Are you serious? Did you lose them?"

"No. I know exactly where they were. They're not worth much, but they're gone. And your watch is valuable. You had it looked at once when we needed to repair the roof. Back then, even with the scratched face, the pawnshop would've given you a few hundred bucks, but I wouldn't let you part with it."

"This is ridiculous," I snapped, trying not to shout. "Lily wouldn't—"

"With all due respect, how can you be sure?" Maya shot back, and I couldn't come up with an answer fast enough. "If you didn't misplace your watch and I didn't lose my earrings, where are they? Where's the money from the Cliff's Head?"

"I don't know."

"Patrick said he'll talk to her when she goes in for her next shift the day after tomorrow, but he wanted to give me the heads-up. She's on her way home now. Before she gets here, do you think we should…" She grimaced and waved a hand. "No, we can't."

"Go through her stuff?" I said. Jesus, she was joking, right?

"No, I was going to say talk to her. But you're right. Maybe we should take a peek."

"Maya, we can't."

"Why not? It's our house and she'll never know. If we don't find anything, there's no harm done, but my ass is on the line if she took the money. I vouched for her. And if she has my jewelry and your watch…well, we have a whole other set of problems to deal with."

Fuck. My mind took a few seconds to wrestle with the options, but Maya was right. If we asked Lily about taking our things, it would give her the opportunity to get rid of them. Worse, if she hadn't taken them—and I didn't for one second believe she had—she'd hate me for accusing her of being a thief. But if she didn't know we'd looked, and it would shut Maya up…

"Let's go," I said.

Once we were in the spare room, Maya checked the closet. I searched through Lily's clothes in the chest of drawers, feeling more and more like a traitor. I kept telling myself this was all a big misunderstanding, but, as I dug through her things, doubts crept in and I wondered how well I knew Lily after all. Yes, I could recall her favorite movie, that I'd given her a bracelet on Valentine's Day and she loved blueberry pancakes, but did I *know* her?

"Found anything?" Maya said.

I shook my head. "I need to be sure."

I got on my hands and knees and looked under the bed. Nothing. But when I lifted the mattress and ran my hand down the sides of the frame, my fingers butted up against something. When I yanked the item out and saw a rolled-up wad of cash in my hand, my heart sank.

"Shit," I whispered, holding it up to Maya. "It's a coincidence, surely?"

"How much is it?" she said.

I unrolled the notes and counted them. "Six hundred and eighty-three bucks. Jesus Christ, what the hell was she thinking? How could she do this?" I lifted the mattress again, told myself I'd find nothing, but the glint of something tucked down the side caught my eye. Dad's watch and a pair of earrings, but those weren't the only things, because nestled between them was a little plastic bag of pills.

"What are those?" Maya said, holding out her hand, and when I gave her the bag her eyes and mouth went wide. "Ash, this is clonazepam."

"What?"

"Benzos. Serious, prescription-only addictive shit. I was given some of these after you left because I had panic attacks. I hated taking them because they made me so dopey."

I stared at her. "What do you mean, 'dopey'?"

She waved a hand in front of her face. "I don't know, I was tired all the time, like I was living in this soupy brain fog. Drowsy, a bit stupid, just...*weird*."

"That's how I've been feeling," I said quietly.

"From your amnesia..."

I shook my head. "No, it's been different. Exactly how you described. I didn't want to tell you, but some mornings...some mornings I can't get out of bed for hours."

"Ash, you don't think Lily...*drugged* you, do you?"

"Why else would she hide that stuff with stolen money, my watch and your jewelry?"

"But why would she give you benzos?"

"I don't know," I said, thinking back to the attack on the beach. What if I'd got it wrong? Could it have been Lily? Had she come here to drug me, try and keep me confused or make sure I never remembered what happened? It didn't make any sense and I was about to speak when we heard the front door open.

"Ash?" Lily called out, her footsteps coming up the stairs. I looked at my sister, saw that her fury-filled face matched how I felt inside, and I knew I couldn't stop the imminent confrontation from becoming explosive. Worse, I didn't want to.

"Oh, hey," Lily said as she walked into the room, frowning

when she saw both of us in here, and her eyes landed on the stuff in my hand. "You found your watch. Where was—"

"Don't," I said. "I know you stole it. Why, Lily? Why would you do that?"

Lily's mouth dropped open. "What are you talking about? I didn't take anything."

"Patrick called not long ago," Maya said, her voice glacial. "You took money from the Cliff's Head last night." When Lily tried to respond she raised a hand. "Don't bother. We found it under your mattress along with Ash's watch, my earrings and the pills."

"What earrings? What pills?" Lily said. "I don't know what you mean."

"Have you been feeding me benzos?" I said, watching her closely, but her frown deepened. "Clonazepam?"

"What? *No.*" Lily's voice went up three notches. Her reaction seemed genuine, but what the hell did I know? As far as I was concerned, she and I had only just met.

Maya held up the bag of pills, one eyebrow raised, her voice low. "You sure about that?"

Lily nodded, her head bobbing up and down, eyes darting from me to Maya and back again. "Yes, I'm sure. I've never seen those before in my life. I'd never do anything to hurt you, Ash. I didn't steal anything, I swear, and I certainly didn't give you any of those pills. You have to believe me."

"How?" I said. "When we found all this stuff under your bed."

"I don't know." Lily's voice filled with panic. "Someone else must have…" She stopped midsentence, slowly turning around to face Maya. "*You* did this."

Maya put a hand to her chest. "Don't put this on me."

"God, I'm an idiot," Lily said. "I thought you'd changed your mind. I thought you'd accepted me, *us.* But you haven't, have you? I was right all along. You can't stand Ash having anyone else in his life but *you*. You got me that job so you could get rid of me. You planted all this stuff in my room."

"Can you hear yourself?" Maya said. "You're insane."

Lily grabbed my hand. "I didn't do this. I'm telling the truth. About everything."

"Are you sure?" Maya said. "Have you told him about Buffalo? About your conviction?"

"What?" Lily and I both said at the same time, her voice overpowered by the volume and intensity of mine.

"What conviction?" I urged, louder still.

"I wasn't going to say anything," Maya said. "Because I didn't want to hurt you, Ash, and I thought maybe she'd changed, but Lily lied about who she is. Her name wasn't always Reid. It used to be Hetherington."

Lily blanched. "I changed it because—"

"You spent time in prison." Maya put her hands on her hips as Lily opened and closed her mouth a few times. "Lily's a con artist. She ran a scam with a guy called Dominic Martel. They had quite the thing going, stole thousands of dollars' worth of expensive cars. It was all over the news."

"Is it true?" I said, my voice hoarse, gruff.

"It was years ago," Lily said, pleading with me. "It was a stupid mistake."

"Did I know about any of this when we were in Brookmount?" I demanded, but she took too long to answer, her silence telling me everything I needed to know. "Why not?"

"Because it didn't matter—"

"Of course it did—"

"How can you be such a hypocrite?" Lily threw her hands in the air. "You lied to me about your name. You never told me about Celine or Kate. You never mentioned Maya, either, and we still don't know why, but you have the audacity to call me out on not wanting to tell you something about my past? How *dare* you." She took a step toward me. "Can't you see what's happening? She's manipulating you." When Maya started to protest, Lily cut her off. "She's manipulating both of us. She lied about the Facebook photo, I'm sure of it now. Think about it. She didn't even tell you I called. The first time I came here when you were out, she almost convinced me to leave town. She's never wanted me here—"

"That's completely unfair," Maya fired off.

"I agree," I said. "It was her idea for you to stay at the house. She got you the job at the restaurant."

"Exactly," Lily said. "It's the perfect way to blame everything on me."

"You're crazy," Maya said.

"What if it was her intention to get rid of me all along?" Lily said, ignoring her again. "You know the saying 'keep your friends close and your enemies closer'? What if she's the real reason you left Newdale?"

"Bullshit," Maya said. "There's no way I'd—"

"Enough," I yelled, my head on the verge of exploding. I looked from Lily to Maya and back again, trying to figure out whom or what to believe. But then I thought how utterly exhausted I'd felt of late, how fuzzy my brain had been, particularly since Lily had moved in. If Maya was right and those pills were clonazepam… "I think you should leave the house," I said to Lily.

"You're right," she said. "Let's all take some time to cool off." I shook my head. "No, I meant you should *leave.*"

"Are you serious?" Lily said.

"Yes. You can't stay here anymore."

She tried to argue but I wouldn't listen. Her shoulders slumped and I looked away until she pulled out her duffel bag from the closet and grabbed her clothes, stuffing them inside as fast as possible. As I watched her pack I almost told her to stop, and we should talk about this, but seeing my father's watch, the earrings, the wad of the Cliff's Head money and those goddamn pills made the words shrivel up in my mouth.

None of us spoke again until we got to the front door, where Lily turned to me.

"I didn't do this, I swear. I'm being set up—" she pointed at Maya, who'd followed us down the stairs and was hovering in the background "—by her."

"Please, Lily," I said. "Just go."

"I'll be at the Harbor Inn," she said. "Think about this, Ash. I've done nothing wrong, you have to believe me." She opened the door before turning around again. "I love you," she whispered, but as she walked away, I now knew for certain I'd never say it back.

30
MAYA

I wanted to celebrate as Lily walked out of our house—our *lives*—and Ash shut the door behind her, resting his head against it. A tiny part of me felt bad for him, but my elation kicked the emotion out of the way, sent it scuttling into the background.

My plan had worked. Simple, effective and carried out with meticulous precision. Everything would now be exactly as it should.

"Why didn't you mention her history?" he said, turning around, his voice sharp, and my face fell as he continued. "Why did you keep it a secret, Maya? You should've told me. I had every right to know."

"I thought about it," I said, my voice low and calm. I'd half expected him to blame me, and I couldn't spoil things by over-reacting. After Keenan had told me about Lily's name, and I'd done my research, it had been easy to ask Ash a few leading questions and figure out Lily had kept her past a secret since she'd arrived in Newdale, which meant she'd probably never told him when they were in Brookmount, either. It had been a gamble, and it had paid off. As the saying goes, "she who dares, wins." "It wouldn't have been fair to bring something like that up when you two were making a go of it," I said. "I mean, we've all made mistakes…"

"I need to see for myself," Ash said, pushing past me and heading to the kitchen, where he grabbed my laptop. "Show me what you found."

Once he'd gone through Lily's history online, he had no choice but to accept she'd betrayed us. Reading about her misdeeds had permanently quashed any lingering doubts he may have had and there was no way he'd want anything more to do with her. Lily would soon be on her way to Maryland, broke and brokenhearted. It wasn't all my doing. She'd had a partial hand in her demise. People shouldn't lie unless they were sure they'd get away with it.

"I trusted her," Ash said. "And I don't understand. What was the point of coming all the way to Newdale to steal a few hundred bucks?"

"I don't know," I said. "Is it a case of once a con artist always a con artist? She could be a kleptomaniac. Maybe the garage she worked for didn't go out of business. Or maybe it did because she stole from her boss there, too? Perhaps that's the real reason she lost her job."

"But why feed me those pills? What for? Did she attack me on the beach that night?"

"God, I hadn't even thought of that, but I suppose it's possible. Or maybe she's just not well—" I tapped the side of my head "—in here."

Ash fell silent, his mind no doubt working through all the possibilities of what Lily had done, and why. He'd question everything she'd ever told him, reexamine everything he'd remembered about their relationship, too. In no time at all his imagination would transform her from perfect human being to psycho bitch he'd had a lucky escape from, and I'd be by his side, helping him through it every step of the way.

"She put my stuff in storage," Ash said, looking up. "I should go and get it."

I frowned at him. "What? Why? What's the rush?"

"Those things are my past, my history. I've got the key and she put the locker in my name but still… What if she tries to throw them away?" He took a deep breath. "I think it's time I spoke to the cops in Maryland, go in person and show them I'm alive. What's the worst that can happen?"

"They charge you?" I said, panic in my voice. "The guy who attacked you tries to finish you off?" I hadn't banked on this reaction. Lily going back to Brookmount, a hundred percent, but Ash wanting to travel there, too? I wasn't prepared. I didn't want him to go.

"I need to put all of this behind me. Going for my things might help."

"If you go, I go. I'll call Patrick, talk to him about taking a few days off."

"I can't ask you to drop everything and come with me."

"Good thing you're not asking," I said, making Ash grin a little, and I promised myself that, very soon, he'd be smiling properly again, exactly as he had when Lily had arrived in town, except this time it would be because of me. "He'll fire Lily the day after tomorrow if she has the guts to go in, which I doubt. Why don't we leave in the morning, get a head start?"

I made the call, agreeing with Patrick I'd take two days off, and when he asked me about Lily I said, "I don't know what to say about her." Dropping my voice to a whisper I added, "But I don't think it's going to work out between her and Ash. It's such a shame."

Next, I went to the laundry room and fished Lily's favorite

sweater out of the hamper, where I'd hidden it earlier that morning. "Ash," I said, walking into the kitchen. "This is Lily's. I'm going to drop it off."

"I'll go," he said.

"You could do without seeing each other right now. I'll hand it in at the front desk."

He didn't argue, which I took as another victory. The damage was done. Hiding the cash, jewelry and pills hadn't just put a dent in their relationship, I'd taken a sledgehammer to it. A couple could never recover from this kind of destruction. I walked over, and put my arms around him, hugging him hard. I'd hated giving him the Benadryl in his beer that night, even though he hadn't drunk it, and slipping him the benzos this last week had been torture, but it had been the only way.

"I'm sorry. I know you were hoping things would work out for you both," I said.

"It's not your fault," he said. "Looks like it's you and me against the world again."

As I went to kiss him on the cheek, he turned his head at the same time, and when my lips brushed against his neither of us moved. Everything seemed to stand still.

I'd waited for another moment like this for so long. Years and years of pretending and patience, buried yearning, love and desire—all of it building and building from the first time I'd set eyes on Ash. I'd had to endure watching him with other girls. Tried to hide my shame of wanting a boy who was my stepbrother. I'd put up with the taunts and gibes and chants when word had got out at school. Believed it wasn't right, it wasn't normal, I was sick in the head.

I'd had a string of boyfriends who hadn't looked like him, and another string who had. And still. Nothing I'd done had been able to sway my feelings for him. He'd stolen my heart and carried it with him ever since. I'd promised him—and myself—I'd do anything for him, and that would never change. Standing there now, I wanted to slide my arms around his neck, pull him closer and press my chest against his. I wanted him to do to me what I'd watched him do to Lily in the garage. As he'd thrust deeper and deeper inside her, I'd imagined it was me. His hands on *my* breasts, his fingers between *my* legs, him whispering *my* name.

It felt like our lips had touched for an eternity, but it was only the briefest of nanoseconds before Ash jerked his head back. "Wow, talk about awkward. Sorry, Bee."

A volcano of heat rushed to my face. After everything I'd done for us, nothing had changed. He'd always see me as his little sister, even though we weren't related by blood. How long would it take for him to realize the one person he needed stood in front of him?

I almost laughed. I'd been here, waiting for him for almost twenty years. Before I could stop it, blind fury washed over me, slamming into my core. When would he finally see what I'd known forever to be the truth? We belonged together, end of story. I didn't want to wait anymore. I wouldn't continue being second, third or fourth best. I was done. We *would* have our happily-ever-after, I'd make sure of it. But not yet, not just yet.

"No harm done," I said, compressing my anger into a tiny little box hidden deep inside me along with another I'd filled with all the secret longing I had for Ash. "How are you feeling?"

He let out a breath. "Furious. Confused. Hurt. Exhausted."

I nodded, gave him my very best sympathetic smile and made my next move. "I'm glad you found out the truth about her sooner rather than later. And I'm glad she's gone. She couldn't be trusted, obviously. She'd never have covered for you the way I did."

I saw his breath hitch. "Covered for me? For what?"

I made my face fall and turned away, pretending to be flustered. "Nothing, forget I even—"

"Maya." The fierceness in his voice surprised me. It was low, almost a growl, a warning I was to deliver the truth. His eyes darted over my face, his expression filled with fear, his eyes pleading. It was exactly how I needed him to be. Vulnerable, exposed and dependent on me. My strategy, telling him some truths, was another gamble, but if I did it properly...

"I lied," I said. "The night Kate died, I lied about where you were."

He looked like he might throw up or sink to his knees, but he did neither as he stared at me, his hands shaking. "We went for a drive," he said. "You and me. Together. That's what you told me."

"I know, but it wasn't true. I went to the beach looking for driftwood and you said you were going out alone because you were angry with Kate. You said you had to sort things out in your mind."

"Angry about what?" he said, but I looked away. "Maya, why was I angry?"

"Because she slept with Keenan," I said quietly. "She cheated and you found out the day before because...because I told you."

He ran his hands through his hair, and I imagined what was going through his head. He'd found out his girlfriend had cheated on him with his archenemy. The next night he'd gone out alone, she'd died, and I'd given him an alibi. He was struggling now. I could practically see the scene of what might have happened forming in his head: him leaving the house at the same time Kate arrived. His accusations. Her denial. Their confrontation. Did he wonder if he'd struck her? Killed her by accident before throwing her off the cliffs to hide what he'd done? Could he picture himself watching her body being swallowed up by the dark waters below, only to be found battered and bruised the next morning?

"Maya," he said, his voice so strained I barely heard him. "Did I hurt Kate?"

"*No.* No, I'm sure you didn't."

"But you don't know for certain?"

"I know *you*. You wouldn't do something like that. It was an accident."

"Was it my idea to lie? Did I ask you to cover for me?"

"No, it was mine. It didn't look good for you. If we'd admitted you'd gone out alone…"

He put his head in his hands and I thought he was going to let out a sob. I felt guilty for telling him about his fake alibi, but it was the truth, same as it being me who'd found out about Kate and Keenan sleeping together. It hadn't necessitated me being any kind of sleuth, not considering how loudly Keenan had bragged about it at the Cliff's Head one night, when he'd—surprise, surprise—had too much to drink. I'd stood in the doorway, out of sight, listening to him boast to his friends about how he'd come on to her and how she'd gone along with it for old time's sake. Once confronted, she broke down, pleading with me it was a mistake, she'd been drunk, and had begged me not to tell Ash.

Of course, I had, but instead of Ash confronting her immediately he said he needed time to think. What the hell had there been to think about? I'd never liked Kate. Not her doe eyes, perfect teeth or her holier-than-thou attitude. Or the fact she was my age. My ugly-duckling-to-swan moment had happened, in the end. While I'd never been beautiful, I was attractive in my own way, and unlike when Ash had gone out with Celine, this time I could see the similarities in Kate's and my looks. It pissed me off even more that Ash was obviously in denial, and I told myself to be patient, that it wouldn't last between them, but just like Celine, everybody had fallen under Kate's spell, and she'd ensnared Ash completely. They'd met when he'd gone paintballing with some friends. She'd shot him in the head and offered to buy him a beer by way of apology. Yes, that was Kate all over. The fun girl, the cool one—an overenthusiastic schoolteacher with a perfectly proportioned body, and a head full of values. Except for her bedding her ex-boyfriend one last time, something I took great delight in pointing out to her.

"This is so fucked up," Ash said, pulling me out of the past. "If anyone finds out you gave me an alibi—"

"They won't. They never have. It's been over two years."

"Jesus, this is why I left, isn't it? Because I killed her?"

"I don't believe you hurt her," I said, allowing a sprinkle of doubt in my voice. "I don't believe it for one second."

"Why didn't you tell me any of this before?"

"Because I knew how you'd react," I said. "Look, today has been crazy. Let's go to Maryland tomorrow. We'll figure stuff out as we drive. We can get your things, bring them here and take it day by day, all right?"

Ash shook his head, his face distraught. "Maya...I don't know if I can stay here. Maybe it would be better if I left town again."

"Better for *whom*?" I said, struggling to keep my voice in check. "Do you have any idea how selfish you're being after everything I've done for you?"

He shook his head. "Maybe...maybe we should sell the house."

"What? *No*. This is my home, Ash. Mom's buried here, and Brad. I won't leave." How could he even suggest selling this place? Had Lily put this idea into his head? How could he betray me like that? "I'm going to drop off the sweater," I said. "We can talk more when I get back."

Before he could protest, I left the house and got into my car, the pent-up anger inside me making it hard to breathe. I drove into town, my rage going from boil to simmer and back to boil again when I spotted Lily's car in front of one of the rooms of the Harbor Inn.

I'd never had any intention of handing the sweater to Fiona, but I knocked on the wrong door at first, disturbing an elderly couple's game of Scrabble. When Lily finally opened up, red-faced and puffy, I held out her sweater and she snatched it from me.

"You bitch," she said. "I know what you did."

"Are you sure you're okay?" I kept my voice low and soft, as if I were speaking to a child. "If I'm being honest, you sound unhinged."

"You, *honest*?" she said, letting out a hollow laugh as she stared at me. "You lied and manipulated us. You fed him those pills to get rid of me, that much is obvious, but I've been thinking. Ash thinks his father hated soccer, and I know that's not true. He clearly remembered the receipt for the Benadryl you said you never bought, but I bet you did. Why would you say those things? What other lies have you been telling him?"

"Nice try. You're the one who never told him about your past, and—"

"Confabulation my ass. Did you really use up all your allergy medicine, or did you give that to him on the sly, too? I've been trying to figure out why you'd warp his truth. Tell him something was a false memory when it wasn't."

"You're sick," I spat.

"And then it hit me," she said quietly. "It's because you don't want him to remember why he left Newdale because it has something to do with *you*, doesn't it? I think I'll ask around. Take a trip to the drugstores. Ask Fiona about Brad's love for soccer. Maybe I'll talk to Keenan. Figure out if you've bought clonazepam before. Make no mistake, Maya. Very soon, everybody will know exactly what kind of a manipulative piece of shit liar you really are."

I stared at her. Lily was more dangerous than I'd thought. Most of us were when we had nothing left to lose, but she'd always been at least two steps behind me. She still was, because I'd prepared for this. Hoped for it, even, if I'm being completely honest. A tingle zipped down my spine and I forced my face to fall for a second or two. I had to let her think she'd got to me, and believed I was scared.

"Let's get a few things straight," I said, lowering my voice to a trembling and not very convincing stern whisper. "One, you'd have to find proof first, which you never will, I can promise you that. Two, you've lost Ash. Again. And three, I'll make sure it's permanent this time." When she opened her mouth to respond I kept going. "We're leaving in the morning to pick up his things. I suggest you go back to Maryland, too. Go home, don't come back and don't contact either of us again."

I turned and marched to my car, and as I drove off, I looked in the rearview mirror. She stood in the doorway, her cold, hard glare boring into me. No point in believing she would follow my advice. I didn't want her to, but I couldn't let her get Keenan on her side. Together they'd be a dangerous combination, and Fiona, too, if she ever told Lily about Dealer Dave.

"One step at a time," I whispered. "One step at a time."

When I headed down our road, and as I got to Keenan's place, I saw him working on his Subaru in his garage, tools laid out, front left wheel on the floor, the car raised with a scissor jack on the old, uneven concrete floor. I parked and walked over. Keenan raised an eyebrow.

"I haven't done anything," he said. "I haven't even seen Ash."

"I know," I said, smiling.

"Then why are you here?" he said with a smirk. "My irresistible charm?"

"I wanted to thank you for the info about Lily." I moved closer. "You were right about her. Ash was so shocked he threw her out. I know you hoped it would hurt him, and it has, but you did him a favor in the long run. She's crazy."

Keenan rolled his eyes. "Christ, that didn't take you long, did it?"

"What do you mean? You didn't think I'd tell him? I've always looked out for him."

He reached for a can of beer, his fifth or sixth judging by the amount of debris scattered across the floor, and attempted what he maybe thought was a sexy wink. "Yeah, sure you have."

"What's that supposed to mean?"

"Oh, come on. Everyone knows you've lusted over him for years. I sure as hell always did. I knew it the moment I found your notebook with all those cutesy double hearts and that—" he made quotation marks "—*Maya and Ash forever* shit."

I let out a gasp. "*You* found my notebook?"

"Not as much as I took it," he said with a laugh. "It was right there, on top of your bag. Besides, who else did you think started the nickname brotherfucker?"

"You *bastard*," I shouted. "It's because of you Ash never wanted—"

"You?" Keenan said, laughing again. "You think that's my fault?"

I wanted to grab the wrench from him and swing it hard enough to crush his skull or take off half his face, but instead, and without another word, I got into my car and drove home.

As soon as I parked out front I pretended to go to the garage before heading for the woods on foot, making sure I stayed hidden from the road, watching where I stepped as I got closer to Keenan's place, so I didn't alert him to my presence by snapping dry branches.

I watched him slide underneath his car on a creeper, and my heart rate picked up. Willing myself to cross the road slowly, carefully, I checked for traffic, pedestrians and dog walkers, but, as always, our lonely street was empty.

Keenan disappeared farther under his vehicle, almost to his knees. I looked around, saw he'd opened another can of beer and had left his cell phone on the floor, that little bit too far out of his reach.

Two quick steps and I bumped the side of his Subaru with my hip as hard as I could. The car wobbled, falling as the scissor jack gave way and landed on the ground with a metal clang.

Keenan let out a scream. It was louder than I'd anticipated, he still had a bit of fight in him. I walked to the garage door and hit the close button with a shirt-covered finger before kneeling beside him. His head was turned toward me, his face red, eyes bulging from the weight of his pride and joy that was now crushing his lungs.

"Help…" he gasped. "Help…me…"

"You ruined my life," I said slowly, smiling as he cried out again and took another breath, much shallower this time. "Now I'm going to ruin the rest of yours, and you'll never, ever know what really happened to Celine."

31

LILY

I couldn't sleep, spent the entire night tossing and turning, trying to figure out what to do. One thing was clear, I wasn't wrong about Maya, and Ash needed to know the truth. I couldn't believe how she'd come here, how she'd had the downright audacity to mock and challenge me, and any doubts I'd had about how deranged and twisted she was had long evaporated. I thought about going back to the house to try and talk to Ash, but knew she'd be there, ready to spin more lies. Somehow, I had to get him on his own, make him see her for what she was: a compulsive liar. But how when they were heading to Brookmount?

The more I thought about it, the clearer my two options became. The way I saw it, the first was getting to Maryland before Ash did. I'd have to camp out at the storage facility and try to talk to him, but no doubt Maya would be there, and my credit card was dangerously close to being maxed out. As things stood,

I wasn't sure I'd be able to pay for the gas to even get there. The second option was to wait until they came back to Newdale. It would give Ash time to cool off and provide me with more opportunity to work out what to say, but it also afforded Maya the same chance to turn him against me even more.

It was almost eight in the morning now and I still hadn't decided. I wasn't due at the Cliff's Head until tomorrow, and I already knew Patrick would accuse me of being a thief. He wouldn't believe me when I said I hadn't taken the money, and no doubt Maya had already told him about the cash in my room. With my history, it wouldn't be hard to convince people I'd gone back to my old thieving ways.

As I debated whether I should go to Brookmount or wait it out in Newdale, my phone rang. When I saw it was Heron, I declined the call, listened to the voice mail she left me a few moments later, my grip tightening around my phone as she spoke.

"Lily, it's Detective Heron. I have news. We believe Jason Whitmarsh attacked Jack on the beach the night he went missing, and we have enough evidence to charge him with manslaughter. A witness will testify Jack was new to the poker group, in fact it was the first time he'd played with them. He won the game fair and square, well, as fair and square as an illegal game can be won, but Whitmarsh wouldn't accept it. He insisted Jack was a hustler and made it very clear he'd get his money back somehow. Anyway, you're no longer a person of interest, okay? Please contact me when you get this message."

I thought about calling her, but what was the point? She was so far away and couldn't help me with the situation here, and, anyway, could I trust her? Would Ash be in trouble if I told her he was alive? Would I be, considering I'd known for more than a week and hadn't told them? Maybe this was just a ploy to find out where I was. How could I be sure they no longer suspected me? No, I decided, I wouldn't call her, not yet. I needed a little bit more time, wanted to tell Ash the details I'd found out about

Whitmarsh and see if it sparked a memory. Except he wouldn't believe anything I said now, not until he understood what Maya was doing to him.

I wondered if I should call Sam for help, but he couldn't do anything, either. I'd texted him about the side effects of clonazepam as soon as I'd got to the motel, and he'd filled me in a few minutes before Maya had knocked on my door with my sweater—a false pretext for a visit if I'd ever heard one. That's when I'd realized *she'd* been giving Ash the pills. I thought about how she'd practically dared me to hunt for evidence relating to Ash's departure from Newdale, something to incriminate her. She'd said there was none but...

I stopped pacing the room as another path crystalized in my mind. With Ash and Maya in Brookmount, the house would be empty. If I could get inside while they were away, I'd have ample time to search the place, see if I could find something that would help me convince Ash his sister was crazy. My mind raced ahead as I packed my things, deciding I'd have to make everyone believe I'd left town in case Maya asked around. There was a dirt track a few hundred yards before her house, an ideal place for hiding my car while I hunted through her things.

Fiona hadn't been at the front desk when I'd checked in last night and wasn't there when I dropped off my key. I was grateful. I didn't want to explain how things hadn't worked out with Ash, and I was going home. Thankfully, my credit card payment for the room went through, and within a few minutes I was in my car, heart thumping at the thought of breaking into Ash and Maya's home. She wasn't stupid, and she'd have moved the spare key, but I'd have to get in somehow, either by jimmying the door or a window. Whatever. I'd make it work.

I drove down the long road and past Keenan's place, which looked abandoned. I kept expecting Maya's Pathfinder to come in the opposite direction, but when I got to the dirt track, I turned and drove up until the path veered to the left, and the road behind me was no longer visible. I got out and continued on foot, staying hidden in the brush as I made my way to the house. I needn't have bothered being so secretive. Maya's car wasn't there. I couldn't be certain they'd already left town, but as I listened, the only sounds filling the air were the gentle noises of chirping birds and the leaves waving in the wind.

I crept across the grass, circling around to the front of the house, trying not to wince as the deck creaked beneath my weight. I couldn't break in until I was sure no one was home, and I rang the doorbell, counting to fifty as I waited. Nobody came. Maya and Ash were gone.

The front door was locked, but when I lifted the flowerpot, expecting to find an empty space, the spare key glinted in the sunshine, another clear sign Maya thought she'd beaten me. My heart sped up again, fear bubbling inside me, but I was here now. I had the time, the opportunity—and I had to act, do *something*.

I pushed the key into the lock. The front door groaned as I opened it farther, and I listened for movement. Although everything was quiet, I tiptoed across the hallway, checked all the rooms on both floors before finally believing I was on my own. I opened one of the front windows a little, hoping it would be enough to hear the crunching gravel if a car pulled up. Keeping one eye on the driveway, I searched through the living room and the kitchen, quickly rummaging through the cupboards and the old dresser, coming up with nothing, not even the receipt from the drugstore Ash had mentioned, which would've been a start.

One thing was certain. Maya wouldn't be dumb enough to leave anything implicating her just lying around. I headed back up the stairs to her bedroom, terrified she'd jump out as I stepped in. I needn't have worried. The only things greeting me were the ticking of a clock and the scent of fresh laundry. I went to her bed and ran my fingers underneath the mattress. No, too easy. Whatever she was hiding had to be somewhere more private. I checked out the obvious places anyway, including the toilet cistern and the bathroom cabinet, but the only things I found were tampons, scissors, nail files, cotton swabs and a couple of bottles of headache pills, which appeared legitimate. So much for hiding things in plain sight.

My impatience grew. I searched through the spare room, and Ash's, too, but still found nothing. Maya was cunning, had a mind with more twists than a corkscrew...or perhaps I'd become crazier than her.

I stood in the house, trying to think of my next move, and as I looked out of the window, it dawned on me I was in the wrong place. If Maya was hiding something, it had to be in the garage. Excitement fluttered in my belly as I headed out of the house and crossed the driveway. The side door to the garage was unlocked, but I didn't ponder why for long, because the enormity—the impossibility—of the challenge ahead settled on my shoulders, weighing me down. There were so many places Maya could've hidden something. Nooks and crannies, boxes and crates. It would take me days to do a thorough search. Even with them out of town I'd never get it done. I was debating whether to give up and leave when I noticed the old orange rug. It had been shoved to one side, exposing the trapdoor to the old room below. An ideal place to hide if you were a kid, but also to stash something you didn't want anyone to find.

I pulled the door open, flicked on the light, and with the blood thundering in my ears, put my left foot on the ladder. I counted the steps as I descended, one, two, three, four—ten in total before I reached solid ground, my heart sinking when I saw the shelving units had been taken out, the empty bottles removed. The room was completely empty. Not only that, but I still didn't know what I was searching for. I was about to climb back up when I heard sounds above me. Footsteps coming closer. There was no time to reach the light switch and pull the trapdoor closed, so I hugged the wall, made myself as small as possible.

"Well, well, well," Maya said as she approached. "What are you doing, *Lily*?"

How did she know it was me? I was standing too far back for her to see me.

In a sickly singsong voice she said, "I know you're down there..." Still, I didn't move. "My mistake." She sighed before flicking off the light, plunging me into darkness as she pulled the ladder up two feet.

"Wait," I shouted, taking a few steps and looking up at her.

She smiled with a coldness I'd never seen before, not in anyone. "There you are... Why don't you come up so we can have a proper conversation?"

I hesitated, but what choice did I have? "I can explain." I put my foot on the first rung of the ladder, knowing she'd relish the tremble in my voice I hadn't been able to hide.

"I'm sure you can. Let's go to the house and talk things through with Ash."

Ash was home? I sighed with relief. Although I knew how furious he'd be at my breaking in, at least I wasn't alone with *her*. I climbed the ladder faster now, but when I reached the third rung from the top she pulled back and swung something in my direction, aiming straight for the side of my head.

Although I saw the piece of driftwood coming, I had no time to react, not even to put my hands up. My upper body was completely exposed as she brought the makeshift club down onto my skull. I cried out as I lost my grip on the ladder and fell. As I landed with a thud at the bottom, all the air left my lungs in a single *whoosh*. My head throbbed. My eyes went blurry. I couldn't move, couldn't speak. Not even when Maya climbed down and stood over me.

"I warned you," she said, taking my phone and keys from my pocket. "You should've listened. If you'd stayed in Brookmount, none of this would have happened."

I wanted to get to my feet, but more of my vision faded, softening everything around the edges. As I heard her climb back upstairs, I held up a hand, silently begging her to come back, to not leave me down there. The last thing I saw was the ladder disappearing out of reach. I tried to scream, but only a small, pathetic sound made its way out of my mouth.

As the trapdoor slammed shut above me, enveloping me in complete darkness, the rest of my strength seeped from my body. Slipping closer and closer to unconsciousness, I had no choice but to stop fighting, and let it take me.

32

ASH

Now that we'd decided to travel to Brookmount, I wanted to leave first thing, but Maya had insisted I take her car to the garage in Falmouth for a long-overdue oil change while she packed and finished off two pieces for Drift. Ultimately, I decided I didn't mind. We'd be spending the next two days in close quarters, and I could do with some time alone first.

I'd left the house a little before eight and it was almost nine thirty now as I sat in the waiting room of the garage, flicking through a shiny copy of a luxury car magazine, trying to distract myself. I stared at a picture of an Aston Martin, imagining a life in which I could afford that kind of vehicle, where I had no financial or other problems. It seemed so impossible, so vastly out of reach it was laughable. No way around it—my world was one giant clusterfuck.

"Mr. Bennett?" The receptionist who'd greeted me when

I'd arrived stood in front of me, his arm outstretched, a phone clutched between his fingers. "I have a call for you."

"Hello?" I said after he'd gone back behind his desk.

"It's me," Maya said. "How much longer will you be?"

"Not long, I think they're almost done. Why?"

"Just wondering. I want to get going."

After reassuring her I'd be there as soon as possible, I hung up and returned the phone to the receptionist. I tried to concentrate on the magazine again but felt a growing sense of unease as I thought about traveling to Brookmount. Would I recognize any of my things in the storage locker? Would a particular item help me remember anything? More importantly, what would the cops say when I walked into the station, very much alive? And what would I do if I saw Lily?

She was right; her lying about her name wasn't the issue, I couldn't be angry about that, or about her hiding a prior conviction. But stealing? Drugging me? I still couldn't get my head around that last one. Why the hell had she wanted to keep my mind fuzzy? It didn't make sense. Maybe she'd taken the pills herself, it was entirely possible, but then why not say so? Whatever her reasons, our relationship, both past and future, was over.

Lily and the trip to Brookmount weren't the only things on my mind. Maya's revelations about my fake alibi sat heavily in my stomach and I'd meant what I'd said—I couldn't stay in Newdale with this knowledge. The place was slowly squeezing me dry, I had no future here. I'd broach the subject about selling the house with Maya again. It would make things easier for her, too. The place was heavy on old memories and upkeep, and her living there alone made little sense. She'd take some convincing to get rid of the house, and it wasn't a conversation I relished, but I needed to get away. Find a job somewhere, move on with my life somehow, and not live with my sister. I needed to put some distance between me and her, too.

Something made me tune into the conversation the receptionist was having with a woman who'd just walked in. She was nodding furiously, leaning forward on the counter, her voice breathless. "It's true," she said, sounding as if she was proud to be the first one sharing some gossip. "They think it happened yesterday. He'd had a few drinks, and was working under his car when the scissor jack gave way…"

"Keenan's *dead*?" the receptionist said, and the woman nodded. "That's nuts. I saw him, what, three days ago? Came in for some parts to fix his car."

I pretended to focus on the magazine again as I continued to listen to their exchange. First indications were Keenan had been trapped underneath his Subaru overnight, and someone had found him after looking in through the garage window. I shuddered as I wondered how long Keenan might have suffered. I hadn't liked him, but that kind of death wasn't something I wished on anyone, enemy or not. My next thoughts went to Fiona, and how she was coping with the news. She'd already lost Celine, now her brother was gone. Maybe Maya and I could stop in at the motel on our way to Brookmount and offer our condolences. It was the least we could do.

Ten minutes later and the car was ready. I paid the bill in cash—sorting out a bank account and credit card were still on my to-do list—and as I turned on the engine, I looked up at the car wash, something Maya's grimy Pathfinder probably hadn't seen in years. The inside of her car was full of empty sandwich and chocolate wrappers, coffee cups and other discarded remains, all of which emitted a slightly offensive smell. While it hadn't bothered me so far, the thought of being trapped inside a rubbish tip on wheels all the way to Brookmount and back held little appeal.

I headed to the car wash, bought a pass and eased into Neutral. Afterward, I parked by the vacuum cleaners, where I emptied all the loose crap before removing the floor mats and grabbing the hose, sucking up mountains of crumbs and sand. The final task was to clean underneath the seats, and when I slid the one on the passenger's side back as far as it would go, I uncovered another slew of waste. As I picked everything up and dumped it in the bin, I spotted a notepad wedged next to the seat. Maya's writing filled the pages, shopping and to-do lists, mainly, which were interspersed with sketches of driftwood art, some of which I'd seen in the garage and at the shop.

When I turned another page, taking in more of her scribbles, a series of pictures flashed in front of my eyes. They came thick and fast, and I had no control, couldn't do anything to stop them. Wincing, I pressed the balls of my hands into my face, which did nothing to block the onslaught of images. In the first, Maya was crying, looking down at me as I crouched by something on the floor. Then it was me, shaking my head as I shouted, "We can't. We *can't!*" Blind panic came next, the memory of it making me want to vomit. And finally, I was looking over Maya's shoulder as she wrote a note slowly, carefully, while I clutched a silver-and-amethyst necklace in my hand. Something I'd hidden where nobody would ever find it.

"No," I whispered, my heart hammering as it found its way up my neck and into the back of my throat. *"No. No. No."* This was more confabulation, another false memory, one my mind had conjured up, stitching my faulty knowledge and random fears into a sick movie. What I'd seen couldn't be real. It *couldn't* be.

I threw the vacuum hose out of the car. It took three attempts before my fingers obeyed my brain, and I fired up the engine. Time continued to work against me. Thick and suffocating, slow as treacle. A second stretched to a minute, a minute to a decade. Although I drove well over the speed limit, only slowing down as I passed Keenan's house, where the driveway was filled with cop cars, it seemed to take a thousand years to get back to the house, where I abandoned the car in the driveway, rushed through the front door and bolted up the stairs.

My chest threatened to implode when I got to my bedroom

and stood perfectly still as I saw the metal bed frame, which now represented everything I'd been afraid of, everything I'd convinced myself I wasn't. I walked over and put a finger on the bottom left bed knob. How easy would it be to convince myself I was wrong? How difficult would it be to walk away, out of the house, out of Newdale, and disappear? I'd done it before. I could do it again. Except…I needed to know. I had to be sure.

I turned the knob, heard it squeak beneath my fingers as it loosened. Two turns, three, four and five. The knob ended up in my hand, revealing a small space in the leg of the bed frame. I peered inside…and there it was. Celine's butterfly pendant. The one I'd given her one summer's day. The necklace she never took off.

I let out a moan as my legs gave way and I sank to the floor, the realization of what I'd done pulling me down like a drowning man. Because I knew. Everything I'd feared, everything I'd tried to run from, but couldn't escape. I knew.

I was a murderer.

33

MAYA

I knew Lily would come snooping. I'd banked on it. It's why I'd sent Ash to the garage as early as possible so she'd think we'd already gone, and the reason I'd hidden in the tree line behind the house, a little off to the side so I could see the driveway. I'd even left the spare key for her, and I'd been right to, because not half an hour after Ash had driven off, the nosy little bitch sneaked through the woods and into my house.

I'll admit it was hard to sit there and wait. I knew what she was doing, prying, going through all our things, but unlike most people, I'd managed to develop an astounding amount of patience over the years. Waiting for the man you love to recognize what's in front of him will do that to a person. I could've laid in the grass for hours, watching, waiting.

It took Lily a while to give up and come outside, exactly as I knew she would because there was nothing for her to find, and my heart didn't begin to race until she entered the garage, which I'd left open for her, too. I had to time this part exactly, make sure I gave her enough leeway to spot the misplaced rug—another little breadcrumb—and climb down the ladder, but I couldn't give her enough time to come back up until I was ready.

Everything had worked out according to plan. Well, almost everything. I'd hoped the fall off the ladder would be fatal. I'd read somewhere killing someone *almost* accidentally felt different from doing so with absolute intent, say with a gun or a knife. Either way, I'd smiled when I'd heard her cry out as I'd slammed the trapdoor shut.

Back at the house I'd called Ash, packed a bag and made sandwiches for the trip, and then I'd contacted Patrick. He hadn't been too happy about extending my time off, but I'd begged him to give me four days, not two, so I could "surprise Ash with more of a road trip." Four days would turn into five or six once I'd taken a knife to the tires on my car, blaming it on the local Brookmount youth, and making sure we were delayed coming home. Of course, that was without the cops asking Ash to stick around. He'd remained adamant he wanted to speak to them, and I'd somehow have to convince him otherwise. I couldn't risk him having to stay there and me returning home alone. Whatever the outcome, without water, Lily—whose phone I'd use to text Patrick in a little while, informing him she was leaving town and quitting her job, another indication of her guilt—wouldn't last until we got back, and then all I needed to do was give Ash a few benzos one night to make sure I wouldn't be disturbed while I got rid of her, her phone, which I'd already switched off, and her car, before anyone realized she was missing. Other than her landlord, would anybody even care?

I wasn't concerned about people hearing her if they stopped by the house while we were away, either. Nobody ever did, but I'd put the rug over the trapdoor and added some boxes of supplies to muffle any of her nonsense. All she could do was scream and shout, and she'd soon tire. Give up when she realized nobody would come.

Standing on the porch now, I couldn't resist going back for another look to see if Lily had woken up, tell her she had to keep quiet if she wanted me to let her out, but I needn't have bothered. All was still. Maybe she was dead after all. It would make things easier for her if she was. I went into the new storage room Ash had built for me, stared at the driftwood pieces I'd carefully laid out on the shelves, thinking that once we got back from Brookmount, it would just be the two of us again. Without all these distractions I'd finish the website Lily had so kindly started to put together for me. I'd work on my art. I'd help Ash find a job locally and do whatever it took to make him see our life was perfect, that we belonged together. We could at last be that happy family we so deserved.

Satisfied everything would finally work out the way I wanted it to, I walked over to the door, ready to lock up, was three feet away when it crashed open and Ash rushed in, his face gray. I peered past him at my car parked askew, realized with the double insulation in the room I hadn't heard him arrive.

"What's wrong?" I moved closer, ready to grab him in case he passed out, but he backed off, standing in the open doorway without uttering another word. He held out his hand, turned it around and opened his fingers one by one. My breath stalled as I saw what he was holding. A butterfly necklace.

"It's Celine's," he said, his voice so low and strained, I barely heard him.

"I've never seen—"

"Don't lie to me," he said, eyes narrowing, jaw clenched. "I bought it for her. Fiona showed me a picture. Celine never took it off. *Never.*" He thrust the necklace closer to my face. "You knew I hurt her, didn't you?" When I couldn't answer he grabbed my shoulders. *"Didn't you?"*

"Let's go to the house."

"Tell me what I did to her." His voice bounced around the room as he grabbed me harder and gave me a shake, his eyes wild. He looked dangerous and powerful, the way I'd felt when I hit Lily with the driftwood, and right then I didn't think I could ever love him more. He was ready for the truth. If I told him now, he'd understand everything about us, and he'd realize why we had to be together. And so I opened my mouth, and began to speak.

34

MAYA

The day Celine went missing was a perfect storm of circumstance. Over the past months she and Ash had spent every day together. They sat on the bus on the way to and from school, her head always resting on his shoulder, his hand on her thigh, their fingers entwined. After dinner, and every weekend, he'd leave the house. Neither Mom, Brad nor I bothered asking where he was going anymore, we all knew, and consequently I spent my days and evenings alone.

Since my notebook had fallen out of my backpack on the bus, and been passed around, the whispers and taunts had intensified. Rude notes with gross drawings had made their way into my locker. Pictures of a naked boy having sex with a naked, dark-haired girl, images of what were supposed to be me, with a penis in my mouth or my butt, the word *BROTHERFUCKER* scrawled underneath. I ignored them at first and threw them in the trash, but they kept appearing.

I didn't tell Ash then, was too embarrassed to show him what people thought I wanted to do with him. They were wrong. I loved Ash and longed to be close to him, yes, but not in that way. Not until we were older and had a place of our own. I imagined a house and two children, a dog and a cat, maybe some fish. He'd have his own business, I'd be a famous artist and we'd be deliriously happy, exactly like Brad and Mom were. They'd come over with gifts for the kids at Christmas, Thanksgiving and for birthdays. We'd take trips together in the summer. We'd be a perfect family.

If I showed Ash the disgusting drawings, he'd never give me the future I wanted, and so I said nothing, and sulked whenever he wasn't at home. When I'd tried talking to Mom about how often he was out, she'd brushed me off.

"Whether you like it or not, you have to get used to him having a girlfriend, Bee," she'd said. "I'm sorry, honey, but the truth is he doesn't want to hang out with his kid stepsister all the time. It's normal, I'm afraid." As if all she'd said hadn't hurt enough, she added, "He's a handsome boy. And Celine's lovely. She deserves to be with someone like Ash."

With a small smile she'd muttered something about having another headache and needing to lie down, but I'd stopped paying attention. The words *kid stepsister* made me want to run for the bathroom and throw up as my world, and the future I'd imagined us having, imploded and collapsed around me. Mom was right, Ash saw me as a child, and worse, his *sister*. In the past months I'd tried everything to change his perception. I'd taken down all my babyish posters and replaced them with grown-up ones we'd chosen together. Brad had helped me repaint my room, covering the sickly pastel pink with an eggshell white, and making an emerald green feature wall behind my bed. I'd sewn new curtains, put the remaining few stuffed animals I'd kept in a box in my closet and stacked my shelves with books I knew Ash liked. But I'd kept my silver star lights and watched them twinkle when I lay there in the darkness, thinking about Ash. Although he'd commented on how grown-up my room appeared, he couldn't yet see me as his equal, and so I'd persevered.

My appearance was next. I'd styled my hair to match Celine's, had it cut a similar length, found the same lip gloss at the pharmacy and used my pocket money to buy it, but still, despite Brad passing a comment about how Celine and I could almost be sisters—yeah, only if I was the ugly one—Ash didn't notice. Even when I stole one of the love letters she'd written Ash, and practiced until my writing looked exactly like hers, he still couldn't see what was in front of him.

I needed him to understand I could be so much more than he thought, if only he'd let me. If only he'd give us a chance. I knew him, understood him. What he liked, what he hated, his favorite food, music and movies. There was nobody on this earth who could make him as happy as I could, but still, he only had eyes for Celine, and every time I saw them together, it stoked the colossal fire of envy burning inside me.

When Brad took Mom out for dinner and a movie one night, hoping it would cheer her up because she hadn't been well again, Ash promised he'd spend the evening with me. Not twenty minutes after our parents had left, Celine called, and Ash suggested she stop by.

"Why is *she* coming?" I said when he hung up, hugging my knees as I sat on the sofa, pulling a cushion against my chest. "Why does she always have to intrude?"

"It's not intruding if I invite her," Ash said, with a hint of annoyance, and him thinking badly of me made my stomach turn. "You know she's having a hard time."

"*I'm* having a hard time," I said, swiping at my eyes with the back of my hand.

He came over and plopped himself on the coffee table in front of me. "Hey," he said gently. "What's going on, Bee? What's happened?"

"It doesn't matter. You won't care." I jumped up, sending the cushion flying. I brushed past him, ran to the stairs and up to my room, where I slammed and locked the door, making the thin walls shake. It wasn't long before I heard his footfalls, followed by a soft knock.

"Bee? What's going on? Talk to me."

As soon as I opened the door, he put his arms around me. "What's wrong?"

I didn't want to tell him everything, couldn't face verbalizing my jealousy, but he asked me again, his voice gentle and calm. I wanted to keep him here, with me, in my room. I wanted us to spend the whole evening together. I wanted him to finally see me, look after me, love *me*.

"They call me names at school," I whispered, fighting back more tears, relieved to finally let go of the secret that involved him. Maybe he wouldn't be disgusted with me, but with them, and we could fight this together. "It's been going on for weeks."

"What kind of names?" Ash said. "Who's bullying you?"

"I don't know who started it," I lied, not wanting him to know I'd been the one who'd stolen Sydney's precious jacket and ripped it to shreds, which had done nothing to stop the taunting. "Someone found my notebook. It got passed around and now they call me a...they call me a...a brother*fucker*."

It was a mistake telling him because he looked as if I'd slapped him across the face, and I wanted to take the word back, erase it from his memory, but it was too late.

"Why would they call you that?" he said.

"Because I wrote 'Maya and Ash forever' over an entire page." I swallowed. "Or two."

"Maya and Ash...?" he said, shaking his head. "Bee, why would—"

"Because I *love* you."

"I love you, too, but—"

I wrapped my arms around him, silencing his next words with my lips. It was a kiss I'd dreamed of for months and months—it was what I needed more than anything in the entire world, the one thing that held the power to make everything okay. Every gibe, every taunt, every horrible note, and all my jealousy faded away to nothing. Ash's mouth tasted of breath mints, but when he tried to loosen my grip on him I held on, not ready to let the moment end. But then I heard a creak on the landing, and a high-pitched, disbelieving voice rang out.

"What the... *Ash?*"

We spun around, both of us startled by Celine, who now stood in my bedroom doorway, the goddamn sparkling butterfly necklace Ash had given her hanging between her perfect breasts. She stared at us, eyes wide, mouth open, before turning and thundering down the hallway.

"*Celine,*" Ash yelled, shoving me to one side. "Wait. It's not what you think."

I wanted to ask him what he was talking about. Our kiss had to have meant as much to him as it had to me. He loved me. He'd said so before I kissed him. It was *why* I'd kissed him. I followed him out onto the landing. He'd stopped Celine at the top of the stairs and stood a few feet away from her, holding up his hands, backing away.

"Don't touch me," she shouted, tears streaming down her face. "How *could* you?"

"It's not what you think," he said. "I'd never do that to you. Not with her, not with anyone. She's just a kid, she's my step-sister. I love you, Celine, *please.* Maya was confused."

I opened my mouth to shout at him, tell him he was wrong, that I wasn't a child, that I loved him, but no words came out.

Celine looked past Ash, her face full of loathing. "You weren't confused at all, were you, Maya? You knew exactly what you were doing. You brotherfucker."

"Don't call her that," Ash shouted, grabbing her arm.

"Get off me." Celine shook him off hard, her momentum forcing her backward, and as she put a foot behind her, it slid on the bunched-up stair runner, making her slip off the top step.

I saw her arms flail, watched as she tried to save herself by attempting to regain her balance. Her hands reached for the banister but grasped only air. Ash lunged forward but he was too late. Celine let out a piercing shriek before toppling backward, bumping down the steep stairs, two, three at a time, a mass of chocolate locks and tumbling limbs. Her head reached the tiled floor at the bottom first, where it made a loud crack, but instead of getting up as I expected her to, she lay there, legs bent, arms outstretched, immobile and still.

"Celine," Ash shouted, stumbling down the stairs, repeating her name over and over, his sobs becoming louder and thicker, the desperation in his voice mounting. It was all for nothing. There was no blood, no open wound, but from my vantage point at the top of the stairs I knew she was gone. Her eyes were open and glazed, her neck bent at a strange angle. She'd broken it, simple as that. One second, she was insulting me, and the next, she was dead.

"Call an ambulance," Ash yelled, and still I didn't move. "Maya. Call someone, *please.*"

I looked at his face, filled with remorse and guilt, and realized I felt none of that. Yes, I was afraid, but afraid of us getting caught, of him being taken away from me. My brain knew I should have felt terrible about what had happened, but I held no sorrow for Celine's death, or how it had occurred. Secretly I was glad, and while that knowledge should have terrified me even more, it didn't.

I walked to him slowly, put my hand on his back. "It's too late."

He let out a loud moan as he put his head to her chest, tried

to find her pulse on her neck with his fingers. "I think she's...
oh, Christ...she's... We have to call the police."

He was the child now. I had to be the adult and take control.
Figure out what was best for both of us, for our family. Brad and
Mom wouldn't be home for hours yet. We had plenty of time.
"If we call the police, they'll send you to prison."

"They won't—"

"They *will*," I wailed, forcing tears because I couldn't cry
proper ones, not for her. I ran my fingers through my hair, pulling on it like I'd seen people do on TV when they were acting
distraught. "We'll both be locked up."

"N-no. I won't let that happen. It was an accident."

"Do you think they'll believe that?" I said. "You've seen the
crime shows. What if there's a bruise on her arm from where
you grabbed her? What if your DNA is under her fingernails?
We have to hide her."

He looked up at me. "We can't," he cried. "We *can't!*"

"We have to. If we say it's an accident and they don't believe
us, it'll be so much worse. And if we tell, it'll tear us apart.
What about Mom? What about Brad? What will they think?
We have to hide her, and I'll cover for you. I promise I'll do it
until the day I die."

When he looked at me again, I could tell his allegiances had
shifted. He was coming back to me where he'd belonged right
from the start. I knew it wouldn't be easy for him to cope, that
he'd blame himself for a long, long while. I realized it would
take time and patience to put this gorgeous boy back together
again. But I also knew I was the only one capable of doing so,
the only person in the whole world who understood. As much
as it hurt my heart to see him broken, it was what strengthened
my resolve. I vowed I'd make his pain go away, that I'd do whatever was necessary to make him happy, no matter what or how
long it took. I'd be there for him.

"We can never speak of this again," he'd said with tears

streaming down his face a month after we'd buried Celine on the grounds, when he'd knocked on my bedroom door in the middle of the night because he couldn't sleep again, the nightmares were too intense. "We'll protect each other. It's the only way we'll get through this. Do you promise me, Maya? Do you?"

As he stared at me now, standing quietly in the garage, I took his hand. "We made a pact that day," I said. "It bound us together, forever. We pressed her fingers on a notepad to make sure we left her prints, and I wrote a letter for her parents, saying she was running away. Then we sneaked into her house and packed a bag with some of her clothes and favorite things. It wasn't hard to make everyone believe she'd left, especially when I went to Boston on a school trip and mailed the postcard."

"Where is she?" Ash said, his voice barely a whisper. "What did we do with her body?"

"She's not too far from where Mom and Brad are buried. Don't worry, she wasn't alone for very long."

Six months, because that's when my beautiful mom had died, and if I hadn't been so distracted by Celine's incessant pandering toward Ash, I'd have noticed she was sick. Maybe I could've saved her. Ash had almost lost it when we'd found out our parents had stated in their wills they wanted to be buried together on the grounds. The guilt of knowing the person whose death we'd covered up would forever lie so close to our beloved parents who were none the wiser almost made him confess everything to the cops. I helped him through that, too.

I never told Ash I thought Celine should be thankful because she didn't deserve the company. That wretched girl was also the reason I'd never sell this house. If anyone found her body, they'd blame Ash. We'd promised we'd do anything to protect each other, and I would rather die than break my word.

In the end, getting away with it hadn't been complicated. People tend to have short memories and hardly anyone mentioned Celine these days. Of course, nobody else knew she was dead, but even with Keenan I could already tell it would be the same. They'd call his death a tragic accident. Poor guy working underneath his car after having a few beers. They'd shake their heads, mourn awhile and say a prayer or two before getting on with their busy lives. That's the way things worked when someone died. People paid attention for a while and then moved on. Forgot. It's how it had been with Mom and Brad. Give it a little time, and hardly anyone cared.

35

ASH

I stared at my stepsister, trying to comprehend what she'd told me, but all the doubt crumbled away as the memories of what happened that night slipped back into place.

Celine had died because of us. We'd hidden it from the world. She was buried on the grounds. How could we have done such a thing? How could we lie to Celine's family for years, pretend their daughter, their sister, had run away? We were abominable, that much was certain now, but looking at Maya, her face a picture of pure calm, I realized she felt no guilt about what we'd done. Given the chance, if we had the ability to go back in time, it seemed she'd make the same decision all over again, and if we'd done something so despicable once…

My legs buckled as I sank to my knees, all my strength and resolve flowing out of my body and into the ground. "What really happened to Kate? You have to tell me—"

"Let's go to the house," she said, reaching for my hands, try-ing to pull me up, but as she did, there was a dull thud from somewhere inside the garage. "Get up, Ash." Maya raised her voice and yanked on my arms again. "Come on, let's go now and I'll tell you everything else."

I was about to move when I heard another thud, followed by what sounded like a muffled cry. Pulling away from my sis-ter, I cocked my head and listened, putting a finger to my lips. As Maya was about to speak, I shushed her and got up, asked if she'd heard the noises, too. She insisted I was imagining it, pulled on my sleeve to steer me toward the front door, but I shook her off, walking farther into the garage. Another thump, another cry. I turned around.

"Maya," I said, slowly. "Is someone in the old room below?"

She shook her head, but her eyes betrayed her, and I looked back at the trapdoor, which had been covered with boxes of Maya's supplies set atop the orange rug. It was definitely where the noises were coming from.

"Who's down there?" I asked her before the realization hit me. "Jesus, is it Lily?" She swallowed, hard, but didn't deny it. "What the hell is wrong with you?" I shouted as I ran to the trapdoor, kicking and shoving the boxes out of the way.

Maya didn't move. "If you open that," she said slowly, "ev-erything will be ruined. She'll tell the police I put her down there. I'll be arrested…"

"What were you thinking?" I yelled, shaking my head. "We were about to leave for Brookmount. We'd have been gone for two days. There's nothing down there. No food, no water. What if she'd *died*? She'd—" I stopped, what had to be a look of com-plete horror and absolute disgust appearing on my face. "Unless that's what you wanted. Was she right? Did you set her up? She wasn't lying after all, was she? You wanted to get rid of her."

"Help me!" Lily screamed, her shouts clearer now that the boxes were gone, and I turned my attention away from Maya, who stepped closer as I kicked the orange rug away. I bent over, my fingers closing over the ring of the trapdoor when another thought punched me in the gut.

"Did you have anything to do with Keenan's accident?" When she didn't ask me what I meant I knew—*I knew*—she'd killed him. And Kate's death, that mustn't have been an accident, either. That's why I'd left Newdale after she died. Maya had to have been the reason I'd changed my identity. It was all because of *her*. I couldn't remember why, not yet, but I'd make damn sure I would because another thing was certain. My stepsister was a sociopath.

I lowered my voice, my words coming out firm, hard and cold. "Here's what's going to happen. You're going to take a step back while I let Lily out. Then we're calling the police—"

"*No, I—*"

"*Yes.* We'll tell them everything."

"But they'll send us to prison."

"Then so be it. I'm done with the lies, with all the deceit. Do you hear me? I'm done."

"How can you say that? I'll never see you again," she shouted, letting out a sob, her shoulders shaking as she collapsed on the floor, and I wondered if this was the first time I'd witnessed her true emotions. There was no telling what she'd lied to me about over the past couple of weeks, or what she'd done, and I wasn't going to give her another opportunity to do more harm.

"I think that'll be what's best for the both of us," I said, watching her blanch so hard I thought she might puke.

"I'm sorry," she said, her voice a mere whisper as she clutched her stomach. "I'm sorry, Ash. I'll do whatever you want. Whatever you say. I'm sorry."

I ignored her and as soon as I opened the trapdoor, I dropped the ladder into the room below. Lily looked up at me, terrified and shaking as she shouted my name over and over. I put my foot on the top rung, ready to climb down to her, but stopped and turned to Maya, a person I should never have trusted, and would never trust again.

"Climb up to me, Lily," I said. "Everything's going to be okay."

36

MAYA

Before Ash stood at the top of the ladder and made that promise to Lily, I already knew all of the trust between us, everything I'd worked so hard to rebuild, was gone. This was ground zero, and I pivoted, transforming my plan into a better, more sophisticated and permanent one. The foundation for it already existed, quite literally, in this garage, something I'd hoped I wouldn't have to use, but now knew I had no other choice.

"Lily," Ash said, reaching for her. "Are you hurt? Let me help you."

He grabbed her hand as she emerged looking like a terrified, wounded animal, ready to step into the arms of her Prince Charming. I saw her fingers wrapped around a belt, realized it must have been what she'd used to make all that noise, throwing the buckle repeatedly at the trapdoor.

How very clever.

She climbed the last few rungs. Blood trickled from a wound on the side of her head where I'd hit her, and her clothes were brown and gray from the dirt and dust. If I'm being completely honest, she looked pathetic, and they were too busy with each other to notice me moving the few feet to my workbench, where my hand deftly closed over one of my power tools.

"She hit me," Lily said, letting out a sob. "She locked me in. I thought I was going to die." Ash put his arms around her, and I almost rolled my eyes at their cute little reunion. When she finally worked up the guts to look at me, she flinched. "You wanted me to die," she whispered.

"Let's get you to the house," Ash said, ignoring me. "Everything's going to be okay now, I promise." When she took a step back and he bent over to close the trapdoor, exactly how I knew he would because he wouldn't want anyone to fall down there by accident, I took three swift strides, pushed my nail gun to Lily's chest and pulled the trigger.

Her eyes widened as the sharp metal pierced her flesh, burrowing straight into her heart. I watched as her mouth dropped open in surprise, and she let out a tiny gasp before sinking to the floor without making another sound. Now I knew what killing someone directly—immediate, precise and efficient—felt like. It wasn't so hard after all.

"Lily!" Ash screamed, too focused on her to notice me lowering the nail gun onto the floor behind me. He dropped to his knees, shouted her name again, pressed his hand over her chest where a patch of crimson had already spread across her shirt.

I didn't have long until he realized what I'd done, so I picked up the heavy piece of driftwood I'd used on Lily, and swung hard, aiming for the back of his head. No, I didn't *want* to hurt him, but sometimes things had to get worse before they got better.

As he slumped, unconscious, over his dead girlfriend's body, I knelt down and stroked his hair. "It's for the best," I whispered. "You'll thank me. I promise you'll thank me for protecting us. For keeping our pact."

EPILOGUE

MAYA

You expected a story with a fairy-tale happy ending? We'll get there, because it's not over yet. Besides, happiness means different things to different people. There isn't one single definition of what it means to be content. In my case, at this moment in time, it's knowing Ash is home, and that he'll always be where he belongs. Here, in our house in Newdale. With me.

It's been three months now, but I'd be lying if I said I was delighted with his progress. He tried to fight me at first when he woke up in the new storage room in the garage, found his hands and feet bound, and realized I wasn't going to set him free. At one point he refused to eat or drink because he'd figured out I'd been giving him more clonazepam to keep him calm, but after almost three days without anything, he begged for water and I was happy to comply. Like I said, I don't want to hurt him.

It took him a while to accept Lily was gone, but I assured him

I was gentle when I laid her to rest close to Celine in a quiet corner of our grounds, where nobody will ever find them. Not as long as we live here, and I've already told him he'll never leave.

In time, maybe I'll let him move back into the house, but for now he's comfortable in the double-insulated storage room, the little nest he helped build for himself. He still has to have his hands and feet tied, I can't trust him enough yet, but the benzos make him relaxed and manageable. I had to increase the dose while I finished the work on the rooms in the garage, and I didn't want to try to put him in the room below. Believe me, I'm not the devil.

The first thing I did was add a steel-reinforced door to the storage room and switch the hinges around to make sure Ash couldn't get to them from the inside. Next I worked on the bathroom, sealing up the original door and thickening the walls with bricks, but not before I'd cut a different opening, giving Ash direct access from his room. After all, he has to be comfortable and able to use the facilities whenever he needs. The work was easy to do once he was passed out, although all this medication still makes him confused, but we'll get there. Soon enough he'll understand this is what's best for him. I promised I'd be patient. We have all the time in the world. Nobody's looking for him.

Most people would be surprised to learn how easy it is to make someone disappear. I checked the weather, made sure I knew when to expect the most torrential rain, a mere two days after I'd killed Lily. Historic levels, they'd said. July Fourth festivities canceled. The threat of riverbanks bursting. An increased risk of accidents. Everyone had been advised to stay home and avoid unnecessary travel and so I let Patrick know I could come in to work after all. And what do you know, while I was there, he found a misplaced envelope with six hundred and eighty-three bucks in his office, where it had "slipped" behind a cabinet.

"Lily must have put it there for some reason and I didn't see it," Patrick had said, putting a hand to his chest as he let out an emphatic sigh before running a theatrical hand over his brow. "Thank God. That would've been so embarrassing. I don't want to lose Lily, she's an amazing worker and everyone loves her. You were right, and I'm sorry for jumping to conclusions like that."

"What she doesn't know won't kill her," I said with a smile. "Actually, seeing as I'm not taking time off, she was hoping I could cover her shifts for the next couple of days. She and Ash are quite the lovebirds and want to go on that road trip together instead. I said I didn't mind and I'm happy to help. And I was wrong. Things between them are working out after all."

"How lovely," he said, beaming. Of course. Everybody loved Lily.

"Between you and me," I whispered, leaning in, "she's moving here permanently and I'm so excited. It'll be like having a sister."

Patrick had agreed to my covering her shifts, as I knew he would, and I sent a message to Lily's phone, telling her about the good news. Once I got home after work, I implemented the next part of my plan, texting Sam from Lily's cell.

The pill stuff was a big misunderstanding. Ash and I are okay. Things are great and back on track!

His reply was swift. Congratulations. I'm so happy for you both.

I'd left it an hour or so, before replying, We're leaving for Brookmount soon. We'll speak to the cops, pick up his things and I'm moving to Maine. I can't wait!

Cue multiple heart-eyes emojis, to which he'd replied with a series of happy faces. The genius of modern technology. You can pretend to be anyone if you have their details, although using her credit card had been a problem. Turned out Little Miss Spender had almost no money left, but I'd found a way around that.

Thanks so much for offering to pay for our flights back home! I texted from her phone to mine. It's the most generous thing anyone has ever done for me.

You're so welcome, Lily. Anything to make you and Ash happy.

I'll admit to gagging a little when I wrote the reply, and again when I used my card to pay for a one-way flight from Maryland to Portland for both her and Ash, selecting dates a week out. Money well spent, in the end.

And then I implemented the final part of the vanishing act.

There's a point between Newdale and Yarmouth, where the road goes over a wide, fast-flowing river, a notorious spot for accidents because it's a long stretch followed by a sharp bend and a bridge. There's been talk about improving it for years, and all the locals know to slow down. Except Lily wasn't a local, and Ash wouldn't have remembered the treacherous curve. It's an easy place to push a car into the river without making the accident obvious. After all, I couldn't have the authorities finding it too quickly, and once I'd smashed the window from the inside and cleaned up the glass, got the empty car in the water and watched it bob around before it slowly tipped forward and disappeared, I shivered with delight. I wasn't sure where it might end up, but with the amount of rain coming down, it would take a long while to be found.

My plan had to be flawless, and the execution of it even better, and so, two days later, I alerted the authorities. I told them I hadn't heard from Ash or Lily, insisting something must have happened to them. I cried and begged them to do something, *anything*, to find my brother and his girlfriend. I played the terrified stepsister so well I deserved all the fucking Oscars. When the police found out Ash had disappeared before, had lived under a fake name in Brookmount and that Lily was an ex-con, their interest in the alleged missing persons case all but disappeared.

I waited, crying on Barbara's, Patrick's and Fiona's shoulders, and, finally, after almost ten weeks—longer than I thought—Ricky came to the house, his mood somber. They'd found Lily's car more than a mile downstream from the bridge, completely submerged. There were no bodies, but Ash's and Lily's bags were in the trunk, her purse containing her wallet and phone still wedged under the seat. I cried when Ricky told me how the driver's window had been broken in their apparent attempt to escape, sobbed when he reassured me they'd do everything possible to recover Ash and Lily, although I had to understand there was a possibility they'd been swept out to sea.

In less than a day the news spread. People rallied around me—making calls, bringing casseroles, stopping by for visits I made sure got cut short. This phase, too, did pass. Before long they got back to their lives, no doubt grateful theirs wasn't filled with as much tragedy. People have stopped coming to see the girl who lives alone in the quirky old house on the cliffs. With all the heartbreak, I think they believe its occupants are cursed.

Patrick offered me some time off, but I wouldn't take it. There's a rumor going around about me officially becoming the manager of the Cliff's Head in the near future. Apparently, the owner wants to open a new restaurant in Portland and have Patrick run it while I take his place here. I know I'd enjoy the role. It's more money, and I'd be good at it, but I have to be sure I still have plenty of time to work on my pieces in the garage, and be with Ash.

I've decided to be completely honest with him, about everything. It's what I should've done from the start. If I'd told him how I felt about him when we met, none of this would've happened. He'd have seen we were made for each other, so now I'm making up for that. He remembers what happened to Celine, and today's the day I'm telling him about Kate.

"She came looking for me at the house that night," I say as I shave his beard after securing his hands and feet to the chair. "She pretended she was out for one of her runs, which was a total lie. I knew she'd waited until she saw you leave, I'd spotted her jacket beyond the tree line. She wanted to convince me not to tell you about her sleeping with Keenan and when I refused she stomped off. I followed her along the cliffs, told her the only way I wouldn't say anything was if she broke things off with you."

"You...pushed...her," Ash says, the effort of talking making his voice faint and raspy. I wish I could ease up on the benzos, but when I tried cutting down, he became agitated and aggressive, something he thinks I bring out in him, which really pisses me off.

"I didn't mean for her to fall, I didn't think we were that close to the edge, but it served her right. You said you might forgive her for cheating on you." I shake my head. "I couldn't let you marry her, but when she died you blamed yourself. You said it was penance for what we'd done to Celine. You thought you didn't have the right to be happy, and it broke my heart. But when I told you the truth, when I explained what happened to take away your guilt and your pain, I woke up the next day and you'd left Newdale. You'd left *me*."

"Because...you're...a...monster," he whispers. "We both... are."

I smile, and as I stroke his cheek he tries to move his head away, so I put my thumb and index finger under his chin, forcing him to look at me. "We belong together," I say. "And I understand now. You could've told the police about what I did to Kate, but you didn't, not even after you left, because you knew I could tell them about Celine. You protected us, just like you promised, because you love me. Tell me you love me, Ash. Help make all this better."

He closes his eyes, tries to move away again, and I sigh. Maybe

I shouldn't have told him about Kate, he wasn't ready after all, but eventually he'll come around. He'll see what I'm doing—what I've always done—is the best thing for him. For *us*. I've known since I was twelve years old that we're destined to be together. For now, it might not be the fairy tale I'd imagined, but I've been patient for sixteen years and I'll do the same for another sixteen if I must. Because it will happen. And when it does, I already know he'll be worth the wait.

★ ★ ★ ★ ★

ACKNOWLEDGMENTS

The acknowledgments section has quickly become one of my favorite parts of novel writing. Not because it means I've finished another book, although that's a stellar feeling, too, but because it's an immense pleasure and privilege to put together a list of wonderful people to whom my infinite gratitude extends.

Let's start with you, the reader. Whether you deal with books in a professional capacity, review them for fun, or simply enjoy novels during your commute or while curled up on your sofa, thank you for picking this one up, and for letting me take you into my fictional world. I hope you enjoyed the ride. Huge shout-outs to the amazing social media and #bookstagram communities who spread book love with infectious enthusiasm and boundless originality. Your friendship and support are precious gifts.

To Carolyn Forde, my savvy, all-round kick-ass agent—thank

you for your support and for being in my corner. I wonder what our next adventure might be. To Emily Ohanjanians, my incredible editor, whose insight and knack for making manuscripts shine is astonishing—I couldn't be more grateful to you, or proud of what we've accomplished thus far.

To the wonderful Harlequin, HarperCollins and MIRA teams, including Cory Beatty, Peter Borcsok, Nicole Brebner, Audrey Bresar, Randy Chan, Jennifer Choi, Heather Connor, Lia Ferrone, Emer Flounders, Heather Foy, Olivia Gissing, Miranda Indrigo, Amy Jones, Roxanne Jones, Sean Kapitain, Linette Kim, Karen Ma, Ashley MacDonald, Leo MacDonald, Margaret Marbury, Lucille Miranda, Leah Mol, Lauren Morocco, Lindsey Reeder, Loriana Sacilotto, Elita Sidiropoulou, Alice Tibbetts, Kaitlyn Vincent and colleagues: you are incredible. Thank you for everything you do.

Huge thanks to HarperAudio, BeeAudio and the brilliant performers who bring my words to life with such grace and enthusiasm, making them their own. Special thanks to Lauren Ezzo and Alex Wyndham, my go-to narrating gurus who blow my mind each time I listen to their work, and to Melissa Moran for completing the brilliant trio. To Brad and Britney at AudioShelf—you know how you crack me up. Keep on doing your fab videos!

The generosity of those who take time out of their busy lives to answer my (weird and wicked) questions always astounds me, and I'm surprised none of you have turned me in to the cops yet. Special thanks to cool A.F. Brady and Sharon Guger for their medical expertise (and to A.F. for reading the first dodgy version of this book), Mary Randall for her library insights and local knowledge of Maine, and fellow author Bruce Robert Coffin for helping me get away with fictional murder…again.

I'm so fortunate to be surrounded by such a fantastic bunch of supportive GTA gal-pal authors, including Sam Bailey (thanks for your plot input!), Karma Brown, Amy Dixon, Molly Fader, Jennifer Hillier, Natalie Jenner, Lydia Laceby, Jennifer Robson,

Marissa Stapley and K.A. Tucker. Love, hugs and thank-yous all round. Huge hugs to Sonica, too—thank you for everything, dear friend.

Farther afield, the immensely talented Mary Kubica and Kimberly Belle were the first to accept to blurb a book for me, an unknown British/Swiss/Canadian combo. Not only that, but they also introduced me to so many other writers, it's become near impossible to name you all without doubling the length of this book. Please know I appreciate every single one of you. Your friendship, help, knowledge, ongoing encouragement, sweet messages of support and strict kicks up the backside whenever I'm throwing a wobbly...you really are the best, and you make the writing community better than I could have ever imagined.

To Wendy Heard—thank you for the early input on the plot for this novel! To Hank Phillippi Ryan, my First Chapter Fun partner in crime, and to Candice Sawchuk—thank you for reading a late version of the manuscript and helping me shape it further. You're amazing!

To my lovely mum, who I miss so very much, and my brilliant dad, my amazing sister Joely, and Simon, Michael and Oli, lots o' love to you all. I wish we could be together more often. To my in-laws, Gilbert and Jeanette, and my extended family all over the world—thank you for reading my books, sharing pictures of them and "making" your friends read them, too. Lots of love to Becki, who continues to champion everything I do from afar. *BFFs forever* is an understatement.

And last but never, ever least: to Rob and our boys, Leo, Matt and Lex. Thank you for putting up with me as I went through the usual love/hate relationship with this manuscript. Thanks also for holding down the fort and keeping me fed and watered while I disappeared into my book. I promise I'll make it up to you with your weight in blueberry muffins, carrot cake and raclette (not necessarily in that order, although after a year like 2020...what the hell).

YOU WILL REMEMBER ME

HANNAH MARY McKINNON

Reader's Guide

1. What do you make of Lily and Ash lying to each other about their past from the moment they met? Should we disclose our entire history to our partner, or are some things better left unsaid?

2. What do you think was behind Maya's obsession for Ash? What was she hoping for? Did you see signs of her obsession early on, and if so, what were they?

3. How do you think the story would have unfolded if Ash hadn't been attacked on the beach? Would he have ever gone back to Maine, or told Lily the truth about who he was? If he had told her, what do you think Lily might have done?

4. What do you think Maya, Ash and Lily were the most terrified of?

5. Maya, Ash and Lily all suffered tragic losses within their families, be it death or being cast aside. How do you think this shaped them, and what might have happened to them if their pasts had been different?

6. Did your allegiances shift at any point during the story? Toward whom, why, and when?

7. What scene was the most pivotal in the story for you? How would the novel have changed if it had been different, or hadn't taken place? What did you expect to happen?

8. What surprised or shocked you the most? What didn't you see coming? What was obvious?

9. How do you feel about stories where evil wins, at least temporarily?

10. What do you expect might happen next to Ash and Maya? Will either of them get what they want?

This is your fifth novel. What was your inspiration for *You Will Remember Me*?

A few years ago, a man from Toronto vanished from a ski hill in Lake Placid while there on vacation and showed up six days later in Sacramento. He had amnesia and couldn't remember much, including the cross-country trip he'd made as he'd hitchhiked across the US. Everything worked out for the man in the end and he found his way home, but it made me wonder—what could have gone wrong? That was the genesis for You Will Remember Me. A while later I had a vivid image in my head—a man waking up on a deserted beach without any recollection of who he was, or what he was doing there. I kept coming back to his story, how he'd arrived on that beach, what he'd do, and how much danger he was in. As I noodled the plot around, I wondered what might happen if he found his way home but had no idea he'd actually left the town years before, and unknowingly walked back into the dragon's den. That was it. I needed to know what happened next, and if he'd survive.

You have three point-of-view characters. Which one did you have the most fun writing?

Can I say all of them? Lily was great because she was determined to be a good person and put her past behind her. All she wanted was happiness and stability. Maya was deliciously evil, probably my darkest character yet, and it was incredibly interesting to spend so much time thinking about why she'd become the way she was, and how she could so easily rationalize her despicable actions. Honestly, she gave me the shivers. Ash was the most challenging character because I didn't appreciate how difficult it is to write someone with amnesia. They can't have memories or flashbacks, yet you don't want scene after scene of them being told their history because it would make for tedious reading. That in itself was a great challenge and really stretched me as an author.

Do you have a favorite chapter or scene?

Oh, my goodness, the ending with the final scene between Ash and Maya, when we discover just how far off the rails she's gone. It's twisted and creepy, and I'll admit to cackling a little as I wrote it (also creepy). This novel allowed me to go even further to the dark side, and explore what people might do, and how they'd justify it to themselves, all in the name of love.

About those dark themes... What draws you to them?

I've identified a few reasons. Ironically, my first book, Time After Time, is a rom-com. When I wrote it, I'd recently moved to Canada, my start-up company had failed and I was miserable. Looking back, I think I was trying to write my own happy ending. Once things got back on track I shifted to suspense. People might not believe this because of what I write, but I'm a very happy, jokey person. Actually, it seems the happier I am, the darker my stories become.

Writing suspense also allows me to dig into my fears from the safety of my keyboard. It enables me to think about difficult, dangerous situations, see what my characters do once they're in them, and how they're changed at the end of that experience.

And finally, I've always been a rule follower, so my books are very much an exploration of what it's like not to be the "good girl." Best of all, none of it is real so I can go as dark and malicious as I please (or my editor will allow).

What research did you do for this novel?

That's such a great question and I'll bet my dubious search history has got me flagged on a few databases somewhere! I think the most unique bits of research were how allergy medication can jumble your memory, and how a person can die while working under a car. Like I said: dubious! I also had to research geographical locations, sought help from medical professionals, poison control and a librarian, to name a few.

I'm continually astounded by how people are so generous with their time, knowledge and expertise when I call on them for help. For example, fellow suspense author A.F. Brady read the entire novel and advised me with the psychological aspects, and Bruce Robert Coffin (a former detective sergeant, and bestselling author) has helped me get away with fictional murder multiple times. Their input was incredible!

Is there a particular author or book that influenced or inspired your writing or decision to write?

I've had a long-standing love affair with both Lisa Jewell's and David Nicholls's books. I discovered Lisa Jewell's first novel, Ralph's Party, at the airport back in 1999 and have read and loved all her books ever since. She has a shelf to herself in my house. I adore how she expertly shifted from rom-com to family drama to domestic suspense throughout her career, and her storytelling always pulls me in.

A friend gave me David Nicholls's One Day when it was published. I devoured it in a matter of days and bought all his other books so I could do the same. His characters are so rich, his dialogue perfect, his stories funny yet poignant, he's an auto-buy author for me.

And then there's Jennifer Hillier... While waiting for my son at our local library I spotted her debut, Creep, on a shelf. Intrigued by the cover, I picked it up, read the blurb, took it home and couldn't put it down. It was a turning point in my writing career. When I was younger, I mainly read thrillers, but after a personal tragedy in my early 20s, I could only stomach lighthearted reads. Creep reminded me of my love of thrillers, and I realized the second book I was working on, The Neighbors, was far grittier than my debut. Jennifer's book gave me that final push I needed to cross over to the dark side. Fun fact: we live in the same town and have become great friends. Jennifer is an inspiration to me and fiercely talented, and I have all her books. I'll read anything she writes!

Tell us about your writing process. Any quirks?

I'm a very structured plotter. I'll start off with an idea—something I read, saw, overheard, or a "what if" situation that pops into my brain. I'll build my main character(s) around that to figure out whose story it is, and I'll ask myself where those people are at the beginning of the story, and at the end. Next come major plot points, and those large stepping stones get further developed into about thirty smaller ones. Each smaller point gets broken down into scenes. I dig deeper into my cast by interviewing my main characters and building a photo gallery...and then, finally, I write. I admire people who don't plot. I like to have a road map of where I think I'm going although my characters don't always let me take them where I'd initially imagined.

What can you tell us about your next novel?

Oh, it's another wicked story, of course. It's the tale of Lucas, who's set to inherit not only the fortune of his kidnapped and presumed dead wife, but also that of his ailing mother-in-law. When he receives a potentially more recent photograph of his spouse, the race to find her is on. Question is, does he want her alive...or would he prefer her dead? I'm having so much fun writing this novel, and I can't wait for you to meet my characters.